PRAISE FOR

The Gentleman Jewel Thief

"The fabled Hope Diamond is the centerpiece of Peterson's charming trilogy, where she mixes one very bad-boy gentleman with a headstrong heroine, a stolen gem, a duel, a band of acrobats, and an exiled French king . . . She peppers [*The Gentleman Jewel Thief*] with steamy love scenes, wild escapades, and a laugh or two . . . [and] keeps the pace flying and readers hanging on to their utter joy."

—*RT Book Reviews* (4 Stars)

"Deliciously fun! What a lovely, witty book—I can't wait to see what Jessica Peterson does next!"

—Kate Noble, author of *If I Fall*

"Sexy and sparkling with wit, *The Gentleman Jewel Thief* overflows with adventure, suspense, and fast-paced action. Jessica Peterson is a fresh new voice in historical romance."

—Shana Galen, author of *The Spy Wore Blue*

The Millionaire Rogue

JESSICA PETERSON

BERKLEY SENSATION, NEW YORK

THE BERKLEY PUBLISHING GROUP
Published by the Penguin Group
Penguin Group (USA) LLC
375 Hudson Street, New York, New York 10014

⊕

USA • Canada • UK • Ireland • Australia • New Zealand • India • South Africa • China

penguin.com

A Penguin Random House Company

THE MILLIONAIRE ROGUE

A Berkley Sensation Book / published by arrangement with Peterson Paperbacks, LLC

Berkley Sensation Books are published by The Berkley Publishing Group.
BERKLEY SENSATION® is a registered trademark of Penguin Group (USA) LLC.
The "B" design is a trademark of Penguin Group (USA) LLC.

For information, address: The Berkley Publishing Group,
a division of Penguin Group (USA) LLC,
375 Hudson Street, New York, New York 10014.

ISBN: 978-0-425-27208-4

PUBLISHING HISTORY
Berkley Sensation mass-market edition / January 2015

PRINTED IN THE UNITED STATES OF AMERICA

10 9 8 7 6 5 4 3

Cover art by Aleta Rafton.
Cover design by George Long.
Interior text design by Kelly Lipovich.

*For my parents, who had an awkward,
often difficult, weirdly imaginative daughter,
and loved her anyway.
This one is for you, Mom and Dad,
even though it makes me squirm
when I think about you reading it.
Love you.*

Acknowledgments

Wow. So many exciting things have happened since book one of the Hope Diamond Trilogy, *The Gentleman Jewel Thief*, was published—things that wouldn't have happened without the help and thoughtfulness of the following people.

My husband, Ben. You know how to throw one hell of a party. I hope to one day repay you by putting you on the cover of my books. In a kilt. I love you.

As always, my talented and inspiring agent, Alexandra Machinist; my fabulous editor, Leis Pederson, who always knows the right thing to say to put my author crazies to bed; and Jessica Brock, my publicist, who has helped a clueless author figure out the ins and outs of book promotion. I look forward to working with all of you in the years ahead!

To Shana Galen and Kate Noble, for their generous offer of time and talent. I so appreciate the wonderful blurbs you provided for *The Gentleman Jewel Thief*. I can only hope to one day be the masters you both are.

To all the bloggers, authors, and readers who have reached out over the past year—especially Alyssa Alexander. Having author friends is really the coolest thing on the planet.

viii ACKNOWLEDGMENTS

And finally, to my family and friends. Y'all are the best, and none of this would be possible without your love, support, and nights spent drinking too much wine. Thanks to all our friends who have made *The Gentleman Jewel Thief* their book club selection; thanks to all our friends who have purchased and read the book. Your kindness means the world to me! Happy reading.

Prologue

THE FRENCH BLUE:
A HISTORY OF THE WORLD'S GREATEST DIAMOND

Vol. I.

By Thomas Hope

Across lands dry and rivers wide, through centuries of blood-shed and the downfall of great kingdoms, the French Blue's siren call has, like forbidden fruit, proven irresistible to royal and common man alike.

It all began in that mythic land across the great sea: India. Nearly three hundred years ago, a blue-gray diamond the size of a snuffbox was mined from the bowels of the earth. The great Shah Jehan, an emperor the likes of which the world had never seen, made an offering of the jewel to the goddess Sita; he commissioned a great statue of his goddess, the diamond glittering from the center of her forehead as an all-seeing third eye.

It was during this time that a Frenchman by the name of Jean Baptiste Tavernier traveled to the court of Shah Jehan. Being French, Tavernier was by nature dirty, wily, a born thief, and, of course, a libertine. Goading the Shah with false gifts and flattery, Tavernier gained his trust, and the love of his court.

It is impossible to know what, exactly, happened next; but it is widely assumed that, just as the Shah pressed Tavernier to his breast as brother and friend, Tavernier betrayed him. Some accounts even posit the Frenchman slit his host's throat; others, that Tavernier poisoned him and half his glorious court.

The goddess Sita was witness to the violence; and when Tavernier pried the jewel from her forehead with a dagger thieved from Shah Jehan's still-warm body, Sita cursed the Frenchman and all those who would come to own the diamond after him.

Sewn into the forearm of a slave girl, the diamond was brought to Europe, where Tavernier sold it to Louis XIV for the princely sum of two hundred thousand *livres*. The Sun King recut the jewel to improve its luster and wore it slung about his royal breast on a blue ribbon. As part of the crown jewels of France, the diamond would be henceforth known as the French Blue.

Alas, the jewel that bewitched the Frenchman and the king would also bring doom upon their heads; Sita would see her curse satisfied. Tavernier, living out his last days exiled in the wilds of Russia, was torn limb from lip by a pack of wild dogs, and buried in an unmarked grave.

Neither were the kings of France immune to Sita's curse; it was on a bitterly cold day in January when the last king, Louis XVI, lost his crown, his fortune, and his head before a crowd of angry Parisians.

And yet Sita's thirst for vengeance is not yet satisfied. The French Blue, along with most of the crown jewels, was thieved in late 1791 from the Garde Mueble, a royal warehouse on the outskirts of Paris. No one knows who stole it, or where it might be hidden away; in a Bavarian duke's treasure chest, perhaps, or the dirty pocket of a serving wench in Calais. The diamond could be anywhere.

While the trail grows cold, Sita's thirst burns hot. The French Blue is far too glorious a gem to remain hidden forever. Only when it is again brought into the light; only when it is claimed by whomever is brave, or perhaps daft, enough to claim it; only *then* will Sita's lust for blood be satisfied, and her curse at last fulfilled.

One

City of London
Duchess Street, near Cavendish Square
Spring 1812

Resisting the impulse to leap from his chair, fists raised, with a great *Huzzah!*, Mr. Thomas Hope thrust the quill into its holder beside the inkwell. He gathered the pages scattered across his desk and settled in to read the *History*.

The gray afternoon light was fading, and he drew the oil lamp closer so that he might read his masterwork without having to squint. For a masterwork it was, surely; how could it not be, after the years Hope dreamed of the diamond, researched its origins and the fantastic claims behind its curse?

But as his eyes traveled the length of each sentence, it became abundantly clear that Hope's *History* was no masterwork. Indeed, it was something else altogether.

Dear God, it was *awful*. Dramatic to the extreme, like an opera, but without the painted prima donna to compensate for its lack of narrative savvy. *The size of a snuffbox.* Whence had come *that* rubbish?

Tossing the pages onto the desk, Hope tugged a hand through his tangle of wayward curls. He was reading too much of that brooding, wicked man Lord Byron, and it was starting to take its toll on his pen.

He didn't have time for such frivolity besides. Hope had a goodly bit of work waiting for him back at the bank, and an even larger bit—a barrel, actually—of cognac to drink this evening.

Literary aspirations all but shot to hell, Hope was about to crumple the pages into his fists, when a strange noise, sounding suspiciously like muffled laughter, broke out over his shoulder.

His blood rushed cold. Not one of his men, the butler or a steward or a cashier from the bank. He was not expecting any visitors, and the hour for social calls had long passed.

Hope glanced across the gleaming expanse of his desk. His eyes landed on a silver letter opener, winking from its place beside the inkwell. Then there was the pistol in the top right drawer, of course, and the bejeweled Italian dagger in its box on the shelf; and his fists, he couldn't very well discount *those* weapons—

He swallowed, hard. Those days were behind him. The time for violence and subterfuge had passed; Hope was a respectable man of business now, like his father, and his father before him.

Respectable men of business did *not* greet visitors with a sock to the eye or a bejeweled dagger thrust at their throats.

At least not in England.

Removing his spectacles one ear at a time, he carefully placed them beside the pages on his desk. For a moment he closed his eyes, pulse racing.

Hope spun about in his chair. The breath left his body when his gaze fell on the hulking figure that loomed half a step behind him.

"Oh, God." Hope gaped. "Not you. Not now."

Smirking in that familiar way of his—one side of his mouth kicked up saucily, provokingly—Mr. Henry Beaton Lake reached past Hope and lifted the *History* from the desk.

"'Forbidden fruit'?" Lake wheezed. "Oh God indeed! That's bad, old man, very bad. I advise you to leave alliteration to the feebleminded, poets and the like. And the curse!"

Here Mr. Lake whooped with laughter, going so far as to bend over and slap his knee with great jollity. "Brilliant, I say, brilliant! Reading your little history, I'd almost venture you believed it. Heavens, what a good laugh you've given me, and how in the gloom of these past months I've needed it!"

Hope snatched the pages from Mr. Lake's pawlike hand and stuffed them into a drawer. "It's a work in progress," he growled. "I wasn't expecting to share it, not yet. What in hell are you doing here, and in daylight? Someone could have seen you."

Lake turned and leaned the backs of his enormous thighs against the desk. He crossed his ankles, then his arms, and looked down at Hope. "Anxious as always, old friend. You haven't changed a bit—well, except for those clothes. You look like a peacock."

Hope watched as Lake's penetrating gaze lingered a moment on Hope's crisply knotted cravat, his simple but exquisitely cut kerseymere waistcoat, and the onyx-studded watch peeking from his pocket.

"And you, Lake, look like a pirate out of *Robinson Crusoe*. What of it?" Hope took in Lake's broad shoulders, the corded muscles in his neck. He wore the black patch over his eye as some men wore a well-cut dinner jacket: with pride and a sort of impudent, knowing smile, confident any female in the vicinity would find him a little dangerous, wholly debonair, and far too tempting to resist.

"Thank you for the compliment." Lake's smile broadened. "And you needn't worry about being seen associating with the likes of me. I used the alley, and came in through the drawing room window."

"Of course you did. Still up to your old tricks, then?"

"King and country, Hope," Mr. Lake sighed, the laughter fading from his face. "Boney didn't stop when you and I parted ways. Someone needed to stay and fight."

Hope looked away, blinking back the sting of Lake's words. A beat of uncomfortable silence settled between them.

At last Lake pushed to his feet and made his way to the sideboard.

Hope watched the man limp across the room, his right leg remaining stiff at the knee. For a moment sadness and regret pressed heavy into his chest. Too many memories; memories that Hope did not care to revisit.

Mr. Lake held up an etched decanter. "Mind if I pour us a finger, or three?"

"I do indeed mind, very much," Hope replied.

But as he expected, Lake paid him no heed. His guest busied

himself at the sideboard, and a moment later returned with a generous pour of brandy in each of two bulbous snifters.

"I've too many engagements this evening to begin with brandy, and at so early an hour," Hope said, but even as the words left his mouth he found himself reaching for the snifter Lake had set before him. Something about the man's stone-set gaze made Hope feel as if he'd need a drink, and then some, after Mr. Lake revealed what he'd come for.

Hope watched Lake lower himself with a wince into the high-backed chair on the other side of the desk. He took a long pull of brandy and, after he felt the familiar fire relax his limbs, asked, "How's the leg?"

Lake finished his own pull before replying. "Good, bad, it's all the same. Scares off the right people, attracts all the wrong ones. I rather prefer it that way."

Hope scoffed, grinning wistfully at his brandy. "And you. You haven't changed, either. Not a bit."

Again charged silence stretched across the desk. Hope gulped his liquor. Lake did the same.

"The outcome of the war in Spain shall be decided in the coming weeks." Lake's voice was low. He did not meet Hope's gaze. "Wellington marches for Madrid; when the battle comes, it shall turn the tide of our fortunes there. For better or worse, I cannot say. That wastrel Frenchman Marmont, damn him, has the luck of the devil. The lives of thousands, tens of thousands, of British soldiers hang in the balance. My men— good men, smart men—they will die. Men like you."

"I was never one of your men, Lake. I was a refugee in need of aid and asylum. You gave me what I needed, and in return I gave you the same." Hope looked down at his glass. "I was never one of your men."

Lake's one pale eye snapped upward. "Yes, you were. You still are."

Hope tried not to flinch as he waited for what he knew came next.

"We need you," Lake said. "Your country needs you. To turn the tide in our favor."

Ah, so there it was. Hope knew he should run and hide, for those very words spelled the death of hundreds of England's finest men.

But with his earnest eye—the one eye the surgeon managed to save, after the accident—Lake pinned Mr. Hope to his chair.

"I would help if I could." Hope splayed his palms on the desk. "But it's the same as it was ten years ago. I was born to count, Lake, not to spy. My father was banker to the great houses of Europe, and his father before that. After I fled the Continent, I dreamed of restoring Hope and Company to its former glory. And now I've done that. I'm a respectable man of business—"

"Man of business, yes, but the respectable bit is questionable."

Hope chewed the inside of his lip to keep from rolling his eyes. "Regardless, I've a lot at stake. People depend on me, lots of people. Clients, employees. I can't risk the livelihood of thousands of families—never mind my own, my brothers, bless their black souls—by engaging in your sort of intrigue. It's bad business. I've worked long and hard to build my reputation. I won't see that work undone, and millions lost along the way."

Hope sipped his brandy, then swirled it in its glass. "But you knew I would say all that. So, Lake. Tell me why you are here."

Lake drained his glass and smacked his lips. "I'm here because of that diamond you write so very *ardently* about."

"The French Blue?" Hope eyed his visitor. "Quite the coincidence, that you should appear out of the ether just as I am finishing my history."

"I thought together we might begin a new chapter of your lovely little history," Lake said. "And you know as well as I do it's no coincidence. You've heard the rumors, same as me. You're going to buy the diamond from her, aren't you?"

Hope looked down at his hands. Damn him, how did Lake know everything? He assumed the existence of the French Blue in England was a well-kept secret. The Princess of Wales made sure of that, seeing as she likely came into possession of the diamond through illegal, perhaps even treasonous, means.

But Hope assumed wrong. He should have known better, especially when it came to Henry Beaton Lake, privateer-cum-spy extraordinaire. The man sniffed out secrets as a bloodhound would a fox: instinctively, confidently, his every sense alive with the hunt.

"Perhaps." Hope swept back a pair of curls with his fingers. "I admit I am looking to expand my collection. And diamonds—jewels—they are good investments. In the last decade alone—"

"Psh!" Lake threw back his head. "You're buying it for a woman, aren't you?"

This time Hope did not hold back rolling his eyes. "I avoid attachments to women for the very same reasons I avoid the likes of you. Much as I admire the female sex."

"You did a great deal more than admire said sex when we were in France."

"That was almost ten years ago, and hardly signifies."

Lake leveled his gaze with Hope's. "The distractions of women aside. You are attempting to buy the French Blue from Princess Caroline. I'm asking you to buy it for me. For England."

Hope choked on his brandy. Before he could protest, Lake pushed onward.

"We've tried to buy the stone from the princess, but she is holding it hostage from her husband the prince and, by extension, our operation. Relations between them are worse than ever. I'm shocked, frankly, that they haven't yet tried to poison one another."

"Would that we were so lucky as to be delivered from that nincompoop they have the nerve to call regent."

Lake waved away his words. "I'll pretend I didn't hear that. If we manage to obtain the French Blue, we could very well change the course of the war. For years now old Boney's been on the hunt for the missing crown jewels of France. We have reason to believe he'd trade valuable concessions for the largest and most notorious of those jewels. In exchange for the French Blue, that blackhearted little toad might hand over prisoners, a Spanish city or two. We could very well save hundreds, if not thousands, of lives, and in a single stroke."

Hope let out a long, hot breath. "You're shameless, Lake. Absolutely shameless. I refuse to be cowed into thinking I'm a selfish bastard for wanting to protect the interests of those who depend on me for their livelihoods, and their fortunes. I care for the thousands of lives you'll save, I do, but—"

"But." Lake held up his finger. "You *are* a selfish bastard, then."

Hope gritted his teeth, balling his palms into fists. "I've too much at stake," he repeated. "Princess Caroline has been a client of Hope and Company for years. She is more dangerous than she appears, and wily besides. I'm sunk if she uncovers the plot. I won't do it."

For a long moment Lake looked at Hope, his one pale eye unblinking. He shifted in his chair and winced, sucking in a breath as he slowly rested his weight on the bad leg.

The leg that had saved Hope from becoming a cripple, or a corpse, himself.

"Not even for me, old friend?" Lake's face was tensed with pain, and glowing red.

Hope shook his head. "Shameless." He laughed, a mirthless sound. "How do you know I'm worthy of the task? I am not the nimble shadow I once was. These days, a daring evening is a few too many fingers of liquor and a long, deep sleep—alone, sadly—in my bed."

All traces of pain disappeared from Lake's face as he grinned. "You are not as handsome as you once were, I'll give you that. But I wouldn't have asked you if I didn't believe you were a capable partner in crime. We shall work together, of course."

"Of course." Hope sighed in defeat. "So. What's the play?"

Lake leaned forward, resting his forearms on his knees, and rubbed his palms together with a look of fiendish glee. "Those engagements you have—cancel them. We make our move tonight."

Two

London
King Street, St. James's Square

A debutante of small name and little fortune would, surely, commit any number of unspeakable acts in exchange for a voucher to Almack's Assembly Rooms. For there lurked unmarried gentlemen of the rich, titled variety, the kind with palaces in the country and interests in exotic things like shiny boots and perfectly coiffed sideburns.

So why did Miss Sophia Blaise's pulse thump with something akin to relief, exhilaration, even, when one of said gentlemen excused himself from her company and disappeared into the crush?

The Marquess of Withington was not the handsomest peer, but he was the richest, and quite the Corinthian besides. His sideburns were surely the most perfect and the most coiffed, and his boots very shiny indeed. Every heiress and duke's daughter would willingly claw out the other's eyes for a chance to be courted by the marquess; such crimes were tolerated, welcomed, even, while on the hunt for this season's most eligible quarry.

Even now, as Sophia teetered awkwardly on the edge of the ballroom, she felt the sting of stares from venomous female passersby. Her two-minute conversation with the marquess was apparently grounds for preemptive attack by her fellow fortune hunters.

But Sophia was nothing if not ambitious. She took a

certain pride in being the object of such naked envy. Perhaps she did have a chance at making the brilliant match to which she'd always aspired, after all. Perhaps the marquess—the filthy-rich, swoon-worthy *marquess!*—was not so far out of reach.

The conversation itself had been a moderate success—his eyes had remained glued to her bosom, yes, but he *had* laughed at her jests—and even in the wake of her relief at his departure, Sophia felt the satisfaction of a job well done.

Now she had only to dread their next interaction.

"It will get easier," her mother counseled earlier that evening, swaying in time with the carriage.

"You mustn't take it too seriously," Cousin Violet said. She took a swig from her flask and let out a small hiss of satisfaction. "Men like Withington are in possession of little wit, and even less intelligence. You've nothing to fear from them."

It certainly *hadn't* gotten easier, or any less serious, as the beginning weeks of the season passed with alarming speed.

For as long as Sophia could remember, she desired two things above all else: to make a brilliant match with the season's most eligible bachelor, and a suitably large castle to go with him. Having grown up in a family teetering on the edge of penury, Sophia desired stability, security, too, and a man like the marquess could provide her all that and more: the titles, the crests, the fortune and fame.

She was not prepared, however, for just how difficult it would be to fulfill her ambitions. Nor did she anticipate how intimidating, how repellent, she would find a goodly majority of the gentlemen who belonged to said titles and crests.

Her first season, in short, was turning out to be quite a disaster. Yes, *quite*.

Sophia's shoulders slumped.

But even as the weight of that sobering truth bore down upon her heart, a flicker of anticipation pulsed there. Faint at first, it flamed hotter as the minutes passed. The hour of her departure from Almack's drew near; which meant, of course, Sophia was that much closer to her *second* engagement of the evening.

And this one, praise God, had nothing at all to do with sideburns or castles.

Sophia shivered with anticipation when at last the family's musty, creaking carriage jostled its occupants away from Almack's door on King Street later that evening, making for the family's ramshackle manse in Grosvenor Square.

"You're smiling." Violet eyed Sophia from across the carriage. "What's wrong?"

Sophia bit the inside of her lip, hoping to hide her grin of excitement. "Nothing out of the usual, Cousin. I very likely offended a marquess. Being the graceful swan that I am, I stepped on Lord Pealey's feet—yes, both of them—during the minuet."

Violet shrugged. "That makes for a better turn at Almack's than last week."

Lady Blaise said nothing as she swatted back Cousin Violet's attempt at another swig from her flask.

Violet tilted her head back and swigged anyway, draining every last drop.

Sophia sighed and looked out the window. *One more hour. One more hour until my escape.*

Grosvenor Square

Pulling her hood over her nose, Sophia leaned against the crumbling brick of her uncle's house and stepped into her boots, one stockinged foot at a time. She straightened and peered into the shadows, long and sinister in the flickering light of the gas lamps. Satisfied no one was about, she stole into the square, pressing to her breast the pages hidden in her cloak.

The night was cool and clammy; there would be rain. Above, the stars hid behind a thin layer of gray cloud, while the light of the full moon shone through like a lone, opaque eye, following her as she moved through the dark.

With each step her pulse quickened. The daring of it all, the risk—reputation, ruination, retribution—was immense. And exhilarating, all at once.

Whatever this feeling was, it far outshone the anxiety, and the disappointment, she'd experienced while in the Marquess of Withington's presence at Almack's.

It was not far to The Glossy. While Sophia had no occasion on which to dwell on such things, it had surprised her nonetheless that establishments such as La Reinette's populated Mayfair as thickly as potbellied peers.

Those potbellied peers, Sophia had quickly discovered, were possessed of wicked appetites in more ways than one.

The Glossy occupied a stately spot between Viscount Pickering's massive pile and the Earl of Sussex's broad, tired-looking townhouse. Now Sophia understood why Sussex was such a jolly fellow, despite a succession of sour-faced wives.

Its namesake shutters were lacquered deep blue, the slick paint glittering in the low light of lanterns on either side of the front door. Sophia slipped past The Glossy's facade onto a narrow lane that descended along one side of the house. She stopped at a hedgerow—wait, yes, this was the one—and ducked into the boxwood's firm grasp.

For several heartbeats she scraped through the darkness, complete and sweet smelling. She emerged onto a small but immaculately groomed courtyard, illuminated by exotic-looking torches standing guard around the perimeter. With light footsteps she crossed to a door, half-hidden by a budding vine of wisteria. She knocked once. Twice.

Waited a beat.

Then knocked twice more.

The door opened. A tall mulatto emerged, his enormous bulk occupying the whole of the threshold. His black eyes sparked with recognition as they fell upon Sophia's half-hidden face.

"Good evening, miss." He bowed. "Please, come in. The madam is waiting for you. Lily will show you up."

Sophia stepped into the hall but did not remove her hood.

The scent of fresh-cut flowers, mingled with a vivid musk Sophia had yet to name, filled her nostrils. She followed Lily, a yellow-haired woman so beautiful it was difficult not to stare, down a wide gallery and up a curving stair.

The Glossy was as lovely as Sophia remembered. Lovelier even than the first-rate homes of the *ton*, for La Reinette eschewed overstuffed severity in favor of feminine flair. Enormously tall ceilings were frescoed in the Italian style, blues and pinks and naked bodies aflutter. Light sparkled from heavy crystal chandeliers. The gilt furniture was upholstered in various shades of ivory and pink. Paintings lined the walls, depicting lovers past in various states of repose—Tristan and Isolde, Diana and Actaeon, Romeo and Juliet.

When at last Lily drew up before a pair of painted doors, Sophia was dizzy, intoxicated by her surroundings. Lily opened the doors and Sophia stepped mutely over the threshold, blinking to bring her blood back to life.

Before she could thank her guide, the doors swung shut behind her. A voice, thick and seductive, called out from inside the room.

"Ah, *mademoiselle! S'il vous plaît, entrez, entrez!*"

La Reinette approached, knotting the tasseled belt of her Japanese silk robe. She dropped into an elegant curtsy, and in her excitement Sophia did the same. La Reinette was more legend than lady; really, how did one greet the mistress to prime ministers and Continental royalty? She was called the little queen—*la reinette*—for good reason.

Madame clucked her tongue and lifted Sophia by her elbows. She drew back Sophia's hood and smiled in that languid way only Frenchwomen could, placing her palms on Sophia's neck.

Her spine tingled at La Reinette's touch. "Good evening, Madame. I am happy to see you again."

"And I am very happy, yes." Madame nodded at a table and chairs set before the fire. On the table, several quills were placed beside a mother-of-pearl inkwell and a quire of fine paper. "Come, let us sit. I am most eager to see the work you have done with my tales."

Sophia settled into her chair and placed the pages, bound in thin red ribbon, on the table. She watched as La Reinette hovered at a sideboard, pouring red wine into elegant goblets. Without asking, Madame placed a goblet on the table before Sophia and swept into the chair opposite.

"Drink it," Madame said. "It is very good, from my country. Not the vinegar that is made in Italy. It helps me to remember. I think it will help you to write."

Sophia brought the glass to her lips, gaze flicking to meet Madame's. In the glow of the fire her eyes appeared wholly black, like a stag's; a striking foil to her pale skin and hair.

Sophia pushed the bound pages across the table. "The edits from our first meeting are complete, and I compiled everything you gave me from the second. I—" Sophia blushed. "I enjoyed this week's tales. Thoroughly. That spy you knew, back in France—the one with the curls, who could fell a girl with his gaze alone? He is my favorite gentleman yet."

Again Madame smiled. "Yes," she said. "He is my favorite, too."

She placed a reticule, woven with pink thread, before Sophia on the table.

"Five pounds, as we agreed, and a bonus." Madame held up a thin, elegant hand at Sophia's protest. "It is no small risk you take, visiting me like this."

"I have come to enjoy our meetings, very much." Sophia squirreled away the reticule in the folds of her cloak. "The adventure you have seen, and the gentlemen you have known—they certainly don't make them like that in England."

Madame raised an eyebrow. "Your prince, you have not found him yet? But this is your season!"

"No prince. Not yet. Perhaps it is not my season, after all." Sophia set down her wine and picked up a quill, examining its sharpened nib. "But I'd rather discuss *your* princes. Where did we leave off last week? Oh yes, the spy, the one with the gaze. Together you were boarding a ship bound for Southampton—"

Sophia started at an enormous sound, the walls set trembling as if by thunder. The *thump thump thump* of heavy footsteps followed—running, whomever the footsteps belonged to was running—and drew closer with each passing heartbeat. So many footsteps it sounded as if The Glossy were being invaded by the whole of the French army.

She ducked at the violent, throaty crack of—dear God, was that a *pistol*? It couldn't be, not here, not in Mayfair, not in the madam's inner sanctum . . .

Sophia's thoughts ran riot. Madame had promised her discretion, protection too, and assured her she would not be seen by any guest, man or woman. But what if, by some accident, she *were* to be seen? And by, God forbid, someone she knew—someone who mattered?

"Are you expecting visitors?"

"No." La Reinette's mouth was a tight white line. She set

down her goblet and twisted in her chair at the sudden racket by the doors.

They catapulted open, banging against the walls.

To Sophia's very great horror, Mr. Thomas Hope sprang breathlessly into La Reinette's chamber, dark tendrils of hair curling from his forehead in a disheveled—and rather dashing—manner. A small but deep cut on his cheek oozed blood in thick, languorous drops.

His wide blue eyes swept over Sophia before landing on the madam.

With an authority that startled Sophia from her staring, he said, "Hide me. Now."

Three

—◆—

It began as a familiar tingle at the back of Hope's neck, a spider of suspicion waking long-dormant senses as Lake, playing coachman, jostled the carriage into evening traffic.

They were being followed.

Darkness had fallen early, but even so Hope could see two blurs of blackness, blacker even than shadow, following them down the lane. Riders, their cloaks billowing about them in a close breeze.

With practiced nonchalance, Hope sat straight-backed beside the window. He yanked his beaver hat over his unruly curls and watched his new friends from the corner of his eye.

They were sufficiently sinister-looking, and held back just far enough, to confirm Hope's suspicion that these men were out for blood.

His blood. Lake's, too.

Why, he couldn't say. Except that half the world was out for Lake's blood, and for good reason.

Hope cursed under his breath. Not two hours with Mr. Henry Beaton Lake and already they courted just the kind of attention Hope wished to avoid.

He banged his fist to the roof. "We've got company."

"Haha!" came Lake's muffled reply. "And so the plot thickens!"

Hope was thrown back in his seat as Lake jolted the team into a canter. He cursed again. Moving this fast through the streets of Mayfair made them as conspicuous as highwaymen on the run.

Bad for business, his arse. If Hope made it out of this little assignment alive, he would be ruined, and quite thoroughly at that.

Amid the shouts of outraged groomsmen and foulmouthed pedestrians, Hope continued to watch the riders. They kept pace with the carriage, the hooves of their horses pounding the cobblestones in perfect synchronicity. With each stride they drew nearer, making Hope's pulse leap.

He tucked a curl behind one ear. "They're gaining."

"I see that!" Lake replied, voice edged with annoyance.

The carriage lurched forward, the horses now in an all-out gallop. Hope swallowed, hard, and watched as the street lamps whisked by with alarming speed. He dug his fingers into the velvet upholstery of his seat. Images of an overturned carriage, his mangled body slung across one of its wheels as Lake skipped away, whistling, filled his head.

"We've got to do something!" he called. "They're going to catch us!"

"Distract them!" Lake growled in reply.

Hope pitched forward onto the floor as Lake narrowly avoided mauling a woman and her husband in full ballroom attire. Lake was many things—spy, mentor, pirate, scoundrel— but a coachman he was not.

"Distract them? How?"

"I can't do everything!" Lake shouted. "*Think*, you idiot!"

Think. Hope gritted his teeth and pushed off the floor into his seat. If the front wall of the carriage didn't separate them, he would *think* about smashing his fist into Lake's face.

By now the riders were so close, Hope could hear their horses snorting with effort as they kept pace. His heart pummeled his ribs, and for a moment panic threatened to drown what little sanity he had left.

Think. Think what? He was trapped in a runaway carriage, chased down by men he didn't know for reasons he couldn't begin to guess. He had a pistol tucked into the pocket of his jacket, yes, but he couldn't very well start a firefight in the middle of a busy lane.

No, there would be no confrontation. At least not here, for all of Mayfair to see. That would be *very* bad business indeed.

What the hell did Lake expect him to do?

Hope dared another peek out into the night. A familiar

stuccoed facade, windows framed by shiny blue shutters, passed by the window. Hope's blood leapt in sudden recognition.

Of course!

The Glossy.

Why hadn't Hope thought of it before? La Reinette was one of his oldest clients, and a friend besides. Her house, being what it was, was filled with secret stairways, trapdoors, and hidden rooms; a more perfect place for avoiding certain capture and death did not exist in all England.

Hope peered down at the lane below. He'd have to jump; if Lake stopped the coach, the riders would be on them in half a heartbeat.

He blinked, fear clawing its way through him.

He blinked again. He had to act fast, or he would not act at all.

He raised his foot and pounded it against the carriage door with all the strength he could muster.

He nearly laughed when the door did not budge. And then on second thought, he nearly cried.

Again and again he pounded against the door until it suddenly swung open, banging violently against the outside of the carriage.

Lake was shouting something; the horses were screaming and the cobblestones of the lane below dashed together with dizzying speed. A rider drew close, his face hidden by the collar of his jacket.

Hope crouched, holding either side of the door opening. Without further ado, he closed his eyes and leapt forward, out into the night.

He landed, hard, on his feet, pain radiating up his shins to land screaming in his knees. He sucked in his breath, wincing, but didn't resist the forward momentum of his body. He ran for The Glossy and leapt over the low wall that bordered the property, clearing it with nary an inch to spare.

Behind him he heard shouts, and the whinnying of horses as the cloaked riders rode after him. Hope pumped his arms and legs harder, harder, so hard it felt as if his heart would break free from his chest. He struggled to breathe, lungs burning with the need for air.

Unfamiliar voices rang out over his shoulder, followed by the crunch of footsteps on the gravel drive. The riders were on his heels and gaining ground.

Hope ducked into the familiar hedge. Too late did he think to draw up his fists to protect his face, as an errant branch poked boldly into his cheek. He gritted his teeth against the sting— perhaps like Lake he would at last have a dashing souvenir of his daring—and pushed through onto the courtyard.

He didn't wait for Umberto to open the door, and instead rammed against it with his shoulder. To his very great surprise— so great, in fact, that Hope lost his footing entirely—the door splintered beneath his weight.

Catapulting arse over head into the foyer, Hope pushed clumsily to his feet. He waved away Umberto's pistol and pointed out to the night.

"Them," he wheezed. "Get them!" He turned and took off running through the house.

Hope climbed the stairs three at a time, but tripped to his knees on the top step at the sound of a pistol shot. His heart turned over in his chest. In the close quarters of the house it might as well have been heavy cannon it was so loud; the chandelier was still shivering above Hope's head as he grappled to his feet.

He tore down the second-story gallery, pulse roaring when he heard the footsteps, heavy, hurried, behind him.

At least one of the riders had made it past Umberto.

Hope swallowed the panic that rose in his chest. He pushed through the tall doors at the end of the gallery, his every sense alive with pain.

And then he nearly swallowed his tongue at the scene before him.

A pretty—*very* pretty—dark-haired girl sat, mouth agape, beside La Reinette.

Why the devil was Miss Sophia Blaise, exhaustingly virginal debutante, meeting with La Reinette in the middle of the night—and on a *Wednesday*?

As the cousin of one of Hope's largest investors—Lady Violet Rutledge and her father were some of Hope's oldest and best clients—her very presence threatened Hope's attempt to keep his clandestine activities exactly that.

So much for discretion. Mr. Lake and his follies were very bad for business indeed.

In a single glance, Hope took in Sophia's expression, equal parts curiosity and horror; the small reticule, heavy with coin, tucked into her long cloak; and her long, ink-stained fingers, clutching at the worn collar of her simple gown.

A puzzle, and an intriguing one at that.

But Hope didn't have time for puzzles. Especially not tonight, with the pounding footsteps of his pursuers drawing closer with each passing moment.

With some effort he turned his gaze to the madam, which she returned steadily, expressionless.

"Hide me," he panted. "Now."

Miss Blaise sprang to her feet, eyes so wide he had to resist the impulse to hold out his hand to catch them should they pop free of her head.

"Hide you?" Her voice rose with panic. "Hide *me*!"

God above.

He did *not* have time for this. But he didn't have time to protest, either; the riders were hot on his heels.

And so he reached for Miss Blaise, wrapping his fingers around her elbow as he tugged her alongside him. He ignored her gasp as he followed La Reinette across the room, the madam's footsteps silent amid those, drawing closer, of his pursuers.

La Reinette drew up before the far wall, embellished in elaborate gilt plasterwork. She placed both hands on one side of a framed painting and pushed.

A panel the width of Hope's forearm swung open to reveal a closet set into the wall. A high shelf held a red lacquer box and a haphazard stack of books.

Everything was covered in a furry layer of dust.

Beside Hope, Sophia gaped at the closet in horror.

La Reinette met his eyes over Sophia's head.

"It is this, or the certain death," Madame said. She reached out and with her thumb swiped at the cut on his cheek. He felt the warm smear of blood on his skin. She pulled back with a frown, rubbing his blood between the pads of her thumb and forefinger.

The footsteps in the gallery grew louder. Hope heard the

labored breathing of his assailants as they cursed their way toward La Reinette's chamber.

Hope pulled Sophia against him, her breast to his belly. With a look that implored her to silence, he wrapped an arm about her shoulders and ducked both their bodies into the closet.

His shoulders—*gah!*—got stuck halfway in. Hope was forced to pull Sophia tightly against him—so tightly she let out a little gasp of pain as at last they slid into the tiny space.

La Reinette shoved the panel back into place, pressing it against the side of Hope's body with such force his shoulder cracked to fit inside.

Darkness settled over Hope and Miss Blaise, along with a hysterical silence.

Well. This was awkward.

"Are you all right?" he whispered.

"No. No, most certainly not all right," came her muffled reply.

"Excellent." He tried to stand very still, not daring even to breathe. "Me neither."

Her chest heaved rather invitingly against his as she attempted to catch her breath. He was suddenly aware of her warmth, her every limb pressed against his own. Knees, forearms, hips, and even her nose, which grazed the sensitive skin at the base of his throat.

He took a deep, steadying breath, inhaling her scent as he did so. She smelled of fresh air and wine; not a hint of perfume. It was lovely, made lovelier by the novelty of it. Debutantes of her shape and stripe usually inhabited clouds of sickly-sweet tuberose and ambergris; he could always smell a fortune hunter long before he saw one.

Needless to say, Hope's deep breath had the opposite of its intended effect.

Hope felt Miss Blaise tremble as the sound of male voices filled La Reinette's chamber. He sensed her rising panic and quickly covered her mouth with his free hand, his own heart racing as La Reinette exchanged words with his pursuers.

There were two men, and they were responding to the madam's queries in rapid-fire French. To Hope's surprise, the intruders spoke the sort of airy, refined French of the ancien régime.

They were well-bred, aristocrats.

Or, at the very least, pretending to be.

In a voice like gravel, one of the men told Madame they were looking for a dangerous man, dark-haired with blue eyes, very tall.

Recognition pulsed in Hope's chest. *That voice!* It was vaguely familiar—he knew it in another time and place, another life—though he struggled to place it.

La Reinette responded to the intruder's queries with convincing bafflement, warning that while she had seen no such man, she would not allow them to bother her clients in the other rooms.

The men ignored La Reinette, and began to ransack the room. Drawers opened, pages scattered, a heavy piece of furniture skidded with a crash across the wood floor.

One of the men was pacing the room, his footsteps growing louder until Hope sensed his presence nary a hairsbreadth from the wall behind which Hope now cowered.

Suddenly the closet was filled with a strange, hoarse scraping noise. The intruder, running his hands along the gilded expanse of the wall.

Hope's heart sank even as it raced faster and faster with each passing second. The man's hands were now passing directly over the wall panel that hid Hope and Miss Blaise; Hope heard the man's labored breathing, the crinkling of his cloak as he bent to inspect the baseboard.

As noiselessly as he could manage, Hope tried to reach for the pistol in his jacket. But Miss Blaise was wound too tightly in his arms for him to access it; he had no room in which to move besides.

The scraping sound of the intruder's hand halted just as suddenly as it began. Hope nearly choked with relief; Miss Blaise remained stiff and shivering against him.

Hope removed his hand from her mouth. As if on cue, Miss Blaise whimpered, a small but succinct sound.

She froze. He froze. The voices in the room went silent.

La Reinette tried to pass the sound off as her own, and began offering her unwanted guests the company of her girls.

But they were not listening.

Their footsteps were impatient and heavy as they hurried

toward the closet, cursing with glee in their native tongue. With their gloved hands they pressed against the panel where it met with Hope's shoulder. He gritted his teeth against the tight burn that laced through his arm. He pulled Sophia against him, and braced himself for—

Well. For whatever came next.

Four

---❖---

Yes, Sophia was in a state of most acute distress; yes, she was, in the next five minutes, likely to face death and dismemberment; and yes, she was in the arms of an apparently dangerous, definitely handsome man, the crisp lapels of his dinner jacket sliding up and down her breasts with each breath he took, his scent of sandalwood and lemon faint but delicious.

Even in the midst of such ghastly circumstances, she marveled at her stupidity. Though the whimper had escaped her lips instinctively, without invitation, she cursed herself for ruining their chances of escaping these goons unscathed.

Never mind the fact that the whimper had nothing at all to do with said goons. She'd whimpered not out of fear or distress or panic. No.

Sophia had whimpered at the loss of Mr. Thomas Hope's touch. Oh, that *touch*.

It was confident and urgent and very warm. A lovely little shiver had raced through her at the sensation of his skin pressed against her own. Combined with the heat of their tangled limbs, it was enough to fill Sophia's head with all sorts of salacious imaginings. How it would feel, for example, if it were his lips pressed against her mouth, instead of his palm. How that palm might make its way down the slope of her neck to cup her shoulder, then her breast—

Good God. La Reinette's tales of romance and adventure had certainly taken root in Sophia's fertile imagination.

But now that Sophia was in the midst of her own adventure—the romance bit had yet to materialize, but she apparently longed for it, madly—she was making a muck of it. Indeed, if she kept whimpering—really, who *whimpered*?— this was going to be her first, and last, adventure. Ever.

Sophia's bare hands were caught between their bodies, her palms pressed against Mr. Hope's broad, solid chest. She felt his heart pounding beneath the layers of his clothes, and pound yet harder when the men chasing him began clawing at the panel behind which she and Hope were hiding.

This was bad. Very, *very* bad.

Panic sliced through her. Instinctively her fingers clenched on Hope's chest, pulling at the fine fabric of his jacket. The first two fingers stilled when they gathered between them something jarringly hard and shapely tucked into his waistcoat.

Her fingers went to work, tracing the outline of what felt to be—oh dear, it was indeed—a pistol.

Her blood jumped. *A pistol!* Hysteria sparked at the back of her throat, stoked to flames by the intruders' incessant pounding against the closet panel. She tried to draw her hand away but Mr. Hope held her too tightly, pressing her hand firmly against his weapon.

La Reinette would have used just such a euphemism in her tales, Sophia thought wildly, and together they would have laughed about it over their pages and their wine.

The thought calmed Sophia, and she wondered what, exactly, would La Reinette, that great admirer of dangerous men, do in this situation?

As soon as she asked the question, Sophia knew the answer.

La Reinette would take matters into her own hands. Literally.

Mr. Hope's pistol pressed invitingly against Sophia's palm. She knew he could not reach the pistol himself, his arms stuck akimbo in the tiny closet. In the darkness she tapped twice on the gun, and while she could not see his face, she felt his eyes upon her. A beat of understanding passed between them; Hope loosened his grip on her so that she might grasp the pistol.

She curled her fingers around the metal, warm after having been tucked against the heat of his body. The weight of it nearly snapped her wrist as she pulled it from Hope's waist-coat. It was bigger than she'd imagined, and felt sinister in her hand.

Another euphemism that would have made La Reinette proud.

"Be careful," Mr. Hope hissed. "Have you ever shot before?"

"No-o?"

"Well," he answered tightly. "There's a first time for everything, isn't there, Miss Blaise?"

The intruders' pounding became unbearable. The wall that hid Sophia and Hope clattered against its frame, and finally splintered with a heartrending *crack*.

"Careful!" Hope breathed into her ear as the light from Madame's chamber flooded the closet.

The intruders, their masked, unshaven faces feral, peered over the debris like two red-eyed raccoons. They pulled what was left of the panel away from the closet. One of them—Sophia knew he was the cigar-voiced man, just by looking at him—sneered and lunged forward.

Mr. Hope propelled their bodies out of the closet, tucking Sophia behind his broad shoulders. She glanced down at the pistol, able to see it at last in the light.

It was enormous.

Not only that. It was enormously complicated-looking.

Oh dear.

The sneering intruder was on them now, swinging at Hope. He ducked just in time, allowing Sophia the perfect shot: the intruder's wide chest was exposed as he fell headfirst toward her.

She stepped forward and raised the gun, using both arms to support its weight. Slipping her finger into the inviting arc of the trigger, she gritted her teeth and pulled.

And pulled.

And pulled.

Nothing happened.

"Deuced thing!" she cried.

Before she could try again, Mr. Hope was behind her, wrapping his arms around her own as he took the pistol in his hand. In the space of a single blink—really, that's all it took—he pulled back what appeared to be another trigger on top of the gun and fired it.

Sophia started at the awesome force of it, the sound so loud that for several seconds afterward she couldn't hear much of anything. A cloud of singed smoke enveloped them, and in the fog Sophia felt the floor beneath her feet vibrate with a single, distinct thud.

The intruder had fallen.

Behind her Mr. Hope was shouting, and La Reinette was shouting back from somewhere in the chamber. Their voices were curiously faint.

And then she and Hope were running, her legs moving as if through water; they were at once heavy and weightless, taking her out of Madame's chamber, through the gallery, and down a narrow, winding stair hidden behind an iron balustrade.

Sophia looked down to see her hand clasped firmly in Mr. Hope's. She looked up to see the gleaming line of his jaw twitch with murderous intent, his dark curls wild around the inviting curve of his ear.

Behind them came the sound of heavy footsteps. One or both of those dreadful Frenchmen were still in pursuit.

Hope increased his pace without looking back, tugging Sophia along behind him. Her heart knocked painfully against her lungs, her every muscle begging her to stop the assault.

Just when she thought she might collapse, they stumbled through an unfamiliar door and out onto a dark lane that stank of refuse and horse manure. The night was close and complete here; Sophia found it difficult to breathe.

"This way!" Hope skidded on the gravel around a corner and broke into an all-out sprint. He glanced back at Sophia, his blue eyes translucent in the darkness.

"Not," he panted, "much. Farther."

She began to fall back, and felt herself become a weight on Mr. Hope's arm. Dear God, she was going to collapse. The air was too thick, her legs too heavy.

But then the sound of hurried footsteps again broke out behind them. Her panic propelled her forward, her gait pulling her in line with Hope.

Together they skidded around another corner and drew up before the dark shadow of an unmarked coach. Tendrils of smoke rose from its recently extinguished lamps.

"Get in!" a man called from the coachman's bench. He snapped the reins, and the horses began to move, leading the carriage out into the lane.

Hope reached for the carriage door and pried it open, trotting beside the vehicle as it quickened pace.

"You. First," he said to Sophia. He pulled her against him and looped his palms through her underarms. "Pull. And I. Will push!"

Sophia reached for the carriage and managed to grasp either side of the door opening. Gritting her teeth against the pain of her exertion, she pulled with what was left of her strength. The force of Hope's push knocked her breathless as she somersaulted into the coach.

Somewhere in the back of her mind she knew her ungainly leap had exposed a goodly bit of thigh, and probably more than that. But such virginal considerations seemed to hardly signify in the face of pistols and feral Frenchmen.

She didn't know why any of this was happening, or where the carriage would take her. But this was just the sort of adventure that she so admired in La Reinette's tales, and if such adventure involved nudity, then so be it.

By now the horses were in an all-out gallop, the carriage heaving violently behind them. Sophia scrambled to her feet and reached out for Hope. He took her hands and with an ungainly leap fell into the coach, his legs dangling out the open door.

When at last she managed to wiggle the rest of his great bulk into the carriage, Sophia collapsed on the floor, gasping for air. Mr. Hope rose to his knees as he reached for the door, which was swinging wildly in time to the coach's erratic movement.

"Who the devil. Was that?" Mr. Hope called out the open door.

"Who the devil is *she*?" came the coachman's shout.

Mr. Hope slammed the door shut in reply, and with a tremendous sigh fell heavily on the ground beside Sophia.

Shoulder to shoulder, they sat together gasping for several beats.

"Oh. Miss Blaise." Hope turned his head to look at her. "You visited La. Reinette on the wrong. Night I'm. Afraid."

Sophia glanced up to meet his eyes. *Those eyes.* He was looking at her closely, carefully. With great interest.

Looking at her like no one—man or woman, save perhaps her dearest mama—had ever looked at her before.

She quickly looked away, focusing her gaze on her lap. A moment ago she believed her heart beat as quickly and as vigorously as it could as she ran side by side with Hope from The Glossy.

Now she knew differently. It seemed with his gaze alone, Mr. Hope could very well coax her heart to explode from the prison of her ribs.

She swallowed. Hard.

"Is this what you do every Wednesday night?" She smiled into her lap. "If I had known bankers lived such exciting lives I would've angled to become one myself."

Mr. Hope paused, taken aback by her words; and then he laughed, laughed and put his hand on her knee. "Oh. Miss Blaise," he said again. "If I experienced such excitement every Wednesday, I daresay I'd be dead."

Sophia stared at his hand in the darkness, feeling the warmth of his fingers through the thin muslin of her gown. They were handsome fingers, broad but well kept and elegant, capable-looking, just like the rest of him.

She felt the heat rising to her cheeks. So much *touching.* It made her want to reach out and touch him back, to feel the heat of someone else's thrill beneath her palm.

Mr. Hope must have noticed, for he cleared his throat and pulled his hand away.

Sophia shifted uncomfortably as a beat of awkward silence stretched between them. She let her head fall back against the side of the coach, and tried not to wince as they clattered over a particularly jarring bump.

"You mustn't tell anyone," she said, closing her eyes. "Everything. Anything. I know Violet trusts you, but—"

"You have my word, Miss Blaise. I daresay I must ask the same courtesy of you. You see, I don't usually—"

The carriage lurched; suddenly the pounding of hooves, not far behind, filled the night.

The Frenchman was back, and in hot pursuit on horseback. Sophia's blood ran cold at the memory of his greedy eyes peeking over the debris of the plasterwork.

"Bloody hell." Hope rose into a seat and carefully pulled Sophia up beside him as the carriage bumped and jostled them against one another. He pounded the ceiling with his fist. "He's back!"

"I *see* that!" the coachman replied.

As if on cue, the rider appeared by the window at Sophia's side. She could see the gleam of his teeth as he grinned at her, holding the reins in one hand while in the other he brandished a pistol—Hope's pistol.

Sophia screamed. She heard the discharge of the gun just as the carriage jerked forward, Mr. Hope pressing her head into his lap. The window shattered and there was a great, billowing sound, like close thunder.

She managed to glance up at Mr. Hope. He was grinning. "He missed!" he shouted.

The carriage bolted left, throwing them against the far wall; then it bolted right, and Sophia nearly careened out the broken window before Mr. Hope grabbed her by her wrists and hauled her back against him.

For what seemed an eternity the chase continued in such a fashion, the coach leaping and groaning as it hurtled toward God knew where. Sophia was possessed of a strong stomach, but even so she felt the threat at the back of her throat of losing dinner more than once. Together she and Hope held on for dear life as they raced through the streets of Mayfair.

At last the sound of their pursuer's horse grew distant, and then disappeared altogether. She dared sit straight, her person once again in the line of fire, only when the carriage drew to a halt.

Hope let out a long, hot sigh. Sophia, however, was too shaken to feel any sense of relief. Or, perhaps, too enthralled.

She looked out the broken window and started, a now-familiar panic tingling to life in her chest.

"Where are we?" Her voice was tight. "We haven't left London, have we?"

Mr. Hope stuck his head out the broken window and considered their surroundings. The night was ravenous here, swallowing everything in its path. New grass and open space filled the air. It was damp; the rain would come any minute now.

"Well. I cannot be sure. But I've never known London to smell like *this*." Mr. Hope ducked back into the carriage, his smile fading as his eyes fell on her face. "You needn't worry, Miss Blaise, I'll have you back—"

The carriage door swung open, revealing a tall, sinister shadow with pale hair that gleamed blue in the faint light of the clouds above. Sophia jumped, nearly landing in Mr. Hope's lap.

"Terrifying, I know," Hope said.

"Terrifyingly handsome, you mean," the shadow said. He raised a lantern, illuminating his face, one side of his mouth kicked up in a devilish smirk. Sophia practically clawed Mr. Hope at the sight of the black patch covering one of the man's eyes, the sinister intent glittering in the other.

Dear God, pirates really *did* exist, despite her mother's assurances to the contrary!

"I thought you said you didn't like women," the shadow said, his eyes—his one eye—never leaving Sophia.

She leaned further into the solid warmth of Hope's chest. It was obvious this man was no coachman.

Mr. Hope tucked back the curls from his forehead and sighed. "I said that I *avoided* women, not that I didn't *like* them. Besides, it isn't what you think."

"Who is she? One of La Reinette's girls?"

"No," Hope replied. He rose to his feet and pushed the shadow from the threshold. Leaping to the ground, Mr. Hope turned and held up his hands.

"Who is she?" the shadow asked again.

Hope put his hands to Sophia's ribs, grazing the underside of her breasts with his thumbs.

She couldn't help it. She had to sigh as he lifted her to the ground. In the dark his hands lingered on her body a beat longer than was necessary.

Her heart hiccupped in her chest.

Too soon, he pulled away.

"I'm not above leaving her here if you don't tell me who she is."

Mr. Hope looked from Sophia to Lake and back again. He ran a hand through the tangle of his curls and sighed.

"If I vouch for each of you," he said, "might I make the introduction? You've my word as a banker and a friend, anything that happens this night shall remain between the three of us."

The shadow harrumphed. "Your word as a banker? Best run for the hills, then."

Sophia swallowed. He was even more enormous up close. His neck appeared to be as big around as her leg.

She glanced at her surroundings. They were stopped on the edge of a poorly tended road, a copse of trees to their left, a fallow field to their right. She hadn't a clue where they were, or why, or if the Frenchman would return to slit their throats.

Sophia looked back to the shadow. She risked everything by revealing herself to him. But she risked even more doing nothing.

There was something dangerous about this man. A character straight out of La Reinette's tales, he stank of intrigue and adventure. She had no doubt she would experience both in spades if she followed him, and Mr. Hope, into the night.

Dropping into a curtsy, she bowed her head and spoke before Hope could stop her. "Sophia Blaise. I am your servant."

To her surprise the shadow sketched an elegant bow. Just low enough, no groveling for him; he was, she realized, a gentleman.

"Well now, that wasn't so difficult! I am Henry Beaton Lake. Tell me, Miss Blaise, since we are on the subject of service; how do you feel about aiding in the fight against those nasty libertines the French? King and country, my dear. Tonight they require your aid."

Severed from rational thought, the word escaped her lips in a rush. "Yes."

"No," Hope said. "You'll not involve her in this."

Mr. Lake shrugged. "She's here. Nothing we can do about that now—begging your pardon, Miss Blaise. Indeed, I do believe this is a most happy surprise, for as I have looked upon your most lovely face, I've been struck by a novel idea. But first you must swear upon your very life that you shall tell no one what we share with you this night. I do so hate killing those who betray our cause." He held aloft the lantern, its yellow light illuminating his wolfish grin.

Five

---❖---

Montague House was a pile of soot-blackened stones and tiny, squinting windows that lent it the appearance of an elderly fellow suffering a bout of digestive distress.

Appropriate, thought Hope, for the residence of Her Majesty the Princess of Wales.

Together with Miss Blaise he ascended the shallow front steps, her arm tucked snugly into the crook of his own. She held her shoulders square, but by the way she rolled her bottom lip between her teeth, he could tell she was nervous.

Oh, that *lip*. A just-bitten shade of pink, swollen from her ministrations. For a heartbeat he imagined himself finishing the job, taking the top lip and working it between his own.

Miss Blaise looked at him from the corner of her eye and caught him staring. He snapped his eyes to Montague House's front door, painted a garish shade of red, and felt himself flush the same color.

"Keep calm." He spoke as much to himself as he did to her. "And as I told you before, Miss Blaise, it is best not to stare."

She arched a brow. "'Miss Blaise'? If I am to play your betrothed, shouldn't you call me Sophia?"

The heat in his cheeks burned hotter. He cleared his throat and gave his cravat a ruthless tug. "Of course. Sophia."

"Of course. Thomas." Her grin was impish, her gold eyes dancing. He blinked. Hope had never seen her like this; during his visits to her family, Sophia always played the proper, if somewhat bland, young lady. But now he saw that mischief suited her. Hell, the girl had attempted to shoot a man not an hour ago. Though the attempt was unsuccessful, Sophia appeared all the more alive and eager for having done it.

Sophia. Thomas. The sound of his given name on her lips. He hadn't been called Thomas in years, not since he left his family and fortune behind in Amsterdam.

And now here he was, risking all he'd earned back with a lie on his tongue and a damnably alluring debutante at his side.

There were no two ways about it. He was mad.

Together with Sophia, Hope mounted the top step and raised his hand, knocking soundly on the door. He stepped back and waited in breathless silence, the muffled sounds of the house loud in his ears. Music, laughter, the strangled barking of small dogs.

Hope swallowed his surprise when a handsomely middle-aged man opened the door and bowed them inside. The butler was exceedingly normal, charming even, for a member of Princess Caroline's entourage.

"You are just in time." The butler took Sophia's cloak, and held out a hand for Hope's hat and coat. "Her Majesty is expecting you."

He led them up a short, squat stair to a wide gallery decorated in the Prussian style. Heavy dark moldings enclosed the space, and enormous paintings and banners hung from the walls in an excessive and self-conscious proclamation of Princess Caroline's exalted lineage.

The music and laughter grew louder and reached a crescendo when the butler paused outside a low, wide doorway, and motioned them inside.

Sophia glanced up at Hope. He nodded and let go of her arm, trailing his hand down her side to rest on the small of her back. He felt her spine harden as she took a deep breath, the butler's voice clear and proud as he announced their presence.

Hope followed her into the small chamber, a tower room with curving walls and a tall beamed ceiling that rose to a fine point high above their heads. Sophia fell into a deep curtsy as he sketched his finest bow. They rose, and he heard Sophia's sharp intake of breath as her eyes fell upon the scene before them.

A pair of nubile young men, eyes narrowed to slits with

drink, were laid out upon a sofa. Hope could tell they were Bavarians by their frilly dress and long, unkempt hair. They said nothing, but peered at Hope with a hostile glitter in their eyes, mouths agape as if waiting for an open pour of wine.

Sophia stood very still beside him. She was trying—and failing—not to stare at the figure seated across the room.

Her Majesty the Princess of Wales rose behind a gilded harpsichord, a passel of spaniels at her feet. Hope didn't know where to look first—the painted eyebrows, arching tragically over her tiny black eyes? The grotesquely huge bosom, bursting from a satin gown that Caroline's meaty girth seemed to be swallowing from the inside out? Or the enormous pearl earbobs dangling from her ears, an unfashionable foil to the fistsized emerald slung from a diamond chain about her neck?

Definitely the eyebrows, Hope decided. They were painted black and far too thick for the princess's round, ruddy face.

"Your Majesty." Hope cocked his lips into a smile. "You look ravishing, as always."

A grin broke out on Caroline's face, the wrinkles about her eyes deepening with genuine pleasure. She smoothed the bodice of her gown with a wide, fat hand. "I am glad you have come to visit, Mr. Hope. So few friends I have now in London, and the gossip." She sighed, looking away. "It is worse than ever. Please, do sit."

Mr. Hope and Sophia sat on a settee across from the reclining Bavarians. One of them had fallen asleep, his head thrown back over the sofa's edge, and was snoring softly. The princess lifted a dog into the crook of her arm, cooing to it, and took a seat in a chair beside Mr. Hope with a frown.

"There, on your face." She peered at the cut, dry now, that made his whole cheek sting. "Whatever happened?"

Hope resisted the urge to bring his fingers to his face. "An unfortunate run-in with. Ah. A fork?"

Caroline wrinkled her nose. "A fork?"

"Yes." Hope swallowed. "A fork."

"Indeed." Caroline leaned forward, the chair gasping beneath its burden, to get a closer look at Sophia. "And who is this? A pretty one."

Hope cleared his throat and glanced at Sophia. "I've some news, Majesty. Though I haven't a clue what I did to deserve her, this lovely woman has agreed to be my wife. Miss Sophia Blaise and I shall be married come June."

Princess Caroline gasped. The dog dropped from her arm with a dissatisfied *yap*, and the princess clapped together her hands in a show of childlike joy. "Oh, lovers, let them love! How marvelous! Miss Blaise, you have my sincerest congratulations. Mr. Hope shall prove a wonderful husband." She sighed. "There must be no greater happiness in life than making a love match."

Sophia smiled, warmth radiating from her features. "He is very kind, and decently handsome."

"Decently?" Hope turned his head to look at Sophia. "Not terribly? Wholly? Drop-dead?"

The little minx shrugged her shoulders. "Decently should do, don't you think, Majesty?"

Caroline tittered in a fit of giggles. "Look at the two of you, squabbling like children in the nursery. It tickles my poor old heart." She glanced down at Sophia's hands, clasped neatly in her lap. "But you have no ring! Of all men, Mr. Hope, *you* should know better than to wed without a diamond! My jewels may be the only companions I have left in this world—aside from Gunter and Frederick there, of course— but they have never disappointed me. Nor has their beauty faded to fat, like a certain gentleman of our mutual acquaintance."

Sophia coughed, covering her mouth with a fist to hide the smile that rose unbidden to her lips. Watching her smother her laughter made Hope want to burst with his own.

He cleared his throat. Hope moved to cover Sophia's hands with one of his in her lap. He felt her start beneath his touch but just as quickly warm to him as her laughter faded.

"That is why we have called upon you," Hope said. "You see, Majesty, I was struck very low by Cupid's arrow the moment I laid eyes upon Miss Blaise."

"Love at first sight." Princess Caroline closed her eyes and, clutching a hand to her ample chest, sucked a loud breath through her nose. "Oh, it slays me, this love! I didn't think you capable of such romance, Mr. Hope, what with the bad numbers and worse news you usually bring me."

"I wasn't. Not until I met Miss Blaise. I loved her from the moment we met, and set out to find the most perfect, most flawless gem, for only such a stone would be worthy of her beauty."

Understanding unfurled across Princess Caroline's features. She grinned. "You have not yet found such a stone. And so you come to me." She fingered the emerald at her neck, and batted her eyes. "Tell me what you are looking for."

Hope settled back into the settee. For a moment he contemplated stretching out his arms and legs in a yawning show of nonchalance, but decided against it. Not only did it smack of melodrama, even in the midst of one of Lake's schemes, it would make an even bigger fool of the princess. She was strange, certainly, but kind, and her happiness for Hope and Sophia's pretend engagement was touching. He hated the idea of pulling the wool over her eyes, especially on behalf of that fat gentleman of their mutual acquaintance—the prince regent.

And so he decided on the second best option: candor.

"The French Blue," Hope said, meeting the princess's dark eyes. "I dare not presume you are in possession of that infamous jewel, but if you are, I've twenty thousand pounds in my pocket I'd give you in exchange for that diamond."

He reached into his jacket for said pocket and produced a fresh, if slightly wrinkled, note. He placed it on the marble-topped side table between himself and Princess Caroline.

Silence clouded the chamber as the Princess of Wales surveyed the note. Her expression was inscrutable. Hope's heart began to pound, and the room suddenly felt scorching, airless. He glanced at Sophia. She was playing with her lip again, damn her, and now the room felt *unbearably* hot, sweat breaking out under his collar and along his temples.

He squeezed her hand in his own and the lip popped free of her teeth. She glanced at him, eyes widening as they fell upon his stricken face, then turned her attention to Princess Caroline.

"I told Thomas that he needn't gift me a diamond, for his affection and attentions—" Sophia stopped as her voice tightened. He watched in fascination as she closed her eyes and cleared her throat. "Well. They have been gift enough, your Majesty."

Sophia then proceeded to burst into sobs.

Hope froze.

What in hell? Either he'd done something to offend Sophia, or she was a *much* better actress than she was a shot.

"Oh, my dear, dear girl." Princess Caroline hurried to Sophia's side and nestled her head into her rather epic bosom. "There there, there there. Ah, *el amor*, it is bittersweet, no? But the lovers. We must let them love!"

She released Sophia with a kindly pat on the cheek. "Stay right here, my dear, and I shall return straightaway. No more tears, only happiness!"

The princess swept out of the room in a flash of pearlescent satin and sour perfume, the dogs' nails tinkling as they followed her out. Hope stared at Sophia, unsure what, exactly, he should do next.

Across from them on the sofa, either Gunter or Frederick snorted in his sleep, while the other drooled on a fine tasseled pillow. Whoever these men were—Caroline's lovers, her cousins, the dukes of Bavaria—they were not very good company.

Hope turned to Sophia, who was sniffling beside him. He offered her his handkerchief. "Are you all right?"

She took the handkerchief but did not use it, and instead picked at it with the fingers of one hand while she held it in the other. "Yes. Quite all right. It was your story of Cupid's arrow that got me. Laid *very* low, indeed."

And then they were laughing, their heads bent together as they tried to suppress the sounds of their mirth. If he'd realized how ridiculous he'd sounded, Hope would never have said the words; but then again he and Miss Blaise wouldn't be laughing just now, hard, over the shared joke.

Just as *real* lovers would do.

Lovers, let them love. It did have a nice ring to it.

As Hope and Sophia were gasping for air, Princess Caroline returned, the posse of tinkling dogs at her ankles.

Her face was grave. In her portly hands she grasped a large, exquisitely carved lacquered box, black with looping curls set in silver.

Hope's heart turned over in his chest as a pulse of excitement shot through him.

The French Blue. After all this time, his misadventures, and the implausible, sometimes tragic, history of which Hope had been a part—after all that, was he at last to lay eyes upon the jewel that had fascinated first his father, then him, for years? And in the Princess of Wales's close, puce-colored drawing room, no less!

Caroline settled into her chair and unclasped the box's tiny gilt lock. With bated breath, Hope watched as she opened the lid and held out the box for Sophia and Hope to see.

"My God," he heard Sophia murmur as they straightened in unison to get a better look.

The box was lined in finest white velvet, so fine and silken as to appear pearlescent in the molten light of the room. Against this background the diamond glittered very clear and blue, a transparent color that reminded Hope of the open-air pools in the sultan's palace in Constantinople, gleaming beneath a wide, hot sun.

The jewel was somehow smaller than he'd imagined, but much more beautiful. Seductive even, like a woman with a wicked smile and sphinxlike eyes. He sensed trouble. He knew he couldn't, shouldn't, could never have her; but this desire, it was unlike anything he'd ever known, and the impulse to indulge it was overwhelming.

Cut into an irregular oval, the French Blue was about the size of a small rose bloom. Hope wondered how large it had been when Jean Baptiste Tavernier had brought it, rough and uncut, to France from India some two centuries before. The Sun King's jeweler had done the diamond justice, however; it was brilliant and near flawless. Hope understood where the curse had come from, understood why emperors had toppled kingdoms to possess the jewel; understood why the French Blue meant so much to Lake, and how much it would mean to Napoleon. This power the French Blue possessed over men, it was nothing short of hypnotic.

At last Princess Caroline spoke, breaking the diamond's spell.

"Will this suit my young lovers?" She glanced down at the note on the table beside her. "I do believe it is a fair bargain."

Hope pried his eyes from the diamond and looked at the princess. "The French Blue went missing some twenty years ago in Paris. Some believed it lost forever to the wars that followed. How did you find it?"

The princess blinked and looked away, her smile small and knowing. "Your twenty thousand only goes so far, Mr. Hope. Suffice it to say I came into possession of the French Blue through channels that shall forever remain unknown to history."

Hope swallowed his curiosity. They were so close—so very close to getting what they'd come for. He knew that if he pushed Princess Caroline any further she might renege on the deal.

Still. Something told him that the story of how Caroline came to own the diamond was an intriguing one, a missing piece of the puzzle he'd been trying to solve for years.

Beside him, Sophia squeezed his hand. He met her eyes. *Let's go*, she pleaded, *before she changes her mind.*

Hope looked back at the princess. It bothered him, this glaring gap in the jewel's history—what if she'd stolen the diamond? Bought if off a French spy? Was *working* as a French spy?—but he knew there would be time to unravel it later.

He smiled so wide it hurt. "It's perfect. Wouldn't you say, darling?"

Sophia demurred, her cheeks a convincing shade of pink. "You are too generous, Thomas. I shall have my wedding gown made to match it, though it's too large for a ring. Shall I wear it as a necklace or a brooch?"

"Oh, a necklace, definitely a necklace. You shall look ravishing, my dear." The princess closed the box and handed it to Hope. She picked up the note, and without looking at it folded it twice lengthwise and tucked it into the puckered crease between her breasts.

Mr. Hope's pulse skittered as he held the box in his hands. *The French Blue.* Here, right now, in his very hands. Hands that began to shake. He squeezed the box, willing them to be still.

"Thank you, Majesty, you have made a dream come true

this night. You may contact me at the bank tomorrow to arrange the transfer of funds."

"I am sorry to see it go, but as you can see, my husband keeps me in penury." The princess flapped a hand at her surroundings. "Your note brings me comfort of mind and of purse, and for that I must thank you. Perhaps you shall name your firstborn after me? Oh, lovers."

The princess beamed at them. Hope shifted uncomfortably in his seat, his jaw beginning to ache from smiling.

"Well, your Highness," he began, "it's been a pleas—"

"Aren't you going to kiss?" Caroline asked, looking from Hope to Sophia. "It is no small gift, the French Blue, wouldn't you say, Miss Blaise?"

Hope laughed nervously and glanced at Sophia. Her cheeks had gone from pink to persimmon, but her hazel eyes slanted invitingly, sparking with something akin to curiosity.

This was trouble.

"Kiss?" Hope said. "Well. That would hardly be proper, given the circumstances—"

"Not proper? Why, there were never more proper circumstances for a kiss in the history of mankind! Now go on. *Kiss!*"

Hope swallowed for what felt like the hundredth time that night. He turned his head to Sophia and met those warm, inviting eyes of hers. His heart raced, his blood wild.

It's only a kiss, he reminded himself. King and country, saving lives, for England, Harry, and St. George—he could kiss Sophia for all those reasons.

But kissing her for *his* reasons—reasons that now danced in that wild blood of his—that was another matter entirely. He'd already broken a promise he'd made to himself by joining Lake in this wild goose chase. Hope wouldn't—couldn't—break another by seducing Miss Sophia Blaise.

And yet here she was, those eyes and those lips. Oh, those lips, they just begged to be kissed. His groin tightened as he remembered her working that bottom lip earlier that evening. How he'd longed to work it himself, the top lip, too, and—

Again the twist of desire between his legs.

The urge rolled over him as swift and sure as the tide. He

couldn't say no, not when she looked at him like that, confident and terrified and curious all at once.

Thomas set the box in his lap and reached out and cradled her face in his palm, his thumb gently holding her chin in place. His eyes never leaving hers, he leaned forward, wondering vaguely if he even remembered how to do it, and do it well.

Six

Thomas knew how to kiss very well indeed.

Not that Sophia had any experience with things like kisses.

But God *above* it was a special sort of heaven, the firm but sensual press of his lips to hers, the obvious care he took in applying just enough pressure but never too much.

It had all happened so quickly. She watched with bated breath as he'd leaned forward, his blue eyes suddenly serious and clouded. Something about the lean slant of his neck as he tilted his head, just so, made her entire being pulse with longing. Mr. Hope—Thomas—was deucedly handsome. Devilishly, deucedly handsome.

When he drew too close, and she could no longer bear the anticipation, her eyes fluttered shut. And then his breath was soft and sweet upon her face, and she felt herself leaning into him.

And then.

And *then*.

Their lips met. The kiss was tender; the warmth of it surprised her, the intimacy of it terrifying. She had to resist the impulse to pull away, and yet her body yearned for more.

Hope's thumb grazed the line of her jaw, and suddenly the kiss deepened, so much so that Sophia could feel it all the way in her knees. Pleasure coursed through her when his lips moved against hers, slowly, skillfully, and she felt herself falling into the kiss, moving her mouth in time to his.

The assault was endless, and Sophia reveled in the sensation of being captured by him, her blood pounding as Thomas arched over her. With each stroke of his lips he turned his head, and with his hand turned her face so that that she matched his movements. For a moment the kiss slowed, and Hope's hand slipped further toward her. She shivered as his fingers brushed the skin of her neck, his thumb tugging at her earlobe; and then those fingers were tangled in her hair, and he was taking her bottom lip between his own.

All the while moving slowly, with great intent and concentration. His touch was sure but soft. She drank deeply, her belly turning over at his passion; hers, too.

Being kissed was wholly different, and God above so much better, than she'd imagined it would be. But even Sophia in her ignorance knew this was no mere kiss, not the kind a debutante would share with a beau. This kiss was too honest and bold. It spoke of forbidden things. Attraction. Desire. A curiosity to push further, and know more.

Through the pounding of her heart and lips, Sophia heard Princess Caroline making an odd, high-pitched sound. Her blood leapt in dismay at the realization her kiss with Thomas would end.

He slid his hand back to cup her jaw. He tugged at her lips one last time, his teeth lingering on her bottom lip before he pulled away altogether.

Sophia opened her eyes, chest heaving in an attempt to catch her breath. Thomas was looking at her, his blue eyes probing and full of concern.

As if he had anything to be concerned about. The kiss— *his* kiss—it was so deucedly good it left her all but shaking.

For a moment she was overcome by a sense of wonder. Where had Mr. Hope learned such sensual skill? And how did she get so lucky as to experience it?

Regardless, Sophia knew one thing for certain.

She was ruined. Not the kind of ruin that got everyone in the upper ten thousand, her mother especially, so excited. No.

She was ruined for whichever poor marquess or earl's son whom she (hopefully) married. For there was no way on God's green earth that anyone could possibly kiss as well as Mr. Thomas Hope, that any man could thrill her with his lips alone as he had done.

She wanted to throttle him for giving her a taste of something that could never be hers.

Looking into his eyes, she also wanted to beg him to do it again, right here in front of the princess, that diamond be damned. Beg him to kiss her again, and show her everything that came after.

She blinked, a small smile creeping to her lips.

Thomas let out a sigh of relief and returned her smile, the creases at the edges of his eyes deepening with laughter.

Why had Sophia never noticed how handsome he was until now?

Together they turned to face Princess Caroline, who was weeping noisily into the bowl of her hands.

Sophia handed Her Majesty the handkerchief Hope had given her moments earlier.

Caroline took it and blew her nose into it, making a very unladylike honking sound as she did so. Sophia bit her lip to keep from laughing.

"Oh, lovers, don't mind me." The princess waved the sodden handkerchief at no one in particular. "That kiss, God save me! I can see the love you bear one another. It is a—a"—here her voice faltered—"a beautiful thing!"

She collapsed into sobs. Mr. Hope wasted no time. He stood and patted the princess on the shoulder, whispering assurances in her ear—something about love, and life's journey, and the prince regent coming around.

Caroline gazed upon him with a watery smile, and thanked him for his kind words. She looked to Sophia, blotting her red eyes with the handkerchief, and sniffled.

"How lucky you are, dear girl, to be loved by a man like Hope," she said. She paused to blow her nose again. "In this world romance is all but dead. But in his eyes, I see it is alive. Oh, lovers!"

Again the sobs; again, Mr. Hope whispering kind words in her ear. The princess wiped at her eyes, smudging one of her eyebrows so that it appeared a slightly askew comma, hung high in the middle of her forehead.

Mr. Hope met Sophia's gaze over the princess's head as he patted her gently on the shoulder. He shrugged, and mouthed *I'm sorry* with a roll of his eyes. He tried, and failed, to repress the boyish grin twitching at the sides of his mouth.

Sophia looked into her lap and held back her own smile.

How many times she'd smiled this evening—well, considering the circumstances, diamond and deception and all that, more than was proper, surely.

It was all Hope's fault. He made her feel giddy, and alive, and safe, as if nothing she did or said would be the *wrong* thing. And what a relief that was.

At last, when the princess cried her eyes to slits, she called for her maids to put her to bed. Bowing his thanks, Mr. Hope held out his hand to Sophia and helped her rise from the settee, the box containing the French Blue tucked into the crook of his arm.

They left the princess with Gunter and Frederick in the puce-colored room, keeping their steps slow and even lest they be consumed by a newborn eagerness to know what, exactly, *did* come after the kiss they shared.

S ophia had known Mr. Hope for years now—in a professional capacity, of course. Most, if not all, of her family's meager fortune was invested in Hope & Co. stock; Mr. Hope had come to their shabby house in Grosvenor Square once a week to meet with Cousin Violet and discuss—well, Sophia didn't quite know what they discussed, though she was relatively certain it wasn't nearly as interesting as the conversations she'd had with Mr. Hope tonight.

But now that Sophia knew him on more *intimate* terms, she suddenly found it difficult to meet his eyes, training her own on her feet. They sat opposite each other in the swaying coach, the French Blue in its shiny box on the seat beside Mr. Hope.

While they both burst into laughter the moment the coach pulled away from Montague House, after they wiped their eyes a charged silence settled between them. Outside, the night was still and humid, holding its breath for the rain that would come at any moment.

Sophia bit her lip to keep from squirming, the lip that was still tingling from Mr. Hope's ardent attentions. In her chest her heart was giddy, her every sense aware of his presence an arm's length away. Her eyes traveled from his boots, dull from tonight's adventures, up the length of his long, shapely legs, to his square knees, set just apart. His thighs were impossibly long and well muscled, filling his fine breeches to great effect.

Really, she must've been blind all these years not to see what a very fine specimen Mr. Hope was. Very fine indeed.

Of its own volition her gaze kept moving up, passing over a suspicious bulge protruding from the place where his legs met his hips; up past the narrow waist to land on his broad, finely wrought chest, rising and falling in long, steady strokes.

She swallowed. It was more than a little impolite to stare as she was, but *my God* Sophia felt as if she were living in one of La Reinette's thrilling tales. And if this was her only chance to know, even for a night, romance and adventure and dangerous, good-looking men, then manners be damned, she was going to know them, and know them thoroughly.

Her gaze traveled up his neck to his face. Her breath caught in her throat when she caught him looking at her, and she burned beneath the intensity of his stare.

"Awful quiet in there! Any casualties?"

Mr. Lake's jolly, muffled voice startled Sophia and Hope into motion, Sophia jolting forward in her seat, and Mr. Hope jolting forward in his to catch her.

Hope groaned and rolled his eyes. "That man is a plague," he muttered. He reached up and pounded the ceiling with his fist. "No casualties!"

Mr. Lake chuckled. "We'll see about that, you devil."

Holding Sophia's elbows in his palms, Mr. Hope shook his head. "Some cheek that man has, calling *me* the devil."

Sophia smiled, doing her best to ignore the heat that pulsed through her at Hope's touch. "I think he means it as a compliment, Mr. Hope."

"Mr. Hope?" He cocked his head to the side, eyes sparking with mischief. "Sounds like a stodgy fellow, old and boring, doesn't he?"

"Thomas." Sophia's smile grew. "I suppose having shared a closet and a kiss, we are to be friends now."

"Friends, yes." Mr. Hope slid his palms down the length of her forearms to clasp her hands. He looked down at her fingers and ran his thumb along the edge of her palm.

That touch.

A shiver of anticipation sparked up her spine.

"I hope you'll forgive me——" He paused, as if deciding what to say next. At last he looked up. His eyes, very blue, seemed to glow in the darkness, earnest with an edge of daring. He scoffed. "There's no decent way to phrase this, I'm afraid. And what I'm about to say—I mean it as a compliment, I do, so I hope you will take no offense. But you are not at all what—whom—I expected. Where has Sophia been hiding all these years? Under Miss Blaise's bed?"

It was Sophia's turn to scoff. She looked down at their clasped hands, trying in vain to ignore the skittish pounding of her pulse. After a moment she looked up and smiled. "And what of Thomas? Does Mr. Hope stash him in the brandy board of his study?"

"Nowhere else to keep a scoundrel like Thomas. The fellow's liable to drink me out of house and home before summer's out. He's got dashedly expensive taste, you know."

Sophia nodded at the box on the seat beside Hope. "So I'm learning."

"But Sophia," Thomas said, leaning closer. "Sophia, I rather like."

Again she looked down at their hands, only to realize that she, too, leaned close to Thomas, so close the tops of their heads nearly touched. "Me, too. But I'm afraid the *ton* would disagree. And my mother—I daresay Sophia would send her into a fit of apoplexy. I can hear her now: 'The *horror*, oh, the *horror*! How my daughter doth deceive me! Jesus, I am ready, take me now!'

"No," she sighed. "Sophia will not do. She may be an adventurer——"

"And quite the actress, might I add."

Sophia grinned, a bittersweet thing that faded as quickly as it appeared. "Flatterer. Any debutante worth her salt knows how to make a scene. I've yet to master the swoon, but I can wail with the best of them."

He lightly squeezed her hands, imploring her to meet his eyes. They were narrowed, his head cocked to the side in curiosity. He was looking at her in that way again, his handsome face glowing with unabashed interest. Sophia didn't know what she'd done, exactly, to garner such attention; there had been none of the batting eyelashes or forced laughter or meaningless flattery she usually employed at Almack's.

Not that such things had proven effective in snaring suitors, anyway.

But still. Sophia did nothing to earn Hope's attention, save tear through the night at his side with giddy abandon.

And any debutante worth her salt knew giddy abandon was not the sort of sentiment that attracted a well-connected viscount or duke's son.

"Besides." Sophia made to drop Thomas's hands, but he held her fast. "No man in his right mind would risk life and limb on an attachment to an adventurer and an actress."

"The *horror*!" Thomas grinned, shaking his head. "No, Sophia, I must disagree. Men and their right minds aside— really, are we even in possession of such things?—some of us prefer adventurers far and away to debutantes."

Sophia looked away, face burning even before she said the words. "Not the sort of gentleman I hope to marry. That I need to marry."

Hope paused. She felt the heat of his gaze as a stifling silence filled the carriage. She hadn't meant to insult him; heavens, he'd shown her a grand time, and a goodly bit of his rather delectable body besides. It wasn't as if Hope had any intentions toward her, the interest in his eyes and the warmth of his touch notwithstanding.

So why did Sophia feel as if she'd just delivered a ringing blow to his handsome cheek? That she'd hurt him in some unknown, but still visceral, way?

"The sort of gentleman you *need* to marry?" Hope carefully released her hands. He sat back and placed his palms on his knees.

Sophia shifted uncomfortably in her seat. "You know my family's circumstances. I don't have much choice. A good marriage will go far to repair our fortunes, and our reputation."

"But you do have a choice. Your family is in the care of Lady Violet's capable hands. She is a savvy investor, Sophia, and sees to your family's fortunes most ably."

Sophia looked out the window. She swallowed. "It's not that I don't trust Violet. It's just—"

The words caught at a sudden, ominous swell in her throat. Good Lord, how many times was she going to weep tonight?

Only this time she wasn't trying to make a scene.

"It's just?" Thomas said softly.

Sophia waved a hand through the air. "Nothing." She pulled a long breath through her nose, hoping to still her wildly beating heart. Across the carriage she met Hope's eyes and managed a tight smile. "I'm sorry, Thomas. I don't mean to burden you with my. Ahem. Dramatics. Most unseemly of me, isn't it?"

To her very great relief, a smile broke out on Mr. Hope's face. "Let us not forget it was your dramatics that saved our arses tonight. Begging your pardon, Sophia." He patted the lacquered box beside him.

Sophia nodded in the French Blue's direction. "So. What's next for you and Mr. Lake?"

"Well." Mr. Hope sighed, an exhausted sound. "London is crawling with old Boney's spies, so it shouldn't be difficult to turn him on to our scent. The more people who learn of the diamond's discovery, the better chance we'll have of getting the highest price from that blackhearted scrum."

"Perhaps you should host one of your balls." Sophia tapped a finger to her lips. "They are the most famous event of the season. Last year's was one of the few events mama allowed me to attend, and I'll never forget the crush. Or how ridiculous you looked dressed up as that Borgia pope. Almost as ridiculous as Violet in the guise of Lucrezia. She drank so much wine that night she fell down the stairs, do you remember?"

They laughed at that, Hope slowly shaking his head. "How could I forget? If I hadn't been there to catch her, I daresay she'd have a very different nose than the one she has now." He took the box from the seat and held it in his lap. "But I do believe you're on to something, Sophia. Perhaps this year's theme could be 'Great Jewels of the World.'" He paused, a small smile creeping across his lips. "Though there might be some confusion as to what sort of jewels I'm referring to."

With startling clarity, Sophia recalled the scratch of her quill against a half-empty page, recording in badly translated English La Reinette's tale of a smuggler's jewels. Their great size, a "treasure trove the likes of which she'd never seen."

Sophia suddenly understood the madam was not talking about rubies or emeralds.

Her face flooded with a violent rush of heat, and she was grateful for the blurring darkness that hung between her and Thomas.

"Yes. Well." Sophia swallowed. "I'm sure you'll think of something."

She turned her head and nearly started. Familiar stuccoed facades filled the window, slumbering Mayfair mansions rising on either side of a wide, well-kept lane. The smells of London—close air, smoke, and a vague, medieval sort of stench—filled her nostrils.

She blinked as a wave of displeasure spread through her.

Tonight's adventure, it seemed, was over.

It was all she could do not to curse aloud. But she wasn't ready for it to end! Not now. There was more to be done. More to know and discover. More danger, and touching, and kissing—

Her gaze darted back to Mr. Hope, who was pressing his beaver hat onto his mess of curls.

"If you are in agreement, I thought Lake might drop us behind the mews," he said. "I dare not imagine what your poor mama would think if the horses jolted her awake to a face like his."

Sophia grinned. "I don't think she would ever recover."

Hope pounded twice on the roof; Mr. Lake coaxed the horses to stop. Hope removed the diamond from its lacquered box and carefully tucked it into his waistcoat pocket before disembarking. He turned and helped Sophia out onto the street, pulling up her hood against the drizzle that had begun to fall.

Lake looked over his shoulder, his one eye glinting in the dark. "Shall I wait?"

Thomas held out an elbow to Sophia. "No. Good evening, Lake."

Lake's eye narrowed. "Are you sure? I don't mind, really—"

"Lake." Thomas pulled Sophia against him. "*Good evening.*"

Lake sighed, shaking his head. "Very well. Until tomorrow, then. Miss Blaise, it's been a pleasure."

With a low whistle, he jostled the horses into motion and was gone.

Together, Sophia and Thomas turned left and made their way down a dark, narrow alley. Hope held her fast, their legs brushing with every step they took. Neither of them spoke, Sophia's thoughts scattered by the heady thumping of her heart.

Ahead, the familiar grim facade of her family's London house loomed where the alley came out onto the lane. If it weren't for Thomas's close—very close—presence, she would've buckled under the full weight of her disappointment.

It really was over. The adventure, her interlude with Thomas, the kissing and the intrigue, the *kissing*—

Hope suddenly turned to her. He tugged none too gently on her arm so that she faced him and stepped forward, pressing his body to hers. She fell back against the wall, her simmering blood at last ignited by the impatience of his movements.

"Sophia." His voice was barely above a whisper; she felt his breath on her face. Even in the darkness she could see the intent in his eyes. They were serious. Warm.

"What were you doing at The Glossy?"

She looked up at him, too terrified, too enthralled, to reply.

"Sophia. I'll have an answer. La Reinette is not the sort of company a lady like you should keep, adventurer or no. She is alluring, certainly. But dangerous, too. Any deal you have made with her will only come back to haunt you."

Sophia swallowed, hard. "I. Well. I. I'm not at liberty to say."

Hope stared at her. Again he stepped forward, pressing his arm to the wall beside her head, and leaned down so that his face was half an inch from hers.

He surrounded her, his enormous shoulders blocking the night from view. Around them came the growing patter of rain.

"Sophia." His voice was little more than a growl. "A debutante in search of a brilliant match doesn't dally about in whorehouses. Tell me. What business do you have at The Glossy?"

The rain was coming down with great intent, rolling off the brim of Hope's hat into her face. In a swift, impulsive movement, Hope pulled his hat from his head, his curls falling rakishly across his forehead.

Sophia let out a breath. If Hope wasn't holding her up with

his weight, her knees would have *definitely* buckled. Good God, never did a man look so delicious in his looming as Mr. Thomas Hope.

"Sophia," he repeated.

She ran her tongue along her bottom lip, suddenly alive with sensation.

The words came before she could stop them, a defense against his questions; a plea of desire.

"Do it again."

Thomas paused. "I beg your pardon?"

"Kiss me. Like you did for the princess. Do it again."

His eyes searched hers, moving from one to the other. With every sense she implored him to action, tilting her chin so that her lips waited just beneath the soft curve of his own. The air between them tightened, pulling them slowly toward one another.

Sophia vaguely heard Thomas's hat dropping to the ground beside her; and then his hand was cupping her face and his hair was falling into her eyes and his skin brushed against hers. He took her lips with his own, an urgent but luxuriously careful caress that drew a moan from the back of her throat.

He moved ardently over her now; no time, no need for introductions or assurances, just desire, sure and swift, beating between them.

Taking her bottom lip in his teeth, he opened her mouth to him, his tongue sliding along the slick insides of her lips. In her veins her blood pounded.

For the second time that night she surrendered to the ruin of Hope's expert touch, his hands and his shoulders, and dear God, this *kiss*.

Seven

—◆—

It was her curiosity that did it, the challenge that sparked in her eyes.

That, and her damnably luscious lips. While Miss Sophia Blaise wasn't entirely guileless—she had, after all, helped him swindle the French Blue from Caroline's grasp—the debutante-cum-actress hadn't the slightest idea how alluring she could be.

Especially with that bottom lip caught between her teeth.

Then there was her sudden, impulsive request. *Do it again. Kiss me.*

Good Lord. What was a decent man to do but oblige the lady, and oblige her most thoroughly?

As for his fear that he'd forgotten how to kiss—it boded well, didn't it, if Sophia asked for another?

Somewhere in the back of his mind he knew she was using the kiss as a weapon against him, a way of avoiding questions she quite clearly did not wish to answer. Her presence in La Reinette's chamber was, to be fair, none of his business.

But when it came to Sophia, Hope did not feel like being fair. Fair was for business, for money, for duels. For cards and the races. For ledgers and war and the shops on Bond Street, the grocer, the steward. Fair was predictable and dull.

No. There was certainly nothing fair about Sophia; her egregious loveliness, her scent. There was nothing fair about the way she stoked his growing desire for her with every word she said, her unexpected bravado and the full, honest sound of her laughter.

He would find out what she was up to with La Reinette, come hell or high water.

Just after he kissed Miss Blaise senseless. Yes. He would find out then.

This time he held nothing back. He kissed her with a passion that was at once foreign and intoxicating, driving deeper, softer; the more of her he possessed and discovered, the more of her he wanted. He felt wild, his body and his heart pushing him forward, his hands cupping her face as he coaxed her lips apart with his tongue.

He'd forgotten just how lovely kissing could be.

Sophia yielded to his caresses, parting her lips. Their kiss deepened, slowed for a moment as he gently explored her warmth. Beneath him she shifted, running her palms up over his chest to land on his shoulders. She slid a hand up the side of his throat, and he groaned when she buried her fingers in the curls at the back of his neck, pulling him closer. With her thumb she gently stroked the cut on his cheek; her touch was featherlight, soothing the wound's sting.

He sensed his own fingers tingling for the feel of her bodice as her breasts pressed far too invitingly against his chest. The impulse—it was nearly impossible to resist. He hadn't expected her to be so willing, so curious, so passionate.

If he didn't stop soon, he knew he'd devour her whole. And while he knew the adventurer in her would very much like to be devoured, the debutante had a reputation to protect, and a certain sort of gentleman to marry.

With one last, lingering stroke of his tongue, he pressed his lips, hard, to hers. And then he pulled away.

For several beats they stood, foreheads touching, his hands still on her face as they gasped for air. Her breath was hot on his face; he slid his last finger down to her throat and felt the ecstatic screaming of her pulse. Her skin was scalding. An invitation for his lips to finish what his hands had started.

He did not want to let her go.

The rain began to fall in earnest, fat, insistent drops that fell straight from a low sky. It was a summer rain, and yet not quite. Not yet. The water was calm but cold.

Not yet.

He slid a wet ribbon of hair from her brow. "You are as a nymph, Sophia. So lovely. So tempting."

Hope dropped his hands from her face. He shut his eyes

against the shouting of his blood to kiss her, touch her, take her, and stepped back, releasing the tension between their bodies.

"I am writing her memoirs."

Hope's eyes flew open at the sound of Sophia's voice. Through the rain he could see the gleam of her eyes, her breast rising and falling as she caught her breath.

Out of all the things she could've said, Hope was certainly not expecting her to say *that*.

"You're a writer?"

Sophia shrugged. "I am no Lord Byron—"

"Thank heaven for that."

"But when I was young, I lived in books. They were an escape." She looked down at her hands. "An escape from my family, the chaos of our house. It wasn't long before I began to write. Stories at first, small things, always in secret. I wrote about romance, adventure, pirates of course. When I was seventeen, my governess discovered one of my pirate melodramas I'd foolishly hidden beneath my pillow. Imagine my shock when, rather than rapping my knuckles with her stick, she asked me to pen her memoirs."

Hope blinked as understanding dawned on him. "Your governess wasn't—"

"Yes."

"Not that Miss Entwhistle, surely—"

"Yes. *That* Miss Entwhistle."

"Dear God. I remember those memoirs caused quite the stir that year." Hope tugged a hand through his curls. "Surely your pirate melodramas were less, er, *explicit* than Miss Entwhistle's tales."

"Not really, no."

Forget his curls. Hope gave his cravat a ruthless tug and cleared his throat. "Well, then. How did you come to work for La Reinette?"

"Miss Entwhistle wrote me some weeks ago, said a friend of hers sought a writer for her memoirs. I had every intention of refusing, I did. But from the moment we met, La Reinette enthralled me. I couldn't say no. The stories she tells! Sometimes I feel *I* ought to be paying *her*."

Thomas furrowed his brow, swiping back his curls with

his hand. La Reinette was his friend and, a decade ago, more than that; she was enthralling, yes, all too aware of the hypnotic power of her beauty.

"Does she mean to publish these memoirs?"

Sophia pushed back her sodden hood. "You know how popular memoirs are these days. The more scandalous, the better."

Thomas stepped forward. He hooked his thumb beneath her chin and lifted her face. Her eyes met his.

"Take care, Sophia. La Reinette may be glamorous, but she resides in a world much different from your own."

Sophia grinned. "If I'm old enough to make my debut, then certainly I'm old enough to look after myself, Thomas."

"I hope you recognize the irony of that statement."

"Please." She placed her palms on his chest. Beneath her touch his heart leapt. "You mustn't tell a soul. I am sworn to secrecy. I shall take care, I promise. Besides, La Reinette guaranteed discretion, protection, too."

"Did she." Thomas frowned. He covered her hands on his chest with his own and sighed. "Very well. But remember what you promised me. And should you find yourself in trouble, you must come to me straightaway."

Pleasure pulsed through him as her grin deepened. "Hm. I think Mr. Lake, with that vicious little eye patch of his, might be better at protecting my prized virtue than a scoundrel like you."

If they weren't standing pressed knee to navel in an alley in Mayfair well past midnight, Hope would've thrown back his head and laughed.

"I've been called many things, Sophia, but never a scoundrel. Though I suppose it *is* scoundrelly to kiss debutantes in dark alleys."

"Scoundrelly, yes. But only in the best of ways."

Her grin was saucy now, playful; her eyes gleamed with pleasure even as drops of rain rolled down the smooth planes of her cheeks.

In the very center of Hope's chest, a puzzling lightness took shape. A lightness he recognized, vaguely, but could not name.

He sighed, biting back the impulse to lean in and proceed with the devouring he'd reluctantly halted a few heartbeats ago. Instead he stooped to pick up his hat and, holding it above Sophia's head, held out his elbow.

Hope sensed her reluctance as she looped her arm through his.

So. She was no more eager for the night to end than he. Hope smiled. He'd done his job, and done it well.

Together they skipped across the lane, the rain mercifully obscuring the sound of their boots on the cobblestones. Sophia led him down the sloping walk that ran along the side of the house, and drew up at last before the kitchen door.

She released his arm and stepped up onto the stoop, turning to face him.

"Well." She clasped her hands. "Thank you, Mr. Hope, for a marvelous evening."

"Thomas. You must call me Thomas."

His name on her lips came out in a soft whisper. "Thomas."

They looked at each other. The lightness in his chest threatened to burst through his entire being. Around them the rain pattered noisily, an opaque curtain that hid this moment from the rest of the world.

Without thinking, Hope leapt forward onto the stoop. With his hand he cupped her face and, drawing close, pressed his lips to her cheek. It was a simple kiss, quick and tender; he couldn't help but kiss her with feeling.

Sophia inhaled, holding her breath as he looked down at her.

"Good night, Sophia." His voice was foreign to him, soft and rough all at once.

Beneath his hand he felt the working of her throat as she swallowed, her eyes never leaving his. "Good night, Thomas," she breathed.

And then, as if waking from a dream, she blinked; she turned and noiselessly scurried into the house.

In her haste, she'd left the door open a crack. He reached for the handle and for a moment allowed his hand to linger there, the metal alive with the memory of her touch. Bowing his head, he closed the door softly behind her. Then he turned and stalked into the darkness.

He took the familiar route in long, hard strides, heart thudding, throat suddenly tight, the pouring rain a welcome antidote to the heat that pulsed beneath his skin.

Thomas.

It had been so long. So very long since he'd been anyone but Mr. Hope, creditor, investor, banker, businessman. Casual acquaintance, trusted but distant friend. This *Thomas*, this man on the lips of a lovely woman, this adventurer—he couldn't possibly exist beside the likes of Mr. Hope. There wasn't time enough in the day, and too many memories besides. Memories he'd spent more than a decade trying to forget.

Hope had left that man behind for a reason. And thus far, forgetting Thomas had served him well.

But now.

He closed his eyes and took a long, deep breath through his nose.

Now all he could smell was the clean, fresh scent of Sophia's skin, the sweet hint of wine on her lips. All he could see were her green-gold eyes, the way they slanted so invitingly as she teased him. He could feel nothing but the warmth of her skin, the opening of her lips, her fingers tangling in his hair.

Could hear nothing but the soft breathlessness of her voice as she said his name.

Thomas.

Nymph indeed.

City of London
Fleet Street
Three days later

M r. Hope held the diamond up to the thick, golden afternoon light that streamed through his office window. He turned the French Blue over in his fingers, wincing as the jewel blinded him with a particularly vicious spark of radiance.

He was thinking of her again. With a smile he recalled Sophia's theatrical sobs, and her wonder at seeing the diamond for the first time. Afterward he'd kissed her, right there in front of Princess Caroline—

"Forbidden fruit, old friend."

Hope started at the sound of the voice, grappling after the diamond as it tumbled from his grasp.

"Dear. *God!*" He caught the French Blue and held it fast in his palm. He looked up and met Mr. Lake's narrowed eye. "Damn you, Lake, how'd you get past my men? This sneaking about has gone on long enough. You're lucky someone hasn't shot you yet."

"Trust me, they've tried. No one's come close, of course—" Hope rolled his eyes. "Of course."

"But I'm deadly good at this 'sneaking about,' as you well know by now. And besides. I like the challenge. Front doors are for ninnies," Lake said, setting a familiar black lacquer box before Hope on the desk.

"If by ninnies you mean normal people, then yes, I concur." Hope carefully placed the diamond back in Princess Caroline's box and shut the lid with an agitated *thwack*. He put his elbows on his desk and clasped his hands. "So. Assuming you haven't come to mock my *History of the World's Greatest Diamond* yet *again*—"

"That's not what I was talking about." Lake crossed his bulging arms and from his considerable height stared down at Hope.

Hope blinked, furrowing his brow. "I don't understand."

Lake continued to stare. "Oh, I think you do."

"Actually, I don't." Hope blinked again. *Forbidden fruit.* What the devil was Lake talking abou—

Ah.

Lake was talking about Sophia.

His face rushed hot, and Hope snapped his gaze to the lacquered box on his desk. Lake was a man of many skills; Hope didn't know until now that mindreading was one of them.

"Sophi—Miss Blaise is none of your business," Hope growled. "Nor is she any of mine, for that matter."

Lake's eyes went as round as his mouth. "Oh. Oh no. I wasn't talking about *her*! I was talking about the diamond." He nodded at the box. "Haha! A telling mistake. Well, then. You've made my point for me—best to stay away from them both, before—well, you know why."

Hope's head hit the back of his chair with a bang. "I hate this game."

"Neither of them belong to you, Hope. Not only is your desire for them useless, it's downright dangerous. Deadly, even.

The French Blue will go to Napoleon,"—Lake pounded the desk with his first finger—"and Miss Blaise will go to a nice marquess with a castle and ten thousand a year. Understood?"

Hope scoffed to cover the sharp, unexpected sting of fury that washed over him at the sound of Sophia's name on Lake's lips. "Perhaps I'll understand when I get back that twenty thousand I loaned you. Deadly my arse." He nodded at a neat stack of correspondence on the far end of his desk, each letter meticulously sealed in Hope's signature blue wax. "The invitations to my ball go out today. 'An Evening at Versailles: the Jewels of the Sun King.' A theme, if I don't say so myself, that is also a decent piece of diplomatic bait. Napoleon will be knocking on your door before the evening is out, make no mistake. And then our assignment is done. What's so deadly about all that?"

Lake glowered. "I didn't come to scold you about keeping your breeches buttoned—"

"You didn't? Really? Because it sure as hell feels like you did."

Lake's face softened into grimness. When he spoke his voice was quiet, serious. "There's a leak. Word has gotten out about our . . ." He looked away. "Ah. *Activities* last Wednesday night."

"What?" For the second time that afternoon, Hope started, fearful his heart might leap from his chest. At once he thought of Sophia, imploring him and Mr. Lake to silence on the side of the road in Blackheath. He'd sworn to keep her secrets safe, that no one would ever learn of her arrangement with La Reinette or involvement in Lake's plot.

Hope knew as well as anyone the *ton* was all too eager to tear apart and shun its own. A debutante who snuck out under cover of darkness to pen an infamous courtesan's memoirs was the stuff of dreams for dour dowagers and their miserable ilk. The gossip and censure would be unbearable; not only would it ruin Sophia, it'd likely destroy her family as well.

Never mind all that Hope had at stake. His reputation, his business, and the countless employees and clients who depended on him. His brothers, Adrian and Henry—though they'd been estranged since, well, since as long as Hope could remember—those wastrels remained his dependents. With the rest of the family gone, Adrian and Henry had no one else to whom to turn.

Lake held up his hand. "Whisperings only. Nothing to condemn us; nothing tantamount to blackmail. Not yet, anyway. But someone knows that we were together last Wednesday evening. And that we were up to something. Whoever he is, he's asking all the right questions."

It was Hope's turn to glower. "So what are we going to do? I made clear to you last time we spoke, it's imperative no one know I am involved."

"Trust me." Lake's eye gleamed with malice. Hope swallowed. "We'll find our rat. And when we do, he'll be *very* sorry he ever opened his mouth But you must take care, Hope. Keep your eyes and ears open. Guard the French Blue with your life. And for God's sake, stay away from that girl. If this rat hasn't already figured out Miss Blaise was involved in our plot, he certainly will if she's seen—er—*associating* with you."

Hope let out a long, hot breath and smiled tightly. "It's always the worst-case scenario with you, isn't it, Lake? If we don't end up dead or ruined or both, I'll do my best to help. But I make no promises."

"All right." Lake cocked a brow before he turned and limped toward the window. With a grunt he heaved it open. "But don't say I didn't warn you. Stay away from that girl."

Hope watched in mute shock as Mr. Lake, pushing aside the damask drapes, grasped either side of the window frame and swung his legs through it. Looking back over his shoulder, he nodded. "I'll see you at the ball. Don't forget, it's important everyone is talking about that bloody jewel. See to it that they do."

With another grunt, he launched his bulk through the window and was gone.

One bad leg.

One good eye.

Really, how the devil did Lake do it?

After Hope managed to retrieve his jaw from the floor, he stood and made his way to the stack of invitations on the edge of his desk. He grasped the letter at the top of the pile, the paper pleasantly smooth and heavy in his hands, and read the address scrawled in looping calligraphy across the page.

His Grace the Duke of Sommer
Her Ladyship Violet Rutledge
Her Ladyship the Dowager Baroness Blaise
Miss Sophia Blaise

Hope looked out the open window. A glorious spring day; the fashionable hour approached. No doubt her ladyship the dowager baroness would be chaperoning Sophia's stroll through Hyde Park. Perhaps they would stop to admire the fine horseflesh—and finer fortuned bachelors—on Rotten Row.

His fingers clenched around the invitation in his hand. He glanced at the gleaming malachite clock on the mantel behind his desk.

Quarter past three. He still had time before the beau monde poured out into the park.

He looked at the pile of pages, bills and wills and all matter of business, that cluttered his desk. An afternoon—and evening's—worth of work, at least.

He looked again at the sunlight streaming through the window.

The invitation had to get there *somehow*. He had a bit of business besides to discuss with Lady Violet.

Yes. Business. *Urgent* business. Business that had absolutely nothing at all to do with Miss Blaise.

But if he should perhaps run into her while conducting said business—well. Such things could not be helped. One *must* be polite, after all.

Calling to his man, Hope tucked the invitation into his waistcoat and made for the door.

Eight

— ✦ —

It had been three days since her adventure with Mr. Hope. *Thomas.*

Three days since he'd pressed his body to hers as they ducked into a closet to avoid deadly assassins. It was so delicious as to be absurd.

Three days since he'd pressed that last kiss into her cheek, searing her flesh with his eager, knowing lips.

And three days since Sophia had seen or heard from Hope last.

She brought her hand to her face, the skin still burning with the memory of those lips. Truth be told, she'd thought of little else but Hope and his diamond since she'd left him standing in the rain outside the kitchen door.

The more she thought, the more she felt. Confused, certainly; she did not understand the first thing about Hope, who was chasing him and why he was involved with that one-eyed monster of a man Mr. Lake.

But even more certainly than that, she felt intrigued. Despite having spent the entire night at his side, Sophia wanted to see him again. Were his eyes as blue and daring as she remembered? Did he laugh as much during the day as he did at night?

And what was it about him, exactly, that made her belly turn over in the most marvelous of ways?

Having drunk deeply his presence, Sophia was thirstier than ever for more.

Who wouldn't be, after that kiss—

"Sophia!"

She nearly fell from her chair. Sophia blinked, the image of

Thomas's night-darkened face leaning in for the kiss replaced far too suddenly by Lady Blaise's look of horror.

"I'm terribly sorry," Sophia said, straightening her spine. "What was that?"

"The *marquess* was just *asking* if you *enjoy* the *theater.*"

Sophia turned to the Marquess of Withington, baring her teeth in what she hoped was more smile than grimace. "Oh, oh yes, my lord. More than you could possibly imagine."

When the marquess had unexpectedly swept into their drawing room a half hour before, boots shining and sideburns trimmed, Sophia had nearly fallen out of her chair for the *first* time that day.

To have the Marquess of Withington call upon one was no small matter. Indeed, to see his gleaming phaeton and pair of matching blacks pulled up before the house had sent a pulse of excitement through her.

And now here he was, patiently wading through what was obviously an excruciating conversation with Lady Blaise and Sophia. She had to give him credit: he was trying very hard not to look at her breasts, and for the most part was succeeding.

Even so. Sophia kept waiting for her initial excitement to return; for the conversation to become enjoyable, or at least easier; for a jest, a joke, a roll of the eyes that would prove the marquess was not the mindless pink he appeared to be.

Thus far, however, he'd proven himself to be exactly that.

"Capital!" Withington's face lit up. "Perhaps you and your mama could join me in my box at Drury Lane. I am partial to Shakespeare—the comedies, of course—but do so love a good opera."

"That would be lovely," Lady Blaise cut in before Sophia could reply. "Perhaps next week?"

"Capital!"

Sophia's smile began to hurt. "I very much look forward to it."

The marquess rose, apparently satisfied. Sophia and Lady Blaise followed him to their feet. "Well, ladies, duty calls; her ladyship my mother is expecting me for tea. It has been a capital afternoon."

He turned to Sophia. To her very great surprise took her hand in his and, jerking into a rather enthusiastic bow, brushed his lips against her knuckles. For a moment his gaze lingered on her bosom before he reluctantly looked up to her face. "Miss Blaise, I do so hope to see you at the theater—"

Over the plane of the marquess's bowed back, a quick, blurred movement in the gallery beyond the drawing room door caught Sophia's eye. A figure, dressed in somber shades of blue and black; she watched as the tail of a jacket disappeared round the edge of the door.

Her heart beat a loud and unsteady rhythm. It couldn't be him. Not at this hour, not today.

Yet. Her heart would not be still.

"Yes, yes, of course, thank you," she murmured as Withington drew up before her.

It seemed an eternity between the time he dropped her hand and his final bow at the door. As soon as the marquess departed, Sophia was moving past her mother, murmuring apologies as she slipped through the door.

Darting into the gallery, she made for the back of the house, where Violet kept her study. Just ahead she heard footsteps, unhurried but firm.

A man's footsteps.

Sophia quickened her pace, walking as fast as her legs would allow without breaking into a run.

She turned the corner, breathless.

There, standing with his back to her in front of the study door, was a familiar figure. With no small appreciation she took in his long, powerful legs, broad shoulders, and the mop of dark, unruly curls that just brushed his collar.

At the sound of her steps he turned his head, right fist raised as if he were about to knock.

In the shadowy light of the hall their gazes collided.

Oh, yes. His eyes were *definitely* as blue as she remembered, and just as piercing. A breathless warmth washed over her, coaxing her lips into an open smile she couldn't have suppressed if she'd wanted to.

A smile that certainly didn't hurt.

"Miss Blaise!" He turned so sharply he lost his footing, falling into an ungainly bow. A wide, flat packet fell from his breast pocket onto the floor.

At once they both dashed forward to retrieve it, their heads nearly bumping as Sophia picked up the packet. Swiping back his hair with one hand, Hope helped her to her feet with the other.

He cleared his throat, his cheeks pink with embarrassment as he attempted to straighten his person. Sophia thought he appeared adorably disheveled; she struggled to resist the temptation to reach out and tuck an errant curl behind his ear.

"Thomas," she said softly. She held out the packet to him. "I did not intend to startle you. Aren't men of your—er—*experience* supposed to be immune to surprise? A sixth sense and all that."

Hope took the packet and looked down at it. While he did not smile, she could tell he was amused. "Seems the only sixth sense I've got is a knack for finding trouble."

"And diamonds. Very *big* diamonds. Besides, what you call trouble others might call—dare I say it?—adventure."

He laughed, looking up at her at last. His eyes were laughing, too, the skin around them crinkling pleasantly.

A beat of silence passed. The color in Hope's cheeks deepened, giving him the look of a shy—albeit devilishly handsome—boy.

She became acutely aware of it then, the tug of desire that moved between them. Bodily desire, of course; but also a desire to *stay*, to ask questions, know more, to understand and be understood.

She recognized the sensation from that night three days ago. But today it felt stronger than it did then. More immediate, a hungrier feeling.

Thomas must have felt it, too. He stepped forward, keeping his voice low. "I wanted—" He paused, embarrassed. "I wanted to write, I did—but I. Well. No, no, that doesn't sound at all right; let me try again. I have thought. Thought about this—er, often. Thought about *you*—"

Sophia waited on the tips of her toes as Mr. Hope tugged a hand through his hair, cheeks flaring with a huff of frustration.

"I'm dismal at this, aren't I?"

"Yes." Sophia offered a small, entranced nod. "But do go on."

"What I meant to say is, I care for—"

Suddenly the study door creaked open, and together they turned to see Cousin Violet, brow furrowed, step into the hall, a ledger cradled in the crook of her left arm. Her blue eyes slid from Hope to Sophia and back again, narrowing with suspicion.

"Did I," she raised a brow, "interrupt something? I wasn't expecting to see you, Mr. Hope, until Tuesday."

They both rushed to speak at once.

"No."

"No!"

"No, most certainly not, no interruption *what*soever!" Thomas looked down at the packet in his hand. He started, as if seeing it for the first time; after half a beat he thrust it forward, offering it to Sophia. "I was just delivering an invitation to my annual ball. Friday next; I do hope you and your family will be able to attend."

"Your ball!" Violet slammed her ledger shut, eyes alight with excitement. "Of course we'll be there. It's the only event of the season that's actually any fun. And your liquor! I promise not to drink as much of it as last year."

She wedged herself between Sophia and Thomas and grabbed the invitation, turning the packet over in her hands and breaking the seal. Sophia peered over her shoulder as she read it.

" 'The Jewels of the Sun King!' " Violet looked up in amazement. "I daresay it's even better than last year's theme! Wherever did you get the idea?"

Over her head, Hope met Sophia's eyes, a smile playing at the corners of his lips. "Come to the ball and perhaps you'll find out."

"You may count on it." Violet folded the page and playfully tapped him on the shoulder. "Are you to be the Sun King?"

"I should think so, yes."

"And your queen? Who is to play her?"

For a split second Hope's eyes widened with panic. A charged silence settled over them; Sophia winced as the floorboards creaked beneath her feet. Violet couldn't possibly know—could she?

Hope cleared his throat and brushed back his curls with his first two fingers. The color in his cheeks rose. "Well. No one at the moment, I'm afraid."

"Are you ill?" Violet drew close. "I've never seen you blush like that."

Again Hope met Sophia's eyes, a plea. "Yes, well . . . no, I mean no. . . ."

Sophia swept between them, looping her arm through Violet's. "After your inquisition, you're lucky Mr. Hope does not rescind his lovely invitation. Besides, we must change if we're to make it to the park on time."

Violet hesitated, searching her cousin's face with those narrowed eyes of hers. Sophia felt herself growing warm beneath Violet's scrutiny, waiting for her to call her and Hope out, question them on the palpably charged air that crackled between them.

Violet was no fool, but Sophia was no witless debutante, either. And so she returned her cousin's gaze levelly, coaxing the heat from her face with every passing heartbeat.

"Very well." Violet turned to Hope. "You're keeping something from me, I can feel it. But I suppose I can wait until the ball to squeeze it out of you. Until Thursday, then."

Mr. Hope bowed. Watching from half a step away, Sophia swallowed in appreciation. Like his person, Thomas's bow was elegant, earnest, and just singular enough to intrigue, rather than intimidate.

He rose. "Until Thursday, Lady Violet." Turning to Sophia, he said, "Miss Blaise. I look forward to seeing you at the ball. It is my sincerest wish that you find it as enjoyable as does your cousin."

She met his eyes one last time, heart thudding in her chest as she read the relief there, and the promise.

A promise, she liked to think, for another go at that kissing business.

"But I don't understand." Violet turned, peering over her shoulder at her reflection in the mirror. "What's a nymph to do with Louis XIV and his jewels? I still think my idea is better. Madame de Montespan makes for a far more intriguing character than a wood nymph. A more dramatic entrance, too."

Sophia glanced in the mirror and, furrowing her brow, bent to smooth the gauze of Violet's train. "My mother would drop dead if you paraded in public as the king's infamously nubile mistress, and you know it. The gauze is scandalous enough, don't you think?"

Violet tugged the neckline of her costume so low the threat of a rogue nipple was very real indeed. She puckered her lips in satisfaction before turning to her cousin. "I suppose. Here, sit; your curls have fallen."

Sophia watched in the mirror as Violet, pins clenched between her teeth, went to work on her hair, fingers featherlight as they tucked and twisted.

Her bravado notwithstanding, Violet would drop dead surely as Lady Blaise if she knew the *real* reason why Sophia so ardently insisted they costume themselves as nymphs for Mr. Hope's ball.

Even now a shiver ran down her spine at the memory of Hope's murmured words, the low, smooth rumble of his voice as he said them.

You are as a nymph, Sophia. So lovely. So tempting.

Would he remember? And more importantly, would he notice her amid the beautiful, perfumed masses that crowded his house?

"There. Lovely." Violet stood back to admire her handiwork. She caught Sophia's eye in the mirror. "Are you nervous? You look nervous. Is it that marquess again, Wart-what's-his-name?"

Sophia blinked, the pleasant reverie of Hope's voice and his lips and the rain dropping from the tip of his nose disappearing in the space of half a heartbeat.

"You know his name, Violet." She sighed. "Withington *is* handsome, isn't he?"

Violet wrinkled her nose. "If fops are your type, then yes, he's very handsome indeed. You always were ambitious, cousin."

"It's no surprise, considering I was raised on Debrett's." She scoffed, but in the mirror her eyes were serious. "I understand that marrying a marquess with ten thousand a year isn't the only dream there is. But my world is very small, Violet. *Our* world is small. What else am I to do? How else can I improve my lot, raise myself, than to marry a man like the marquess? I couldn't very well start a bank, or run a business, like Th—like Mr. Hope. There *is* no other dream for a girl like me, poor and nameless, than to seek a title and live in a great house. A house that doesn't leak when it rains."

Violet rolled her eyes.

"What?" Sophia pouted. "I thought that was a very good speech."

"The house doesn't leak *that* much." Violet playfully tugged on a loose curl at Sophia's ear. "Besides, you're young. Perhaps it's a blessing your first season is . . ." She paused, searching for the right word. "Off to a slow start. Perhaps it's a sign you should take the time to discover what other dreams, as you call them, exist. There's got to be others besides marrying that marquess of yours."

Sophia placed her hands on the vanity and rose, sighing. "You're an heiress with a fondness for books and brandy. Not all of us are so inclined to ignore the opposite sex."

Especially, Sophia thought, when said opposite sex kissed one as if the world were about to end.

Violet took one last look in the mirror, patting her hair. "I don't ignore them, cousin, I mock them. And you forget whatever meager fortune I am meant to inherit is in peril." She turned and looped her arm through Sophia's. "But enough of this boring talk of our troubles. Hope asked we arrive early—"

"He did?"

Violet paused, eyeing her cousin. "Yes. Though I haven't a clue why. Do you?"

Sophia's shoulders shot to her ears. "Why would I know? He's your acquaintance, Violet. Not mine."

But even as she said the words, a new wave of excitement rippled through her. They were to be guests of honor, then. Perhaps Hope *did* remember.

"Hm. A mystery, then. How so like him! Clever man."

Violet led Sophia down to the front hall, where Mr. Freeman, the butler, waited with a letter on a small tray.

"For you, Miss Blaise."

Sophia furrowed her brow. "For me? That's silly. A letter, and at this hour? No one ever writes to me."

It was addressed simply as *M. Blaise* in a gnarled, unfamiliar script. She freed her arm from Violet's grasp and opened the letter somewhat clumsily with her gloved fingers.

"What is it?" Violet asked casually as she straightened the embroidered edge of her own glove.

Sophia inhaled sharply as she read for a second time the

letter's three uneven lines. Her heart began to pound thickly in her chest, a rush of panic prickling at her temples.

For a moment she froze, throat closing with fear.

"Sophia?" Violet was looking at her now. "Is everything all right?"

With hands that trembled, Sophia folded the letter. "Do you know who sent this, Mr. Freeman?"

"I'm afraid I do not, Miss. Found it tucked into the kitchen door. I asked the maids, but they did not see or hear any visitors. Curious."

Sophia swallowed. "Curious, yes."

"What does it say?" Violet asked.

"Nothing important." Sophia managed a tight smile.

Lady Blaise scurried into the hall then, her face and gown a matching shade of pink as she struggled to catch her breath.

Sophia had never in all her years been so relieved to see her mother. She slipped the note into the elbow of her glove and turned to greet her.

"Good heavens, Mama, whatever is the matter?"

"My," she huffed, "gown. It's a bit. *Tighter* than I remember." Violet raised a brow. "A bit?"

"Oh, hush, you. I can't wait until you get old; we'll see who is laughing then." She padded to the front door, waving her fan. "Come along, we mustn't keep Mr. Hope waiting. I hear from Lady Dubblestone that Withington is to attend. Oh! And rumor has it that wastrel Beau Brummell is to make an appearance, though everyone knows he is falling out of favor with the regent, and did you know he soiled himself at the race this past week . . ."

Sophia settled stiffly into the carriage beside Violet, who, as annoyed as she was at Mama's endless tittering, seemed to have all but forgotten about the mysterious letter.

Good. This sort of trouble was above and beyond even Violet's expertise. The sort of trouble that Sophia had hoped to avoid all along.

Nine

— ✦ —

"I look ridiculous."

Mr. Lake shrugged at Hope's grimace. "But I thought you liked costumes? In France you were all too eager to don a disguise. Remember the time you played a one-armed butcher—"

"*This*," Hope pointed to the towering wig of black curls that wobbled on his head, "is a rather different scenario, don't you think? The wig, the shoes—it's a bit much, even for me. And dear *God* my head hurts."

Lake waved away his words. "Small price to pay for king and country, my friend. Though it does make you wonder how old Louis managed it. Fellow must've been bald as a bat to want to wear a wig like that."

"He was a glutton for punishment, no two ways about it." Hope took a deep breath, resisting the urge to itch his head. "Actually, I'm beginning to think we have quite a lot in common."

They were on the terrace, an open bottle of French cognac, smuggled into London not two days ago, resting on the stone balustrade between them. Over the tops of neighboring houses a cloudless sky faded to dusk, the edges of the horizon glowing faintly with the last of the day's sun. A curving peel of moon swam noiselessly through the blue above their heads.

Sounds of last-minute preparations floated through the open ballroom doors. The hurried steps of a dozen footmen; the famous opera soprano he'd hired, practicing her aria; the clink of crystal; the murmuring of kitchen maids as they laid out the refreshment tables.

The sounds pleased him. Nearly five years ago to the day he'd hosted his first costumed ball with the intention of attracting wealthy—and well-known—clientele. A generation before, the Hopes were among the most prominent families in Amsterdam, bankers to and social equals of princes, dukes, even sultans. Their home in Groenendaal Park was one of the finest in the city, its rooms alive with a never-ending progression of teas, soirees, balls, and exhibitions.

It had all ended abruptly, one tragedy after the next. But the memory of his family, their home, and the people whom they had welcomed and entertained there, had kept Hope warm throughout the years of misadventure that followed. When he at last landed on his feet in London, he set about resurrecting the glamorous heyday of the family he so sorely missed.

The ball was an absolute triumph. By the third year, Hope counted among his clients the greatest and wealthiest titles of the *ton*. Though some of the more stalwart members of society refused to socialize with one who (God forbid) *worked* for a living, an invitation to Hope's costumed soirees was nonetheless a coveted one.

This year was no different; he'd done everything in his power to ensure its success. Hell, Hope had even convinced that infamously slippery rake the Earl of Harclay to attend. Tonight's ball was, Hope knew, going to be the biggest and best he'd ever hosted.

Surely there was no greater stage on which to play out Lake's plot to snare Napoleon with the French Blue.

Lake lifted the bottle of cognac to his lips and took a short, ruthless swig. He wiped his mouth with the back of his hand and, as if reading Hope's thoughts, said, "When Bonaparte's men make contact, send for me straightaway. And don't lose sight of that diamond."

Hope reached out and swiped the bottle from Lake's hand. "And you. Don't drink all my cognac. It's bloody impossible to get these days." He took a pull and, retrieving the cork from his waistcoat pocket, pounded it back into place with the heel of his hand. "Who do you think is going to steal the French Blue, anyway? Everyone who's coming tonight can buy their own damned jewels. If I were to peg anyone, it'd be you. Besides, I hired twenty extra men to patrol the ballroom, just in case. Trust me, Lake. *Nothing* is going to happen."

"I don't have to remind you there are no more famous last words than those."

Hope rolled his eyes, deciding a change of subject would best keep him from throttling his unwelcome guest. "Speaking of words. Any word on our leak?"

"No. But I can't shake th—"

They both turned at the sound of female voices coming from inside the ballroom.

"Ah," Lake said softly. "Appears your first guests have arrived."

"Indeed." Hope strained for a look inside, but straightened before the weight of his wig toppled him to the ground.

"Be careful, Hope. And good luck."

"Same to you. I'll be in touch in the morn—"

Turning back, the words caught in his throat. Lake was gone, nothing but the cool evening air in his place.

Hope peered over the edge of the balustrade and sighed. "One of these days you're going to hurt yourself, old man," he murmured.

Taking the bottle in his hand, he turned and made his way through the doors into a gallery, narrowly avoiding disaster when with his gilt-tipped walking stick he tripped a footman carrying a tray of petit fours. Hope apologized profusely, rolling his eyes in the direction of his wig as if that should explain everything.

He handed off the cognac to another passing footman with instructions to decant it so that Hope and his most important clients might enjoy it later that evening. Straightening his person as best he could with a two-stone wig on his head, Hope strode into the ballroom to welcome his first guests.

Three ladies stood in the center of the room, heads tilted back as they admired the spectacle of his very own Versailles. Lady Blaise, behind whose ample figure her wards were hidden, took a step forward, revealing a young woman with elegant posture, her gown a diaphanous creation of ivory gauze. Pale rosebuds, the same blush that now rose on her cheeks, were tucked into the swirl of her dark hair.

For a moment he stood watching, wonderstruck at her beauty, her daring.

So she *did* remember.

You are as a nymph, Sophia. So lovely. So tempting.

Did she think of that night as often as did he? These past weeks had been an exercise in frustration; without fail, his thoughts would wander from rents and markets to the slope of Sophia's cheek, the curious innocence of her touch. In the midst of appointments—important appointments, during which the fate of hundreds of thousands of pounds was decided—Hope would miss entire swaths of debate, enraptured as he was by the memory of their time together, the tantalizing possibility there would be more to come.

And now here she was, more lovely, impossibly, than he remembered. His heart tightened in his chest; his pulse took off at a gallop.

From across the ballroom she turned her wide hazel eyes to him. He saw his own anticipation mirrored in their gleam; but there was something else there, a worry, a fear.

A desire to know what troubled her overwhelmed him. He crossed the ballroom in three long, purposeful strides, a smile on his lips as he welcomed them to his ball.

Their conversation was brief but merry. Hope's admittedly excessive praise of Sophia's costume—"A nymph, I presume? What a marvelous conceit. A goddess of the wood, and of the hunt. The Sun King was a great hunter, and would have delighted in such a creature. We go together, you and I"—drew a look of consternation from Lady Violet, but he couldn't help himself.

Sophia said very little but kept her gaze trained on Mr. Hope, as if she were trying to tell him something. He nodded in reply. When the crowd thickened, it would be easy enough to pull her aside without being seen.

The ladies continued to gawk; when Hope waved over the men he'd hired as guards, one of them bearing Princess Caroline's black lacquered box, he thought Violet's eyes might pop out of her head.

It was a rather clever idea if Hope didn't say so himself. Mr. Lake was right to suggest that advertising the French Blue's discovery would only increase its value: the greater number of people who saw it, the greater number who would want it, speak of it, inflate its size and beauty. And what better way to advertise the beauty of the jewel than to display it slung about a beautiful woman's neck?

Better yet that said beautiful woman did and said as she pleased without a care for what others thought. Lady Violet was certainly one of a kind; Hope had yet to meet another woman with a taste for brandy and high-stakes gambling. She'd have everyone and their mother talking of the French Blue well before the night was out.

Hope laced the diamond onto a collar of gems he'd borrowed from a client's wife and carefully lifted the brilliant garland onto Violet's neck, the French Blue glittering from her breast. When he clasped the garland, his fingers grazing the nape of her neck, he felt her shiver.

"Are you all right, Lady Violet?"

"Yes, quite. What a thrill to wear the Sun King's diamond, truly," she said, and shivered again.

Hope's idea worked. As the ball began in earnest, dancers stomping and men laughing and women gossiping behind gossamer fans, it seemed no one spoke of anything but the Sun King's fifty-carat blue-gray diamond. It would only be a matter of time before Napoleon would knock on his door, begging for the jewel.

Assured the job was done and nothing, indeed, could possibly go wrong, Mr. Hope set out for Sophia. He hoped and prayed that whatever burdened her had nothing to do with their shared adventure.

His every sense told him otherwise.

Hope stopped once to accost the Earl of Harclay, that rakehell, who in turn was accosting Lady Violet, ogling her bosom as if he'd like to eat it. Only after Lady Violet assured Hope, in so many words, that she could look after herself, thank you very much, did he move on.

He found Sophia at last bobbing about in a cotillion. Hope smiled at her obvious awkwardness as she twirled clumsily around the Marquess of Withington, who, in his satin breeches and azure-velvet coat, cut an annoyingly dashing figure.

Hope's smile faded as his head began to pound with an unfamiliar urgency. It was the wig, yes, the bloody thing; but he recognized the prick of jealousy, too. It felt at once silly and terribly serious, more serious than silly as he remembered Sophia's halting speech about a brilliant match, Lake's admonition that Sophia would marry a titled gentleman with ten thousand a year.

His fingers clenched around the smooth, rounded finial of his walking stick. The metal felt hot against his skin, a welcome distraction from the entirely unwelcome feelings holding him captive. He breathed deeply, fighting back with every rational thought he could muster.

He was a man of business, first and foremost. He could not forget the hard work that had seen him to this moment; nor could he forget the work that had yet to be done. He was the bank. The bank was his life, a living tribute to the family fate had left behind.

And with Lake's plot in play, Hope had more to lose than ever. These feelings, the attraction he felt for Sophia, were dangerous. He'd dedicated his life to Hope & Co.; and in that life there was no place for a lovely, witty, beautifully terrible dancer like her—

Hope found himself at her side just as the dance was ending. When she turned to him, color high, lips parted in a half smile, he knew he'd made the right decision.

Or perhaps the worst decision ever.

"Miss Blaise." He reveled in the satisfaction of knowing her eyes were upon him, taking in his bow with no little appreciation. "The next dance. Might I have it?"

She eyed the wig towering over his person. "Are you sure you're able to dance with that—that *thing* on your head? It might pose a hazard to the other guests."

Damn it, Hope had forgotten about the wig. It was liable to cause a good bit of damage staying right where it was; should it move, the destruction could be catastrophic.

He pulled the monstrosity from his head, sighing with relief as he did so. "Forget about the wig. Dance with me."

Sophia glanced at the marquess, hovering just out of earshot. "We're in the middle of a set, you see, and I couldn't very well abandon his lordshi—"

As if on cue the dashing marquess stepped forward, wiping his brow with his sleeve. He smiled ebulliently at Hope. It was all Thomas could do not to sock him in his dashing jaw.

"Mr. Hope! Capital ball, good man, capital ball! And your costume!"

Hope smiled tightly. "Let me guess. Capital?"

The marquess threw his head back and laughed as if Hope had cracked the funniest joke he'd ever heard. "Capital, yes, how ever did you know?"

"A lucky guess. Listen, my lord." Hope pulled him close. "You must tell no one. But I've a stash of cognac in my study, smuggled in from France not two days ago. It's reserved for my best clients only—you included, of course."

"Capital!" Again the marquess wiped his brow, looking with some reluctance at Sophia. "After Miss Blaise's spirited dancing, I find that I *am* rather parched, though we're only halfway through the set . . ."

"Have no fear. I shall merely take your place and join you when the set is through."

"Are you quite sure? I wouldn't want to take you away from your cognac. And Miss Blaise, I couldn't very well leave her—could I, Miss Blaise?"

Sophia looked levelly at Hope, her lips curling into a grin. "Please, my lord, go find your refreshment. It won't do to have you parched."

Hope shoved the marquess off the ballroom floor as gently as could be managed, tucking the wig and cane into his hands as he went. "If you don't mind giving these to a footman, I'd be much obliged."

He turned back to Sophia.

Dear God she was beautiful.

And now, finally, she was his. At least for a little while.

"Well then, now that that's all sorted out—shall we dance?"

Sophia stepped forward. "Yes. Though you may regret asking me—I'm not very good at it."

"So I noticed."

Hope turned at the sound of commotion near the orchestra. That cad the Earl of Harclay—really, the man was far more trouble than he was worth—was tossing a reticule heavy with coin into the lap of the first-chair violinist. Hope couldn't make out what he was saying, but suddenly the ballroom was erupting with gasps and shouts as the master of the dance called for a waltz.

Hope looked at Sophia. They both rushed to speak at once. "A waltz?"

"That's impossible!" Sophia's eyes were wide. "A debutante can't be seen *dancing* the *waltz*! I don't even think I know how."

But the music was already starting; despite the risks to Hope's sanity and Sophia's reputation, he wrapped an arm around her waist and tugged her to him. With his other hand he drew out her opposite arm and together they moved—or, rather, stumbled—through the first steps of the waltz.

"Let me go!" she hissed. "I'll dance the next set with you."

Hope looked down at her with a smile. "Too late, Miss Blaise. Follow my steps—yes, that's—no, no, the *other* foot—no, the other *other* foot!"

He tripped over her misplaced foot and together they lurched forward, nearly toppling Lord Harclay and Lady Violet before Hope in his terror turned and righted his and Sophia's bodies.

"Dear God," Hope gasped. "If I'd been wearing my wig I daresay we'd both be dead!"

To his very great pleasure he watched as, despite her protests, Sophia dissolved into breathless laughter, closing her eyes against the force of it.

When she opened them she met his gaze, a small smile lingering on her lips as her steps, praise heaven, fell in time with his. He held her to him and they danced together, the music so loud, so insistent in its rhythm, Hope lost himself for a moment. He had cognac in his blood and the most beautiful woman at the ball in his arms; the plot was in play and business could only get better.

But something was not quite right. That fearful gleam had returned to Sophia's green eyes, and a shallow crease now appeared between her brows—though, to be fair, it *did* seem to require enormous concentration on her part to land the three steps of the waltz.

"What is it?" He turned, pulling her close enough so that he might murmur in her ear. "My promise remains the same, Sophia. I gave you my word then, the same as I give it to you now. Anything you say shall remain between us."

Beneath his hand on her back she stiffened. As they turned once, twice, three times, she glanced over her shoulder, watching with wide eyes the couples that twirled around them.

He pressed his lips to her ear. "I will know what it is that's bothering you. Tell me, Sophia, so that I might help you. You've my word."

"That's just it, Thomas." She looked up at him. "You may have given me your word, but someone knows. Knows about *us*. About what happened that night."

A clammy sweat broke out along his collar as he pulled her close, imploring her with his eyes. Just as he'd suspected. "Who threatened you?"

"I don't know. It—it was a letter. I didn't recognize the seal, or the script. It said something—" She paused, eyes wet. "Something like, 'two queens, the ace of diamonds, soon you will have a royal flush.' I've got it in my glove; it arrived this evening, just as we were leaving to come here."

"Well." Hope's throat tightened ominously. "Whoever wrote it has a terrible sense of humor."

He turned course sharply, making for the gallery at the far side of the ballroom. He saw nothing, felt nothing save the desire to get Sophia alone, to make sure she was safe, to talk and together tease out the source of these threats.

As he sped through the tangle of couples, Hope cursed himself for ever allowing her to join them in the first place. Yes, it had been mostly Lake's doing, but in his lust-filled haze Hope had done little to stop it. Sophia was intelligent, certainly, but she was also innocent. She hadn't a clue about the enormity and depth of the cesspool into which she'd dipped her pretty toe.

If Hope didn't put a stop to her adventuring, it would swallow Miss Sophia Blaise whole.

The music was reaching a crescendo, the ballroom a whirl of white satin and kerseymere coattails. There was laughter and whispered conversation, couples flush-faced from the heady thrill of such unexpected privacy in the midst of an epic crush.

Surely, Hope reasoned, no one would notice if he whisked Sophia away for a few moments? And even if someone did, he could pass it off as business—

His heart went to his throat at the enormous, shimmering crash that sounded just above their heads. In one swift, sure movement, he tucked Sophia into his chest, covering her head as shards of glass rained down on them.

He watched in mute horror as three lithe, shadowy figures catapulted through the gallery windows into the ballroom. They swung through the air and landed on the trio of enormous chandeliers that illuminated the crush. Handling the daggers held fast in their teeth, the intruders began sawing at the silken ropes from which the crystal monstrosities hung.

Panic, wild and hot, pounded through Hope. *My God, my God, what the devil is happening?*

The music came to a jarring halt as stunned silence settled over the ballroom. A beat later the crowd erupted in screams, shouts, swoons. Hope watched, trembling with fury, as the sinister-looking men he'd hired to guard the French Blue suddenly turned on his guests, waving their pistols as if they'd very much like to use them.

Traitors.

He'd been betrayed. The *why* was obvious enough: King Louis XIV's plum-sized diamond was no small prize.

But the *who* was more difficult. Had Napoleon's men foiled their plan? Was it one of Lake's own, working against his master? Or was it a band of ambitious petty bandits, hoping to make the theft of a lifetime?

A shot sounded; more screams. Against his chest Sophia was shaking. He did not answer her whispered questions.

"Who is it? Are you all right? What's happening, Thomas, please!"

He held her fast against him, pressing his back against the gallery wall. The crush roiled with chaos, bodies climbing over one another in attempts at escape.

From above came an ominous groan. The first chandelier now hung from a thread, the bandit hard at work severing the last bit of rope.

"Move aside!" he screamed, gesturing wildly with his free arm. "Move, quickly, everyone must *move!*"

With a thrumming *snap* the chandelier broke free. The thief somersaulted away, landing with inhuman lightness in a far corner.

The chandelier landed with a piercing crash, sending shards of crystal and gilt across the ballroom. People dashed about, streaming out of windows and doors like water in a flood.

Thomas, please, I must find my mother, and Violet—

"Not yet." It was all he could manage. He held her fast; in his confusion, his terror and his rage, she kept his head—just barely—above the water.

The second chandelier came thundering down, followed in quick succession by the third. Plunged into darkness, the ballroom descended into a pit of writhing shadows. The roar of panic was unbearable.

Under cover of blackness, Hope began to move, Sophia held close in the crook of his arm. Against his ribs he felt the furious working of her heart, her breath hot and fast on his collar.

Together they waded into the dark, Hope offering a hand to those he could reach. To his very great relief it appeared no one was seriously injured.

Across the ballroom came another shot, more screams; running footsteps.

The thieves. It would only be a matter of time before they found the diamond, and then, he knew, all hell would break loose; no doubt they'd shoot anyone who blocked their path to escape.

She couldn't stay, not with everything at stake. Her life most of all.

And Hope. He couldn't leave for the same reason.

He released Sophia, grasping her by the shoulders so that he might see her face. Pale, eyes wide and wet. No tears, but she did not meet his gaze. She opened her mouth as if to speak, but he shook his head, bending his neck so that their noses nearly brushed.

"Look at me, Sophia. *Look at me.* Go find your mother and get out of here. Do you understand? If you stay you'll end up hurt or worse. There's a hidden door the servants use toward the front of the ballroom. Use that, it will take you out to the street."

She swallowed, searching his eyes. "And what will you do?"

"Don't worry about me. Go. Now. Watch you don't trip over the chandeliers!"

Taking her by the arm, he pushed her toward the door,

watching as she haltingly made her way across the ballroom. A strange twist in his chest left him momentarily breathless.

But he wouldn't make the same mistake twice. Her reputation—never mind her life—was now in peril after she'd played a role in their plot. He would not stoke that fire by courting her involvement once more.

Just as Sophia was fading into black, he saw her loop her arm through that of a portly woman wearing a drooping feather headdress.

Her mother. Thank God, she'd found her mother. He watched as, making for the servants' entrance, they disintegrated into the darkened chaos of the ballroom.

He took a deep breath, closing his eyes against the impulse to follow them out, to see to their safety.

The diamond, he reminded himself. He had to secure the diamond, or all would be lost.

Hope turned to the ballroom, screams and shouts echoing off its tall-coffered ceiling.

And then there was a scream—well, a voice, really—that he recognized.

Lady Violet.

The French Blue.

He took off at a sprint, dodging his way to the center of the ballroom. From a knot of heads and legs Violet rose, the Earl of Harclay holding her by the elbow. Beyond came the sound of running footsteps—the thieves, Hope knew, making a run for it.

Violet's hand was at her neck.

A neck that was bare.

"The diamond! Lord Harclay, the diamond—it's gone!" Violet shouted, before promptly turning to the earl and vomiting on his very fine shoes.

Serves him right, Hope thought, for all the trouble he's caused tonight.

Hope turned, waving his arms in the direction of the intruders' fading footsteps. "Stop them! They're making off with the French Blue! Wait, you bastards, I'll have you hanged!"

But even as the words left his lips, Hope knew it was too late.

The French Blue was gone.

Ten

Sophia swung through the kitchen door into the stable yard, her mother huffing two steps behind. Above them they heard the cacophony of Hope's ballroom: muffled shouts, the crack of pistols, shattering glass.

"Sophia," she panted. "What in. God's name. Happened up. There?"

"I don't know," Sophia replied, before saying, more softly, "but I do mean to find out."

Across the yard, the mews were just as dark and disordered as the ballroom. Guests flung themselves into any carriage they could find; grooms scurried about helplessly as a great knot of traffic blocked the lane that led out into the street.

Sophia scanned the mess but, praise heaven, did not see the Rutledge family's dusty old coach among those vehicles trapped by the crush.

"Come, Mama, this way. Only a bit longer, I promise."

She tugged her mother around toward the street, Lady Blaise all the while moaning in staccato sentences about her poor nerves, and poor Hope, and where in God's name was Violet? They'd all better hope she was not with that handsome libertine the Earl of Harclay, or they would be ruined, the whole family . . .

Sophia tugged harder, mind racing all the while. The French Blue had been stolen, that much she knew, and by thieves with a flair for acrobatics. Whoever plotted the theft was no tenderfoot; he was one to make an entrance, and did not shy away from drama.

Then there was the mysterious note tucked into the crook of her glove.

Sophia's life, up until now a dull study in decorum and Debrett's, was suddenly full of excitement.

Not that a heady dose of fear didn't accompany said excitement. It was with shaking hands that Sophia led her mother round the dark corner and out onto the graveled half-crescent drive in front of Thomas's house.

There were people everywhere, crisscrossing the drive with cries for the constable, the mayor, smelling salts. Her mother was beginning to limp with the effort of keeping pace. Sophia had no doubt whatsoever that Lady Blaise would topple to the ground in an appropriately dramatic swoon if they didn't find shelter, and quick.

Over the din Sophia heard her name. She turned.

Relief flooded through her at the sight of her family's scuffed-up old carriage, the scuffed-up old coachman waving to her from the street.

As they sidled up to the vehicle, Sophia told him the story in so many breathless words. Together she and the coachman lifted Lady Blaise into the carriage, where at last she succumbed to that swoon she'd been saving all night.

Sophia collapsed against the coach, drawing deep, hungry breaths of the cool evening air.

The coachman held out his hand. "Best be goin', miss, before the real trouble begins."

Sophia looked at the man, swung her head to look back at the house. It was ablaze with light and life, guests still pouring out the front door. She wondered where Thomas was, and if he'd managed to stop the thieves before they could escape with the diamond.

The diamond that she'd helped him win from Princess Caroline. Her chest swelled with pride and something else—something softer—as she remembered how well they'd played that game together, she and Thomas. He never wanted to involve her in his plotting, she knew that, but she knew also that he was grateful for her presence, and that she played no small part in the success of his scheme.

Perhaps, she thought, eyeing her mother as she moaned softly in her stupor, she might again come to the rescue tonight. Surely Hope would need all the help he could get if those scalawags the acrobats had indeed made off with the French Blue. The more bodies involved, the more ground they could cover in their search.

La Reinette would surely dive in headfirst, wouldn't she, and seduce those she encountered along the way?

Surely indeed.

Besides. While she still trembled, heart in her throat, after so much action, the last thing Sophia desired was to go home to a quiet house for a quiet evening in. With her pulse racing as it was, she knew sleep would elude her. And there were her mother's hysterics with which to contend . . .

"Miss?"

Sophia blinked, turning to the coachman.

No. She was not ready for tonight to end just yet.

She smiled as she reached between them to gently shut the carriage door. When he tried to protest, brow furrowed with concern, she merely held a finger to her lips and shook her head.

"Very well," he said softly. "But the scene ov a crime ain't no place for a lady. You've only to send for me, miss, and I'll come straightaway."

She placed a hand on his shoulder in gratitude. Dipping her head, she stepped out into the fray.

It was like fighting against a monstrous tide. With no small effort she mounted the front steps, the press of the crush pushing her backward so that with every two steps she lost twice as many.

She tried slithering between bodies—she was an adventurer now, after all, and slithering seemed the adventurous thing to do—but her attempt was only met with sharp elbows and panicked feet, driving her ever backward until she stumbled down the same steps she'd spent precious minutes climbing.

Letting out a hiss of frustration, Sophia followed the crush out onto the drive. She veered to the left, retracing her steps back to the mews. If Hope and his men had made it out of the ballroom yet, they would be running for their horses to begin the chase.

A chase. She felt ridiculous even thinking the word.

Sophia ran to the mews as fast as her feet would carry her, pushing her way into the stables, where dozens of coaches and four times as many horses and grooms were still tangled in an impossible knot.

"Thomas!" she called. She turned this way and that, narrowly avoiding a run-in with an enormous black horse and its equally enormous rider.

The rider heaved expertly at the reins, jerking the horse onto its hind legs. Sophia gasped, cowering with her hands held out above her head.

"Christ, Sophia, is that you?"

She peeked between her splayed fingers to find none other than Thomas Hope glaring down at her, blue eyes cold, nostrils flaring with anger.

"I told you to go home. This—all of this—it is none of your affair." Though his voice was deadly calm, quiet even, she felt his simmering wrath as surely as if he'd howled the words.

She put down her hands, struggling beneath the weight of his gaze to remember why, exactly, she'd chosen to stay. Something about adventure, and what La Reinette would do, and oh, yes, the role she played in coaxing the jewel from Caroline's grasp—

"It is as much my affair as it is yours." Sophia would win this fight, come hell or high water. She was *staying*. "I daresay without my help, none of us would be in this mess in the first place."

Thomas peered at her, looking as though he could not decide whether her words amused or dismayed him.

She wrinkled her nose as she reconsidered the words. "Wait. No. No, that didn't come out at all right. What I meant to say is, you and I work well together, Thomas. Our success at Montague House proved that. Neither of us is nearly as good without the other. So let me help you. Whatever it is that you need, let me help you."

Thomas put a hand on his thigh, tugging his skittish mount into stillness as he ran a hand through his tangle of curls. He sighed. "I don't have time for this, Sophia. The thieves got away. The French Blue is gone. I am out twenty thousand pounds, never mind my debt to England. I'll not ask you again." He leaned forward in his saddle. "Go *home*."

"And I'll not ask *you* again." She stepped in front of his horse, hands on her hips. "Let me help. And don't think for a moment I wouldn't let you run me over. I'm not going anywhere until you accept my offer."

"Don't you have your mother to see to? And what of your cousin?"

"You know as well as I do that Violet can take care of herself. And my mother—well, suffice it to say she won't get out of bed until day after next, at the earliest."

Sophia watched as Hope's fingers tightened around his thigh. She bit back a smile of triumph.

She was staying.

A handful of horsemen rode up behind Thomas.

Thomas held up a hand in greeting. "The lot of you head east, toward the Thames. The thieves are nimble and likely faster than we'll ever be on horseback or even on foot. Tell no one what has occurred this night. Godspeed, gentlemen."

Sophia looked up at Hope. "And what about us? Where are we headed?"

"To where this whole mess began," he said grimly. He reached for her and, wrapping his fingers around her right arm, pulled her none too gently onto the horse. He settled her into the saddle in front of him, turning her so that her back was to his chest.

She heard a muted tear as he pried her legs apart, pressing his body against her so that she now rode astride the horse, the backs of her thighs resting against his knees.

So much for the nymph costume. No doubt the damage was beyond repair.

Never mind her dignity. That, along with her composure, had gone out the window long ago.

It was terribly uncomfortable, not to mention awkward, to be situated upon a horse with a fuming gentleman pressed far too invitingly against one's backside. Perhaps Sophia should have thought this whole staying business through. Then there was the very real threat of injury or death or, even worse, ruin to consider. What would the Marquess of Withington think, really, if he knew she'd run off into the night with Mr. Thomas Hope—and not for the first time?

This was not the wisest decision she'd ever made.

But as Hope wordlessly urged the horse into motion, holding Sophia tight between his arms as he handled the reins, it suddenly didn't seem so terribly unwise. While her head swam with all manner of things—panic, the waltz, just where on earth were they going, and would they find the diamond there?—she felt safe pressed against the warm firmness of Hope's chest, the long, lithe muscles of his legs.

Perhaps, while not the wisest decision, it *had* been the right one.

And so Sophia held on for dear life as Hope guided them through the darkened city streets. Her heart pounded in time to the horse's forward thrust, Thomas's body colliding with hers with each giddy leap.

The night was cool and clear and wide open. Sophia saw where they were headed long before Hope reined in the horse's frantic pace. Just past a familiar facade, its blue shutters glittering in the light of a vivid moon, Thomas veered left down a shadowy pathway.

They rode into The Glossy's small but neat mews. A groom, trying very hard not to gape at the breathless couple before him, held the reins while Thomas dismounted. The horse grunted with relief.

Hope turned to Sophia, his movements precise and ruthless as he hooked his hands around her waist and brought her to the ground. Glaring at the curious groom, Thomas whipped back his shoulders and removed his jacket.

He shrouded Sophia in the fine folds of its fabric, tugging at the collar so as to hide the better half of her face. Pressing a coin into the groom's palm, Hope murmured his thanks and guided Sophia into The Glossy.

Sophia was glad to have Hope's jacket. Stepping foot into the house's palatial hall, a chill ran through her, strong and visceral, as if she'd plunged through ice into a frozen lake.

For the first time Sophia did not feel welcome here.

She had not returned since that night she ran breathless out the door, struggling to keep pace with Hope as he sprinted toward the street. Nor had she yet worked up the courage to write La Reinette who, for obvious reasons, could not send a letter to Sophia at her uncle's house.

This much Sophia knew: the events of that night forever altered the rules of their arrangement. Both she and Madame had bared parts of themselves that were very much at odds with what each wanted from the other. Could Sophia trust La Reinette to provide the discretion and safety she'd promised?

And could Madame, in turn, trust her memoirs to a debutante possessed of a real terror for her reputation while, impossibly, exhibiting a taste for less than wholesome nighttime activity?

The arrangement couldn't possibly continue. Not as it had before—well, before *this* happened.

And then there was Madame's relationship with Mr. Hope to consider. Were they in business together? Master and servant? Friends? Allies? Or were they—

No. It was none of her business. She and Thomas were on the hunt for the stolen French Blue—nothing more, nothing less—though what La Reinette had to do with any of that, Sophia hadn't a clue.

Hope charged into the madam's room without knocking.

"What do you know?"

Sophia started at Hope's growl. He stalked to the far end of the room as if it were his own, pacing behind La Reinette as she sat before her painted vanity.

With exaggerated slowness the Little Queen dabbed the edge of her mouth with a handkerchief, patting back an errant curl. In the mirror her color was high; Sophia noticed the bed was unmade, its coverlet curled invitingly around rumpled sheets.

It shouldn't have surprised Sophia, this still-warm evidence of the skill that made La Reinette famous. Still, she looked away, training her eyes on something, *anything*, other than the bed; embarrassed, as if she'd interrupted the act itself.

Madame rose and turned to face them, the diaphanous robe tied about her trim person revealing as much as it concealed. She looked, Sophia thought, as effortlessly lovely as she always did.

What was it about Frenchwomen and their effortless everything? Really, it wasn't fair.

La Reinette's black eyes, inscrutable, took in her visitors' disheveled appearance, Hope's white satin breeches and red-heeled shoes; her gaze lingered a moment on the jagged rent that split Sophia's skirts. Sophia, face burning, was overwhelmed by a sense of guilt. As if she'd somehow committed a crime against the madam in her own house.

Sophia gathered the loose edges of her costume in her hands and looked to the floor.

"Your diamond." Madame turned to Hope. "Someone stole it, yes?"

He returned her gaze levelly. "The time for playing coy with me is long passed, Marie. I know well enough that London's secrets—the ones worth knowing, anyway—pass through this room. So." He clasped his hands behind his back. "*Tell me what you know.*"

She stepped forward and took him by the shoulders, halting him midstride. "Look at me, *mon chéri*, I do not play coy. That is the lucky guess I had, that the diamond, it is stolen. You should be wiser in these things. You display this beautiful jewel before all the world, *oui*? And what, you think no one will want it for themselves?"

"I cannot afford to lose the French Blue. Either tell me what you know—"

Madame scoffed. "Or what?"

In the beat of silence that followed, Sophia sensed something dark moving between La Reinette and Hope. Something heavy and well worn.

More secrets. So many deuced secrets.

At last La Reinette released Hope, making for Sophia. She took her burning face in her palms. "And you, *ma bichette*, more adventure for you! Soon you will write your own memoirs." Her thumb grazed the rib of Sophia's cheek. "Tell me. When it was taken, this diamond of *monsieur's*. Tell me what you saw. Were you together with him?"

Sophia swallowed. An odd question, yes. But clearly La Reinette knew something they did not. She glanced at Thomas, his blue eyes glowing in the dim light of the room. He nodded. *Go on.*

"Well." Sophia returned Madame's gaze. "Mr. Hope and I were dancing the waltz—"

Madame arched a brow. "A waltz? But then, did you intend to kill off all the nice ladies in your ballroom? I imagine many of them hit their heads, yes, when they swooned? That dance, for you English it is too much. Too much of the *passion*."

"Not amused." Hope closed his eyes and sighed, pinching the bridge of his nose. "Not amused, Marie, not one bit. See here, Miss Blaise and I were dancing, and then all of the sudden . . ."

Hope told his story, about the acrobats flying through the windows, his treacherous guards; he told her about Violet screaming, *It's gone, the diamond, it's gone!*, and then added, strangely, an anecdote about her losing her dinner on the Earl of Harclay's shoes.

Like that rapscallion had anything to do with the French Blue and its sudden disappearance from Hope's ballroom. Sophia hoped Violet had managed to escape that wicked man's presence. Though heaven knew he was handsome enough to slay even the most upright of the female sex. Perhaps Sophia *shouldn't* have left Violet to her own defense. For there was no defense, really, against a face like Harclay's.

La Reinette listened to Hope's tale closely, all the while holding Sophia's hands in the warm comfort of her own.

"It is unfortunate, this thing that has happened to you tonight," she said when Hope had finished. She held a finger in the air and made for her escritoire. "But the fear, let it leave you. These devils steal from you, yes, but we will take their own trick and use it for us. I will make inquiries, discreet of course. *Le bleu de France* will be yours again, *monsieur*."

Madame sat at the desk and took out a fresh sheet of paper, dabbing a swan feather quill in a pot of blue ink. Sophia bent her arm, intent to brush away a stray eyelash, when a small but succinct *crack* sounded from the crook of her elbow.

The note.

Of course.

If La Reinette was mistress of secrets, as Thomas implied, then who better to untangle the mystery of Sophia's note?

"There's something else," Sophia blurted. Hope's gaze snapped toward her, a warning; but she ignored it, drawing from her glove the tiny square of paper. "A note. It came to my house this evening—someone stuck it in the kitchen door. Do you think it has anything to do with the theft?"

Madame frowned as she unfolded the note, smoothing it over the blank page on her escritoire. "That night you came to me, here in this room. Who knows of it, besides us? I do not ask from you an explanation of why those men were after you. But you must tell me this."

"Virtually no one." Hope spoke before Sophia could reply, warning her off with narrowed eyes. "You, an associate of mine, one or two others. And then, of course, the men who chased us. As far as I know, no one has seen or heard from them since."

Madame nodded absently, her attention fixed on the note. "I have been watching for them, but they have disappeared—*poof!*—into the air. Let us hope they have gone back to the hole they came from, yes?"

"What of the note?" Sophia asked. "D'you think they wrote it?"

"Perhaps." Madame pursed her lips. "Perhaps not. I do not recognize the hand. But now, those men who chased you—they are the first suspects. Perhaps all this"—she waved a hand among the three of them—"is connected. We shall find out, yes?"

Thomas leaned in to grasp the note, which he tucked into the lapel of his jacket. "Thank you, Marie. As always I appreciate your. Er. *Expertise* in these matters."

La Reinette offered Hope a small but meaningful smile. So meaningful that Sophia felt as if she were eavesdropping on a private conversation.

"As always, *monsieur*, it is a pleasure to help you."

Hope was offering an arm to Sophia when La Reinette suddenly turned, finger to her chin. "Oh yes! I cannot forget. You, Hope, must watch over our dear friend the *mademoiselle*. The two of you, you were close, yes, in those last moments before the theft? The thieves, they may try to use her against you. Forget this chase tonight; you will find nothing. Go home, keep her safe. That note, I do not like it."

Sophia started, a pulse of fear racing through her. Dear God, just what did La Reinette mean by that?

"Thank you, Marie," he repeated, voice edged with impatience as he tugged Sophia out of the room. It was obvious, as head of his own bank, Thomas was rather more used to giving orders than receiving them.

"And do take care!" La Reinette called after them as they made their way out of the room. "These devils may want more than your diamonds, *monsieur*!"

Eleven

———— ✦ ————

City of London
Hope & Co. Offices, Fleet Street

Hope shoved aside the detritus on his desk, setting in its place two heavy-bottomed crystal glasses and the only bottle of port he'd managed to rummage from his sideboard, crowded as it was with brown liquors of every shape and stripe.

From the stricken look on Sophia's face, he could tell the last thing the girl needed was a kick in the arse from an especially potent Scotch. Port, surely, was a better bet. Ladies drank port, didn't they?

And even if they didn't, Hope sure as hell did. He needed libation.

Several libations, in fact.

And even then he wasn't sure he'd be able to erase the fact that the French Blue—*the French Blue*, the Sun King's fifty-carat diamond, and quite possibly England's ticket to victory on the Continent—was stolen, right from under his nose.

The weight of his anger, his helplessness and his guilt, was suffocating.

The port. Yes. That would help.

At least a little.

Hope watched Sophia watching him as with swift hands he twisted the corkscrew into the mouth of the bottle, tugging the cork free with an airless *pop*.

In the soft glow of the lamp her eyes were enormous,

depthless; he could practically see thoughts cross her mind as she thought them, brow furrowed.

Part of his anger was directed at her. Why didn't she listen to him when he told her to run, to seek safety with her family? He had a stolen diamond to find, God damn it, and she would only slow him down. As La Reinette had so eloquently reminded him, whoever was after Hope was deadly, a very real threat. If those men dared take his diamond, perhaps they would not hesitate to take his life, too.

And now that Sophia was with him, she was also in danger. That bloody note proved nothing good came of her involvement in his plots; that nothing good came of her involvement with *him*.

Even so. Now that the damage was done and the night was darkest, Hope found he was relieved, glad even, to have her with him, to share a drink—many drinks, on his part—with her in the cool quiet of his office at Hope & Co.

He would take her home after the first glass. At least that's what he told himself as he helped her dismount in the mews behind the building. La Reinette was right to say Sophia was in danger; nevertheless, she *was* an unmarried debutante of gentle birth, and such creatures usually shied away from staying out all hours of the night with tradesmen like himself.

Hope poured each of them a glass and passed one to Sophia. She straightened, grasping the glass eagerly in her gloved hand.

He was, apparently, not the only one in need of a drink.

He held up his glass but could not think of a toast. Sophia waited impatiently, biting her bottom lip against an exhausted smile.

"Forget it," she said at last. "I can't wait any longer."

"Praise God. Me neither."

Over the rim of his own glass Hope watched Sophia take one, two long, luxurious pulls, wincing a bit as she guided the glass into her lap.

"That's good." Again she brought the cup to her lips. "That's very good, Thomas."

She set the empty glass on the desk and fell back into the chair with a contented sigh. With her hair and costume askew, a milky white thigh peeking through the makeshift slit in her skirts and lips purple-red from the port, Sophia appeared more nymph than debutante.

"More?" he asked, grasping the bottle.

She nodded. He poured.

They drank in silence. At once he felt the port working its magic way through him, the ache in his shoulders and neck easing with every sip he took.

After his second glass he grew courageous enough to step round the desk, trailing his hip along its edge until he drew up beside Sophia's chair. He refilled both their glasses and, setting the bottle on the desk behind him, leaned the backs of his thighs against the desk, facing her, and crossed his arms.

"I bet you wish you were at home, in bed. Don't you, Sophia?"

Sophia blinked, as if he'd just insulted her. She crinkled her nose. "No. Why? Do you?"

"What, home in bed? Your bed? My bed? What?" he scoffed, suddenly flustered. "No-o?"

So much for the debonair adventurer. After a glass or three of port he was no smoother than a randy fifteen-year-old boy.

He gulped his port. Yes, it could only make things worse, but what else was he supposed to do when she was looking at him like *that*, with those eyes and that hair and that goddamned thigh . . .

Hope cleared his throat. "What I meant to say is, don't you wish you'd kept dancing with that marquess of yours? Stayed safe and sound in your family's house? Seems the moment I step in, a whole heap of trouble follows."

He nearly winced as the words left his lips. Where the devil had *that* come from? Speaking of randy fifteen-year-old boys: the marquess was a perfect example, yes, but that hardly signified. He and Sophia had shared a dance; and if they shared more than that, well.

It was none of Hope's business.

Still. Even in his own ears the words smacked of jealousy. It was an unfamiliar feeling; Hope was not a jealous man. Especially when it came to women.

So why the sudden, hot tug in his belly at the memory of Sophia stumbling through the steps of a reel at the Marquess of Withington's side?

You know my family's circumstances. I don't have much choice. A good marriage will go far to repair our fortunes, and our reputation.

Hope recalled Sophia's words, her dreams of a brilliant match.

A match with a titled, fortuned man like the marquess. A man who couldn't be more different, in family, history, circumstances, than Hope.

Well, except for the fortune part. Hope trumped the marquess there.

Nevertheless.

Sophia, praise God, had the grace to ignore Hope's comment, but not without a small smile.

"I like your kind of trouble." She looked down into her glass. "I wish you'd stop feeling guilty, Thomas. You didn't drag me into this; I joined you willingly. Whatever trouble I'm in has been of my own doing. I daresay if I hadn't run into you my first season would prove awfully dull."

"I suppose," Hope said carefully, "I should take that as a compliment?"

Sophia raised her glass and clinked it against his own. "You should. Cheers."

She finished her port with a hiss, and waved away Hope's attempts to refill her glass. Her color was high; she shifted in her chair, crossing her legs invitingly so he could see just enough skin to drive him wild, imagining the vision of more skin, more leg.

Her eyes, gold in the low light of the room, caught on an array of pages that hung precariously off the edge of his desk. Brow furrowed with curiosity, she bent forward in her chair. Before he could stop her she reached for them, lips curling into a grin as she read the first line.

"*A History of the World's Greatest Diamond*, by Thomas Hope." Her eyes danced as she met his own. "I did not know you were a writer!"

He tried again to take the pages from her, but she snatched them from his grasp. "Yes, well. It's not quite finished, you see . . ."

Hope waited with bated breath as Sophia read one page after another, her smile at times fading, others growing, as her lips moved silently in time to the words. By the time she set her empty glass on the desk and gathered the pages in a neat pile, Hope's heart was racing.

"Well?" he asked weakly.

Sophia cleared her throat, setting the *History* on the desk. "Well."

Her gaze met his. She let out a sound—a sob, a sigh?—and only when Hope felt the rise in his own belly did he recognize it as laughter.

And then they were laughing together, tears gathering at the edges of Sophia's lovely eyes as she recited that bit about forbidden fruit, and Hope nodding yes, yes, it *is* terrible, isn't it?

"Not all of us, *Miss Blaise*, can be bestselling authors!"

"Bah!" Sophia wiped her eyes with her first finger. "Hardly signifies, when I am merely a vessel; the stories aren't my own. I only wonder why you wrote such a history? Why the French Blue? Aside, of course, from your interest in all things extravagant."

Hope sucked a breath through his teeth and rocked back on his heels. The laughter faded from his belly. He closed his eyes for a moment, willing his voice to remain even. This was nothing, a story. He could, his apparent lack of narrative prowess aside, tell a damned *story*.

"Before I was born, my father traveled to the court of Louis XVI. He'd gone on business, a meeting with the minister of finance; but he was taken by the beauty of the court, the allure of such excess. He was especially enamored of the jewels; jewels, he said, like he'd never seen before. When I was little he would tell me stories of the French Blue, the whisperings he'd heard at court of its curse, its journey across the seas. My father saw him wear it once, Louis, on a brooch hung from a ribbon slung about his chest. He never forgot that, my father."

"Incredible," Sophia whispered, shaking her head. "To have been witness to the spectacle."

Hope looked down into his glass. "I had hoped to make the journey myself someday. I wanted to see King Louis wearing *le bleu de France*, just as my father had. He promised, my father, to take me; and I promised to accompany him. We were to go together, he and I.

"Of course." Hope swallowed, hard. "Of course we never

went. But when I heard the Blue was in England, and in Princess Caroline's possession, I knew I'd been given a second chance. At last I would know the diamond as my father knew it, albeit without poor old Louis in the picture."

He sighed. "And now the French Blue is gone."

"I am sorry." Sophia's voice was soft.

"No. *I* am sorry to have ruined our merrymaking with yet *another* terrible tale." He held up the bottle. "More port?"

Despite her protests he refilled her glass.

"Are you sure you're all right?" she asked.

He held out the glass and met her eyes. "Very much so, thank you, Sophia."

She looked at him for a beat; satisfied, she took the glass in her hand and tossed back her head to look at the room. "Quite the office you've got. Looks more like a museum. Or an art gallery."

Glad for the change of subject, Hope swept his eyes over the priceless antiques, the Turkish carpets and Italian masterworks that decorated the space. "Do you have a favorite?"

"Yes." She rose to her feet, the port in her glass sloshing a bit as she made her way to stand in front of the fireplace. Pointing to the gilt-framed painting that hung above the mantel, she said, "This one. It's beautiful."

Hope joined her in front of the fireplace. Together they admired the painting, its vivid colors, the ethereal luminescence of the two figures reclining across the expanse of the work. It was beautiful, yes.

Beautiful in that sensual, explicit sort of way that made the old masters of the Renaissance so famous. Mars, in all his well-muscled glory, was naked, asleep after the rigors of physical love; Venus, curvy and luscious, lounged beside him in a diaphanous gown not dissimilar to the one Sophia now wore.

Hope blinked at the familiar twist of desire between his legs.

"Botticelli is among my own favorites," he said. "This is his *Venus and Mars*. Do you know the tale?"

Sophia cocked her head to the side, her purple-stained lips pouty in concentration.

Dear God. Was she trying to kill him?

More port.

"Star-crossed lovers, yes?" she said.

"Yes," he replied. "An ancient Romeo and Juliet, if you will. Venus is married to Vulcan, the king of the gods. He's powerful but—if you'll excuse my crudeness—impotent. It's no surprise, then, that our fair Venus falls in love with Mars, who, as you can see, is a rather handsome fellow, flowing locks and all that."

Sophia turned to Hope with a smile. "If his were a bit darker, they'd look just like yours."

Hope cleared his throat for what felt like the hundredth time that night. He was glad the glow of the fire was dim, for beneath the cover of semidarkness he felt himself blushing.

"You can see here"—Hope pointed to a trio of satyrs making off with Mars's spear—"that the artist is suggesting Venus's love for Mars disarms him. That his love for her in turn is so great, so powerful, that it leaves him defenseless."

Sophia turned to him. "That love," she said softly, "conquers all."

"Yes." Hope looked at her, his belly turning over at the soft slant of her eyes. "That love conquers all. Even, it seems, the matchless god of war."

For several breathless moments they looked at one another. Beside them the fire sputtered and cracked. Sophia's face, in shadow one moment, dancing light the next, was lovely, those lips of hers parted slightly. An invitation.

No. No. Not tonight. There was too much to do, and the French Blue, it was gone, stolen at his own ball—he had to keep a clear mind, focus on the task at hand—

More port. While it was making him forget everything good and right, his manners and his decorum and his sense of duty, it also helped him to forget his grief. The diamond, his father—they disappeared in the presence of Miss Sophia Blaise.

Sophia blinked, a look of—was that disappointment?—darkening her features. She placed her empty glass on the mantel and began to wrangle free of Hope's jacket.

"Too warm?" Hope asked, setting aside his glass to help.

In reply Sophia shot him a smoldering look over her shoulder.

That twist between his legs pulsed to a full-on rush of heat.

Warm? Dear *God*. A drop in the old proverbial bucket.

Hope stepped back, holding the jacket awkwardly in his hands, unsure what his next move should be.

Again that look in Sophia's eyes.

Harry, England, and Saint George. The diamond, and Napoleon; the twenty thousand pounds he'd put down to set the plot in motion, the bank and all the lives at stake, keeping her safe from the men after her—

It all went out the door when Sophia stepped forward and took the jacket from his arms, spreading it out on the carpet before the fire. She took her glass from the mantel and held out her hand.

"I like it here," she said. "Let's sit."

Hope, embarrassingly, let out a groan. "Just one—" He loosened his cravat. "Just one moment, Sophia."

He dashed to the desk, grabbing the bottle of port; turning back to the fireplace, he took his own cup from the mantel and held it between the fingers of one hand along with the bottle. With the other hand he took Sophia's, and together they began to sink to the floor when she stumbled over her dress, caught beneath her foot. She pitched backward; Hope's arm darted out just in time, grasping her by the arm.

"Oh," she gasped. "Oh, dear. That port's strong, isn't it?"

He guided her to the floor beside him. "No stronger than usual. Are you all right?"

Sophia stretched out her legs toward the fire, propping her weight on her free hand. Hope followed suit, her mirror image. Her slippered toes grazed the tip of his boot, once, before she moved her foot.

"Yes." Sophia held out her glass. In the moving light of the fire her color was high, eyes wet and willing.

He swallowed. And filled her glass.

He held the bottle up to the fire. Damn it. Almost empty.

"Did we finish the whole bottle?"

Hope splashed what was left into his glass, and looked up at Sophia with a smile. "Just did."

"Goodness." She brought the glass to her lips and took a long pull. "We should probably slow down, shouldn't we?"

He laughed, and she laughed along with him.

Again that heated silence. Propped on his hand, he was close enough to reach out and touch her, swallow her in a kiss.

Just as he was leaning in, she surprised him by speaking up.

"Might I ask you a question, Thomas?"

He pulled back slightly, praying she did not sense the foolish thing he'd been about to do. Putting aside his glass, he ran a hand through his hair and grinned. "Since when have you asked my permission to do anything, Miss Blaise? Go on, then."

"You and La Reinette. How—how do you know her? And why go to her about the French Blue before anyone else? I did not realize she was a woman of such great. Er. Importance."

Well. Out of all the things she could've asked, Hope wasn't expecting *that*.

He narrowed his eyes. Was that a reflection of his own jealousy he heard in her words? More likely Sophia was merely trying to piece together the details of the plot.

Still. Though it shamed him to admit it, some small part of him was pleased she might be jealous. Perhaps—*perhaps*—he intrigued her as much as she intrigued him.

Perhaps a small part of *her* cared for him, even.

He did not dare follow that thought any further.

"Ah, La Reinette." Hope wondered how much he should tell Sophia about his long, and often complicated, relationship with the mercurial Frenchwoman. "How much do you know?"

"Only that she's got a taste for pirates, and has a habit of attracting dangerous—albeit handsome—men."

"Well, then." Hope pulled back a curl with his fingers. "I shall begin at the—er, beginning, then.

"Marie and I are very old friends. We first met ten—no, twelve years ago, in Paris. I was working with Lake at the time, doing—well, it doesn't matter. Suffice it to say my line of work brought me into contact with Marie around the time Napoleon overthrew the Directory."

"Who is she?"

Hope sighed. "No one knows, really. She keeps her own secrets even better than she keeps everyone else's. I *do* know she rose to prominence during the Revolution, when it was rumored she—how do I put this?—*befriended* several high-ranking nobles. It wasn't long before she was the *maîtresse-en-titre* to the likes of royal dukes and German princes.

"More than that, she was their confidant throughout the bloodshed that was to come. Marie became involved in all sorts of intrigue to save her lovers. She was discreet, intelligent, too. But even she was not immune to the danger of those times. Back then France was a fearful place, you see; *madame guillotine* exacted terrible justice. Everyone was afraid.

"And so when the danger grew too great, I helped La Reinette escape to England. Together we found asylum in London. I loaned her the funds to establish The Glossy; she in turn became my first client and an advocate of Hope and Company besides. It wasn't long before I could count all of her high-ranking clients as my own. She operates, you see, in perhaps the most rarefied circle in all of England."

Sophia nodded. "Rubbing elbows with London's finest, La Reinette would be the first to hear of any plot against you."

"I wouldn't call what she does 'rubbing elbows,' exactly," Hope said, tugging at his cravat. "But yes. If anyone of any importance had designs to steal the diamond, she would be the first to know about it."

"And the note," Sophia said. "I know the diamond is of utmost importance, Thomas. But I do hope La Reinette can help us uncover who wrote that letter. Not only does he threaten us, he threatens my family, too."

Hope met her eyes. For the first time, she appeared frightened. "We'll find him, Sophia. I'll do everything I can to keep your family safe in the meantime."

Sophia looked down at her glass, shaking her head. "And here I thought myself an adventurer. My God! She wouldn't be afraid. Not after the things La Reinette must've seen, and the people she's known."

"So now you understand, Sophia," Hope said, finishing what was left of his port, "it is no small thing that she chose you to write her memoirs. If—when—they are ever published, they will be a sensation. You must be possessed of great talent."

Sophia scoffed. "Indeed, I beat out several other applicants for the assignment. Zero, to be exact."

"Marie wouldn't have taken you on if she didn't see something in you she liked."

"Well." Sophia tipped her head back, draining the last drop of her port. "We'll see if La Reinette still likes me enough to finish what we've started. Everything's—" Her voice softened. "Everything's changed, you know."

Hope turned his head to look at her. The words left his lips before he could stop them. "Yes. But some things, I hope, for the better."

A beat of charged silence settled between them, long enough that Hope would've squirmed if it weren't for the goodly amount of port hard at work in his blood.

Her face was open as she looked back, lips slightly parted as she waited. Willing. Curious.

Christ. He needed the port now more than ever. Up until this moment it had kept his hands and his mouth busy.

But now. Now they were left idle, set ablaze by the not insignificant amount of said port he'd imbibed in the last few hours.

He didn't like how much he liked not thinking about the diamond, or the bank, or the world outside. How much he liked thinking about Miss Sophia Blaise instead.

The silence grew unbearable.

And then, embarrassed—terrified, in Hope's case; terrified that he would do something he'd regret, that would compromise everything for which he'd worked so hard, but dear *God* he'd never wanted anything so badly—they both moved to stand at once.

Sophia bent her knees, the whole of her bare leg exposed as Hope took her by the arm and hauled her up beside him.

A lovely, lithe, impossibly shapely leg.

For some inexplicable reason, both Hope and Sophia were breathless as they stood, not daring to touch, before the fire. Hope trained his eyes on Botticelli's masterwork above the mantel, balling his hands into fists to keep from reaching out for Sophia, indulging the desire that pounded unabated through his body.

But staring at Venus only made his struggle worse. Had she always been this sensual, the goddess, her legs so visible through the transparent gauze of her gown?

If those damned Frenchmen, those acrobats, or the diamond's thief—heaven above, Hope was a wanted man—didn't kill him first, then this Venus at his side, brought to startling, sensual life, would certainly be the death of him.

Sophia turned her head and met his eyes, her breast working as she struggled to catch her breath. "Thomas," she said, her voice barely above a whisper. "We should—I should—"

In one swift, ruthless movement he reached for her, curling his hand around the back of her neck as he pulled her to him, lowering his lips onto her own.

Knowing as he did that, once he'd started, he would not be able to stop.

Twelve

---◆---

T hank God Thomas kissed Sophia first, before whatever she was about to say slipped from her tongue. *I should go. I should stay. We should kiss, and keep kissing until whatever happens after that happens.*

No, it would not do at all; she did not trust herself with a bellyful of port and Mr. Thomas Hope looking at her like *that*.

Like he was racked with thirst that could only be slaked by swallowing her whole.

Sophia had only known Thomas—truly *known* him—for a week or two. But in those two weeks they'd each shared more of themselves than either of them ever had with anyone else. He knew her secrets, and she knew his. Well, a goodly amount of them, anyway. Together they'd shared adventure, cheated death, and outwitted villains, touching and talking and *kissing* along the way.

She felt as if she knew him better than she knew even her dearest friends.

Even so. One did not discuss the goddess of love over a bottle of wine with a frightfully unmarried member of the opposite sex. Never, never, *never*.

And yet.

It could've been the port—no, it was most *definitely* the port—but the memory of Hope's kiss, his touch, pounded through her with every breath she took. The longer they talked and drank, drank and talked, the press of the evening's events faded. In their place rose a dizzying—oh, that *deuced port*!—fire, its embers bursting to flame when he'd looked at her for several long, silent heartbeats, his eyes darkened by pain, struggle, something heavy with which he was grappling.

When they'd stood, chests heaving, before the fire, Sophia wasn't sure if Thomas would lean in or turn away.

When he'd leaned in—well.

Whatever reservations she had dissolved into desire when his lips met hers. This was no innocent kiss; his deadly intent was as palpable as the heat that radiated from his body.

Beneath the knowing gaze of Botticelli's Venus, Hope opened Sophia to him. His hand slid from her neck to her cheek, and together with his other hand cradled her face, turning her head in time to the strokes of his kiss.

When she matched him, caress for caress, he let out a deep, contented moan and stepped closer, pressing his body against hers. His flesh felt at once familiar and frightening. The warmth of his emotion, the terrific hunger of his desire—she recognized these things in her own response to the kiss, yes.

But if they were both flooded with longing, who would stop them from sinking into one another, from giving in and giving up everything that they wanted, that they were?

Hope's lips were traveling across her jaw now, pressing into the exquisitely tender skin of her neck. She inhaled his scent, clean lemon, spicy sandalwood. So lovely, so inviting . . .

No. Stop. The words were there, the debutante still alive somewhere inside the tangle of her limbs.

Thomas kissed her neck, teasing her with his teeth, his tongue, sending bolts of white-hot pleasure through her.

The words were lost. Her eyes rolled shut as she tilted her head back, surrendering to Hope's desire for her, the sensation of his mouth moving over her as if he knew where she wanted to be touched before she knew it herself.

So this—this was *it*. What came after kissing. The *it* Sophia had been warned against since she was old enough to listen.

But no one warned her *it* was going to feel like *this*.

As Thomas touched her, explored her with tender fingers and urgent lips, she felt her body unfurling beneath his hands. Her shoulders relaxed; the tension between her eyes and along her spine loosened.

Thoughts of her family, her fears for them, scattered like

shadows from a struck match. Here it was only Sophia and Thomas and the gasped breaths between them.

Here there was no war to wage, no marriage to make. The rules were what she made them. Here she was flesh and blood and heart, nothing else, nothing to pretend or force.

She suddenly felt light, alive. *Honest.* As if the walls of her pretending and forcing and worry had fallen, at least for a little while, to her feet.

The release was intoxicating. Coupled with the port—or, perhaps, in spite of it—Sophia felt as if her feet might leave the ground.

Hope's hands adored her, slow caresses as they moved down from her face to her shoulders. She inhaled when his hands slowly, oh, *slowly* traveled the length of her ribs, his thumb grazing her breast before dipping to her belly, tugging her further against him as he held her by the hips.

His lips were on the neckline of her gown. Sophia arched back, digging her hands into the inviting mass of his dark curls. She let out a long, hot breath, willing herself to remember this moment.

It would never be like this again. It couldn't.

Thomas raised his head, straightening so that he loomed over her, his eyes ablaze. He dragged his hands back up over her hips, hooking his thumbs beneath her ribs.

"Hold on to me," he growled. Without waiting for a reply he lifted her, a familiar, guttural tear sounding between them as her skirts—what little was left of them, anyway—were rent into a dozen pieces. He pressed her back against the wall beside the fireplace, holding her with one arm while coaxing her legs about his hips with the other.

Lightning shot through her at the feel of Thomas nestled between her legs. She felt open and vulnerable.

She felt like *more.*

Pulling his face close, she covered her mouth with his, and he moaned again, this one so deep and strong she felt the vibration of his chest in her own. She followed his example and moved her lips to his cheek, his chin, the place where jaw sloped to ear and neck.

She sensed the tension coiling inside him; vaguely she wondered if she was hurting him, if she should stop—

Sliding his hands along the backs of her thighs, he gathered her backside in his palms and lifted her away from the wall. She gasped as he took one, two unhurried strides across the room, setting her at last on the edge of his enormous, gleaming desk.

Sophia looked up at him, wondering what could possibly come next. There was a wicked gleam in his eye she'd never seen before. Thomas, it seemed, knew *exactly* what came next.

He leaned in, and she closed her eyes and surrendered to the rush of his lips against her. He ran his hands down her bare legs, the scrape of skin against skin sending a shiver up her spine; he pulled back his hands, allowed them to linger on her hips a moment before trailing them up her sides, over her breasts. She released his mouth, sucking in a breath at the exquisite sensation that rushed through her as he buried the fingers of his right hand into the neckline of her bodice.

With his teeth he nipped at her bottom lip. And then he was tugging at her bodice, pulling it up and over her skin, baring her breast to his touch.

Sophia gasped. "Thomas! Thomas—"

He put his first finger to her lips, pulling open her mouth as he met her eyes and lowered his head, kept lowering it.

She watched in breathless wonder as he took the hardened knot of her nipple into his mouth, sucking in a breath at the pleasure that pulsed between her legs.

As if under a spell her body arched further against him, her fingers tangling in his hair, encouraging him as he licked, then teased, scraping his teeth against her nipple with excruciating finesse.

In her veins she felt her blood rising, pooling between her legs. It felt good to have Thomas pressed against her there; good, and not nearly enough.

He went to work on the other side of her bodice, coaxing her breast free. While he moved his lips to this unexplored skin, he worked the other with his fingers, rolling her nipple between his thumb and forefinger.

Sophia's breath caught in her throat. She threw back her head, biting her lip against crying out. The more he touched and pulled, the more unbearable it became.

When she lifted her head, her gaze landed for a moment

on Botticelli's Venus, watching the scene impassively from across the room. How did she appear so calm, Sophia wondered, after Mars had done *this* to her moments before?

There was no shame or regret in Venus's eyes; only knowledge, a breathlessness in the pose of her head as if she would nod her assent. *Go on, go on, explore so that you might know.*

Hope's finger traced a line of fire along the inside of Sophia's bottom lip. In her mounting frustration she bit the tip of his finger, crying out as he returned the favor on her nipple.

She was pulling at his hair now, the silken curls catching on her fingers. Thomas released his mouth, feathering kisses across her breast. He lowered his hand to her hip, meeting her eyes.

Sophia should shake her head, push him away, end the encounter as a lady of good manners ought. Through the pounding of the port and of her desire, she knew this could only end badly. She was only as good as her virginity, at least in the eyes of those who mattered.

But here, now, blessed by Venus and drunk on wine, that lady of good manners felt as far away as the moon. Here and now under Hope's spell she was only Sophia, filled for the first time with the will to follow her own desires, rather than everyone else's.

Yes, she breathed, and ran her thumb along the ridge of Thomas's brow.

He did not waste any time. Grasping her hips in his hands, thumbs grazing the inside of her thighs, he got down on his knees. She watched with bated breath as he reached up with one hand, placing it squarely over her heart.

"Lie down." His voice was barely above a whisper. He gently pushed back her torso, guiding her down, and bent her knees so that her feet rested on the edge of the desk.

"Is this," she panted, "the sort of work you usually do at your desk?"

From his perch between her legs he scoffed. "Oh, this, and every now and again the odd bit of paperwork."

Sophia laughed, his humor alleviating her shyness at opening herself to him so freely, so wholly.

He tugged her skirts aside, revealing the length of her legs. One at a time he removed her slippers, then her stockings and the ribboned garters that held them in place. His touch was light, deliberate, a thrilling foil to the hard expanse of the desk pressing up against her spine.

Thus having untangled Sophia from the intricacies of her footwear, Thomas moved farther up her legs, over her thighs and hips to her belly. He hooked his fingers into the waistband of her drawers, and, grinning at Sophia's gasp, ripped them off, dropping them to the floor beside her slippers and stockings.

She was completely naked. Well, save for the scraps of gauze wrapped about her middle that were all that was left of her costume.

Not only that. Hope's face was mere inches from that most private place between her legs, the place she'd been taught to simultaneously ignore and worship as the source of all her worth.

He pressed on the inside of her thighs, inching her legs wider. She closed her eyes, unable to bear the thought that he didn't like what he saw.

"Sophia." The word was kind but spoken firmly. "Open your eyes. I want you to see how beautiful I think you are."

Her eyes flew open. "Beautiful?" She lifted her head as if to look herself. "Really?"

His hands crept closer to her center, his thumbs grazing her dark, slick curls. "Oh, God," he groaned. "You've not the slightest clue, Sophia."

Between her legs she felt a tug, at once painful and intensely pleasurable.

And then, just when she thought it couldn't get any better, that she might explode or die or swoon or all three, Thomas touched her.

It was his first finger, brushing lightly the very tip of her sex—the place that she quickly discovered was the center of all this delicious, maddening sensation.

She cried out, the agony of her pleasure at his touch overwhelming. He splayed his other hand palm-down over her belly, willing her to be still as he touched, and kept touching. The hand slid forward, caressing her breast, plucking at her nipple. A sharp stab of pleasure shot through her. She was on fire, every inch of her burning; her hips now worked against him, pressing harder, wanting more.

"Easy, Sophia," he purred. "Easy."

His finger slid from the top of her sex down to its middle where it gently, slowly, began to ease its way inside her.

She shot upright, eyes wide.

"No." Thomas pushed her back down. "Soon, soon. Patience, darling."

Patience. How was she supposed to have patience when he tortured her like this?

Pressure mounted around his finger as it delved deeper yet. His other hand slid back down her belly to rest where her legs met; and then with his thumb he began stroking that *place* again, the place that hurt and thrummed and sang the most.

In and out, he was inside her, over her, in her, all at once. A hard, tight sensation rolled through her, so poignant she gritted her teeth against it.

And then he was lowering his head, brushing his lips to the inside of one thigh, then the other, moving closer, closer, so very close . . .

Her eyes fluttered shut at the featherlight touch of his mouth on her sex. A new wave of pleasure coursed through her, potent but different somehow; it was forbidden, erotic, the idea of it alone enough to make her moan aloud.

His lips, his tongue, were moving faster now, circling again and again that bit of flesh. His teeth nicked her, gently pulling, caressing to the point of pain.

She watched his head moving between her legs, earnestly, slowly, her fingers once again finding purchase in his silken curls, now damp with sweat. He groaned against her; her desire spiked at the vibration of his lips, the vibration of her own.

The rising tide of heat inside her—it was impossible to escape.

It was coming now, whatever it was that came next; she felt the muscles in her legs tense, her shoulders flatten against the desk. She took a shallow breath in, closing her eyes as she searched in vain for something, anything to hold on to.

Her eyes flew open as the rush came, a tumbling, pounding thing. She cried out as pulse after pulse of sensation rounded through her, the ripples of pleasure slowly fading into a satisfaction so immense she felt limp beneath its weight.

Sophia sputtered for breath, pushing aside wisps of hair from her slick forehead with shaking fingers.

Dear God. Even La Reinette's stories hadn't prepared her for *that*.

Thomas's eyes appeared over the ridge of her sex, blue and serious; his mouth came next, not quite a smile; his lips glistened with her arousal. He waited for her verdict.

When her gaze met his, a warm happiness rolled through her. She longed to reach out, to touch him and hold him to her. But while his eyes were serious they were wild, too; she recognized the rising tide in him, those excruciating last moments before the crash.

She did not trust her touch. His hands and his lips were knowledgeable and fast. Hers would be clumsy. Where to even begin? Perhaps it was best to defer to Thomas. *He* would know what to do next.

And so she grinned, palms held fast to the desk. "Yes." She breathed. "Yes!"

He returned her grin. His eyes gleamed wickedly; and then he was sinking down again, moving toward her.

Sophia started at the feel of his fingers on her sex. She fought the urge to squirm; but as his hands began to move in earnest, she relaxed, the spark of her desire ignited again.

There was more? But how? Could she possibly do that *again*—

Just as she felt herself swelling against him, Hope suddenly froze, his thumb poised just below the jointure of all this delicious sensation.

Sophia did not dare to breathe, listening instead to the racket that reverberated just beyond the office door. Grunts, heavy footsteps, a shout or two for good measure.

Christ in heaven. Not this again.

Their gazes locked, eyes wide as the racket drew nearer.

In the space of a single heartbeat Hope was on his feet, gathering her slippers and stockings and undergarments in the crook of his elbow. With an efficient tug at the scraps of her costume he covered her breasts, her legs, wincing as that curious hardness between his hips brushed against her.

"I'm terribly sorry, Sophia." His voice was hushed. He met her eyes, holding out his free hand. "Seems we've become fast favorites of thugs and thieves and the like. I wonder who it could be this time."

Sophia blinked, virtually blinded by the haze of desire that hung between them. With no small effort she swung her legs over the back of the desk and with Hope's help ducked into the alcove occupied by his tall-backed leather chair.

"Please, *please* do as I say for once and stay here," Thomas said, handing her the misshapen bulk of her unmentionables. "There's a pistol in the top drawer there." He paused. "Though, on second thought, you may want to leave the shooting to me."

If Sophia's thoughts weren't still storm-tossed she would've stuck out her tongue at his jest. Her heart worked furiously as alternating waves of disappointment and relief and fear crashed through her.

Disappointment that she and Thomas could not finish what they had started. It seemed with every new sensation his body wrought she always yearned for more, and more yet. What heavenly part of him came after his fingers and his mouth?

Relief that she did not, in fact, experience said part. She was not entirely ruined. Not yet.

And fear—well, fear for the obvious reasons. Thugs, thieves, the revelation of her carefully guarded secrets.

Secrets that now included a rather heady, half-naked interlude on Mr. Thomas Hope's desk.

"Sophia."

She met his eyes once more. Licking his port-stained lips, Thomas's face momentarily softened, his eyes very full as he struggled to find the right words. "Sophia, I—"

She jumped at the slam of the door. Thomas darted upright; she saw him yank at the crotch of his breeches before stepping in front of the desk.

A familiar voice rang out across the chamber.

Thirteen

—◆—

"We found them." Lake shoved a short, broad-shouldered figure into the room, the man's face blackened with soot. "Acrobats from a traveling troupe playing at Vauxhall. Ran 'em down in a tavern in Cheapside."

Hope carefully arranged the knot of his hands in front of his legs and tried to think of anything, *anything* but Sophia.

"And you're sure these are the men who attacked my house?"

Lake stepped forward, waving his pistol at the perpetrator's enormously calloused hands, his thick, corded neck. He pulled back the sleeves of the man's shirt, revealing the bulge of his forearms that were nicked with dozens of small, oozing cuts.

"I've never been wrong." Lake winked. Hope bit the inside of his cheek to keep from throttling him. "We've a few of his friends waiting outside."

"Good." Hope turned and made for the sideboard. All the better to hide the rather alarming condition of his breeches, a condition he could not subdue no matter how hard he tried. "We cannot interrogate them here; no one at the bank can know of this, not yet. Though I'm sure the gossip will be rife by morning. Take them to my house and wake the kitchens. I'm going to need coffee. A *lot* of coffee."

"Consider it done. I assume you've all the accouterments available there—pliers, hot pokers, an axe?"

Hope tried not to smile at the acrobat's high-pitched squeak of terror.

"No pliers, I'm afraid, but Cook does keep a rather interesting collection of paring knives. Might we experiment with those?"

"Oh, yes, let's do." Lake shoved the man back into the hall outside the office where the rest of his officers waited.

"Well?" he said after a moment, waiting for Hope at the door.

Hope waved him away. "I'll meet you back at my house. I've a few. Ah. Matters to which to attend here first." He pretended to busy himself at the sideboard. For the first time in his life—well, no, that wasn't true, exactly—suffice it to say he could not remember the last time he went green at the very sight of liquor.

Of course today would be that day.

As if on cue, the clock on the mantel struck five o'clock. Hope glanced out the window to see darkness fading to gray dawn.

The night—this night, spent in the half-naked company of Miss Sophia Blaise—was over.

But his troubles. *They* were just beginning.

Hope looked over his shoulder to see Mr. Lake backtracking into the room, moving too noiselessly, and with far too much finesse, than his injury should allow. His eyes took in Hope's coat, laid out before the crackling fire, lingering a moment too long on the Botticelli above the mantel. At last his gaze landed on the massive expanse of Hope's desk.

"I say." Lake furrowed his brow and bent over to retrieve something from the floor. "What's this?"

Hope watched in horror as Lake dangled a satin garter between his thumb and forefinger.

The banker reached out and snatched the garter before Lake could get a better look. "It's mine."

"It's yours? What the devil do you mean to do with it, *Miss* Hope? Use it to tie up those b*eau*teous curls of yours?"

Hope cleared his throat as he shoved the garter into his waistcoat. "Jealous, are you, of my flowing locks?"

"Ha!" Lake snorted. "I may be ginger-haired, old friend, but the ladies certainly don't seem to mind." He leaned over the desk, eyes narrowed, nose in the air. He was a bully, yes, but Lake was no fool. If Hope did not stop him, he would sniff out Sophia. And when he discovered her pink-cheeked, her costume in telling shreds, she would surely die of shame and embarrassment.

And, lest Hope ever forget, there was Lake's wrath to consider.

There was no telling what the man would do once he discovered Hope was further jeopardizing an already complicated plot.

"Well, then," Hope said briskly. He took Lake by the shoulder and turned him away from the desk. "Remember the coffee. And have those little bastards brought down to the kitchens; I don't need to tell you that no one must know they are in my house." Lake opened his mouth, but Hope pushed him out the door before he could speak. "Oh, and send for Lady Violet. What with the diamond being stolen from about her neck, she might shed some light on our proceedings. I shall join you directly, *old friend.*"

Hope shut the door and leaned against it, clamping his fist around the knob. He waited, heart thudding, until he heard Lake's staccato shuffling down the stair.

He let out a long breath. "The coast is clear," he called out softly, making his way to Sophia. "You may come out now."

Hope helped her to her feet, trying all the while not to stare at her adorably disheveled appearance. Her hair was askew, lips bright red. Attempting to straighten her costume, Sophia only made the damage worse and revealed, to Hope's delight, far more bosom than was polite.

"That was close," she said, stepping into her slippers. "We're off to your house, then?"

Hope looked at her. She blushed. Adorably, of course.

His shoulders sagged. "I don't suppose I could convince you to end our adventure here, could I?"

She leaned in, a small, suggestive smile on those damnably alluring lips. "Not if you want to keep that garter as a souvenir. Besides, we've already come this far. The more ears you have to the ground, the better chance you have of recovering the French Blue."

Hope sighed. He couldn't say no, not when she stood before him in the gown he'd torn to shreds. Not when she smiled at him like that.

"All right. I've got to write a few letters to my friends at the papers. Buy us some time before word gets out of the theft. Once my clients hear of it—those who weren't at the ball, anyway—they'll panic. Then we'll send for your mother and meet at my house."

Only as he sat down to pen said letters did Hope realize

he'd said *us*—"Buy *us* time"—as if he and Sophia were true partners in crime.

It seemed Sophia was now an integral part of the plot, whether Hope wished it or not.

D espite Lake's supposed expertise in such matters, the interrogation of the acrobats proved a failure.

Until, that is, Lady Violet strutted into the room. A fuming Lord Harclay—what was *he* doing here?—at her side, she trailed perfume and the promise of forbidden things in her wake. The baby-faced men, their hands bound behind their backs, sat up straight in their chairs. With a strategic batting of the eyes, Violet squeezed the story out of them in five minutes flat.

Interestingly, while the acrobats admitted to crashing Hope's ball, they knew nothing about the French Blue.

"We was down the pub, yeah?, when a man wiv a fake-like beard, teeth rottin' out ov his head, yeah?, sat down," the lead man said. "Said he'd give fi'ty pounds to the each ov us for making a right nice mess of your fancy-pants party. Twen'y-five before, twen'y-five after."

"And what of the other twenty-five pounds the man owes you?" Violet asked. "Have you received it yet?"

The acrobat shook his head. "Nah. Seein' as we been caught, we ain't expectin' to see the rest. Though that ain't exactly fair now, is it?"

But when Violet asked them about the diamond, the man responded to her question with a blank stare; his companions, impossibly, appeared even more puzzled. And unless they were better actors than they were acrobats, Hope could tell they spoke the truth.

Across the room he met Lake's gaze.

So now they were looking for a man disguised in a strap-on beard and, from the sound of it, ill-fitting wooden dentures.

A description that encompassed a solid half of the inhabitants of London during the bustling months of the season.

Splendid.

"Discover any further information about this man," Hope said, knowing all the while his offer would come to naught, "and I will gladly pay you the twenty-five guineas he still owes you."

Head throbbing and heart sunk, Hope charged from the room.

"Keep them in your custody," he growled over his shoulder as Lake followed him out into the servants' hall. "In the extreme unlikelihood that we find this bearded, gap-toothed son of a bitch, those acrobats of yours might help us untangle his plot."

Without waiting for a reply, he mounted the stairs two at a time. He needed more coffee and a bath; as it was Friday, a goodly amount of paperwork awaited him at the bank before the start of the weekend.

Mr. Hope sighed. He wasn't used to dreading the day like this. His work was difficult and often frustrating, but he enjoyed it nonetheless. It was what he did, and who he was. He rarely, if ever, desired to be anywhere but the offices of Hope & Co. on Fleet Street.

And so the tug to remain at his house, and take his coffee in the upstairs drawing room where Sophia now waited, shocked him.

That he imagined taking more than his coffee, even with her mother there in the room—well, it quite frankly *petrified* him.

In his rational mind he knew there was no time for such things, and besides, his relationship with Sophia had progressed far enough. Too far, even.

As much as Hope loathed Lake's habit of barging in uninvited, thank God he interrupted Hope's interlude with Sophia before they'd done something they would both regret. Hope knew he would have done it, and done it again and again and again. And where would that leave the two of them today?

He dare not imagine the possibilities.

And so off to his study he went, nodding at a footman along the way for a pot—no, make it two pots of coffee and whatever potion Cook had on hand for a headache.

Slipping into the quiet, tobacco-scented calm of his study, Hope was about to close the door behind him when a sudden, inelegant movement at the desk caught his eye.

The Marquess of Withington sprang to his feet and dipped

his dark head in a single, elbowy jolt. He held his hat in his hands.

Hope's mouth went dry as he ran a hand through his curls. A visit from one of his largest investors and clients before nine o'clock on a Friday morning was *not* a good sign.

That said client was also courting Miss Sophia Blaise, procurer of impeccably timed sobs, temptress of Hope's restless dreams, had nothing to do with Hope's rising ire.

No, absolutely nothing at all.

At least that was what Hope told himself as he attempted a smile.

"My lord! Welcome. What an—*unexpected* pleasure. You must forgive my mess; it's been a busy morning, as you might imagine." Hope made for his desk. "Please, do sit."

Withington nervously eyed the leather-backed chair, but did not move. "My apologies for visiting you unannounced, and at so ungodly an hour. Thank you for seeing me, Mr. Hope. I shall make quick work of the business I have come to discuss, though I confess it—well, I'm afraid it's rather. Um. Unpleasant."

"Rather the opposite of capital, then?"

Missing the jibe, Withington furrowed his brow. "Capital? Heavens, no."

"Go on, then."

Withington jerked his cravat into disarray; his face burned pink. "The events of last night were. Um. Rather terrifying, actually. My mother lost her wig and her dignity and was up half the night howling like a madwoman because of it."

Good Lord. As if Hope didn't feel bad enough. "I do apologize for any grief her ladyship has suffered on my behalf. I understand it is no comfort, but I take full responsibility for last night's events. My clients—" He swallowed. "My clients are very important to me, my lord. You've my word I will do everything in my power to see that justice is done, and her ladyship compensated for any trouble I may have caused."

Withington passed his hat from one hand to the other. He looked as if he would burst into tears at any moment. "You don't know my mother, Mr. Hope. There is no compensating her. Not when she's. Er. In *this* sort of state."

Hope stood awkwardly beside his desk and cast a longing

glance toward the sideboard. "Well." He cleared his throat. "I've been on the hunt for the stolen jewel since the moment it was taken from me. Make no mistake, Lord Withington, I *will* find the French Blue. It's only a matter of time now. And you will be glad to know this whole—er, series of *unfortunate* events will have no impact on your funds."

Well. At least he could *hope* there'd be no impact. But if he and Lake didn't find the jewel, and soon, all hell would break loose—

"I'm sorry!" Withington blurted. "You have always done right by my family, Mr. Hope. If I had it my way—well, I'd have a different mother, I tell you that much. But I'm afraid I've no choice in the matter. I must." Oh, God, the man was going to faint. "I must move my accounts to—er—a different bank. I'm terribly sorry, Mr. Hope, *terribly* sorry."

Hope bit back his panic. At least one hundred thousand pounds were in those accounts.

This did not bode well for the hours and days ahead. At this rate, Hope & Co. would shutter its doors in a week or two, maybe less.

"I'm sorry," Withington repeated. He looked up to the ceiling, as if trying to recall a memorized bit of Chaucer. "Everyone knows that Hope and Company is only as great— no, that's not it. Only as *good* as its reputation. And I'm afraid your reputation will suffer on account of this. Um. Unfortunate incident. I cannot risk it, Mr. Hope. I've three sisters, you see . . . and my mother, of course, the old bat just refuses to die . . ."

Hope could hardly breathe for the sudden swelling of his throat. Those were his mother's words, probably hurled at the poor marquess over breakfast this morning. Hope would've felt sorry for the fellow if Withington wasn't pushing him to the brink of ruin.

If Withington wasn't after the woman Hope held in his arms mere hours ago. The woman who set his mind, his body, alight with desire.

"I told you," Hope said, trying not to grit his teeth. This jealousy, it made him feel wild, and he did not like it. "I will sort out this diamond business. Your funds shall not suffer, my lord. Do not forget how well I have safeguarded your family's fortune for years now. I've made you thousands, tens of thousands—"

"I know. And I appreciate your efforts; they have not gone unnoticed. It pains me to say this." Withington looked away; the fingers that held his hat were white. "But I must sell my Hope and Company shares and withdraw my deposits. I've already visited Fleet Street, and the transfer is under way as we speak."

Hope's breath shook as he tried to calm the panic, the rage, too, that rose in his belly. It took considerable effort not to leap across the desk and take his lordship's close-shaven neck in his hands.

The marquess was not being rude, nor unkind; this was a matter of business, and Hope never lost his head over business. So why this sudden urge to do violence to a kind, if odd, fellow whose only crime was harboring a *tendre* for Miss Sophia Blaise?

Hope swallowed the answer to his question and straightened. He had to get the marquess out of here before bad things—things Hope would forever regret—happened.

"Very well. I will see to the transfer straightaway, my lord."

Withington's shoulders fell back from his ears, and a breath of relief escaped from his open mouth. Thanking Hope, he jammed his hat on his head and hesitated, as if he would bow; remembering himself, he thumbed his hat in that abrupt way of his and exited the room.

Standing behind his desk, Hope fingered a heavy crystal paperweight as his fury burned to new heights. The Marquess of Withington was a client, an investor, no more than that; he couldn't possibly know of Hope's acquaintance with Sophia.

His desire for the woman Withington courted in earnest. The woman his lordship would in all likelihood take for his wife.

Even so. His presence this morning was like salt in a wound; nothing like adding insult to injury, and at so early an hour.

He took the paperweight in his hand just as Mr. Daltrey poked his head into the room, bearing coffee and biscuits.

Hope dropped the crystal with a dull thud onto the desk.

He sighed. "Your timing, Mr. Daltrey, is, as always, impeccable. Come in."

He sat at his desk, staring out the window at a brightening day, and drained cup after cup of coffee. It was bitter and hot but slowly burned away the knot in his throat. As he drank he found himself thinking about his father, a man who'd always occupied the shadows of his thoughts but rarely appeared center stage.

The elder Hope was brilliant beyond imagination: philosopher, inventor, theologian, and collector. How he'd managed to find the time to grow the family's smallish business into a world-renowned banking house, and be a husband and father besides, Thomas hadn't a clue.

He remembered when he was five, his brother Henry had been born sometime in the night, and the house was in a tizzy over a beautiful new baby. Forgotten by his governess (and everyone else), Thomas had hidden behind the drapes in his nursery and cried himself into a stupor, whimpering for his mummy.

It had been his father who discovered him. With a smile the elder Hope had taken his son in his arms and kissed his cheeks.

He'd clucked his tongue and said, "But my dear Thomas, surely you know by now it's best to leave the crying to babies! Besides, they cannot eat chocolate."

Thomas's sobs halted at the mention of *chocolate*. "They can't?"

"Absolutely not! If they do, their lips turn green and fall off. Ghastly, I know. But you and me, we can visit the chocolatier as often as we like."

"And still keep our lips?"

His father had laughed. "Yes. And still keep our lips."

Later that night, with a bellyache from eating far too many of Monsieur Cormier's truffles, Thomas held his father's hand as he met Henry for the first time. Though he wished he'd wake so that they might properly be introduced, Thomas kissed him anyway, and hugged his mummy with a smile.

"You naughty boy." His mother grinned and wiped a smear of chocolate from his face with her thumb. She met her husband's gaze. "Someone's been to visit the monsieur."

His father shrugged, then turned to wink at Thomas. "I don't know what you're talking about, darling."

Hope closed his eyes against the hot press of tears, dropping his cup onto its saucer with a clatter. God, how he missed them; how he wished his father were with him now. What would John Hope do? How would he seek out the diamond while assuring investors and keeping the bank afloat?

And what would he say to his son, still half-drunk on Miss Sophia Blaise's touch, about the choice between duty and following one's own desire?

Part of Hope believed his father would call him a fool. He'd remind him of all he'd sacrificed, and everything he'd been through, to make his dream come true of seeing Hope & Co. flourish once more.

But another part of Thomas, the part that recalled with startling clarity the sound of his father's laugh, believed his answer might be more complicated than that.

Hope rose abruptly, pushing the thought from his mind. The day was in full force now; there was much work to be done.

He dressed and made for Fleet Street.

Fourteen

— ✦ —

Heart pounding, Sophia set down the paper. She reached for her cup and saucer, which—*drat!*—made a terrible clatter in the grip of her shaking fingers.

"Dearest," her mother said, looking up from her needle-point. "Are you unwell?"

Sophia set the tea back on its tray and arranged her features into what she hoped was a smile. "I am quite well, Mama, thank you. Just a bit—"

"Tired? Regretful? Plagued by guilt? Yes, well, that *does* tend to happen when one leaves one's unconscious mother in a carriage to run about *unchaperoned* in the dead of night."

"Mama," Sophia sighed, too exhausted to resist the impulse to roll her eyes, "I already told you, Mr. Hope needed my help—"

"Regardless," Lady Blaise sniffed, returning to her embroidery hoop, "that does not excuse what you have done. We had better pray the marquess makes an offer before word gets out of your *nocturnal activities.*"

With her bottom lip Lady Blaise blew a lock of hair from her forehead. "If I survive your first season, I daresay I shall fill the bathtub with champagne and drink it. Every"—a furious tug on the thread—"last"—another tug—"*drop.* No one appreciates how difficult it all is for the poor mamas. Debutantes these days! If I behaved as you did last night, my father would've locked me in the cellar and thrown away the key. Mark my words, it is the end—the *end* I say!—of my sanity and my soul. And your cousin—I cannot even *begin* to speak on *that* subject . . ."

Lost as Lady Blaise was in the heat of her diatribe, Sophia hoped she would not notice her daughter slipping the gossip sheets into the folds of her skirt. God forbid Mama discover the news. Sophia would be spending the rest of her life in that cellar of Grandfather's.

The lines of text glared in her memory. She'd run her thumb over the words, smearing the ink as if she might erase them.

Like any debutante worth her salt, Sophia devoured the gossip pages first thing every morning, always before she tucked into breakfast but never after her first cup of tea. And like any debutante, she shamelessly enjoyed the faux pas and *affaires de coeur* of London's most fashionable, if indiscreet, aristocrats.

That is, until the indiscretion was her own.

It has been revealed by Mr. C. that a certain debutante S. has been ghostwriting the memoirs of a royal more accustomed to the company of men.

Fear bolted through her, clouding her belly with dread. Sophia understood the entry for what it was: a threat. While readers would glance over the lines, thinking them nothing short of a riddle, Sophia knew that the advertisement was the first of many. Doubtless more would be revealed with each new entry—*S.* would become Miss Sophia Blaise of No. 8 Grosvenor Square; *royal* La Reinette, notorious madam of The Glossy in Mayfair.

The clock was ticking. Sophia did not know how much time she had, or who this Mr. C. was, but she would try her damnedest to stop him.

Besides. The devil hadn't a clue whom he'd crossed. The indiscretions that made Sophia the target of his wrath also worked to her advantage. She hadn't outrun caped assassins and outwitted a Princess of Wales on accident. If anything, her adventures at Mr. Hope's side had taught her she had more to offer than her pretty manners and mediocre dancing.

Courage. Cunning. A way with strategically timed sobs.

Oh yes. Mr. C. would be sorry he ever threatened Miss Sophia Blaise.

Still, that did not mean the burden of discovery weighed

upon her any less. The threat of losing everything that mattered was greater than ever. Her reputation, the glamorous match, the brilliant life she'd wanted for as long as she could remember—if she didn't move quickly, it would all be lost.

"The marquess." Sophia looked to her mother. "I believe we should accept the invitation to his box at Drury Lane. This evening, perhaps?"

Later that evening, Mr. Hope was at his desk at Hope & Co., when a breathless groom delivered the note.

Found thief. At Duchess Street, come as soon as you get this.

It was unsigned, but Hope recognized the wild scrawl of Violet's hand. He leapt to his feet, nearly toppling the chair as he grabbed his coat and raced down the stairs.

"To my house," he called to the coachman, "and quickly!"

Hope stared unseeing out the carriage window, his only awareness of the Friday evening traffic outside an occasional jerk this way and that as the driver careened onto backstreets.

His mind raced. Violet had found the thief. How? Who was he? What evidence did she have? A confession, perhaps. Or, even better, the diamond itself.

But Hope knew better. Violet would have mentioned such a thing in her note. And besides, it was too easy; he had the distinct feeling this chase would be long and messy. A fitting end, as it were, to his *History of the French Blue*.

The carriage had hardly come to a stop before Hope leapt onto the drive and up the wide stone steps of his house.

Mr. Daltrey, his butler, greeted him at the door. "In the library, sir."

Hope darted down the hall. "We shall require shackles, Daltrey, and a bottle of champagne!" he called over his shoulder.

Charging through the library's mahogany doors, Hope stared in dismay. Lady Violet was pacing before the fire, hands clasped at the small of her back. Mr. Lake, wet hair plastered to his skull, sat nearby, his bare shoulders wrapped in the thick folds of a blanket.

There was no one else in the room.

Violet raised her head at the sound of his entry. "You may cut the acrobats free. For I've reason to believe I've found our thief."

Hope removed his hat and watched Lake and Violet exchange glances.

"Pour us a drink, Hope," Lake said, nodding at the sideboard.

"I don't want a drink."

"Yes"—Lake looked him in the eye—"you do."

Hope sighed in exasperation. Truth be told, he was still recovering from last night's port, and needed a nip like he needed a hole in his head.

Nevertheless. Something was afoot, and the dull gleam in Lake's eye told Hope he wasn't going to like it. Not one bit.

"What the devil happened to you, Lake?" he asked over his shoulder as he poured three glasses of American whiskey. "You look like you fell—well, like you fell into a lake."

"Very funny." Lake took his glass. "As a matter of fact, it was the Serpentine."

Violet laughed. "And at the fashionable hour, too. Poor Lady Caroline, I don't know if she'll ever recover!"

"Lady Caroline." Hope thought for a moment. "Lord Harclay's sister?"

Violet ignored Lake's glower. "She was chaperoning Lord Harclay and me as we took our turn about Hyde Park this afternoon. Halfway through our stroll, Mr. Lake mysteriously appeared from behind a tree, and next thing I knew Lady Caroline was careening into the Serpentine. The two of them get on splendidly. If I didn't know any better, I would think they were very old friends indeed."

Hope glanced at Lake. Good God, was the man actually *blushing*? "You forget, Lady Violet, that Mr. Lake doesn't *have* any friends. Especially friends of the female variety."

"My friends are none of your business," Lake suddenly snarled. "Lady Caroline had the misfortune to fall into the river; I jumped in after her. No one was harmed. End of story."

Hope bit back his laughter; he'd never seen Lake so uncomfortable. Clearly that was not the end of the story.

"I am sorry to have missed this stroll of yours," Hope said

with a grin. "Apparently it was quite eventful. You didn't find our thief, too, in the midst of all your adventures?"

Lady Violet took a deep breath. She met Lake's eyes one last time before settling her gaze on Hope. "Actually—"

"You did?" He wrinkled his brow. "You *did.*"

"I did indeed. You see, Mr. Hope, I've good reason to believe that William Townshend, the Earl of Harclay, stole your diamond."

Mr. Hope choked on his brandy. "Really, Lady Violet, now is not the time to jest. Why, Harclay is not only an *earl*, and one of the most powerful peers at that; he is also one of my largest and most faithful clients. Tread carefully."

Violet resumed her pacing. "I would not dare make such an accusation if I wasn't convinced it were true. Just as you would not dare forget my entire inheritance is invested in Hope and Company stock. I understand, Mr. Hope, how much you have at stake; I, too, risk everything in this."

"But how?" Hope gulped at his whiskey. "And, more importantly, *why*? I know for a fact the man's got more money than all the pharaohs of Egypt. Combined."

"It makes perfect sense," Violet replied. "Only a man of Lord Harclay's hubris is bold and brash enough to thieve a diamond in the midst of a ball. Don't you see? The man is desperate for a thrill. Look at how he gambles, wagering small fortunes on this trifle and that. It's only money to him; he's got plenty of it, and is willing to spend thousands in the pursuit of excitement. Harclay is rich, he is clever, and he is bored. A more potent combination for a crime such as this does not exist."

Hope stared down into his empty glass. Bloody hell, she was right; it *did* make perfect sense.

A gentleman jewel thief, moving in plain sight for all the world to see, risking the gallows in his search for a thrill.

Hope remembered the earl ogling Lady Violet at the ball, the French Blue glittering invitingly from her breast. Arm in arm, the two of them had waded through the crush, bodies pressed close as Harclay called for that fateful waltz.

And then all hell had broken loose, the ballroom plunged into darkness as the acrobats and Hope's traitorous guards harassed the perfumed masses.

It was genius, really. In the midst of the chaos, the earl

could've easily swiped the diamond from Lady Violet's neck, and her none the wiser.

That *bastard*.

Hope resisted the urge to hurl his glass across the room. He would have to take his own advice and tread carefully. As yet there was no proof; and besides, Hope couldn't risk running off yet another client, never mind the infamously rakish Earl of Harclay.

"I pray you're wrong, Lady Violet." Hope leaned against the mantel and looked into the fire, draining the last drop of his whiskey. "But if Lord Harclay is indeed our man, we need to find out where he's hiding the diamond. And we mustn't forget the diamond collar; I borrowed it from a . . . friend who misses it very much."

Indeed, a cousin of the Tsar's had loaned Hope the collar; and the last thing he needed was batty old Alexander coming after him with all the might of the Russian army.

Lake nodded his agreement. "There's no negotiating with a man who wants for nothing. If what you're saying is true, Lady Violet, the only way to get back the French Blue is to take it. I can canvass his house; and Hope, you might search his records for any mention of a recent acquisition . . ."

Violet swallowed her whiskey in two long gulps and wincéd. "No. I'll do it."

"Are you sure that's wise?" Hope turned to face her. "You just said you've got quite a bit at stake here."

"I said I'll do it. Lord Harclay and I—" She stopped and looked away. "Trust me. I've a much better chance of finding the French Blue than the two of you."

"Are you and—" Hope cleared his throat. "The earl—er—fond of each other, or courting, perh—"

"No."

The vehemence of her reply startled Hope. He met Lake's gaze. This was a bad idea and they both knew it, but what else could they do?

"Very well," Lake said, rising. "Don't say we didn't warn you. The earl is a dangerous man, my lady, and you could very well be harmed—or worse—on the hunt for the jewel."

Violet looked at Hope levelly. "I'm the one who lost the French Blue. And I'm the one who's going to get it back."

Fifteen

—◈—

Sophia smoothed the pale silk of her skirts and wondered how much earsplitting opera, exactly, one could endure without losing one's hearing.

The marquess's box, while of prime location and excellent prominence, only made matters worse; they were so close to the stage Sophia heard every footstep, every murmured endearment, and, of course, every agonizing aria.

Beside her, the marquess raised his glass of claret and tried not to wince as the prima donna screeched a crescendo. "Capital, isn't it?"

Sophia nodded enthusiastically, unsure whether he was referring to the opera or the claret. "The best I've had—seen! Do you come often to Drury Lane?"

"Oh, yes," the marquess shouted above the din. "I am rather fond of Shakespeare's comedies. The operas—they are good, too. And you, Miss Blaise. Do you enjoy the theater?"

Sophia sighed, realizing they'd had this *exact* conversation in her uncle's drawing room some weeks ago. "Yes. Yes I do."

Even with actors yelling declarations of love at one another on the stage, the silence that settled between Sophia and the marquess was painful. A pulse of longing shot through her at the memory of her conversations with Mr. Hope; how easily words and thoughts flowed between them. There was no pretense, no desire to impress. She could be honest with him, and much to her surprise, she was fond of her honest self; Hope's, too.

Sophia wished, for a moment, that Hope were her escort tonight.

And felt ashamed as soon as the wish was made. She shouldn't feel this way about a man like Thomas Hope. She didn't want to *want* him like this, especially when the season's greatest catch sat in a chair mere inches from her own.

The marquess had kindly invited her to his box so that they might become acquainted—and, with any luck, more than that. It was an invitation for which her fellow debutantes would gladly sell their souls, surely. And the marquess—he wasn't such bad company. Not as bad, at least, as tonight's opera.

Sophia turned and caught Withington looking at her, a soft gleam in his dark eyes she recognized but could not place. His gaze was not lascivious or lustful, though she could tell the poor chap struggled not to look at her breasts. Rather she saw in his eyes curiosity, a steady declaration of interest that belied his boyish exclamations.

Understanding rolled through her, swift and startling.

He *liked* her!

The Marquess of Withington actually *liked* her.

All along, Sophia assumed the marquess hunted her for the same reasons she hunted him; practical, if not cynical, reasons. After all, what sort of fool believed affection, much less love, had anything at all to do with marriage?

While she claimed no great fortune, her uncle *was* a duke, and she supposed her face qualified as passably pretty. Withington would bring his fortune, and she would bring her hazel eyes and that greatest inheritance of all, her goodly-sized bosom.

But to her very great surprise, the marquess was proving far more honorable in his courtship. He called on Sophia, and strolled with Sophia, and invited Sophia because he genuinely *enjoyed* Sophia, no matter the subject of their conversation.

Withington looked away, blushing as he sipped nervously at his claret. His movements were ungainly, severe, as if he were a puppet and his strings were jerked too taught by an overeager master. While certainly odd, his lordship's awkwardness was also endearing; proof, perhaps, of the goodness of the heart that beat beneath his expensively clothed breast.

Sophia sipped her own claret, though it was shame, rather than embarrassment, that flushed her cheeks.

She had to salvage the evening. Not only because it would serve her well in obtaining that brilliant match—a match she needed to make, now more than ever—but also because Withington deserved kind company; wit, too. He was a gentle man, and right now she was making a mess of his good intentions.

The marquess deserved better. He deserved her honest self.

"I've recently acquired a predilection for port," Sophia said, ignoring her mother's gasp from the row behind. "Perhaps it might be amusing to arrange a tasting of sorts?"

Withington grinned so widely Sophia thought his face might split in two. "Well, Miss Blaise, I did not know ladies drank port! Capital news, I say, capital indeed! We shall arrange the tasting straightaway. We might have it on the terrace at my house, if it please you? The weather seems to have taken a turn for the better."

"Yes," Sophia said, smiling. "That would please me very much, my lord."

"Capital! It shall be a great pleasure to have you at *my* home for a change. Begging your pardon, Lady Blaise." He winked at Sophia before turning to her mama. "Of course I find your *salon* a most capital affair. The tea, it is so very. Yes, so very good."

Sophia bit her lip to keep from laughing. She was going to like this Withington fellow; and could only hope he would like the honest Sophia in turn.

One week later

Sophia tapped her slippered foot on the floor of the carriage, glancing out the window at a darkening sky.

"Where the devil is she?"

Lady Blaise clucked in disapproval. "Heavens, mind your tongue! I don't know where you learn these things—"

"Cousin Violet," she answered matter-of-factly. "We've an invitation to dine at the *Earl* of *Harclay's* house, and we're going to miss it, all because of her. If I've got to wait another minute—"

"I hardly doubt the marquess would approve, especially

after that dreadful comment of yours about having a taste for port. Really, where *do* you—"

"Cousin *Violet*," Sophia repeated through gritted teeth. "She's never late. Nor does she ever take such care in her toilet. Poor Fitzhugh dressed her in every gown we own between the two of us. I don't care what Violet says about searching the earl's house for the missing jewel. She is fond of him, I can see it in her eyes—oh, oh thank *heaven*, there she is!"

Violet appeared at the front door, her satin gown shimmering in the light of the gas lamps. She was coiffed and perfumed and pulled within an inch of her life, pink rose blooms tucked into the gleaming mass of her dark hair.

She looked dazzling.

And Violet did not dazzle for nothing.

"Well, aren't you coming, Violet?" Sophia poked her head out the coach window. "We're going to be late!"

Violet waved away Sophia's words. "Mr. Hope always arrives at a fashionably tardy hour. You won't miss a minute of his company, I promise."

Sophia resisted the urge to stick her tongue out at her cousin.

Alas, the urge proved too strong.

"So*phia*!" Lady Blaise rapped her none too gently with an ivory-handled fan.

Sophia fell back into the coach, a familiar fire in her cheeks.

"What's this about Mr. Hope?"

"Nothing." Sophia kept her eyes trained on her lap. "He's to be a guest of Lord Harclay's, that's all. Violet seems to think I've set my cap at him."

Lady Blaise tensed, her eyes widening before she could stop them. "Well. Have you?"

"No!" The force of Sophia's response surprised both of them. She cleared her throat and tried again. "What I meant to say is, it is a joke, mother *dear*est, nothing more. What foolishness! Dearest Cousin Violet has perhaps been at her flask again." Sophia's laugh was flat and grating. "Hope is a *banker,* for God's sake."

Even as the words escaped her lips, she hated herself for

saying them, thinking them, *believing* them at one point or another.

This snobbery, this heartless betrayal of all she'd shared with Hope—these things were at odds with the woman she was now. It wasn't her. Not anymore.

And yet, cowed by her mother, she did not deny them.

Lady Blaise relaxed into her seat and sighed with relief, hand on her breast. "Thank heaven, Sophia, you had me worried with all this talk of caps and tradesmen. And here you've managed to snare a marquess. Not just any marquess, either. *The* marquess. Ha! Now *that* is a good joke."

"Yes, the most amusing thing I've heard all day," Sophia said, watching through the window as Violet kissed her father on the cheek. He offered in turn an unsteady salute. Poor Uncle Sommer; he had not been himself for years now, and his condition was only getting worse. Violet certainly had her hands full. She was good, her cousin, for all her eccentricities.

Good, because she had chosen to stay with the family, while Sophia longed for nothing more than to escape it.

S ophia's pulse leapt as the old family carriage pulled onto Brook Street. Truth be told, Violet wasn't the only one sent into a tizzy by the arrival of Lord Harclay's invitation three days ago. Sophia smiled as she recalled Violet turning bright red whilst reading the note—something about money and champagne and settling their accounts.

All the ingredients for an appropriately scandalous evening out. Whatever her intentions, Violet had most *definitely* set her cap at that libertine the earl.

Over Violet's shoulder Sophia had managed to catch one last line—"*others of our mutual acquaintance shall join us*"— and knew, *knew*, that Mr. Hope would be among them.

Even now her heart danced in her chest at the thought of seeing him again. She had not heard from him since leaving his house the morning after the theft; that was nearly a week ago. Much to her disappointment he had not come to say good-bye after interrogating the acrobats with Violet and Lord

Harclay; Sophia in turn did not write him following her harrowing debut in the gossip sheets, perhaps out of spite, perhaps because she knew there was nothing either of them could do.

The French Blue, of course, remained at large.

Besides, the marquess kept her busy, calling most afternoons, offering invitations for the evening. While talk of an offer was assiduously avoided, Sophia saw in Withington's eyes he meant to do right by her. And what did one cryptic entry in the gossip rags matter when she was engaged to be married to a marquess?

Still. She often found herself thinking about Thomas. She wondered what occupied his time, what he did and whom he saw. Had he had much success in his search for the French Blue? What of La Reinette, the cloaked riders, Sophia's mysterious note?

And then there was the memory of his touch, his mouth and hands on her body in ways that made her ache when she thought of them.

Some days the longing to hear from him—a letter, a call, a stroll, *anything*—was unbearable.

And so it was no surprise that Sophia's entire being thrummed in anticipation as the carriage drew to a stop before the immaculate facade of Lord Harclay's residence in fashionable Hanover Square.

Even in the midst of her own excitement, Violet noticed her cousin's distress. As they dismounted, she took Sophia's hands and pulled her close.

"Do not worry, cousin," she said quietly, her blue eyes gleaming. "Tonight shall be great fun. Mr. Hope was asking about you today."

Sophia's heart skipped a beat. "He was?"

"Oh, yes." Together they mounted the front steps. "It was actually rather adorable. At the end of our meeting he tied his tongue in knots trying to ask, without asking, if you were to attend tonight's dinner. He had a certain spring in his step after I assured him you were."

The butler, a young, handsome man by the name of Mr. Avery, led them into the drawing room. He held the door open and motioned them inside.

Sophia swallowed, hard, to keep her heart from leaping

into her mouth. Violet patted the top of her hand and smiled. They were here at last.

At last.

Stepping over the threshold, Sophia blinked, turning her head; and there he was across the room, shifting his weight from one foot to the other, coupe held carelessly in his right hand, the left grazing a well-sculpted thigh.

In her veins her blood rushed as Mr. Hope met her eyes. His were bluer than she remembered, soft and serious and so lovely she could hardly bear to look. There was a tug, vaguely familiar, in the knot of her belly—the tug between their bodies, at once sweet and terribly overwhelming.

His lips were parted, face taut as if he, too, suffered from stolen breath. And still he did not look away; for a moment his eyes flashed with hunger, and she remembered his hands between her legs, the intoxicating tenderness of his fingers.

Hope set down his glass, eyes never leaving hers, and made to move in her direction.

"Miss Blaise? Begging your pardon, Miss—"

Sophia started, turning to face the footman at her side. He held aloft a tray of delicate coupes.

"Would you care for some champagne? An excellent vintage from his lordship's cellars."

"Oh, yes please." She took a coupe and smiled tightly. "Don't go too far."

Drinking deeply, Sophia let out a long breath. She squared her shoulders in a failed attempt to gather her wits, knowing she had to face Thomas whether or not she possessed the power of speech.

She turned, expecting Mr. Hope's fine form to be revealed to her in new detail, but met instead with her mother's round, radish-red face. Lady Blaise's eyes slid from Sophia to Hope and back again, lips pursed. Her gaze settled on Sophia, displeasure evident in the sharp, single swivel of her head.

No.

Lady Blaise blinked, a smile appearing as if by magic on her lips. She turned to the woman at her elbow, who wore her exotic looks—tall, taller than Sophia by a head or two, and very thin—as one would a tiara of diamonds: elegantly, confidently, as if she owned them and not the other way around.

Mama introduced her as Lady Caroline, the Dowager Countess of Berry and the Earl of Harclay's elder sister.

"A pleasure to make your acquaintance, Miss Blaise." Lady Caroline returned her bow, nearly mauling the champagne-bearing footman as she tripped over the hem of her gown.

Sophia grabbed Lady Caroline by the arm, catching her just in time before Lord Harclay's excellent vintage ended up on the rug.

"Oh, goodness, how clumsy of me! I wish I could say it was the first mishap of the day. My brother, the dear, wouldn't even let me dance after my coming out. He was worried I'd kill someone. Can't say that I blame him—I'm all thumbs, you see, and I can hardly walk without slaying either myself or my neighbor."

Sophia smiled. Lady Caroline certainly *looked* elegant, but was, apparently, anything but.

She liked her straightaway.

"I'm afraid I can relate." Sophia sipped her champagne. "I'm not much of a dancer myself. I dare not imagine how many poor gentlemen's toes I've broken this week alone. It's a wonder Almack's hasn't banned me for life."

"Oh, but Sophia, she is good at other things." Lady Blaise cast a warning glance her way. "Like. Er. Conversation! Yes. She's very good at that."

"Splendid!" Lady Caroline clapped her hands together. "I made your cousin's acquaintance the morning after Mr. Hope's ball. That Lady Violet, she's got pluck! And a rather wicked way about her. Perhaps the three of us might take tea together? I'm just out of mourning, you see, and would love the company."

The dinner gong sounded, and Mr. Avery stood by the door as he made his announcement. With a bow he motioned for the guests to follow him to the dining room.

Mr. Lake's hulking figure suddenly appeared at Lady Caroline's side. While he was smoothly sinister as always, more so, perhaps, dressed in fine eveningwear, an uncertain softness took captive his features as he looked upon her.

Sophia watched the working of Lady Caroline's throat as he grazed the bare skin of her arm with his fingers. Sophia looked away, face burning. She didn't know what she just saw, but she certainly knew she wasn't supposed to have seen it.

Wordlessly Lake moved past them, holding his arm out to Cousin Violet.

Sophia blinked, running through the calculation in her head. If Lake escorted Violet to dinner, and Lord Harclay his sister the dowager countess, that left Mr. Hope for Sophia and Lady Blaise.

That also meant she and Mama would be seated on either side of Mr. Hope at the dinner table. The three of them, stuck together for the length of the meal.

Thank God the earl had a well-stocked cellar.

She felt the heat of Hope's gaze as he moved across the room toward her. Anticipation, prickly and fast, shot up her spine, and for a moment she closed her eyes, reveling in the sensation as much as it pained her.

And then Thomas was at her side, bowing his greeting before holding an elbow out to Lady Blaise. She shot Sophia another look of warning over her shoulder—as if one were not enough—and took Hope's arm with a lukewarm smile.

"Miss Blaise." His eyes swept the length of her pale lavender gown, the strands of tiny pearls that hung from her neck. Even as she looked away, a grin rose unbidden to her lips. "You look lovely."

"And you." She took his arm. "You look like you haven't slept since we saw you last."

He scoffed as he led them down the corridor, the sounds of swishing skirts and murmured conversation echoing around them.

"That bad, eh? I was hoping my youthful good looks might compensate for the hell I've put myself through these past days—begging your pardon, Lady Blaise." Thomas sighed. "I suppose I'm not as youthful as I once was."

"Or good-looking."

Mr. Hope smiled. "Yes, that, too."

Lord Harclay's dining room was lit to full splendor, great chandeliers sparkling upon an enormous table set with the earl's family silver, the century-old gilt china. Sophia was relieved to see several footmen hovering in the perimeter of the room, each man wielding an uncorked bottle of wine.

Settling Lady Blaise in her seat, Hope turned to Sophia.

He pinned her in place with those deucedly blue eyes of his, offering his hand as a footman shuffled her chair into place.

She took it so that she might steady herself, the warmth of his palm seeping through the fine kidskin of her glove. She inhaled sharply at the firmness of his touch, the familiarity of it. Desire sliced through her.

Mr. Hope took his seat beside her, the heat between them so palpable Sophia was surprised the table linens didn't catch fire.

The food was splendid, the wine, delicious. Sophia spent the better part of the meal chatting with Lady Caroline, who sat at the head of the table to her left, while Mr. Lake sat in uncharacteristic silence across from them.

It pleased Sophia to hear her mother's laugh as Mr. Hope shared some jest or another. He *was* charming, and even in the midst of all his troubles appeared to be in good spirits. While he and Sophia did not so much as meet eyes during the meal, Sophia was aware of his every movement, every word, hypnotized from the corner of her eye by his handsomeness, the beauty of his manners, and his happy way with the other guests.

He was putting on a show, certainly; testing out Cousin Violet's theory that Lord Harclay was the thief. From what little she knew of the earl, Sophia had no doubt he was guilty. A more notorious rake in all England there was not; he was a gambler and a drinker besides, and it was rumored he'd fought more duels than could be counted on hands *and* toes.

It was obvious the man was far too intelligent for his own good, and doubtless at the age of one-and-thirty he'd drunk London dry of its every amusement and vice. Perhaps he'd thieved the diamond out of boredom, perhaps for a thrill. No matter his motive, Sophia was convinced he'd done it.

But Mr. Hope, she knew, must proceed with great care; he stood to lose everything on such an accusation. Violet had explained that Lord Harclay was Hope's wealthiest client, with well over a hundred thousand pounds in deposits at Hope & Co. The loss of such a client would be nothing short of catastrophic.

While the proceedings at dinner were delicate, the amount of wine consumed at the table was not. Each course brought with it its own French varietal, and by the end of dinner Sophia's head was swimming, her awareness of and desire for Thomas scorching through her unimpeded.

She was at once disappointed and relieved when Lady Caroline stood and invited the ladies to retire. The gentlemen rose to their feet, chairs scraping hoarsely across the floor. Sophia followed, determined not to look in Mr. Hope's direction lest he deliver the knockout blow.

Too late.

She met his eyes, which flicked for a moment to her lips before settling on her own. Sophia sensed the energy coiling inside him. He was struggling not to reach out, pull her to him, finish what he'd started in the room where Mars and Venus lay.

Head swimming, Sophia abruptly turned, catching her hip on the edge of the table. A beautiful cut-glass pitcher of lemonade—full, because no one had touched it—tumbled off the table and landed with a terrific clatter on the floor.

"Oh dear." Sophia's hand went to her throat. "I'm terribly sorry, Lord Harclay, I don't know what happened—how terribly embarrassing—"

Harclay waved away her words. "Think nothing of it, my dear."

Face burning, Sophia made for the door, followed by her mother.

"No more wine for you!" Lady Blaise hissed.

Violet swooped to the rescue, looping her arm through Sophia's as they scurried through the gallery. "We're all foxed, no shame in admitting it."

Sophia managed to smile in thanks, her thoughts a riot as Lady Caroline led them to a drawing room done up in bottle green velvet. She took a deep breath, trying with all her might to think of anything, *anything* but Mr. Hope, his blue eyes, the desire that simmered between their bodies.

It would not do; no, it would not do at *all*. If Sophia wanted to make it out of Lord Harclay's house alive, she would have to focus her attention on something else.

Like the marquess.

Yes. Yes, Lord Withington would do. They had arranged to meet up in his box at Vauxhall Gardens tomorrow night, and Cousin Violet caught wind the marquess spoke of nothing but their port tasting.

Port. That bottle she and Hope had shared beneath Venus's benevolent gaze, the sweetness of his lips as they'd plundered her own. Had it really been only a week since he'd kissed her? It felt like an eternity. No, longer than that . . .

Sophia jumped at the pinch on her arm, turning to see her mother glowering at her side.

She swallowed for what felt like the hundredth time that evening.

And knew that whatever trouble she'd already caused tonight, there would be more of it.

Much, much more.

Sixteen

Having lit his cigar, Hope waved the match between his thumb and forefinger and took a long pull. Smoke whirled over his head, the earthy reek of tobacco filling Lord Harclay's dining room.

"So." The earl's eyes glittered through the haze. "Lady Violet tells me you've made progress in your search for the diamond."

Hope exchanged a glance with Mr. Lake, who sat brooding at the far corner of the table, his face obscured by smoke. What in hell was wrong with *him*? He hadn't been himself all evening.

No matter. Hope had bigger problems, one of which was sitting just to his right, chomping merrily on his cigar.

Man had a set of stones on him, Hope would give him that. The earl, he knew, was baiting him, testing Hope's limits. It was all part of his deception, a deception that, judging from the smug look on his face, he was enjoying immensely.

Hope gulped what little brandy was left in his balloon and flopped further into his chair, running a hand through his hair so that it hung haphazardly across his face.

Two could play this game.

"Great progress, yes." Hope pulled on his cigar. "Lady Violet has proven quite wily, though I cannot say I condone her methods. Alas, I think you'll agree"—he winked—"ladies often have the upper hand in these sorts of . . . What shall we call them? *Situations*."

Hope bit back his smile as Lord Harclay's face darkened. The earl took one, two long pulls on his cigar, narrowing his eyes against the column of smoke that rose from his lips.

"Now now, Mr. Hope. I agree we must give credit where credit is due. But we must also acknowledge the fact that Lady Violet could run circles around any of us, even on the best of days. She is"—he paused, a small, secret smile unfurling across his lips—"most unusual and invigorating company."

Ah. So Hope's suspicion that Violet was—er, *fraternizing*, to put it kindly—with the enemy proved true. While she was indeed more intelligent, and more daring, than most anyone he'd known, could Hope trust her to choose the diamond and their livelihoods over her affection, whatever its nature, for the Earl of Harclay?

Hope brought his cigar between his thumb and forefinger and examined it, smoke curling languidly into the air. "Make no mistake, my lord, I'll find the French Blue—and our thief. And when I do, I have no doubt he'll be very, *very* sorry he ever crossed me."

Lord Harclay's lips twitched, but he had the grace not to scoff. "My offer of aid stands, Hope. The news bodes ill for my fortunes as it does for yours. I've men and money at my disposal. You need only ask."

"We've men and money of our own." Lake pounded his cigar into the ashtray, making what was left of the silver and the crystal jump on the table. "Besides. I rather enjoy the hunt. Not as much as I enjoy the kill, of course. The kill is my true skill."

Hope grinned tightly. Whatever was wrong with Lake, he was going to get to the bottom of it. "Let us hope more so than your poetry, Mr. Lake."

"Ah! My poetry." Lake smiled at him from across the table, a mirthless thing. "*That* I learned from you, old friend."

Hope tugged a hand through his hair to keep from reaching for Lake's neck.

The earl, eyes glittering with triumph, put out his cigar and stood. "Let's join the ladies, shall we? My new billiards table has just arrived. It's proven quite amusing; even Caroline likes to play. Perhaps we might teach Lady Violet and Miss Blaise? If Miss Blaise is anything alike to Violet, I daresay it shall make for great sport."

Hope tensed at the sound of Sophia's name on Lord Harclay's lips. While the earl did not insult her—his words were,

Hope knew, meant as a compliment—Hope was overwhelmed by the fierce urge to protect her. Possess her, even; Hope longed for nothing more than to take the earl by the throat and tell him in no uncertain terms that Sophia was his, damn it, and that a thieving prick like him had no right to even think her name, much less speak it.

Biting the inside of his lip, Hope took a deep breath through his nose. *Tread lightly. Harclay is your largest depositor. Think of the bank, all you've dreamed and accomplished in its name.*

"Let's do." Hope set down his cigar and rose. "I've yet to see one of these new-fashioned tables. Is it still lined with felt? And the pockets, I've heard they're all the rage now."

Lake slid to his feet with the speed and grace of a tiger on the prowl—had he always moved like this, like a healthy man, a whole man not crippled by injury?—and together with Hope followed the earl out of the room, Hope all the while resisting the urge to slip the pocketknife from his waistcoat and sink it between Harclay's proud, well-formed shoulders.

The earl's billiards room was as tastefully appointed as the rest of his home. Nearly as long and wide as a town coach, the billiards table occupied the majority of the space, while an equally enormous brandy board took up the rest.

Across the room, Lady Violet was arm in arm with Harclay's windswept sister, Lady Caroline, their heads bent in deep conversation. As soon as he entered, Violet halted mid-stride and met his eyes. He replied with a quick, grim shake of his head.

Nothing. The earl revealed nothing.

Though that didn't mean Hope absolved Harclay of all guilt. Quite the opposite, as a matter of fact: Harclay's assiduous hospitality, his offer of aid, and his fawning over the ladies present were suspicious for a selfish man such as he. In all their years as banker and client, the earl had never extended Hope an invitation to his home in Hanover Square. Until now, of course.

Hope had yet to untangle the intricacies of Lord Harclay's plot; but a plot there certainly was, Hope had no doubt. He merely needed proof, and then he would be free to make his move.

Violet nodded, slipping her arm from Lady Caroline's and making to walk toward him, when the earl stopped her in her tracks. He murmured something in her ear; she flushed pink.

Dear God. If Hope didn't know any better, he would say they were well acquainted indeed. Perhaps even more than that.

He resisted the urge to separate them, to warn Lady Violet off lest the earl do her irreparable harm. But if anyone could snare Harclay at his own game, it was Violet; she was smart and witty and could hold her liquor better than any man this side of the Channel.

Besides, Hope knew the lady would take offense at the intrusion. Violet wanted to prove she was capable of remedying the mess she believed she'd caused. And while Hope knew she was not guilty in the slightest, she *did* stand to lose everything on the outcome of their hunt for the jewel. Who was Hope to question her methods, or dictate instruction? He would have to trust her, whether or not he understood what in *hell* she was doing.

He balled his fingers into fists.

Tread lightly.

He turned, his pulse leaping at the knowledge that she would be there. *She.* The one he'd wanted to claim. Still wanted.

The one for whom he'd nearly thrown it all away.

Sophia sat on a far settee, color high as her mother sat purse-lipped beside her. Lady Blaise had two eyes and a brain; doubtless she'd witnessed Hope's interlude with Sophia in the drawing room earlier, their shameless ogling of one another. And doubtless she was displeased. For what lady in her right mind wanted a man like Hope—tradesman, orphan, foreigner—for her only daughter?

He felt her disappointment as his own. He knew it; Lady Blaise did, too: Sophia deserved better.

And yet he couldn't stay away from her.

In the golden light of the candelabra, Sophia looked lovely. Her lips were stained plum from French wine; the long strands of pearls at her neck gleamed a shade paler than her cheeks. Her eyes, wide and wet, reflected the fire's flame. When she turned them to him, his blood rushed with heat.

"Ladies." He nodded his head in greeting. "I hope I did not bore you overmuch with my company at dinner."

Sophia grinned. "No more than usual, Mr. Hope. Oh, look, Violet and Lord Harclay are pairing up for a go at this billiards nonsense. Shall we join them?"

Without waiting for a response she held out her hand. He took it, ignoring Lady Blaise's bland smile of dismay, and tucked her arm into the crook of his own.

Alone, at last! If they weren't in polite company he would've danced a jig. Hope was not prepared for the force of his happiness at having Sophia by his side; he'd missed her more than was proper or good. Much more, indeed, than he cared to admit.

He had told himself to keep his distance. It would not do to further embroil her in the worsening crises that now dominated his every waking hour. While the matter of the jewel thief was being resolved, that of Sophia's mysterious note and the bastard who threatened her and her family was not.

Still. To draw her to him was akin to the beating of his heart: an impulse, an inexplicable necessity over which he had no control.

There were four, maybe five steps from the settee to the billiards table. Hope had no time to waste.

"Sophia." God, what to say to her? There was so much, he felt about to burst. "I. Er. I want you to know that just because I haven't—haven't been in contact doesn't mean I don't think of you. Often." *All the time.*

He watched the working of her throat. "That is kind of you to say, Thomas. And how goes the hunt for the French Blue?"

"Fine. Awful. I don't want to talk about that bloody diamond anymore. Not when I'm with you."

Sophia turned to him, bottom lip between her teeth. "So what *do* you want to talk about?"

Hope swallowed. Truth be told, what he wanted had nothing at all to do with talking.

He lowered his voice. "What I'm doing—I do to protect you, Sophia. Every time I enter your life I make a mess of things. If I'm not careful I could very well ruin that brilliant match you've always wanted. I hear"—he swallowed again—"your courtship with the Marquess of Withington progresses apace."

Her eyes snapped to meet his. "Where did you hear that?"

"I am banker to the most prominent arbiters of the fashionable world, Sophia. That you have captured the attention of this season's most eligible bachelor has not gone unnoticed. I daresay you've sent every debutante and her mama into fits of rage and jealousy. The marquess is no small prize—as his banker, I would know."

Sophia drew to a stop, pulling Hope to her side. She looked at him, eyes narrowing as if she fought back tears. She opened her mouth, but thought better of it; quickly she looked away and resumed their stroll.

"Any word from La Reinette?" Her voice was barely above a whisper. "Whomever is after me tightens the noose; there was a short but direct attack printed in the gossip pages a few days ago. It's only a matter of time before he reveals that I am the author of a courtesan's salacious memoirs."

Hope's grip on Sophia tightened. "I'll get to the bottom of this, Sophia, you have my word. If you should come to any harm on my account—" He looked at her. "I won't let them touch you."

She returned his gaze levelly. "Then let me help you. We can smoke these men out together, you and I—"

Sophia jumped at a sudden, deafening *thud*. Hope turned just in time to see Lady Caroline, cue poised above the billiards table, launch a cue ball smack-dab into the middle of Lady Blaise's forehead. With a strangled cry, Lady Blaise toppled over on the settee; her arms flailed as she landed none too gently on the floor, and was inundated in the foaming lace of her petticoats.

It all happened so quickly Hope could hardly keep pace. The earl, that son of a bitch, was at Lady Blaise's side in an instant, cradling her head in his hands as he cooed soothing words.

"Bring water," he called to the footmen, "and smelling salts. Lots of smelling salts!"

Across the room, Hope met Mr. Lake's gaze. Was Harclay's sudden tenderness all part of the act? Over brandy and cigars the man was rotten, callous, vainglorious in the extreme. And yet here he was, gently whispering sweet nothings into a wounded old woman's ear.

The man was a paradox.

Sophia, her attempts to help having been shooed away by the gentleman, watched the proceedings in mute horror, letting out a small sigh of relief only when the earl helped Lady Blaise to sit upright. Her gaze landed on Hope and Sophia, still arm in arm before her. While her eyes rolled a bit in her head, her mouth settled into a tight, colorless line.

Waving away Harclay's offer of a bed and rest, she allowed him to haul her to her feet. "That is most kind of you, Lord Harclay, most kind indeed, but I would hate to put you out. No, I believe I'll be quite all right, if you'll just help me to my carriage. Come, Sophia, it's time to leave."

Hope reached out to help one second too late. As if he were King Arthur and she the Lady Guinevere, Harclay swooped Lady Blaise into his arms and without so much as a grunt carried her from the room.

If Hope hadn't wanted to strangle the earl before, he certainly was possessed of the urge now.

The rest of the party followed, Lady Caroline wailing her apologies, Sophia trotting behind in breathless silence.

As if by magic, Sophia's family coach was brought round the front of the house. With great care, Harclay deposited Lady Blaise onto the carriage's cushioned seat. Together they laughed at some private joke, Lady Blaise's eyes twinkling despite being hit in the head by a cue ball.

And then everyone was shrugging into his jacket or her pelisse. As they made their way out the door, Hope noticed Lake and Lady Caroline hanging back in the entry hall. They glared at one another, hungrily.

The earl and Violet, meanwhile, were staring drunkenly into one another's eyes as he helped Violet into the carriage; the horses shuffled and huffed.

Hope's heart hardened at the knowledge the night was over. For a moment he pressed Sophia to him, as if to say, *I am not ready to let you go.* She met his eyes, and from the flickering heat he saw there, Hope could tell Sophia was not ready to let him go, either.

How was it the hours he spent in her presence passed as minutes, seconds, even? He'd been looking forward to this evening for days; and now, in the space of half a heartbeat, it was over.

"Good night, Miss Blaise." He did not dare say more: that

he wanted to see her again, tonight, tomorrow, and the day after that, and the day after that, too. When it came to Miss Sophia Blaise, it was never enough.

Her hand lingered in his as he helped her into the carriage. The sound of Lady Blaise's snoring broke the silence; Sophia bit her lip to keep from laughing.

"Good night, Mr. Hope."

They met eyes one last time. He knew he was grinning like a fool, but he didn't care. Sophia was happy, and he was, too.

A poignant, bittersweet sort of happiness. He could not bear to see her go; the torture, it was singular and far too painful to witness, especially with brandy in his belly and a gallon of wine besides.

Hope pressed a yellow boy into the groom's palm with instructions that his coach be sent back to his house—yes, yes, he was quite sure he wanted to walk, the night being as fine as it was.

He turned his back and stalked into the darkness.

Seventeen

———— ✦ ————

Sophia watched Mr. Hope's shoulders disappear into the shadows of Brook Street. Beneath the layers of satin and lace and wine her blood thrummed, skin burning from his touch. She'd never wanted anything more in her life than to follow him down the lane, allow him to swallow her in his arms, put his hands on her as he had that night on the shining expanse of his desk.

Beside her, Mama snored softly, the trauma of tonight's events apparently too much to bear.

Across the coach Sophia met eyes with her cousin; Violet pressed her first fingers to her lips and reached for the latch.

Heaven above, she was going back in!—back to the Earl of Harclay's lair.

If Violet was going, then Sophia was, too. Perhaps it wasn't too late to catch up with Mr. Hope.

"You wouldn't dare. And if you go, I want to come with you," Sophia hissed.

Violet returned Sophia's gaze; her dark eyes were pleading. "Next time, Sophia, I promise. I'll be home before dawn."

Before Sophia could protest, Violet bolted from the carriage.

Mama snorted in her sleep. The coach creaked into motion.

Sophia collapsed against the squabs in defeat. Violet and her deuced theories about Harclay being the jewel thief. Seemed more like an excuse to have all the fun, and stay out all hours of the night.

Next time indeed. Next time Sophia would escape first and never look back.

                              *   *   *

I t was well past midnight when they arrived home. Together
  with the driver, Sophia brought Lady Blaise to her room.
She and Fitzhugh undressed Mama and tended to her injury,
which, as one might imagine, was no small task.

An hour after Sophia fell into bed, exhausted, she lay
awake, unblinking in the darkness, thoughts and body alive
with the memory of Mr. Thomas Hope.

She'd been about to confess everything to him in that
moment he'd brought up the marquess. Yes, their courtship proceeded apace, and yes, they had become friends, good friends.
She liked to think she and Withington genuinely enjoyed one
another's company.

In an *innocent*, companionable sort of way. Though their
acquaintance was awkward at first, it had blossomed into
friendship; and while that friendship was lovely and good, it
was certainly no romance.

Sophia did not feel for the marquess the heat, the desire,
the longing to know and do and say more that she did for Mr.
Thomas Hope. Tonight made her realize that while she felt
affection for Withington, her feelings for him would never go
beyond that.

Because whatever was *beyond that*—well, she felt it for
Thomas. Dear God, merely occupying the same *room* as Hope
made her heart soar and blood rush.

She couldn't explain it. All Sophia knew was she'd never
felt this way for anyone else—including, it seemed, the Marquess of Withington.

Sophia threw off the covers. It was suddenly stifling in her
chamber, her sheets and night rail damp with sweat. She hob-
bled to her feet, exhaustion ringing in her every limb, and
made for the window.

With no small effort she hauled it open. She closed her
eyes and took a deep, contented pull of fresh air.

And was then promptly hit in the nose by something cold,
hard.

Her eyes flew open, landing on the narrow alley below.
There in the shadows stood a figure, its hooded face turned
toward Sophia.

"Mademoiselle." La Reinette's accent was immediately recognizable, even in a whisper. She dropped the rocks she held in her hands and motioned for Sophia to join her. "Your timing is very good. Come, quickly, we hurry."

Sophia blinked, meeting with mixed success as she attempted to clear Thomas and his fingers from her thoughts.

"Is everything all right?"

"Yes!" Madame hissed. "Come, quickly! They will see me."

Sophia nodded, darting through her chamber as she tossed whatever she found—morning gown, spencer—over her head.

The routine came back to her in a heady rush. She tucked her boots into the crook of her arm; then she listened at the door, sliding into the hall when she was satisfied the house was abed. Down the stair, and down again, tiptoeing through the servants' hall to the kitchen's back entrance.

La Reinette waited just beyond the stoop, hood pulled low. When Sophia appeared the madam looked up, her dark eyes reflecting the shallow light of the night sky above.

They moved through the darkness in silence, Sophia's heart alight as they traced the familiar route. She'd missed this: the clean night air, the gas lamps flickering silently as Sophia's thoughts swirled with scenes from Madame's latest adventure.

The Glossy blazed with light and laughter, a glowing star amid the sea of stony silence that was Mayfair past midnight. La Reinette led her past the back rooms, crowded with men in embroidered waistcoats and the beautiful, butterfly-like ladies who attended them, to a study at the front of the house.

"Come in, *mademoiselle*, we are safe to talk here."

Pulling back her hood, Sophia stepped over the threshold. Her eyes fell on a familiar figure seated in the slight wing-back chair by the fire. He rose to his feet and turned, running a hand through the dark coils of his hair.

"Tho—Mr. Hope!"

He fell into a brief, unsteady bow. The light in the room was low, but Sophia thought she saw his cheeks flush pink.

"Miss Blaise." His gaze slid accusingly to La Reinette. "I did not know you would be here."

The madam closed the door and swept into the room, waving away his words. "The news I have, it concerns the both of you. Miss Blaise, she has as much right as you, *mon chéri*, to know these things I have learned. You are naïve, yes, to think you keep her safe by not sharing your secrets."

She slid into the cane-backed chair behind a small desk. "Do not forget, *Monsieur* Hope. She is smarter than you."

"Bah! Of course she is. Smarter than me, and most everyone else." Hope met Sophia's gaze. Her face grew warm when she saw that yes, yes he *was* blushing, and rather adorably at that. "That doesn't make the danger we're in any less real."

"And so I must help you fight against it." Sophia held up her hand to keep him from interrupting and turned to La Reinette. "What news do you have, Madame?"

The Little Queen unclasped the round golden locket that hung from her neck, a tiny key falling into her outstretched palm. With the key she opened the first drawer in the desk and retrieved a square of rough paper.

She placed the letter on the desk and slid it toward Sophia and Thomas.

"S'ouvrez-le."

Open it.

Sophia met Hope's gaze.

"Go on, then." He nodded at the desk. *"Plus de secrets, mademoiselle."*

Her blood leapt at the effortless confidence of his French. *No more secrets.*

Sophia reached for the note and unfolded it. She recognized the bold, shaky hand at once; the same hand that penned the threatening letter she'd received some days ago.

She stepped toward the fire, holding the page with trembling hands before the light. Like the previous note, this one was written in flowery, well-formed French.

To the Little Queen of my heart,

My dearest, how long it has been since we saw each other last! You left us so suddenly—even now I burn when I think of you leaving my bed before I had finished—it is a terrible crime to leave a man thus. How thirsty I was then—I swore I would have you again—these years in Paris, they have been cold. But I never forgot your little

*trick, sweet dove. I never forgot what you did to me. I do
not think you have, either.*

*But fear not, my queen, for at last I am delivered of
my suffering—I am in London now—and I would have
you finish what you started a decade ago. How old we
grow! I think you will agree that life—it is sometimes
not worth living at such an age.*

*I shall come for you. Soon. Do not be afraid—it will
be quick, and I hope you will feel no pain, sweet dove.*

*In Good Friendship,
G. Cassin.*

Sophia looked up from the letter. "Who is Cassin? And
why does he wish . . . wish you harm?"

Her query was met with silence. She looked from La Reinette
to Mr. Hope, a chill creeping in her limbs as she took in his
expressionless pallor. His eyes were trained on the madam; she
returned his gaze steadily, but from the pucker of her lips,
Sophia could tell she was afraid.

Slowly Sophia folded the note in her hands. "No more
secrets, remember?"

"Guillaume Cassin." Hope's voice was quiet, ominous. "A
name I never thought I'd hear again."

"Why? Who is he?"

"He is a man I knew a long time ago. In a different life,
before I came to England."

He took the letter from Sophia, read it; swallowed its contents in the space of a single heartbeat.

He looked up, crumpling the paper in his palm before tossing it into the fire. "We've got to leave. Now."

"Wait." Sophia stepped toward him. "A name you never
thought you'd hear again? Why?"

Hope's face was grim. "Because he's dead. That's why."

Eighteen

———— ✦ ————

L a Reinette leapt to her feet. "But it is safe here, *monsieur*, I have paid extra men to guard the house—"

"We're leaving. *Now*."

Without waiting for a reply, Hope grasped Sophia by the elbow and blew through the door. She trotted to keep pace with his enormous stride as he led her out into the mews, the madam a few breathless paces behind.

He whistled to the coachman sitting atop a waiting carriage. Though the vehicle was unmarked, its gleaming sides were lacquered a deep shade of red that spoke of discreet luxury.

Hope opened the door and all but lifted Sophia into the coach, helping La Reinette inside before settling into the seat beside Sophia. He pounded twice on the roof and they tore off the drive and into the night.

"We were perfectly safe, yes, back in my study," Madame sniffed, smoothing her ruffled skirts. "What, do you think I would let that animal make a mess of my house, scare off the clients? Never."

"He did before." Hope stared at her. "It was him, wasn't it, that night you shoved Sophia and I into the closet? Cassin, and whatever fools he's paid to do his bidding—they were the riders who gave us chase. How did you not recognize him?"

La Reinette's eyes widened in disbelief. "He wore the— the—" She made a tying motion at the back of her head.

"He wore a mask," Sophia said, trying not to smile at the quaint gesture. "Makes sense to me."

Hope dug a hand through his hair. "How did I miss it? I knew I recognized that voice."

"It has been a long while," Madame said. "A long while for the both of us. He is back from the dead."

"*He.* Would someone please tell me who *he* is?"

The carriage bolted left, and Sophia careened across the bench. Thomas grabbed her by the wrist and righted her, his fingers leaving traces of fire on her bare skin.

His touch, it seemed, electrified her no matter the circumstance. Heavens, even in the midst of an escape from an enemy risen from the dead, Hope's hands set her entire being alight. He could with his fingers alone make her forget everything, *every*thing, her good sense and her manners and all that she'd hoped and wished and dreamed for her whole life.

She wished he'd touch her again.

This time with his lips.

La Reinette and Hope met eyes across the coach. For a long moment they looked at one another without speaking. Sophia sensed tension between them, as if this were a subject neither party wished to broach.

"Guillaume Cassin, he was my admirer a long time ago," La Reinette began. "He inherits a very old banking house, yes, the best in all France. First he loans money to the king. Then he loans money to the emperor. Until I killed him."

Sophia's breath left her body. She stared at La Reinette as if seeing her for the first time. "You *killed* him? As in. *Shot* him through the *heart* killed him? Or just. Er. *Metaphorically* killed him. With your. Er. Eyes or wiles or whatnot?"

La Reinette smiled, a hard, rueful thing. "Ah, it is a bit of both. He fell in love with me. But I," she gestured at Hope, "I was working for *monsieur*. And *monsieur* wanted Cassin dead. So, yes. I killed his heart and then I killed the body. *Monsieur* was there, weren't you?"

Hope shifted uncomfortably in his seat, looking out the window as if he might leap from it. "Yes. Yes, I was. Not my favorite memory; thank you, Marie, for the kind reminder.

"It is quite simple." Hope sighed. "I worked for the British. Cassin worked for the Empire, as banker and as spy. His hands are stained with the deaths of hundreds, thousands of men. I won. Except I didn't, apparently."

"I slit his throat," Madame said without blinking. "The blood, it was everywhere. It is an impossible thing to survive."

Sophia closed her eyes against the well of tears. *I slit his throat.* As if that explained everything. As if the words were not at all connected to the horrific act itself.

No, no. Contrary to Hope's belief, this didn't feel simple at all; as a matter of fact it was deucedly complex, especially in the small hours of the morning. Something didn't make sense; there were missing pieces to this puzzle, *big* pieces, though Sophia couldn't begin to guess what they were.

"But what's this Cassin got to do with us?" she said. "He can't be the thief, the man who stole the French Blue. Could he? But we've pegged the earl . . ."

La Reinette shrugged. "Perhaps. Perhaps no. Cassin has come to settle the score, take blood for blood. The French, we have vengeful hearts. First he will kill me. And then he will come for you, *monsieur.* Already he threatens your woman."

"But how?" Hope burst. "How the hell does Cassin know about Soph—about Miss Blaise? We—she—we do not belong to one another."

Sophia's heart twisted at the words he left unspoken.

Miss Blaise belongs to someone else.

"I said before," Madame continued. "Cassin is a smart man. He will ruin those you care about, yes, and you, you watch in agony. Only then will he come for you."

Hope drew a long breath through his nose. The stubbly skin along his jaw twitched as silence stretched between them; at his sides his hands were balled into fists.

When he spoke at last his voice was low and mean. "I want you out of London, Marie. Tonight. It isn't safe for you here; it will only be a week, maybe two, before I get my hands on Cassin. I think it best you travel in disguise."

La Reinette turned her head to look out the window. Outside the coach the night was black.

"These wild days," she said. "I thought they were past."

"Yes," Hope replied. "Me, too. And they will be, once I take care of Cassin. Promise me you'll leave tonight. Do you need money, horses?"

The madam turned back to him and shook her head. "What do you think me, an imbecile? I will not leave a penny for that man to steal. My coach, it is unmarked, like yours."

"But where will you go?" Sophia asked. "Surely the roads cannot be safe."

"You will go to my house in Surrey," Hope replied briskly, "and wait there for further instruction. Do you understand?"

La Reinette raised a brow. "You do not give me an order, do you, *monsieur*?"

"Christ have mercy." Hope let out a hot breath, tugging a hand through his hair. "You women shall be the end of me, mark my words. Go where you want, then, but keep out of sight. I don't need to tell you Cassin is a dangerous man, and cunning besides. If you are not careful he will find you. Do I have your word?"

Madame stared back at him, her black eyes expressionless. Sophia wondered what she was thinking, how she stayed so calm in the face of all this danger. Heavens, she'd *slit* a man's *throat*, only to face him yet again after he'd come back from the dead. Just the thought of it made Sophia want to howl with terror.

"Yes," La Reinette said at last, gaze never leaving Hope's. "You have my word. Take me back home, yes, for I must pack my things."

They rode in silence as the coach backtracked to The Glossy. Sophia's thoughts were a riot, a hundred questions forming as she replayed all that happened, and all she'd learned, in the past few hours.

More than anything she longed to know what would become of them after it was all said and done; what their lives would be like, and would she ever see either La Reinette or Mr. Hope again?

When at last they reached the corner closest to Madame's establishment, she called for the driver to stop. Placing a hand on the latch, she looked back upon Sophia and Hope, and was about to make her exit, when Sophia reached out, impulsively, and placed a hand upon her arm.

"Madame, it has been a great pleasure making your acquaintance these past months. There are few things I enjoyed so much as visiting with you, listening to your stories, the things and people you have known. What an honor it has been"—Sophia swallowed—"to have put those stories to paper. I am better, and happier, for having known you. Thank you."

La Reinette ducked back into the carriage. She took Sophia's hands in her own and smiled, eyes shining. "No, *mademoiselle*, I am to be the one giving you thanks. Perhaps one day, when this is all done, we might meet again, yes, so we might finish what we started. Go safely, *ma bichette*." Madame's gaze flicked to Mr. Hope. "And do not let him order you about very much, yes?"

Hope groaned. "That's quite enough of that. Good *evening*, Marie."

Madame's smile deepened as she winked at Sophia. Squeezing her hands one last time, La Reinette slipped from the coach.

The driver nodded at Hope's murmured instructions, closing the door softly against the snorts and sighs of the horses as they struggled to catch their breath.

Once the door was shut and she was alone with Thomas, Sophia collapsed against her seat, blinking slowly as wide, hot tears coursed down her face and neck.

Perhaps it was saying good-bye, letting go of all she and La Reinette had accomplished; perhaps it was the awful circumstance in which Sophia found herself, the threat of ruin and death very real indeed; or perhaps it was her exhaustion, coupled with her thrumming desire for the man who sat so close beside her she could smell the heat of the valet's iron on his shirt. Whatever it was, Sophia could not swallow her tears.

She inhaled, a shaky, embarrassingly pitiful sound, and wiped her nose with the corner of her hood.

Mr. Hope took her bare hand in his, holding it as he lightly ran his thumb over the ridge of her knuckles.

"Sophia." He sighed. "Sophia, please. I can bear your domineering and your complete and utter disrespect for everything I say and do, but please, Sophia, I cannot bear to see you weep. It's as you say—neither of us is nearly as good without the other. We are an unbeatable pair. It's going to be all right."

She scoffed. "You don't really believe that, do you?"

"Well, no. But you must agree we've great luck when we're

together. Please, Sophia, don't cry. Here." He held out a hand-kerchief. "I promise it's been washed since you used it last."

Sophia blotted her eyes. "I"—sniffle—"am never one"—sniffle—"to weep. Too much"—sniffle—"work to be done."

"Never? Not once during your first season?"

"Not"—sniffle—"once. I have yet to meet a gentleman at Almack's worth"—sniffle—"crying about."

Thomas smiled. "For one who never weeps, you put on a hell of a show for the Princess of Wales. Those sobs of yours were most convincing."

"I learned from the best."

He arched a brow. "Your dear mama?"

"My mother would give Mrs. Jordan a run for her money."

Sophia leaned her head against the cushion and took a deep breath, steadier this time. A beat of silence passed between them. From the corner of her eye she caught Hope's gaze.

"No secrets," she said at last. "Tell me."

His eyes were transparent pools of blue in the dim light of the coach. They were clear, honest; devoid of his usual strug-gle over what he should and should not share with her.

Thomas looked down at their clasped hands and Sophia looked down, too. His enormous hand swallowed hers; the warmth of his calloused skin soothed as much as it inflamed her.

"I haven't told anyone this story." His voice was low, soft. "Even Lake doesn't know the whole of it."

Sophia swallowed. It was no small thing, what she now asked of him. London knew very little of Mr. Thomas Hope, and he'd worked hard to keep it that way; the mystery sur-rounding his name served him well.

But now he volunteered that information to her freely. Her, and her alone. It was an admission of trust and friendship; it was a gesture of goodwill.

No one had trusted Sophia with so much as a schoolroom secret in all her life. And here was Thomas, one of the richest and most important men in England, sharing with her things he'd never told anyone else.

She felt the smart of tears begin anew at his faith in her.

As if reading her thoughts, Hope squeezed her hand. With

his free fist he reached up to pound the roof, calling for the coachman to drive until he told him to stop.

Thomas turned to her, using the knuckle of his first finger to wipe away what was left of her tears.

For a moment his gaze flicked to her lips. She knocked her shoulder against his, shaking her head. "No. After, perhaps. But tell me your story first."

Nineteen

— ❖ —

Thomas looked down at their joined hands, tilting his head as he considered her proposal. The sharp angle of his smooth-shaven jaw caught an edge of moonlight and gleamed blue; the muscle there jumped, rippling beneath the skin.

"We—my family and I—we were to flee Amsterdam before the French arrived," Hope said. "But we were too late. I was the only one to escape; I left my family behind. Later my brothers, Adrian and Henry, would follow me to London. But the terror—it changed them. We aren't close, my brothers and I."

Sophia swallowed. "I'm sorry."

"My family, my city." Hope squeezed her hand. "I left them behind, and was lost for years. Henry Lake found me, and offered me asylum in London."

"And in return?"

The sides of his mouth kicked up. "And in return, I gave him the name of the banking house that supplied Boney with funds for the invasion of England."

"The invasion of England?" Sophia started. "You knew about that?"

"Only the bank that was lending Napoleon the money to do it. Cassin & Sons, based in Paris. I knew of Cassin through my father's connections back in Amsterdam."

She drew back. "So you and Lake, with La Reinette's aid, went after Cassin, and in so doing saved England from Napoleon?"

Hope shrugged, as if during that fateful night in Paris he'd been a mere tourist, out for a merry jaunt about town, rather than savior of king and country. "Perhaps. Perhaps not. I doubt the invasion would have happened whether we took out Cassin or not. But it was a great victory for England, and for Lake."

Sophia looked from Thomas's face to their hands, clasped in her lap. She wanted to ask about his family—who they were, *how* they were, how he'd lost them—but she remained silent, holding his fingers tightly so that he might feel her warmth.

"We boarded a ship bound for London in Calais. The storm took us at the first glimpse of English coastline. Lake saved me from a fallen mainmast. That's why he walks with a limp now."

Sophia nodded. "He must love you, to have risked his rather enormous neck to save your own."

"He left his family, too, not long before I did. We were as brothers then."

"And now?"

Thomas's grin deepened. "I could loathe someone so much only if I loved him, much as it pains me to admit it. When he appeared in my study after all these years—it was more loathing than loving, yes. But now? Now I'm glad he's back, though I cannot say the same for my accounts at the bank. He's the only family I've got left. The only family with whom I'm in contact, anyway."

Thomas at last looked up to meet her eyes. "I came to London for them, you know," he said. "For my family. So that their dreams might not die with them."

"You've done well by them, Thomas."

He scoffed. "Hardly. They deserve better."

"And you. You deserve to be happy. Your parents, your family—they would want you to be happy."

"What does my happiness matter, when they will never know life, how it is to breathe summer's fine air? And my brothers!" Thomas harrumphed, though she saw his eyes flash with hurt. "It's a miracle their debauchery hasn't led them to an early grave."

"They are grown men, Thomas. Adrian and Henry can look after themselves."

"That's just the thing." He turned to look at her. "They

can't. All things aside, they are my blood. My responsibility. Without me they would be out on the street."

Sophia looked away. She understood the heavy burden of his guilt, and why Hope cared as much as he did for the bank. It was not a matter of fortune, or prestige; for Thomas, it was a matter of *family*. He worked so long and so hard out of love for those he'd lost.

At heart, she realized, Thomas was a family man. Which was a tragedy, in a way, because in his dedication to the bank, the family he left behind, the brothers from whom he was estranged, he would never start one of his own. Looking at him, Sophia knew he would make a wonderful father, fiercely loving, patient, kind.

She ached for him in ways she didn't know she could ache. This struggle of his, it was no small thing. And his story, the past he'd longed to forget—it was bloody, full of heartbreak and loss.

"You've done well by them," she repeated. "Better than I've done by my family. All my life I wanted to escape them, to leave. Leave behind the terrible mess of our lives and start over."

He released her hand. "You'll get your chance, Sophia."

Sophia shifted in her seat, clasping and unclasping her hands before finally clasping them again, squeezing her fingers so tightly it hurt.

"It's probably best if you leave London, too," Hope said at last. "It's not safe for you, either, now that Cassin has connected you to me and knows who you are."

Sophia was glad for the change of subject. She swallowed and her throat loosened. "Don't be ridiculous. I cannot leave London, not in the middle of the season. And besides, Violet won't let us go anywhere before we find the French Blue."

"Ah, yes, I'd forgotten about Lady Violet and your mother. Well, then." Hope ran a hand through his hair, the curls falling rakishly across his forehead, and sighed. "You must take extra precautions. I'll send men to your house."

She looked up to meet his eyes. They glimmered preternaturally in the low light of the vehicle; the skin around them crinkled, as if Hope was holding something in, keeping whatever it was he felt to himself.

"You don't need to do that, Thomas—"

"Of course I do." Thomas said briskly. He sat up, straightening his jacket, and gave his cravat a vicious tug. "I'll do everything in my power to keep you safe."

Again they met eyes. Again that same, guarded expression of his. He could reach out, shove the door open, tell her to leave and never come back; he could reach out and take her face in his hands and ravage her lips until they bled.

Sophia held her breath and waited.

Twenty

—— ✦ ——

H ope couldn't stop staring. With her dark hair loose about her shoulders, the gentle curves of her body just visible beneath the flowing mass of her cloak, Sophia was unbearably lovely. She appeared as he imagined she would after a long, ardent tumble between the sheets of his bed.

Good Lord.

He swallowed the impulse to invite her back to Duchess Street to enjoy exactly that.

Hope shifted in his seat, tugging discreetly at his breeches lest she be exposed to his indecency.

He'd just told her what he never meant to tell anyone. He should run for the hills—or she should, now that he thought about it—especially after that confessional bit about not deserving much besides success at Hope & Co., the regret that plagued him over his strained relationship with Adrian and Henry.

Telling her all he had was a confession in itself. Sophia deserved to know; as La Reinette said, it was pompous of Hope to think he could keep Sophia safe by hoarding his secrets.

But more than that, he told her because he *wanted* to. Because, despite his every effort to focus on the bank, the missing diamond, his falling fortunes, it was Sophia who occupied his thoughts day and night.

In confessing his past, he'd also confessed his affection for her.

They rode the few blocks to her house in silence. He did not dare touch her again—if he did, that tumble between the sheets would occur in no uncertain terms—though he was acutely aware of her presence, the scent of her skin, as she swayed in time to the carriage beside him.

Exhaustion weighed him down besides. In the space of a single night, Hope had experienced every emotion under the sun and then some. He remembered the biting anger that washed through him over port with Lord Harclay; the despair that plagued him as he told Sophia of his past; the desire that tugged between their bodies in Harclay's billiards room.

It was enough to drive a man mad.

The coach stopped a block from the house. Hope helped Sophia to the ground and walked beside her the rest of the way, until they reached the familiar stoop at the back kitchen door.

Hope tapped the stoop with the toe of his boot as Sophia stepped up, turning to face him as she had the night they'd coaxed the French Blue from Princess Caroline's grasp.

"And so we find ourselves here yet again," he said, eyes trained on his boot.

"Doesn't feel at all the same, does it?"

He met her eyes. "No. It feels—" He paused, searching for the right word. At last he spread his arms. "It feels *more*. Everything we—I—felt then, but more of it. Good God if I don't burst."

Her lips parted, her eyes suddenly serious. "Yes," she said quietly. "That's exactly it. I feel as if I might burst."

Her bottom lip trembled, and for a moment Hope feared she might weep again. How he longed to fold her in his arms and comfort her, tell her it would be all right.

"Sophia—"

Before he could say anything further, she pressed a kiss into his cheek. "Good night, Mr. Hope."

She pulled back, meeting his eyes one last time.

Turning, she was about to open the door, when he grabbed her by the wrist.

"I'm not that man anymore, Sophia," he said quietly, impulsively. "That man I told you about, back in France. That isn't who I am."

She looked at him, her face inscrutable. "Thank you, Thomas. For telling me your story."

And then, as she had that night those weeks and weeks ago, she turned and disappeared into the house.

And just as he had that night, Hope reached for the doorknob. Only this time he stopped short of grasping it.

The memory of her touch—it was too much to bear.

M r. Daltrey poked his head through the breakfast room door the next morning, eyes wide as saucers.

"Is something amiss, sir? I just heard—well, I dare not repeat what I heard, but it sounded like someone was shouting."

Hope clutched the paper in his hands as if he might tear it in two. "My apologies, Mr. Daltrey, but I couldn't help shouting after reading *this*."

He tossed the wrinkled paper across the table and pulled his spectacles from his ears, clutching the bridge of his nose between his thumb and forefinger.

"'Rare jewel snatched at banking scion's ball,'" Daltrey read, his voice as chipper as a springtime swallow's.

And then, upon having considered the words: "Begging your pardon, sir, but Holy Christ in heaven! The news—it's made its way to the papers, then!"

"Yes," Hope said without looking up. "The news has made it to the papers. I held them off for as long as I could. But a story this juicy couldn't be kept secret forever."

"Begging your pardon again, sir, but what the devil do you suppose you'll do now that everyone knows? Can't be good for the bank."

Hope met the man's gray eyes at last, a tight smile on his lips. "I suppose we'll just have to hunt down the thief, won't we?"

He sighed. "And no. The news is certainly *not* good for the bank. In fact"—Hope sighed again—"it's entirely possible there will be a run on Hope and Company this very morning. Once my clients—those who don't already know, that is— discover I cannot safeguard my own fortune, I daresay they won't trust me to safeguard theirs."

Mr. Daltrey went pale as a sheet, and seemed to waver

a bit on his feet before straightening. "Will the bank fail, sir?"

Hope threw back what was left of his coffee and stood. "Let's hope not, old man, or the both of us will be out of a job. Have my horse saddled—I haven't the time to wait for the coach."

He stalked across the room, and was about to make his exit when he stopped suddenly, turning to Mr. Daltrey. "One more thing. If I happen to make it back alive tonight, please have my best cognac decanted. The '73, I think it is. In the off chance my clients don't beat me to a pulp, I've a mind to do it myself."

C ollapsing into one of a pair of wingback leather chairs before the fire in his study, Hope gulped all four fingers of his cognac in a single swig.

On the mantel, the clock struck half past three in the morning. He'd been at Hope & Co. all day, putting out fires when he could, solemnly watching them burn when he couldn't.

By his last calculation (somewhere around one o'clock, after the last investor left carrying a two-stone sack of guineas), Hope & Co. had suffered losses in the *hundreds* of *thousands* of pounds.

Another week like this one and Hope would be bankrupt. The run on Hope & Co. was coming—it was, at this point, only a matter of time.

He let his head fall back on the chair, the cognac setting alight the tightness in his throat.

This was bad. Worse than he thought it'd be. If he didn't find the French Blue, and soon, he could lose everything—

"That's dashed good, old man, very good indeed!"

Hope leapt from his chair, his gaze landing on the enormous shadow that lurked just beyond the brandy board.

Mr. Lake stood with a balloon in his hand, swirling the priceless cognac as he held it up to his nose. "What is it, an '87?"

"God *damn* you, Lake! Really, I don't understand your aversion to the front door. My reputation's already in shreds—" Hope threw up his arms in defeat. "Bah! Never mind."

"So it's not an '87, then?"

Hope glared at him. "No. '73."

"'73! Good God, man, who'd you have to kill to get your hands on such a treasure?" Lake took a pull, smacking his lips in appreciation. "Going out with a bang, eh?"

Hope refilled his glass, then turned and slumped back into his chair with a sigh. After a long pause, during which he drained said glass, he said, "Today was a bloodbath. All but a handful of my investors pulled out their money; the deposits fared better, but not by much. D'you happen to have an extra hammock on your pirate ship? I might need a place to sleep."

Lake stepped into the light of the fire, taking a seat in the chair opposite Hope's. "We're all of the same mind, old friend, that the Earl of Harclay is our man. Violet's getting close now; it will only be a matter of time before she digs up the diamond from wherever that bastard is hiding it."

"Even so." Hope brought the empty balloon to his lips and tilted it back, draining the last drop. "There's a very real chance my reputation never recovers from this debacle."

"Oh, believe me, it will. Especially when everyone knows you as the hero who saved England and her brave soldiers from Napoleon's clutches."

Hope's eyes darted to Lake. "Old Boney's contacted you, hasn't he?"

"Turns out word of your 'Jewels of the Sun King' soiree was slow to reach Bonaparte, on account of his location somewhere in the wilds of Russia. Which happens to work to our advantage, you see, for the little shit has yet to learn of the diamond's disappearance."

Hope sat up in his chair. "What did he say? Has he offered terms in exchange for the jewel?"

"Not yet." Lake yawned, stretching his feet toward the fire. "I can't share all the details. But suffice it to say I was privy to a conversation this evening, during which France's 'best wishes for the prince regent's continued good health,' and something or other about forging a friendship out of the 'ashes of our enmity' was discussed."

"So at the very least Napoleon's willing to negotiate. Excellent news, Lake. The best news I've had all day. Except, of course, we *don't have the damned diamond*."

In the light of the fire, Lake's eye glittered. "For one whose name is Hope, you keep very little faith."

"The irony is not lost on me."

"Of course not. You're a poet. A very bad poet; but a poet nonetheless."

Hope's grip tightened on his balloon. "You've done something, haven't you? What is it this time? Blackmail? Poison? Mistaken identity?"

"Mistaken identity! Now that's one I haven't used in a while. No, no, a bit of blackmail, perhaps. Relatively harmless, of course, but rather effective, at least in my experience. I've no doubt the earl will hand over the French Blue by week's end."

Hope sighed and stared into his empty glass. "Let's pray Hope and Company can make it that long. Anything I might help with?"

Lake shook his head. "Just trust that I know what I'm doing. And keep away from Miss Blaise. I saw the way you looked at her at Harclay's dinner; we don't have time for such distractions. Like I told you before, you're only placing her in harm's way."

Anger, hot and sudden, boiled in Hope's belly. "That's rich, coming from you! I saw the way *you* looked at Harclay's sister, Lady Caroline. You were sullen all evening. What," Hope said, mocking, "is she the one that got away?"

Lake froze, humor draining from his features in the space of a single heartbeat.

Christ above. Lake, in love? How had Hope not known?

"Oh." Hope paused. "So Lady Caroline *is* the one that got away. I did not mean to make light—"

"I know what you meant." Lake stood. "Lady Caroline is none of your concern. We are—we *were*—"

"Let's leave the ladies to one another, shall we? I shall not concern myself with Caroline if you do the same with Miss Blaise. Do we have an agreement?"

It was Lake's turn to glare. Hope had never seen him like this; clearly he'd struck a nerve. Lake must have known Caroline in the years before he left London and met Hope. He was intrigued—were they enemies? Lovers, betrothed even?

Hope pushed the thoughts from his mind. Too much going on in there as it was; there wasn't time to become involved in yet another plot, another tangle, another mystery to be solved.

"Agreed," Lake said darkly. And then, after a beat: "Your box at Vauxhall Gardens. Do you still keep it?"

Hope started at the sudden change in subject. "Yes, though I can't say I've had much time for amusement these past weeks. Usually I fill the seats with my more daring clients. Why do you ask?"

"Those acrobats we captured after the theft—the ones Harclay hired to distract your guests while he thieved the French Blue? They're performing at Vauxhall tomorrow— well, I guess now it's *this* evening. Send invitations to Harclay and Lady Violet and whomever else you see fit to attend."

Hope arched a brow as he put the pieces together. He recalled Lake's interrogation of the acrobats the morning after the theft, and the troupe leader's words about the man who hired them.

Said he'd give fi'ty pounds to the each ov us for making a right nice mess of your fancy-pants party. Twen'y-five before, twen'y-five after. We's still waitin' on that last payment, yeah?, if any of yous know where I can find tha bugger.

"Ah." Hope smiled. "So you plan to put the acrobats face-to-face with the fellow who still owes them money. But Harclay was in disguise when he went to them. How are they going to recognize him?"

Lake winked, his good humor reappearing as if it'd never been gone. "Leave that to me, old man."

Hope sighed, cupping his face in his hand as if he were considering the proposal.

Of course he'd say yes. Not only did he have next to nothing to lose at this point; he knew also that if he invited Lady Violet to his box, perhaps her cousin Miss Blaise might accompany her.

Even in the midst of his exhaustion, Hope's blood leapt at the prospect. He couldn't, he shouldn't, but dear *God* he longed to be near her again. Even for an hour, an evening. What harm, really, could come of that?

"Very well. I suppose I'll just skip bed altogether and send the invitations out first thing." Hope yawned and ran a hand through his hair. Good Lord, even his *hair* felt tired.

"We'll find the French Blue, Hope, mark my words. And when we do I will set everything to rights. You'll see."

"I pray you're right."

"I'm always right."

Silence settled between them. Hope yawned again, near delirious with lack of sleep. Though he longed for bed, there was one more matter to discuss with Lake.

The matter that would sink them both if they did not address it, and soon.

Best get it over with as quickly as possible.

"There's something else we need to discuss." Hope cast a longing glance at the brandy board and swallowed. "It appears Guillaume Cassin has returned from the dead. He knows it was us, Lake. He knows we were behind the plot to have him killed. And now he's come back to kill *us*. And, quite possibly, Miss Blaise."

Lake bolted upright, his crippled leg bending curiously at the knee Hope knew to be forever stiff, and choked on his brandy. "*Guillaume Cassin*—back from the dead? But that's impossible!"

"Apparently Madame did not sink her dagger deep enough."

H ope & Co. fared little better the next day. The offices on Fleet Street were a riot of shouts, queues, curses, and wishes for death. Hope's meeting with Viscount Richards had nearly come to blows; the viscount's person grew so red Hope feared his heart might burst forth from his mouth.

It was not, needless to say, a pleasant day at the office.

At last—dear God, *at last*—the hour arrived. Hope had grabbed his things and was in his coach before the clock reached its eighth and final strike.

Hope watched through the window of the coach as familiar sights passed. Westminster Bridge; the muscling, muddy waters of the Thames; and, finally, Vauxhall Gardens.

The lanterns that lined the walkways and pavilions were already lit, blinking through the trees like so many fireflies.

Hope emerged from the carriage and breathed deeply. It was a lovely summer night, the chill of spring gone at last. The sky was wide and fading, though the light from the sun would linger for some hours yet.

He paid the entrance fee, wondering vaguely if he could even afford the three shillings it cost for the evening's entertainment.

Once in his box, he took a seat closest to the stage and ordered food and drink from a liveried waiter. Knowing he was on display before the *haute ton*, Hope took pains to appear relaxed and happy, smiling as he sipped his arrack punch and tried not to gag on its bitter, biting taste.

His gaze landed on a supper box across the stage from his own. There, seated side by side, faces wide as if they'd been laughing, were Sophia and the Marquess of Withington.

Hope's heart lurched, veins flooding with heat. It was none of his business, their acquaintance; Sophia had been nothing but honest when it came to her intentions and the marquess.

Still. The facts of the matter did nothing to assuage Hope's wildly pounding pulse, the possessiveness that took captive his every sense.

Thomas watched as Withington passed her a tiny coupe of punch in that strange, halting manner of his. She brought it to her lips, sharing a witticism as she did so; Withington erupted into laughter, jerking an arm around to slap his knee; she smiled, satisfied.

Sophia looked beautiful, dark hair coiled fashionably about her head, the low neckline of her ivory gown trimmed in an alluring, wispy sort of gauze that emphasized her eager bosom.

A bosom that even the well-mannered marquess could not resist, try though he might.

Across the expanse Sophia met Hope's eyes. For a moment she hesitated, her smile fading. He was desperate to know what she was thinking, what Withington made her feel.

She raised her hand and waved. Hope's heart twisted in his chest. He waved back, smiling tightly; and promptly directed his attention elsewhere.

As if this day could get any, *any* worse.

He felt the stares as the beautiful half of London filled Vauxhall's supper boxes. Their curiosity was sharp and shameless. Everyone, it appeared, had heard of the French Blue being thieved from right out under his nose.

Was he bankrupt? Would he lose everything? Perhaps his house in Duchess Street would go up for auction . . . a lovely pile, yes, and of prime location, but those antiques of his, they are rather odd . . .

But Thomas Hope had not become a banking tycoon on his good looks—ha!—alone; a decade in the business had shaped his heart and head accordingly.

And so he slapped a jolly smile on his face and threw back punch as if he had not a care in the world. He nodded at acquaintances and flirted with old women; he tipped the waiters generously and complimented the food.

Mr. Lake joined him not long after and was all too happy to join the act, especially the arrack-punch bit.

Only when Lady Violet burst into the room, Lady Blaise and Sophia on her heels, did Hope's facade waver. His blood thrummed at the knowledge that Sophia was near, and would be his for the next hour or two; and yet some small part of him was angry with her.

Angry, perhaps, for sharing her company with that marquess. The idiot fellow didn't deserve her. Neither did Hope, but that was beside the point.

The small party exchanged greetings. Thomas came at last to Sophia. All thoughts of bankruptcies and auctions and stolen jewels flew from his mind as she met his gaze, lips parted, eyes full.

She was so damned beautiful.

But when he said, "Hello, Miss Blaise," her beautiful face fell, as if she was expecting more. He furrowed his brow, searching for any clues as to what *more*, exactly, might be.

"Thank you, Mr. Hope, for your lovely invitation."

Hope bowed, the words leaving his lips before he could stop them. "You are most welcome. It is my sincerest wish that you find it more enjoyable than the marquess's. Rather dull fellow, isn't he? Overly fond of the word 'capital.' "

For a moment she looked at him, too stunned to speak; he couldn't tell if it was pain or pleasure that flooded her dark eyes.

"Well," he hastened to add, "in my humble opinion, at least. 'Capital' *is* a popular word these days . . ."

He prayed it wasn't pain. After all she'd been through on his account, the weight he'd placed upon her shoulders, he couldn't bear to see her cry. Not again.

Hope stepped forward, lowering his voice. "Sophia, I—"

He turned at the sudden commotion toward the back of the box. Lord Harclay and his sister the Dowager Countess of Berry had arrived; already the earl was stalking toward Lady Violet, a smug grin on his infuriatingly handsome face; while Lake and Lady Blaise pounced on the dowager countess at the same time, as if she were the last especially well-frosted crumpet on a plate.

Hope turned back to Sophia. They exchanged a meaningful glance, Hope reining in the impulse to accost her with his lips.

But he couldn't, he shouldn't. The weight of his worry returned with crushing force: if he didn't move, and quickly, Hope could very well lose everything by dinnertime tomorrow. He needed to find the diamond so that he might stanch the bleeding at Hope & Co.

And he couldn't accomplish that by spending his time with Sophia, no matter how alluring, how lovely she was.

"I'm sorry," he said, and turned to the Earl of Harclay. Turned his back on her.

Twenty-one

———— ✦ ————

Disappointment rushed through Sophia as she watched the outline of Thomas's broad, sloping shoulders move across the box. The gleaming velvet of his coat, black and well cut, stretched over the expanse of his back as he bowed before Lord Harclay. His face was hardened into a smile, blue eyes studiously vacant of the emotion that occupied them mere heartbeats before.

Hope and the earl exchanged words; and while they appeared friendly enough, Sophia sensed a predatory sort of energy between them, two lions circling one another, sizing up strength, weakness, willingness to charge.

And here men thought *women* were the catty sex. Not so, at least not tonight. Hope's biting comment about the Marquess of Withington's invitation was the perfect example: a mean-spirited admission of envy cloaked in wit and anger. How unlike him, brilliant, levelheaded businessman that he was, to exhibit such raging emotion.

And good Lord, it had thrilled her to no end. It was shameful, she knew, to take pleasure in Thomas's pain; but the fact that he was *jealous* of the marquess was no small thing. It meant Hope, despite his recent chilliness toward her, desired her as much as she desired him. It meant he adored her more than he cared to admit.

Not that they had time to indulge said desire. Cousin Violet was in a tizzy over the failing fortunes of Hope & Co. and, by extension, their family. With the bulk of their money invested in the bank, the sudden plummet in the prices of its shares had hit them hard. Though Violet was never one to air her worries, Sophia could tell she was under great duress. That Violet harbored a not-so-secret fondness for the source of said duress—the earl *was* a terribly handsome fellow—certainly didn't help matters.

And then, of course, there was this Cassin fellow intent upon the murder of Sophia's reputation and Thomas's person. There had been yet another attack in this morning's gossip pages; only by the grace of God had Sophia managed to conveniently misplace the paper before Lady Blaise could read it.

A certain S.B. of which we wrote some days ago is in possession of a most naughty pen. Perhaps the scandals of which she writes are those she has been witness to herself. For a debutante, she is proving a worldly creature.

Sophia glanced across the gardens to the Marquess of Withington's box. She didn't have much time now before her great secret was revealed, and in the worst manner possible. If she meant to marry the marquess, she'd better do it, and do it quickly, before all the world knew of the delicious perversions of her pen.

Scattershot applause broke out in the supper boxes. Sophia started when a troupe of acrobats, their squat faces sickeningly familiar, took the stage.

They were the acrobats that crashed through the windows at Hope's ball; the same acrobats hired by the thief to distract Thomas's guests while he went to work stealing the French Blue.

Her eyes darted to the Earl of Harclay. He stood frozen at the front of the box with Cousin Violet at his side, their clasped hands tucked discreetly into Violet's skirts. The acrobats were waving to the crowd now, their gazes lingering at last on the earl as if they knew, they *knew*, he was their man.

The breath left her body as Sophia watched the scene unfold. It was like something out of La Reinette's tales; all they needed was a pirate and a half-naked governess to complete the drama.

Harclay dropped Violet's hand and tucked her behind him,

away from the acrobats' glares. Across the box, Lake was biting back a snicker while Thomas watched in stony silence;
Lady Blaise frantically fanned herself and Lady Caroline sat
very still in her chair at the table.

Sophia's thoughts raced. Lake and Hope must've revealed
to the acrobats that the Earl of Harclay was the man in disguise
who hired them—and still owed them money. Doubtless the
acrobats, knowing they had the wealthiest earl in London in
their pockets, would blackmail him or worse. Sophia's belly
turned over at the possibility that Violet, having been seen by
the acrobats in the earl's company, would somehow be involved
in the plot.

She understood why Lake, and Hope, too, set these events
in motion. They thought by exerting pressure on Harclay in
the form of blackmail and potential ignominy, they might
coax the earl to return the French Blue. But it was a gamble,
certainly, that nothing would go awry in the meantime. What
if the acrobats took the twenty or so pounds the earl owed
them and went on their merry way? And what if, God forbid,
Violet were to be harmed, blackmailed herself, or worse, held
by the acrobats for ransom?

Sophia closed her eyes against the panic that took wing in
her chest. When she opened them she found Thomas staring
at her, his face hard as ever but his eyes pleading.

Pleading for patience, perhaps; forgiveness, understanding.

A spot of softness in his strengthening resolve to keep
them apart.

A nother sleepless night. Sophia tossed and turned, the
darkness stifling as her thoughts drifted time and time
again to Thomas and those hauntingly beautiful eyes of his.
Her body ached for him; it felt like an eternity since he'd put
his hands on her last.

Sophia stumbled to the window, half hoping La Reinette
would be waiting in the shadows below, and slid it open.

The night was warm and quiet.

Quiet, save for the strange rustling noise off a bit to the
right.

Blinking, Sophia poked her head out the window just in time to see the Earl of Harclay launch headlong into Cousin Violet's window, one down from her own.

Sophia blinked again, catching the tip of the earl's shiny Hessian boot before it disappeared into the house. She heard Violet whispering some curse or another before closing the window behind her midnight visitor.

Ducking into her chamber, Sophia listened as several telling *thuds* reverberated through the wall between her chamber and Cousin Violet's. Whatever Lord Harclay was doing, he was doing thoroughly.

Well, then.

An interesting development, to be sure.

Sophia flung herself upon the bed and with a sigh of frustration tugged a pillow over her head. It was to no avail; she still heard Violet's fluttering sighs and Harclay's groans of pleasure. It was a miracle their ardent—er, *affections* did not wake the whole house.

She should be scandalized, should knock on Violet's door and warn her against fraternizing with the enemy. Then again, Sophia was guilty of walking a fine line herself; wasn't she the one courting the attentions of a well-fortuned marquess while dreaming at night of a different dark-haired gentleman, one with eager hands?

A gentleman she wished would climb through *her* window, and do to her whatever it was that Harclay was doing to Cousin Violet.

Clutching the pillow over her ears, Sophia closed her eyes. She and the marquess were to attend Almack's tomorrow; yes, she would think of that. They'd become friends, she and Withington. Even his notoriously sharp-tongued sisters had taken a liking to Sophia. All was going well, and could only get better.

Perhaps, *perhaps* he would propose by the end of the summer—or, at least, before she was outed as the author of La Reinette's memoirs—and all her dreams would come true: the extravagant engagement ball, the envious tittering of the *ton*, the titles and the castle and the fortune. The things she'd dreamed of all these years would at last be hers.

Sophia closed her eyes, willing herself to sleep.

And woke that morning with a start when she realized she'd dreamt not at all of a glamorous turn at Almack's on the arm of the Marquess of Withington.

No.

It had been Thomas Hope who'd taken captive her dream, whispering into her ear all the things he wanted to show her.

All the things he had yet to make her feel.

Twenty-two

---✦---

City of London
Fleet Street

Standing with both hands on the desk, Hope stared at the open ledger and swallowed the panic that threatened to choke him.

Five more investors had sold their Hope & Co. shares, causing the price to plummet; a dozen or more depositors had pulled their funds from the bank, leaving his liquid assets dangerously low.

Another week like this, and he'd be through by month's end. The bank for which he'd sacrificed everything would no longer be solvent; he'd be as poor and disheartened as he was when he first arrived in London nearly a decade ago.

Hope glanced at the pile of newspapers beside the ledger. The news certainly didn't help. No matter his entreaties, the bribes he offered, Hope's friends at the papers printed headline after headline about the disappearance of the French Blue. The public, they said, couldn't get enough of the story: a cursed jewel, thieved in the midst of the season's most lavish ball—for an editor, it was the stuff of dreams.

Hope pushed aside the papers, tugged the spectacles from his head. He had to find the diamond, now more than ever. The Earl of Harclay was the thief, of that he had no doubt; but Lake's scheme to take back the stone, whatever it was, didn't seem to be working. If only Hope could get his hands on that bastard the earl—

Hope's head snapped to attention as the doors at the far end of the room were flung open, revealing the tall, broad figure of none other than Lord William Townshend, the Earl of Harclay.

Speak of the devil, Hope thought wryly, and he doth appear.

The earl's face was hard; Hope could tell the man's immaculate sense of self-control was on the verge of breaking.

Neither man made any pretense of greeting the other; Hope did not bow, and without so much as a how do you do, Harclay began speaking.

"I need to make a withdrawal. And quickly."

A withdrawal? For what? Perhaps Lake's scheme *was* working.

Though that didn't make Harclay's demand sting any less.

Rage, hot and sudden, burned through Hope. He rose, his eyes never leaving the earl's. His voice, when he spoke, was deadly quiet. "I assume you've seen the papers?"

The earl's face darkened. "I don't have time for this. I don't mean to be rude, Hope—"

"Eight days. I've been in the headlines for eight days straight. Each headline worse than the last; by now all of London must think me a brainless buffoon. Never mind the success of my business before the French Blue incident. Now I am being judged on one bloody night of theatrics; a drop in the proverbial bucket, as they say. And my business—it has suffered greatly, Harclay." Hope balled his hands into fists. "Greatly indeed."

To Hope's very great satisfaction, he saw the earl's dark eyes flash with pain. "I understand your frustration, Hope."

His rage pulsed hotter. "I don't think you do. You see, when Lady Violet came to me with her little theory about you being the thief, I very nearly dismissed her out of hand. Why would Lord Harclay do such a thing, I thought, and to me of all people? I've guarded his investment, shown him generous returns."

Hope knew this was his chance; his chance to pressure the earl into giving up the diamond. If he froze Harclay's accounts at the bank—accounts that held virtually all the Townshend family fortune—perhaps the earl, unable to pay so much as the grocer's bill, might be convinced to hand over the French Blue.

It was the only card Hope had to play.

And he wasn't about to pass up his chance to play it.

"But we've no other suspects, you see," he continued. "And as I've watched my clients vanish, scared off by my seeming incompetence, as I've watched the value of my company plummet—well, I need someone to blame. And I'm afraid that someone is you."

Understanding, swift and terrible, raced across the earl's expression. Hope could tell the man had begun to panic.

Good. Let the son of a bitch suffer.

Now he knows how I have felt all this time.

The earl made no move to deny the accusation. Lady Violet had been right all along.

The Earl of Harclay was the thief.

"Please, Hope, listen to me. I'll give you anything, anything at all, but it is imperative that I make this withdrawal, or Vio—"

"No."

The Earl drew back in shock. Now this—*this* was good sport. Watching Harclay flail about in distress was the best bit of theater Hope had seen in years.

"No? What do you mean, *no*? I've well over a hundred thousand at this bank, and I demand access to those funds!"

"I've frozen your accounts until the French Blue is returned to me. You'll not see a bloody penny before, mark my words. And if you did not steal my diamond yourself, as you claim, then this shall certainly prove motivation for you to help us find the man who did."

Harclay drew back, eyes wide. For a moment Hope wondered why the earl needed the money, and what he intended to do with it; clearly the man was desperate. Had it been Violet's name on his tongue before Hope had interrupted him?

Hope shook the thoughts from his head. He had no sympathy for this miscreant or his troubles. Hope had plenty enough of his own.

The earl was shouting now, red-faced, eyes murderous. "I need that money. Seventy-five pounds, and I swear I shan't ask for more until the diamond is found. I'm in trouble, and so is Lady—"

"That's your problem." Hope felt his limbs begin to shake with anger. "Now get out of my bank before I summon my men."

Harclay crossed the room in two impatient strides. Hope

did not draw back; he met the earl face-to-face, so close he thought for a moment Harclay might butt him in the head.

"If you do this, Hope, you'll have blood on your hands."

Hope called for his men, who materialized out of the shadows at Harclay's side. A man reached for his arm, but the earl flung him off, violence in his every movement.

He jabbed his finger into Hope's chest. "You'll regret this, Hope."

T he poet in Hope had a feeling blood would be spilled this night. Watching a yellow moon rise high over the sprawling expanse of London, that vaguely familiar spider of suspicion had crawled up his back as he stood out on his terrace.

Since that night he sent La Reinette from London, he had no word from her. Cassin, it seemed, disappeared just as quickly as he arrived; Hope wondered what that bastard was waiting for, what tricks he kept hidden up his sleeve. The thought of him ever hurting Sophia, of ruining her and her family, made Hope's blood rush with rage.

What if Cassin planned to make his move tonight?

What if that move meant taking Sophia, holding her hostage, revealing her secrets, going so far as to bodily harm her or her family?

His rage burned so hot for a moment it blinded him.

It was Wednesday, which meant that Sophia and her family would be at Almack's.

Gah, Hope hated Almack's.

But not as much as he hated Cassin; hated the thought of Sophia tangled in his web of treachery, of violence.

In a rather Shakespearean state of mind, what with the blood and the spider and the moon, Hope stalked through the French doors into his office. He slipped the bejeweled Italian dagger into his waistcoat pocket and called for his coach.

Twenty-three

— ❖ —

H aving secured the affections of this season's most eligible bachelor, Sophia thought she might loathe attending Almack's a little less. Perhaps—dare she even hope such a thing!—she might even begin to *enjoy* it. The marquess, in all his sideburned, shiny-booted glory, showered her with attention, and filled her dance card with his name.

And truth be told, she did enjoy his company. He was as charming as ever, introducing her to family and friends as they trolled arm in arm through the crush. It was half past nine and already the Assembly Rooms were humid with laughter, sweat, and swearing; the marquess navigated it all with an ease peculiar to those with blessed births and noble blood.

In that moment, Sophia was possessed of everything she'd ever wanted. A marquess on her arm, a new gossamer gown on her shoulders; the promise of a glittering future and a fortune to go with it.

But the jealous stares and whispers of her fellow debutantes left her feeling hollow and vaguely embarrassed; it was not at all the satisfaction she'd been craving since she was old enough to know what a season was. And while her affection for the marquess grew, it was a companionable, rather than romantic, sort of affection. The kind she felt for Cousin Violet and Fitzhugh; the kind indulged over tea and charades and gossip.

The kind that had nothing at all to do with love.

The dancing was about to begin. Across the ballroom, Violet and that devil the earl were already paired up, her color high as he brushed his lips to her ear. A wave of longing washed through Sophia as she watched them. The earl touched

Violet confidently, adoringly, as if he understood her inside and out. Violet appeared at once flattered and flabbergasted by his affection.

If Sophia didn't know any better, she would say her cousin was in love.

She bit the inside of her lip, smiling tightly as the marquess introduced her to yet another of his classmates from Oxford.

She wished Hope were here, so that he might touch her like the earl touched Violet. Because Thomas's touch was confident and adoring, too. The best kind of touch.

And then, over the Oxford classmate's spindly shoulder, Violet caught sight of a familiar head of dark, unruly curls.

It can't be, not now, not tonight. What the devil is he doing at Almack's?

As if in answer to her wish, Thomas Hope appeared. Something unfurled inside her as she looked into those blue eyes of his. Her heart began to pound, and without willing it her smile grew.

The master of the dance was calling for a cotillion; Withington abruptly turned to Sophia, jerking out his arm.

"A cotillion!" he beamed. "Capital! This one you're rather good at, Miss Blaise."

Sophia swallowed, eyes flicking for a moment back to Thomas. "I make no promises, my lord. How many pairs of your shoes have I ruined thus far?"

The marquess laughed good-naturedly as he led her into the ballroom. "Two. Let's make it three, just for good measure."

"Yes, let's do."

They elbowed their way onto the dance floor. Standing across from one another, they bowed as the master called for the music to begin. Sophia returned the marquess's grin, and almost missed the strange gleam in his gray eyes.

Almost.

She recognized that gleam. It was the same gleam in the earl's eyes as he'd looked upon Violet heartbeats before.

Sophia's pulse took off at a sprint.

The dance began. Sophia moved through the steps haltingly at first, mind racing as she whirled once, twice, clapped and clasped hands with the marquess. What did Withington mean looking at her like that? Did it mean—dear God, it couldn't, it was too soon, didn't these things take more time?—what she thought it meant?

Withington set her out to the edge of the floor; she turned slowly, as if on air, and for a breathless moment her gaze landed on Thomas.

Of course. Out of all the hundreds and thousands of beautiful people pressed into Almack's, it had to be him. He had to be standing there, just so, in a place where she might find him.

Thomas was looking at her, his face tight, eyes full. Even from here she sensed the heat, the longing that radiated from him. There was a flicker in his eye, sharp and clear as glass, different somehow from Withington's; or perhaps it was Sophia's response to it, the way it made her feel, that was different.

She saw something else in Thomas. Something she recognized in her own heart.

Desire. Regret, too.

The music moved and Sophia moved reluctantly with it. She turned to face the marquess, and he was stepping forward the same moment as she was stepping back. She lost her footing, ankles crossing at the wrong moment, and she felt herself falling.

Withington caught her just in time, his grin deepening.

"I'm sorry, my lord—"

"Enough with this 'my lord' business." The marquess took her hand and together they turned. For one whose movements were awkward and severe, he was a rather fine dancer, as if in the crush of the ballroom he might at last, at last, be himself. "I'd prefer it if you called me Withington, like the rest of my family."

Sophia bit back her surprise.

It was no small thing, that she should call him so familiar a name. If their fellow dancers heard his request, they would assume the two of them were good as engaged. Only his lordship's mother—and, eventually, his *wife*—would ever refer to him as 'Withington.'

"You don't think 'Withington' is a bit too familiar?"

"Miss Blaise." He pulled her close, his hand slipping to the small of her back. His touch felt foreign, firm enough but not at all electric. Not the way Hope's touch felt. "You and I, we do not have the opportunity to be alone very often. You must," he spun her about again, "forgive me for saying these things, and at Almack's of all places."

"What," Sophia clapped, "things?"

They turned to face each other. Withington was blushing, bashful little lines forming around his mouth. "I hope you do not think me forward, Miss Blaise, but surely you must know by now how I—how I feel about you."

Oh dear.

"I've very much enjoyed the time we've spent together, however brief. That idea of yours, the port tasting, it was the most capital event I've attended. Ever. I—I mean this as a compliment, I do, Miss Blaise, but I never expected to enjoy a woman's company as much as I enjoy yours."

Sophia closed her eyes against the lump in her throat. "That is kind of you to say, my lord."

"Withington. Please, Miss Blaise. It would mean a great deal if you'd call me Withington."

But I shouldn't mean a great deal. Not to you.

"Of course." She smiled tightly. "If we are to be friends, then I must be Sophia to you."

Out of the corner of her eye, Sophia saw Violet twirling about the Earl of Harclay, both grinning like loons. For a brief, wild moment, she wondered what her cousin would do, what she would say to Withington's heartfelt confession.

Truth be told, Violet would likely duck and run.

But then again, Violet was not possessed of the ambition to make the match of the season. She didn't want to make *any* match, period.

"Sophia." The marquess smiled, stepping back, then forward. "I know we've only recently become acquainted, but I—well I—I'd like to think we get on well, and enjoy each other's company."

She glided past him, narrowly avoiding his left foot. "We get along splendidly, you and I. And I cannot deny I *do* enjoy your company, very much."

And that was true. After showing him her honest self, Sophia *did* enjoy the time she spent with Withington, more than she enjoyed the company of her fellow debutantes, her supposed friends.

Then why did saying so feel so wrong?

Sophia turned and had her answer.

Mr. Hope's eyes were steady as he watched her. The moment their gazes met, she lost all sense of time and place. This yearning, it was unlike anything she'd ever known; strange, for as yet she didn't understand what it was, exactly, she wanted from him, *needed* as surely as the air she breathed.

With all this bosom-heaving breathlessness and longing, it was a wonder Sophia hadn't fallen flat on her face in the midst of the dance. Blessedly it drew to a close, the music climbing to a stupefying crescendo before ending on a clipped, joyful note.

Sophia let out a breath she didn't know she'd been holding. Curtsying before the marquess, she rose to find him standing very close. His face was serious even as his color was high.

"What I meant to say, Sophia, is this." He kept his voice low, even as the crowd around them erupted in applause. "It is my wish my intentions toward you become public. My affection for you only grows; my family, they adore you. *I* adore you. If you'll have me, I'd—"

There was a sudden, vicious tug on her arm. Sophia spun about to see Mr. Hope, his dark face completely transformed from moments ago. Her belly dropped to her knees as the hair at the back of her neck pricked to life. Something had happened.

Something was wrong.

"What?" she panted. "What is it?"

His head dipped toward her, his lips brushing her ear as he murmured a single, devastating word.

"Violet."

Twenty-four

———✦———

"Violet?"

"There isn't time," Hope murmured in Sophia's ear. "Come with me."

Over her shoulder, Sophia nodded her apologies to the marquess, who looked as if she'd just stabbed him in the heart. Hope felt a twinge of guilt at the smirk that rose to his lips.

A *twinge*.

His hand on the small of her back, Hope gathered Sophia against him. Together they shoved their way through the crowd, gulping fresh air as they tumbled out onto the street.

Farther down the lane, Hope watched the vague outline of a lone rider disappear into the darkness, the tails of his coat waving behind him like a standard.

It was the earl, in hot pursuit of whoever had taken Violet.

Hope turned to see Harclay's gleaming carriage loom just down the lane; its team of matching Andalusians was short one horse—the horse Harclay now rode to God knows where.

"What happened?" Hope caught the man lingering beside the coach. "Where is the earl going?"

The man turned; Hope recognized him as Harclay's butler, Mr. Avery. Beneath Hope's touch Avery stiffened, but his eyes gleamed with recognition; after a moment he nodded.

"Mr. Hope, I am glad to have found you. I don't know exactly what happened, only that the Lady Violet was taken from the ball by a man, perhaps two, and shoved inside a waiting hack that took off before I could stop it."

"Taken?" Sophia gulped. "As in—as in *kidnapped*?"

Avery looked to Hope before replying. "Yes, Miss Blaise. I'm afraid so."

"Oh, for God's sake!" For a moment she went limp against him. Though she made no sound, Hope felt her shoulders moving in time to her sobs.

He glanced across the street; there were too many people about, too many prying eyes.

"It isn't safe here. I shall see Miss Blaise and her mother home"—Hope squeezed Sophia when he felt her stiffen in protest—"and we shall await word from you or your master. Or, for that matter, Lady Violet's return."

"Excellent, Mr. Hope. Godspeed, then."

Avery turned and made his way down the lane. Hope watched his sturdy figure disappear into the riot of horseflesh and hackneys.

That spider of suspicion—it had just bitten Hope in the neck.

Twenty-five

---◆---

When at last, after spending the better part of three hours sobbing, Lady Blaise fainted—or fell asleep, Hope couldn't quite tell—he got up from his chair by the fire and stretched his arms.

"Are you sure you don't want to sleep?" he asked Sophia. "I'm happy to keep watch."

She hadn't moved since they'd returned to the house hours ago, and sat hunched over on a nearby settee, staring into the fire with her chin propped upon her fist.

"No, no. It is you who should be sleeping. Violet said you haven't seen your bed in days."

Hope felt the color rise to his cheeks at those words on her lips. His bed. God, how he missed it. God, how he longed to take her there now, and touch her in ways that would help ease her worry.

"Bah! Who needs sleep? I feel fresh as a daisy."

"Liar." Sophia grinned, meeting his eyes.

"Well. Nothing a few pots of coffee can't fix, at least."

Hope sat down and held out his hand. Sophia glanced over her shoulder; and, certain her mama and uncle had indeed gone up to bed, quietly placed her fingers in his palm.

"Thank you. For staying. I know you've seen enough trouble these past weeks—and now, ha!" She laughed mirthlessly. "Now Violet has been kidnapped. It's like something out of a play, isn't it?"

Hope scoffed, digging into his pocket to retrieve the ridiculous dagger he'd hidden there. "Try me."

This time her laugh was genuine.

Silence, at once tense and exhausted, settled between them as they gazed into the fire, the hiss of dying embers suddenly too loud to bear.

"I—I assume you've no word of—of that man, Cassin?"

Hope squeezed her hand, gently this time. He looked down at his feet and shook his head. "No. Nothing. I did see the gossip pages, though. I'm terribly sorry, Sophia. Know I'm doing everything possible to keep you safe."

He swallowed. "I want nothing more than to keep you safe."

Sophia made a choking sound. He snapped to attention, only to see her tears begin anew.

"Oh, dear." He ran a hand through his hair. "Did I say something? What is it, Sophia? Please. Please tell me. Seeing you cry makes me want to—to—"

He looked down at the dagger he held in his hand.

"It makes me want to pry out my eyes with this dagger. I'll do it, I will!"

"I'm not," she snorted, weeping with greater vigor, "*crying*. It's just—just—put that thing away, Thomas."

Sophia took a great pull of air, letting it out slowly as she closed her eyes in an apparent attempt to calm herself. She dropped his hand.

"I'm sorry."

Hope leaned back into the chair. "Don't be. Violet will come home, Sophia. Harclay knows what he's doing. He wouldn't let her come to any harm. Besides, he's an earl, for God's sake. No one crosses an earl. It's tantamount to being God, or at the very least Jesus—"

"That's not—" She looked down at her hands, thinking better of what she was about to say. "Thank you, Thomas, for your words of comfort. She'll come back, I know she will. She's *Violet*. Very much like being God, as you say."

The fire before them was dying; its merry crackling had subsided to small, silent licks of flame.

Silence stretched between Hope and Sophia. A silence filled with all the things he should say. All the things he *wanted* to say.

He pulled his thumb and forefinger across his closed eyes.

This waiting, it was terrible; he felt Sophia's pain as if it were his own. He'd lost more than his share of loved ones.

And he did not wish that kind of suffocating grief on anyone. Least of all the lovely creature on the settee beside him.

Hope felt as if they were wasting precious time. They were alone, they were close, they had nowhere to be. Such moments were fleeting; he knew in the coming days and weeks there would be fewer and fewer of them.

And like the fool he was, he opened his mouth and spoke the first words that came to mind.

Sophia, too, moved to speak, their words tangling as each of them stopped, only to start at the same time yet again.

"So, the marquess—"

"Do you usually attend Almack's—"

A clap of thunder sounded outside, rattling the window-panes. Sophia leapt to her feet, eyes wide; when the pounding became louder, halting abruptly seconds later, she dashed through the drawing room door. Hope followed a few steps behind; he wanted to be close enough for comfort, but not too close so as to intrude upon a moment between cousins.

He was relieved to hear, just before he stepped into the front hall, a muffled cry of relief, followed by a curse as Sophia squeezed the air out of Violet's lungs in a tight embrace.

Hope closed his eyes and sighed. Thank God.

Violet was back. She was back, and in one, foulmouthed piece.

Thank God.

L ady Blaise held Violet's face in her hands one last time, smiling tearfully as she pinched her niece's cheeks. Mr. Hope had long since left, wishing them good evening; now the ladies were free to touch and prod and tease one another as they pleased.

"I hope this means we'll never have to attend Almack's again," Violet said, grimacing after a particularly poignant pinch.

"Once Sophia makes her match," Lady Blaise winked at her daughter, "we shan't step *foot* in those dreadful rooms. Shouldn't be too long now."

Violet arched a brow. "You're really going to do this, then? Marry that marquess—Worcestershire? Withering?"

"Withington. You *know* it's the Marquess of Withington, Violet. And no. Yes. Nothing is as yet set in stone. We haven't talked much of our intentions, much less an *engagement.*"

"Haven't talked *much*?" Violet said. "That means you have talked about it. What did he say?"

"Yes, what did he say?" Lady Blaise dropped her hands from Violet's face and turned to Sophia. "I saw him speaking to you during the cotillion. Poor man, he blushed so furiously I feared blood might spurt from his ears!"

Violet and Mama crowded round her, their faces upturned as they waited for a reply. Sophia swallowed, feeling stifled as the ladies drew yet nearer, the air between them thrumming with anticipation.

"Well." Sophia cleared her throat. "It was nothing, really. A few words about feelings—"

"Feelings! Gah."

Sophia's shoulders slumped. "That's lovely of you, Violet, really *lovely*—"

"Oh, come here, you silly goose." Violet laid a hand on Sophia's cheek. "I don't mean to make light of your *feelings*, dearest. It is your feelings that concern me most. I know you've always been a snob about whom you want to marry—"

"Violet," Lady Blaise warned.

"Let her finish, Mama. Violet offends everyone; we must not take it personally. You may proceed."

"Thank you, Cousin." Violet all but rolled her eyes. "As I was saying. I know you've always dreamed of making a splash, and marrying your marquess at St. George's before the queen and all that. But I've seen you with Mr. Hope—"

"Violet!" Lady Blaise sputtered in disbelief. "Really, now you go too far—"

"All right, all right," Violet demurred. "But I do wonder, Cousin, if having known Mr. Hope hasn't changed those dreams of yours."

Sophia drew a shaking breath. Was it anger that now rose in her chest, or something else—something akin to pain? Her throat suddenly felt tight; she wondered if she had any tears left. First Hope, now Violet—honestly, how many people would make her weep tonight?

She felt exquisitely tender, and very tired. Weary, as if her heart might give out beneath the great burden of all she'd felt and witnessed these past hours.

Sophia narrowed her eyes at Violet. "Did your captors steal your soul, too? Since when is Lady Violet Rutledge, cardsharp and self-declared spinster, a *romantic*?"

Violet returned her gaze steadily. Sophia had never seen her blue eyes so soft, so full of—dear God—was that *love*?

It shocked Sophia to see Violet thus altered. Shocked her, because she recognized that look in her cousin's eyes.

Sophia had seen it in her own, glancing in the mirror as Fitzhugh had dressed her earlier that evening.

The words left her lips before she could stop them, hand flying to her throat. "*Good heavens!*"

"What?" Lady Blaise's eyes went wide. "Tell me, Sophia, what is it?"

Sophia looked to Violet. A small, knowing smile crept across Violet's lips. She turned to Lady Blaise, looping arms. "Come, Auntie George, it's been one hell of a day. Let's to bed, shall we?"

"We shall." Lady Blaise looked pointedly at her daughter. "Cousin Violet's nerves are on edge, Sophia, after a traumatic event. Tomorrow she won't remember a thing she's said, and neither should you. Like the ravings of a deranged lunatic, Violet's words are nothing but meaningless jumble."

Violet scoffed, leading Mama up the stairs. "Deranged lunatic. Such an imagination you have, Auntie George! Come along, now."

With one last, piercing look at Sophia, Lady Blaise turned and followed her niece upstairs.

For several minutes Sophia stood unmoving in the front hall. In the center of her being her heart worked furiously, sending waves of sensation to every corner of her body. The weariness she'd felt earlier dissipated as readily as a summer storm, replaced by a fierce restlessness that demanded action.

She needed to see him. Now. Tonight.

Before decisions were made and futures decided, she needed to see him.

Him, the man she loved.

D oor, stairs, cloak, boots.

Sophia stole out into the darkness, working through the route to Duchess Street in her head. She moved quickly, breathless with impatience as she ducked in and out of shadow. Worried her courage would desert her, she moved yet faster, all but oblivious to the sights and sounds of the night around her as Thomas took captive her every sense.

So consumed was she by rather explicit imaginings of a half-naked Hope that she nearly missed the patter of footsteps just off to her right.

Sophia plastered herself against a nearby wall, waiting with bated breath as the footsteps drew nearer. A shadow passed not six inches from where she stood, so close she thought it certain she'd be found out; but the shadow moved on, quickening its pace as it drew out into the street. The scent of tuberose hung in its wake.

Out of the darkness another shadow approached, this one vaguely familiar: tall and broad, with a loping gait and confident, almost cocky, swing of his arms.

Was that?—no, it couldn't be.

Could it?

Sophia watched wide-eyed as Cousin Violet flung herself into the Earl of Harclay's outstretched arms. For several heartbeats they clung to one another, heads moving rapturously as they kissed the sort of kiss to end all kisses.

Sophia drew back against the wall, heart pounding. Violet was doing more than fraternizing with the enemy; and by the way she kissed him, she was doing more even than *that*, too.

How like Violet to be in love with the man she hunted. Sophia rolled her eyes. They stood to lose everything, all of them, and here was Cousin Violet, assaulting the thief's lips as if they, and they alone, were responsible for the crime.

Perhaps it was all part of Violet's plan. Perhaps she was drawing the earl close so as to better aim her dagger.

Violet was, after all, far more cunning than even the devious Harclay.

Perhaps.

Besides. Sophia was in no position to judge. Wasn't she the one courting the attentions of a marquess while stealing into a banker's bed at night?

That deuced diamond had thrown them all into a state of chaos. Sophia hadn't felt like her status-obsessed self since she first laid eyes on the French Blue that night in Princess Caroline's drawing room. Perhaps there was truth to Thomas's *History*; perhaps the diamond *was* cursed, and they were all doomed to suffer poetically gruesome deaths.

When at last Cousin Violet and Lord Harclay came up for air, he tucked her into the crook of his arm and together they stalked down the street. Doubtless he would take her to his pile in Hanover Square and ravage her thoroughly in the comfort of his enormous four-poster bed.

Which brought Sophia back to her own intentions to ravage and be ravaged in turn. If Violet and Harclay were to indulge in a doomed affair, then by God Sophia would not be left behind. She had her own hopeless, foolish, irresistible liaison to see to.

By the time she reached Duchess Street, she thought she might burst with anticipation. If she had known how thrilling illicit love affairs would be, Sophia would've dreamt of them rather than miraculous matches with viscounts. It was too late for that. Too late.

But she had one last chance. Here, just for tonight, she would forget all that. Just for tonight, she would give in wholly, indulge every whim and fantasy.

And then tomorrow she would return to said miraculous matches, her mama, the marquess and his affections, his proposal, which she knew would come any day now.

Tonight, however, she would be Hope's. Her body, her heart, her every wish and desire—she'd surrender everything she had. Just this once.

Just tonight.

If, that is, Sophia could actually *get* to Hope.

She should've known the house would be a fortress following the theft. Surveying the property from a nearby corner off

Duchess Street, Sophia picked out at least a dozen men patrolling the crescent-shaped front drive. The tall iron gates on either side of the house were closed; toward the back of the building, Sophia picked out two windows glowing with low light. Otherwise, the house was dark.

Moving with as much care as her screaming pulse would allow, Sophia stole across the street, hiding in the shadow of a stone pillar that marked the corner of Hope's property.

She was about to turn and make for the mews, when she was grabbed from behind. Her assailant spun her around with such force it knocked the wind from her lungs, her hood falling back from her face.

"Please," she managed, panic filling her chest as her eyes fell on a familiar face.

"Miss Blaise!" Daltrey whispered, his white hair glinting in the moonlight. "What are you doing here, and at this time of night!"

Relief rushed through Sophia at the sound of his voice, even as she wondered why Thomas's butler was playing sentry in the wee hours of the morning.

"I don't trust these fellows," he said, reading Sophia's thoughts. "Not after those men betrayed Mr. Hope at his ball. I keep watch on them while they keep watch on the house. Come, let's get you inside. Mr. Hope will be pleased to see you."

Daltrey ushered her through the servants' entrance at the back of the house. He led her up a narrow set of stairs to a small drawing room on the second floor. Aside from the fire in the grate, there was no light.

"I'm not waking him, am I?"

"Psh!" Daltrey removed Sophia's cloak and carefully draped it over his forearm. "I think Mr. Hope's forgotten how to sleep, poor fellow. He will be curious, however, as to the purpose of your visit. It isn't safe to be about, and *without chaperone*, so late."

Sophia swallowed, her clasped fingers coiling over and through one another. She couldn't very well tell Daltrey the *true* reason for her visit; she could just imagine him fainting from horror as she said, "I have come to seduce his lordship, Mr. Daltrey. Might you point me in the direction of his bedchamber?"

And so, recalling with no small fondness the evening she'd spent in the Princess of Wales's drawing room, Sophia scrunched her face and stuck out her lip and let out the most pitiful sounding sob she could muster.

"Oh. Oh, heavens, Miss Blaise, I did not intend to upset you." Daltrey took a step forward, holding his arms awkwardly out before him as if he would embrace her. "There, there, Miss Blaise, there, there."

"It's just"—sob, along with a hysterical heaving of her bosom—"it's been so. So very difficult. My delicate sensibilities have been *assaulted*, yes, assaulted, and I—oh, dear, I feel a fainting spell coming on!"

Mr. Daltrey tapped her lightly on the shoulder, prodding as if to make sure she were still breathing. "Well. Er. I am terribly sorry, Miss Blaise, for whatever distress I have caused you. I shall lead you to Mr. Hope straightaway so that he might— er, address whatever it is that. Um. *Assaults* you so. There, there, come with me."

Sophia held up a hand to hide her smile of triumph as Mr. Daltrey steered her from the drawing room and up another flight of stairs.

At the end of a wide paneled gallery, Daltrey paused before a door. He leaned his ear against it, listening for a moment before pulling away in a huff.

"He's not here. Wait inside, Miss Blaise, and I shall locate the master of the house directly."

Daltrey held open the door. With a nod of thanks, Sophia slipped into the room, the door closing behind her with a small, quiet click.

For a moment she stood at the threshold, marveling at the room around her. Wiping a tear from the corner of her eye, she nearly laughed at the exquisite beauty of Hope's bedchamber.

On the near wall, a dying fire burned in a stone fireplace as high and wide as Sophia was tall. The small circle of light it emitted was bruised red, almost purple. Beyond that was utter, complete darkness.

Even so, she could make out the shape of the room's sumptuous appointments: the biggest bed she had ever seen, its pristine coverlet ironed and fluffed to a most welcoming proportion; Persian rugs of every color and shape; carefully curated paintings, hung from silken tassels to cover every square inch of the walls.

Sophia took a step forward, her heart soaring as the audacity of her actions settled upon her for the first time.

She swallowed her fear. She'd come this far. She was not about to go back. Not when she felt like this.

She swam to the darkest corner of the room, running her hand along the smooth, hard surface of a bedpost, the stack of leather-bound volumes on a bedside table.

"Sophia."

She started at the voice, nearly knocking the volumes to the floor. Turning, she saw nothing but darkness.

"You shouldn't be here. You shouldn't have come."

His voice was low, strained; as if something strong, something he wanted to repress, coiled inside him; as if he were a bowstring pulled taut, waiting for release.

She took a step toward him; he made no sound. Though she could not see him, she felt the stirring between their bodies, that familiar anticipation rushing through her with blinding force.

"I came for you," she said.

"It is foolish of you to be out alone, and at this hour."

"I don't care, Thomas." She paused. "I came for you."

"Please, Sophia—"

"No." She wished he would come forward so that she might see him. She wanted nothing more than to *see* him. "Please, Thomas. I did not come to talk."

She heard his sharp intake of air, sensed his mind racing under cover of darkness. For a moment she hesitated. Would he refuse her? He would be right to do so, of course; this was a bad idea, a dangerous idea, and he knew it.

Sophia waited for what seemed like an eternity, her limbs beginning to tremble as if she'd bared to him her body as well as her soul.

There was a rush off to her right, the air suddenly alive with his scent; and then his hands were on her shoulders, brushing her skin as they moved up her neck. She nearly cried out at the tide of sensation that slid through her, his touch firm and impatient as if he owned her.

As if she were his and no one else's.

Twenty-six

———— ❖ ————

As soon as Thomas drew near, his impatient hands drawing her close, he disappeared, leaving her reeling in the darkness.

She turned this way and that, looking for any sign of where he might be. "Thomas, please—"

"I thought you did not come to talk." That voice of his; a growl that at once frightened and titillated her.

A wave of heat pulsed between her legs. Dear God, why wouldn't he touch her again, where was he, why was he *hiding* like this—

There was a tug at the back of her head as Thomas gathered her hair in his hand and pulled. She could not see much of anything, but she could smell him, sandalwood and a bit of lemon as he reared over her, pulling back her head and sinking his teeth into the soft flesh of her throat.

This time Sophia *did* cry out, her eyes wide as they searched the blackness. Nothing, nothing. Nothing save the sensation of his lips moving over her skin, his fingers tugging the pins from her hair. He buried his hand in her loosened waves, pulling, and pulling yet harder, arching her against him.

Beneath her skin her blood pulsed hot and wild. He'd never touched her like this, had never been as wildly possessive. There would be no going back from this place; no time for second thoughts or the heavy lives that awaited them outside these walls. He would have her, and she him, and in so doing they would forget everything but each other, and the desire that stretched between them.

At least for tonight.

Thomas's lips found hers, and Sophia's eyes fluttered shut in an agony of pleasure as he kissed her. It was forceful, this kiss, forceful and tender all at once. She felt the darkness falling in on them as the kiss deepened, blocking out everything but the sensation of his nearness. The backs of her knees relaxed; the tug between her legs was deliciously poignant.

Her body, her mind—the surrender was coming.

He took her bottom lip between his teeth, letting out a hiss of satisfaction at her moan. For a moment he released her mouth, resting his forehead against her own. His breath was warm and hard on her skin, coming in deep, long draws. She felt the flutter of his eyelashes on her eyelids, moving slowly, softly; she reached up and thumbed the scar on his cheek, no more than a slight ridge now. How long ago that night in Madame's closet seemed.

And then his hand was cupping her face, and he was kissing her again, moving over her with exquisite concentration. Her pulse rushed in her ears as he tugged at her hair. She could stay here, kissing him like this, forever, her mind blank except for the sensation of her body tangling with his.

Sophia's eyes flew open when Thomas pulled away, his hands leaving traces of fire where he'd touched her. She gasped for air, trembling in the darkness as she waited. What little light there had been from the fire was now gone; the room was a river of black, the only sound a small rustling somewhere in the dark.

She gasped at the sudden, vicious tug at the back of her gown. He was pulling at the laces with impatient fingers, pressing his body against hers. A shiver ran the length of her spine when his lips found the tender skin at the back of her neck, caressing her with his lips and tongue.

Her laces sighed softly as he pulled them free, working his way from her neck to the small of her back. Thomas slipped his hands inside her gown and coaxed it apart, pulling it over her shoulders and hips. It fell in a gust of chill air to her feet.

Thomas wasted no time. His lips moved from the ball of her shoulder to her collarbone and neck as he spun her to face him.

She reached for him, her fingers tangling in the fine rumpled linen of his shirt. She drew it upward and he stepped back from her body, allowing her to pull it over his head.

The sound of her palms scraping over the expanse of his bare chest filled the air between them. Sophia could see nothing, nothing but the dim outline of his person; but beneath her fingers his heart was warm, beating hard and healthy, the feel of skin on skin wildly thrilling. She ran her hands through the wiry hair at the center of his chest, over the smooth, turgid flesh of his neck, down the thick, lean expanse of his belly.

Thomas growled the lower she went, a low sound of warning. He hooked his thumbs into the neck of her chemise and drew it over one shoulder, then the other, moving with brutal straightforwardness that left her breathless.

He set both his hands on her hips, pushing down her pantalets along with the chemise; the air felt tantalizingly cold against her burning skin.

And then he was running his palms up the sides of her ribs, sending waves of exquisite longing through her. Her blood leapt as his thumbs moved over her belly and up to her breasts, scraping her hardened nipples once, twice, three times, taking them between his thumb and forefinger and pulling, *my God, my God, please*—

He dug a hand into her hair, bringing his lips to hers as he pulled her naked body against his own. She moaned into the kiss, her hands drinking him in, memorizing every slope, every muscle and sinew, for this would be the only time—the last time—she would ever have him like this.

Sophia curled her fingers into the waistband of his breeches. He bit her bottom lip, as if to say *yes*; she worked the buttons free one at a time, Thomas's mouth deepening its assault with each button she managed to undo.

She freed the last button; and then with a violence of which she didn't know she was capable, tugged them over the bulge between his legs, down, down the length of his enormous, hardened thighs.

For a moment he broke the kiss, stepping out of the breeches one leg at a time before kicking them to some unknown corner of the room.

And then he stood before her; she sensed the working of his chest, the air moving out of his lungs and into her own. Though she could not see him, she knew he was as naked as the day he was born.

As naked as she was, their bodies warm with desire.

He made no move, allowing that desire to burn to new heights between them. He was waiting, she knew, for her answer to his unspoken question.

Sophia stood very still, her breathing the only noise in the room. She would not turn back, not now, not when she felt so full she might burst. Never mind her conflicted desires outside this darkness; here, now, she felt wild with certainty.

She wanted Thomas. She wanted to surrender to him, to say *yes* to all the things she'd forbidden herself to feel and know these past weeks.

Sophia took a deep, shaking breath. This was her chance. Her chance to let him fill her being, her every sense. Her chance to forget the French Blue, the marquess, villainous Frenchmen, and La Reinette. Cousin Violet, *her family*, her writing, and her fellow debutantes at Almack's.

As she exhaled, it all fell away, the armor of her ambition disappearing in the darkness. In its place rose a bursting relief, a lightness she'd never experienced.

Yes. Dear God, yes.

Sophia stepped forward, her bare skin brushing against his for the first time. Fire shot through her, her entire being pounding with a craving so complete, so overwhelming, she could think of nothing and no one but *him*. Nothing but what was to come, what he would make her feel.

So *this* is what La Reinette was talking about in her memoirs. This thunderous feeling, this warm, wondrous taking of breaths, of confidences, of innocence. Being *taken*, and taking in turn—yes, this would be Sophia's greatest adventure yet.

Thomas gathered her against him, bending his enormous arms to cradle her in the curve of his body. One of his hands slid to the small of her back, his fingers clutching her skin; the other found its way to her face, guiding her lips to his.

Slipping his tongue between her lips, Thomas pulled her against him. She felt the leap of his cock against her belly, his pubic hair brushing the angle of her hip. The flesh between her legs throbbed, going from warm to hot to fiery in the space of a single breath.

His lips moved from her mouth to her jaw, working their

way down her throat to her collarbones and finally across her—

Oh God. Her eyes slammed shut as his teeth nicked her right nipple, then her left, his lips moving over her hungrily. His hand slid from her cheek down to her breast, running his thumb over the hardened point of each nipple. She arched back, digging her hands into the tumble of his curls, pulling against him, crying out for more.

His other hand moved from the small of her back down the slope of her backside, his fingers slipping between her buttocks to find the source of all this sensation.

Sophia gasped as he moved to cup her with his palm, his fourth finger finding its way inside her as his first two fingers worked that heady place at the tip of her sex. His fingers traced lines of fire, parting her folds with an expert touch while with his mouth he teased her nipples, pulling and biting, stoking her desire to breathless heights.

She felt herself tightening against him, that rolling tide of screaming pleasure very close, *heavens*, very close, if he'd just touch her one more time—

Thomas's hand slid away from her sex, moving down the backs of her legs, the other scraping up the length of her spine. In one swift movement, he lifted her into his arms. She opened her mouth to protest, but in the space of a single heartbeat he was tossing her onto the bed, the coverlet sighing contentedly as she landed on its surface. She searched the darkness for Thomas, but she saw a blackness so complete she wondered for a moment if his expert ministrations had blinded her.

But then she heard him at the foot of the bed; he was pulling at her boots, dropping them one at a time to the floor with a dull *thud*. His fingers moved up her legs, carefully sliding her silk stockings off her feet and onto the floor.

He grasped her by the ankles and tugged her toward him. Sophia felt the bed bow beneath his weight as he reared over her, trailing kisses along the length of her body as he made his way up: one for each knee, the inside of her thigh, her hips and belly, the left breast and right nipple, the place where her collarbones met.

She gasped as he bit into the flesh of her throat, her body screaming for release as he at last took her mouth with a force that knocked the breath from her lungs.

Of their own volition, her legs snaked around his hips; she felt the nudge of his cock against her sex, its slick warmth begging for more, *more*. She closed her eyes, allowing her need to swallow her whole.

Thomas placed his elbows on either side of her head; his curls fell into her face and eyes as he worked her mouth with his lips and teeth and tongue. Still he made no move between her legs. She wondered what he was waiting for; she felt as if she might lose her soul if he did not release her from this agony, this lovely, breathless moment of unbearable anticipation. He felt warm and impossibly enormous against her flesh. She wanted to know what it felt like *after* this forbidden moment passed; what it felt like *after* he was inside her.

Sophia bucked her hips against him, forcing his hand; above her, he froze.

In response he grabbed both her hands in one of his and thrust them above her head, pinning her to the bed. She cried out, writhing against him; but he held her fast, his other hand moving over the plane of her belly to rest between her legs.

Holding her hostage with the bulk of his body, he opened her, his fingers gliding through her wetness with ease. He slipped one, two fingers inside her, moving as if to ease the tightness he felt there. With his thumb he circled the tip of her sex, slowly at first, faster and faster as she pressed against him, her cries turning to whimpers as her legs went rigid with the approach of her climax.

His fingers worked feverishly now. The tide, it was coming, so powerful she felt as if she were falling through the darkness that surrounded her. She opened her eyes to see flashes of light and color, her back arching against the weight of her rising pleasure.

Thomas broke the kiss, his head moving down, down to her breast. He took her nipple in his mouth, circling it with his tongue in time to his touch between her legs. Her entire body clenched tight as a fist; and then—

Then.

A rush of blood, a thundering wave that pounded through her. Sophia let out a gasping breath, her limbs throbbing with the impact of her release. Her head fell back between her arms as her body reverberated with the fading pulse of her orgasm, her muscles loosening bit by bit in time to the slowing of her heart.

Thomas released her hands, gathering her against his chest as the throbbing subsided. She breathed in the scent of his skin, the wiry hair of his chest tickling her nose as she placed her hands inside his shoulders. His skin felt warm, firm but yielding; his heart was pounding so furiously she wondered if it had worked its way through his breastbone to lie right here beneath her palm.

Sophia curled into Thomas's embrace, finding comfort in his strength, his steadiness, after the riot that rolled through her moments before. He pressed his lips to her forehead, smoothing her long waves down the length of her back. His touch sent a shiver down her spine, and he pulled her closer, kissing her nose, her closed eyelids, and finally her mouth.

The kiss was gentle at first, a question; when she responded with rising vigor he pressed back in kind, running the length of her outline with his hand. He cupped her breast, lightly teasing her nipple with his thumb, and she felt that familiar twist of desire flame back to life low in her belly.

She couldn't, it seemed, get enough of Thomas; couldn't draw him close enough. She breathed him in, lemons, soap, that familiar spice. Her thirst for him was without depth.

He slipped his tongue between her lips. Gently he laid her on her back, rolling on top of her to rest on his elbows. His breath was warm on her cheek; she shivered at the expanse of their contact, his flesh pressed to hers from knee to nose.

Thomas dipped his head, trailing his lips along the edges of her mouth, her jaw, her neck. She closed her eyes and willed herself to remember this moment. What his mouth felt like on her skin, the heady trail of fire ignited by his lips. She'd never, not in all her life, felt something so poignant—a sensation that reverberated on both sides of her skin.

Above her he shifted, moving his leg to rest between her own. He paused, waiting for her answer. Sophia put her lips to the hollow between his earlobe and jaw; he tensed, sucking in a breath; and then with his knee he was coaxing apart her legs, settling himself between them.

Reaching back one hand at a time, he bent her legs so that he might fit more snugly against her. Again she felt his cock prodding her flesh, the tip warm and eager and far too large for its own good.

Without thinking, she reached down, curious to know how large, exactly, he was. Thomas let out a hiss as she wrapped her hand around his shaft, drawing a breath of surprise at the smooth, hard feel of him, the pulsing energy of his desire for her.

Carefully Thomas pried her fingers from his manhood, guiding her hand instead to the tip of her sex.

"Here," he said. Placing his hand over her own, he moved their fingers together over her slick flesh. Sophia gasped again at the unexpectedly intimate feel of her own body. This—this didn't feel at all shameful.

No. This felt dashedly *good*.

Thomas's hand moved down, sliding his cock down the length of her womanhood to rest just beneath where her hand worked. With his first two fingers he gently opened her, nudging himself inside her.

He kissed her mouth. She kissed him back, lips fervently working over and through each other.

She drew a breath, easing the tingle of nerves in her belly, and surrendered.

Twenty-seven

———— ✦ ————

Hope closed his eyes, breathing in the feel of her flesh, ripe and willing, against his own. His body hummed with a passion that radiated from the very center of his chest; he wanted to be gentle and fervent with her all at once; he wanted to make love to her well, thoroughly, for this would be his only chance.

She was very wet, the curls of her sex slick and soft as he brushed them with his fingers, wet and very tight. He would have to go slowly, and with great care. The idea of hurting her—

Well. He would never forgive himself.

Slowly, very slowly, he slid inside her. For a moment her fingers stilled above the joining of their bodies. She breathed in short, shallow gasps; for a moment he worried she was afraid, but then thought better of it.

Sophia wouldn't have to come to him if she were afraid. Not like this.

His kiss softened, and she moaned into his mouth. Her fingers resumed their meandering, and with his hand Hope guided himself further inside her.

Breath by breath, inch by inch he moved forward. Her flesh tightened around him as her climax approached, and he sucked in a breath for what felt like the hundredth time that night.

Dear God she felt lovely; if he wasn't careful, he'd spill his seed in the space of the next heartbeat—and lest Sophia think him some randy adolescent, he was determined to make this last as long as he could.

He couldn't see a thing, not with the fire burning so low,

but the darkness only sharpened his desire; for what he could not sense with his eyes he did with his hands, his mouth, his skin. She was *here*; she was *his*.

Sophia's kiss grew messy, and she moved her lips over his jaw to his ear and throat. He winced at the shock of pleasure that ran through him, meeting the barrier inside her at that same moment.

He felt wild with the need to possess her, to make her his, at least for this moment.

At least for tonight.

Thomas gently bucked his hips, sinking to the root. Beneath him Sophia pulled back, sucking a breath between her teeth; he sensed her flesh tightening with pain. He bent his neck so that his nose grazed hers. In the dark he could make out the gleam in her eyes, wide with uncertainty.

Where their bodies were joined he grasped her hand and together their thumbs moved over her flesh. Her eyes fluttered shut, a moan of pleasure in her throat.

He pressed his lips to hers and began to move, slowly at first, soft, languorous strokes; Sophia rose to meet his caress. She did not hesitate; her movements matched his own, her hips riding against his as their hands tangled in her sex between them.

She sighed, a happy, luxurious sound, almost a laugh, and Hope felt in the midst of his merciless desire for her a tightening in his belly and his throat. She was impossibly beautiful, this woman, and he wanted nothing more than to make her laugh. To make her happy.

Sophia bucked against him, arching her back and baring her breasts to him. He devoured one nipple, moved to the other; and then he saw stars as her sex clenched around his cock, a series of viselike pulses that drew him to the point of his own orgasm.

Thomas pulled out just in time, gritting his teeth against the strangled cry in his throat as he spilled his seed on the smooth edge of her hip. Sophia was gasping beneath him, clawing at the skin of his chest as her legs gathered around his buttocks. Her hands slid over his shoulders to his back, pulling him to her.

He let out an exhausted sigh, and together they fell into the

warm cocoon of his bed, their bodies slick with sweat. The
scent of their lovemaking hung heavy between them.

They lay tangled, his leg crossed protectively above her
own. As he struggled to catch his breath, his chest brushing
the hardened points of her nipples—*Christ*, was she trying to
kill him?—a sensation, loud, overwhelming, rushed through
him, as if a flood had broken through the levee at the very
center of his being. He closed his eyes, wrapping his arms
about Sophia so that she might help him bear it; and found
that having her so close, her head tucked into the curve of his
neck, only made the sensation pulse brighter, the flood rush
faster.

In his chest his heart felt enormous, painfully so; it was
working double as Sophia's breath tickled the skin of his
chest. Pressing a kiss into her hair, he rested his chin on the
top of her head.

He was in love with her.

And now that he had the courage to admit it to himself at
last, it was too late.

Not that he ever had a chance in the first place. This was,
after all, the same Miss Sophia Blaise who dreamed of earls
and castles and crests.

And while Thomas was in possession of none of these
things, he was, at the moment, in possession of something—
some*one*—he wanted more than he'd ever wanted the bank,
the fortune, the paintings, and the titled investors.

This desire, *this* love—he felt it in his bones.

Even if she was never his to have.

Pain sliced through him, hot, wild, leaving him breathless.
The thought of letting her go, of releasing her from his bed so
that she might end up in that of the Marquess of Withington—

He bit back the angry surge of his blood. Sophia was his
for tonight and tonight alone—that much Thomas understood. And he wasn't about to waste the precious few hours
they had together burning with jealousy.

And so he quietly gathered her to him, trailing his lips
along her forehead. He pulled back the coverlet, wiggling
both their bodies beneath its warmth. His pain was matched
only by the contentment of curling his body around hers, their
limbs coiled in sheets damp from their exertions.

The contentment of knowing, though they spoke not a word, that Sophia loved him in turn.

T homas leapt from the bed at the pounding on his door. Light, gray and watery, filled the room; it was almost dawn. He started, as if seeing the contents of his bedchamber for the first time. In the complete blackness of the disappearing night Sophia had taken captive of his every sense; nothing but her sighs, her rising body, and the beating of her heart had filled this room.

There were her clothes, puddled on the rug; a stray silk stocking hung from the back of a nearby chair. His breeches and shirt were scattered in a far off corner.

Well, then. The maids were in for a treat when they made their rounds later that morning.

Beside Thomas, Sophia bolted upright in bed, the sheets falling from her bare chest to reveal her breasts.

Hope swallowed. They were just as lovely, perhaps even more so, than he'd imagined last night in the dark. Her long, wavy hair was loose about her shoulders, tousled just enough to indicate he'd made quite thorough love to her.

He swallowed again at the familiar tightening between his legs.

"Come back later," he called, watching Sophia's cheeks flush pink as she covered herself with the sheet. "I'm afraid I'm indisposed at the moment."

Daltrey's voice was heavy. "I am sorry to wake you, sir, but I've just received news I believe you and Mi—*you* might want to hear straightaway."

Hope ran a hand through his hair with a groan. "All right, give me a moment."

He put his hands on the bed and leaned forward, grazing her nose with the tip of his own.

There was too much and yet nothing at all to say. Sophia had come to purge them both of the affection they bore one another by indulging it wholly, passionately; to slake her thirst by drowning in him for one night, and one night only. One night to forget the terrors that tightened the noose around each of their necks, the worries that bound them to fortunes and futures they did not choose.

And now that the night was past, Sophia would go back to her life, and her marquess; and Thomas to his bank and the missing French Blue and the memory of a family long gone; they would go back without regret.

Or so was the intention.

Before he could stop himself, Hope dipped his head and pressed his lips to hers, taking her bottom lip between his teeth. Good God she was delicious. Perhaps they had time for one more—

"Mr. Hope!"

Hope dropped his head and groaned. "I am very sorry," he said, meeting her eyes. He saw in them his own confusion; sadness and desire clouding the irises, turning them a darker shade of green. Christ, how he wanted to hold her face in his hand and kiss her until it was only desire he saw in her eyes. Desire for him and no one else.

Sophia slid under the sheets, pulling them over her head. Shrugging into a robe, Hope stalked to the door and wrenched it open.

"Well?"

Daltrey stood on his toes, peering for a moment over Hope's shoulder. Hope pulled the door shut behind him with a look of consternation. "Out with it, Daltrey. I'd like to get back to bed."

The butler cleared his throat, proffering a scrap of paper in his gloved hand. "It's the Lady Violet, sir. She's been shot in a duel."

Duchess Street

Hope stretched out his legs before the fire, the exquisite heat helping to calm the dull chill of horror, of rage and of sadness, that plagued him all day and into the night.

Lady Violet had not been dueling herself, though it wouldn't have surprised Hope if she had. Feisty, that one, with a mouth on her that would make a sailor weep. What a breath of fresh air she'd been after all the dour dowagers and witless heiresses he'd encountered over the years; Hope had liked her straightaway, even more so after he discovered her passion for brown liquor rivaled his own.

No, it was the Earl of Harclay and Mr. Lake who'd exchanged insults, and then bullets, that morning. Violet had the misfortune of trying to end such foolishness at the very moment both parties discharged their Manton dueling pistols. Apparently it was Harclay's bullet that lodged between her ribs, though the details on this were vague at best.

Sophia had burst into tears when she'd heard the news. They'd arrived at her house just as Violet's body was being brought in by the surgeon; already she was unconscious, her wound vicious-looking and black with blood.

His belly clenched at the memory of it. Though the surgeon reassured Sophia her cousin would be fine, just fine, his face was grim. Even Lady Blaise in the midst of her hysterics knew better than to believe him. Violet's condition was serious.

Hope had resisted the urge to throttle Lake, bloody idiot, then and there. He'd crossed the wrong man this time; Harclay was one of the few who could go toe to toe with Lake and best him at his own game. Lake had, after all, given up the earl to those beastly acrobats, which led to that business of Lady Violet being kidnapped; the earl couldn't have been pleased about that.

Then, of course, there was Lake's odd relationship with Lady Caroline, the Dowager Countess of Berry and the earl's sister, to consider.

Really, just what the devil was Lake up to? He had some explaining to do.

And so Hope waited in his study for Lake to appear through a window, or perhaps through the chimney this time; he would know Hope wanted to see him.

He did not have to wait long. As the clock on the mantel struck eleven o'clock, Lake silently moved from the darkness into the half-moon of light put off by the fire.

For a long moment Hope stared him down. His face was drawn, his skin pale; dark circles ringed his eyes, red from lack of sleep. While he longed to throttle the man, yes, Hope felt pity for him, too. He was selfless, Lake, and savagely loyal; but even such a creature as he had his weak moments, his bouts of extreme and utter stupidity.

He *was* a man, after all.

And this was one such bout.

"What happened?" Hope said quietly.

Lake sank into the chair opposite Hope's. He put his elbows on his knees and hung his head. "I went to visit Lady Caroline last night at her brother's house. It was foolish of me to have been there, but I will not say it was a mistake. I was climbing down from her window—"

"Really, your aversion to *front doors* borders on the insane."

"And the earl, he and Lady Violet, they were—well, you know. They were leaving the house just as I was; an hour or two before dawn. We met in the drive. He was insulted I would dare visit his sister, and she just out of mourning. He was *especially* insulted that Lady Violet was kidnapped after I sold him out to the acrobats."

"And so he challenged you to a duel. Why didn't you refuse him?"

Lake shook his head and scoffed. "I may not play the part, old friend, but I am the son of a baron. I cannot refuse a challenge when my honor is at stake."

"Honor?" Hope arched a brow. "You were climbing through a widow's window in the middle of the night. Somehow I doubt you and the dowager countess spent the wee hours of the morning brushing up on the Bible."

The sides of Lake's mouth twitched. "It isn't what you think. Well, it *is*, but Caroline and I, we—"

"Unless the two of you are secretly married, whatever you are or aren't doing is an insult to her honor as well as her brother's."

Above the ball of his enormous shoulder, Lake met Hope's eyes.

Hope sank further into his chair. "Oh God. You are secretly married, aren't you? But how—"

"That's beside the point."

"I hardly think you being secretly married to a *countess* is beside the point."

Lake pushed himself upright with a groan, wincing as he twisted his arms about his torso. "I'm getting too old for this dueling nonsense."

"Your *nonsense* has placed us further away from the French Blue than ever. I hardly think the earl will be inclined to hand over the jewel after shooting his—his—bah! After shooting Lady Violet in the ribs."

Lake groaned again. "He doesn't have it. Not anymore."

Hope pitched forward in his chair. "Doesn't have it? The French Blue? Christ above, Lake, what the devil do you mean by that?"

"That's an awful lot of religion in one sentence."

"I swear to God, I'll—"

"All right, all right." Lake held up his hands in surrender. "Lady Caroline knew where her brother was hiding the diamond."

Hope nearly choked. "But how? He could be hiding it anywhere!"

"Says when he was younger he used to hide all his naughty bits in a drawer with his socks. As a boy he'd keep rocks and bugs and even a pigeon in that drawer of his to safeguard them from his governess. When he got older the bits were less innocent, of course—a well-thumbed copy of *Fanny Hill*, a few fashion plates of girls without the fashion—but it was always the same. He hid his secrets in that drawer."

"My God." Hope ran a hand through his hair. "All this time, and that damned diamond was in his *sock drawer.*"

"Last night Caroline took me to his dressing room, and together we rummaged through his socks. She swore we'd find it."

"But it wasn't there."

"Exactly, it wasn't there. At first Caroline and I were perplexed; she swore there was nowhere else he'd keep the jewel. You mustn't forget Harclay stole a fifty-carat diamond in the midst of the season's most well attended ball for the mere thrill of it. He could care less about money. Makes sense a careless daredevil like him would keep his prize in his sock drawer."

"But the diamond *wasn't there.*"

Lake held up a finger. "Right. And Caroline was convinced it wouldn't be anywhere else, so I ran through the possibilities. He came to you after the kidnapping, didn't he, to ask for money?"

"Yes." Hope furrowed his brow. His eyes went wide as

understanding, swift and startling, smacked him square in the forehead. "The acrobats must've blackmailed him. Asked him for more money. But after I'd frozen his accounts, he didn't have access to nary a penny. So he traded the diamond for Violet's safety. Christ!"

"I don't believe Jesus has anything to do with it, but yes, I've every reason to believe Harclay traded away the diamond."

Hope fell back in his chair. "Christ," he repeated. "That means we're back to where we started, doesn't it? The diamond could be anywhere by now. Anywhere. This is bad news, Lake, very bad news indeed. If only I had known!—well. Too late for that. But I don't know how much longer Hope and Company can hold out. I need a good headline, Lake. I need good news so the bank might be saved. We've got to find the French Blue."

"I know," Lake said quietly. A vein jumped in his temple. "You aren't the only one with something to lose, old man. The French have grown impatient. They know something is not right; they are demanding the diamond, and soon, or they will go elsewhere in their search. So yes. We *must* find the French Blue. I am doing everything in my power, Hope, to set it all to rights."

Hope let the back of his head fall against his chair and stared at the ceiling. "Just when I thought it couldn't get any worse. Let us not forget our friend Cassin."

Lake scoffed. "At this point I'm tempted to let him kill us so that we might be put out of our misery."

"Ha! Wishful thinking."

"Wishful indeed."

For several moments they sat in silence. Hope contemplated the shadows on the ceiling, flickering in time to the beat of the fire. He was surprised he was possessed of enough energy to sense the sinking in his belly so keenly.

"Sophia," Lake said. "How is she?"

Hope cast him a sideways glance. "Forbidden fruit. Your words, not mine."

"Perhaps I've changed my tune. Forbidden fruit is, after all, the best kind."

Twenty-eight

Two weeks later
Grosvenor Square

Hope fingered the limp daffodils in the cut glass vase by the library window. They were a gift from the Marquess of Withington; Hope remembered him sweeping awkwardly into the house some days ago, flowers tucked under his arm. He'd jerked to his knee like a knight-errant and gravely offered them to Sophia. Hope hadn't even tried to keep from rolling his eyes. They were a hell of a way from Camelot, and he had no patience for King Arthur or his silly pantomime of courtly love.

Hope ran his thumb along the inside of a yellowing stem and sighed. Born and raised in the city made famous by its ruinous fervor for tulips, Hope was well versed in the language of flowers. The daffodils were an interesting choice; popularly known to embody rebirth, new beginnings, they were also a symbol of unrequited love.

Which meaning had the marquess meant to convey? By all accounts Sophia returned Withington's favor; when the fashionable half of London wasn't discussing the theft of the French Blue, it was whispering behind gilded fans and half-closed doors about the marquess's imminent proposal. *Why her?* they wondered. And: *What a fool he is, to pick her when he could have any other!*

Hope, of course, begged to differ.

Without thinking he snapped the sagging flower from its

wilted stem with his thumbnail. Its petals loosened into his palm, releasing an earthy scent, water and green and air.

Sophia's scent.

He gathered the petals into a fist, inhaling deeply, before releasing them onto the windowsill. The afternoon light was waning; she would be down soon, and he wanted to be ready.

Settling into a settee by the empty fireplace, he tucked the bottle of port into his coat and waited for what felt like an eternity. He listened to the sounds of the house, the crunch of gravel as vehicles passed below the open window. Summer had arrived at long last; and while the air was warm, Hope had been plagued by a chill these past days. The port—yes, that would help.

On the back wall the clock sprang into action, six strokes before it fell silent again. His heart skipped a beat at the sound of footsteps on the stair. He sat up, smoothing the dark kerseymere of his breeches.

He heard the whisper of her skirts at the threshold, followed by the click of the door as she closed it behind her. She sighed, a low, defeated sound; her steps were light on the carpet.

Blood thrumming, Hope shot to his feet and turned to face her.

Sophia started, her hazel eyes blinking wide in surprise. "Mr. Hope!"

Ah, that stung. The banker's name on her lips.

"Miss Blaise." He fell into a bow.

"I did not know you were here. Violet received your letters; when she is well enough she would like to thank you for your kindness in person."

Hope rose, meeting her eyes. The knot in his belly tightened. Though her eyes were red and wet, the sleeves of her print-cotton gown pulled up about her elbows, she looked beautiful. The light from the window set fire to the wisps of dark hair that framed her face; her lips were parted just enough to reveal the rosy-pink forbidden flesh of her mouth.

Nymph. He remembered her dressed in that diaphanous gown the night of the ball, the peek of a milky-white thigh through the fabric.

Hope cleared his throat. "I sent them as soon as I received word she'd woken. I cannot imagine your relief at knowing the Lady Violet would." He searched for the right words. "Would be all right."

"Yes." She looked down at her clasped hands and scoffed. "I knew she'd come back to us, if only to return the earl's favor and shoot *him* in the ribs. Though I must give credit where credit is due. Harclay didn't leave her side, not even to change clothes. At last my mother, bless her, convinced him to bathe. He left only after Violet sent him away."

Hope raised a brow. "Duel notwithstanding, I thought they were getting along rather swimmingly, the earl and Violet."

"Apparently not. The diamond is still missing; our fortunes continue to fall. Though Violet hasn't slept or ate since he left." Sophia looked up, a tight smile on her lips. "But now you have come to call. I usually take port at this hour, though I'm afraid our supplies are rather low, what with the earl having plundered the cellar these past weeks. That man has a *deuced* thirst."

Hope untangled the bottle from his jacket and held it aloft. "I thought that might be the case, so I brought this. Might I interest you in a nip?"

Sophia met his eyes. "How did you know?" she said.

Because I know you.

"Because I've been keeping my own vigil. Over Violet." He set the bottle on a round table near the far window and went to work with a corkscrew he pulled from his waistcoat pocket. "Over you."

"Over me?" she scoffed.

"Yes," he replied smoothly, though his heart beat a loud and unrelenting rhythm in his chest. "I pass your house every evening on my way home from the bank. These windows, they face the street. I see you standing there by the window, glass in hand. Always at six o'clock."

"Well." Sophia swallowed and took the tiny crystal coupe he offered her. "I cannot say if I am more flattered or terrified that you know the schedule of our days here. But I am willing to give you the benefit of the doubt."

"How kind of you."

She smiled. "I do try, Soph—Miss Blaise."

Hope looked into her eyes as he held his coupe out before him. "To Lady Violet, that she may be recovered. I've missed her, you know."

Sophia touched her coupe to his and together they downed the port. Hope's eyes nearly rolled to the back of his head with pleasure at the familiar burn in his throat. It helped loosen the tightness there; loosen the tangle of his thoughts.

"I've missed *you*." His voice was low, more intimate than he'd intended. But there it was: the truth.

Sophia's eyes flashed with uncertainty. After a beat she held out her coupe. "Another, if it please you."

"It would please me very much." Hope went to the table and refilled their glasses to the brim. He turned and motioned to the sill by the open window. "Please, let's sit."

Sophia sidled onto the ledge, pushing aside the gauzy curtain as it billowed in the breeze. She took the coupe from him, their fingers brushing, and stared down at it.

Hope lifted his knee onto the sill and leaned into it. An errant curl swirled about her forehead, her skin glistening in the yellow light of the dying sun. He reached out, intent to brush back the curl, but stopped himself.

"Sophia," he said.

She met his gaze; her eyes were wet. "Please, Thomas . . ."

"It was your wish that we not go on as we had. After the night in my room I understood what you wanted. *Why* you wanted it. And I had every intention of respecting that, Sophia, I did. I had told myself it was better for the both of us. You have your season, and your match to which to see; and I of course have the bank and that bloody diamond. I am sorry to break the vow we took that night—the vow that we should leave everything we felt in that bed, in those hours. But despite my best efforts I cannot leave it there."

"Thomas, you cannot . . . *we* cannot . . ."

Thomas looked out the window, looked back at Sophia. She bit her bottom lip to still its trembling.

He ran a hand through his hair and sighed. The breeze felt cool on his skin, suddenly warm on account of the workings of his heart.

"I only mean to ask how you have been, Sophia."

Sophia turned her head to look out the window, bearing the soft flesh of her throat. Thomas watched the jump of her pulse there; it matched his own. It took his every effort not to cradle her neck in his palm, not to hook his hand along her jaw and ear, to tangle his fingers in her hair.

"I am well." Again that tight smile. "Now that Violet is back, the house is less lonely, and the weather, it's been lovely."

"After our meeting. After that night. I . . . I didn't hurt you, did I?"

She turned and met his eyes. For a beat his words hung between them.

"No, Thomas. You didn't hurt me. I confess," here her cheeks burned pink, "I was a bit sore the next day. Hardly mattered, what with Violet bleeding from her chest."

"No." The word came suddenly, more vicious than he intended. "It matters to me. I wanted to make you feel as well pleasured as you made *me* feel that night. I wanted you to have everything you came for and more." *I wanted to be your first, your last, your only.*

Again she looked down at her glass, still full, and let out a sound somewhere between a scoff and a sob. "If you have any doubts as to your . . . your *pleasuring* that night, Thomas, allow me to put them to rest. Well pleasured. Well touched. Well lov—it was all done well. Better than that."

He let out a sigh of relief. "Good."

"I haven't had the chance to thank you for what you did. You didn't have to see me that night. I know what I asked was rather . . . unconventional. Not to say unexpected." She raised her glass and looked at him. "Thank you, Thomas."

His pulse leapt. As he pressed his glass to hers he felt the familiar tug between their bodies, that irresistible pull that moved in the center of his being.

"Thank *you*, Sophia, for blessing me with your friendship. I will not forget that kindness."

She smiled. Her eyes welled but she did not weep. "I am not leaving for the moon, you know. We might still be friends after all this," she waved her hand, "is over."

"Yes." He swallowed. The sun was waning now; evening had set in. The light reflecting off Sophia's skin burned gold to yellow to blue.

"And everything else." His eyes flicked to her midsection,

hidden beneath the tiny pleats of her gown. "It is well? I took the appropriate precaution, of course, but no plan is foolproof."

Sophia's cheeks went from pink to red. "Yes, all is well."

"You're sure of it? It's early yet."

"Yes, Mr. Hope, I'm sure of it. Yesterday I . . . well. Needless to say I received all the proof I needed, praise God."

Hope tipped back his coupe. "Yes, yes indeed. Praise God."

The breeze tickled a loose curl at his temple. He brushed it back. Looking at Sophia, her lips stained red from the port, a swift pulse of desire curled through him. Desire for her body, desire to *possess* her.

For a moment he selfishly wished all *wasn't* well. That in the darkness that night, as he'd joined his flesh to hers, they'd created something bigger than themselves. Miss Sophia Blaise, carrying his child. He knew they'd make a beautiful baby; her dark hair, her shapely lips, his eyes, perhaps, his long fingers and unruly curls. With his child in her belly, Sophia would be *his* and his alone. He'd have an excuse to take her under his protection, and give her his name.

Mrs. Sophia Hope.

He ached for it to be true. For her to confess, so that he might have an excuse to whisk her away to the altar and then, with any luck, to Italy for an extended honeymoon. Or would she like Greece better? She *did* have a soft spot for pirates, so perhaps Morocco was the ticket . . .

Impulsively he reached for her, taking her face in his hand. In the dying light of the window, something glinted at her breast. He looked closer to see a thin gold chain, from which hung a ring bearing a small but exquisite yellow diamond in the shape of a heart.

Which was ironic, as at that moment Hope's own heart seemed to lose its shape as it exploded in his chest. He felt bits of bloody flesh settle on the shelf of his ribs, his breath dying in his lugs.

Sophia's gaze flicked from the diamond to his eyes, her features loosening as if they might collapse.

"I believe congratulations are in order," Hope said, trying his damnedest to keep from choking on the words. "The Marquess of Withington is a lucky man. A good man. When did the happy event occur?"

Sophia drew back, taking the ring between her thumb and forefinger and pulling it across the length of the chain. "He proposed just this morning. I . . . I confess I did not know what to say. He was so lovely, and kind . . ." She looked away, her throat working as her eyes fluttered shut.

"Anyway," she shook her head, "he insisted I keep the ring while I considered his offer."

"How very chivalrous of him." Hope's gaze wandered to the sagging dandelions across the room. Unrequited love—bah! Nothing more than wishful thinking. What lady in her right mind wouldn't love ten thousand a year and a castle in the country?

He swallowed what was left of his port. "When you do say yes, the papers will be aflutter with the news. Perhaps my old friends won't run another headline about the French Blue for a day or two. God knows I could use the break."

"*If* I say yes."

"*When* you say yes. Your family stands to lose as much as I do if we don't find that blasted diamond and prove to my rather unadoring public that I can indeed safeguard the bank's assets. Your marriage to the marquess may be your family's only hope."

Sophia threw back her port with a wince. The sadness in her eyes evaporated, replaced by a gleaming mischief. "'My family's only hope'—why, that's awfully grim stuff. You've been reading Shakespeare again, haven't you?"

Hope stiffened. "Perhaps."

"The tragedies? I bet you've been penning a poem or two as well. Something about that forbidden fruit you and Lake are always talking about."

Hope, suddenly warm, tugged at his collar and cleared his throat. "As you can imagine, the tragedies *have* suited my mood these past weeks. But what with the bank so far under water, I've hardly had time to pen poetry. *Poetry.* Bah! I gave that up long ago."

Even Hope wasn't convinced by his denial. Judging from Sophia's arched brow, she wasn't, either; she was grinning, the pallor of her sadness disappearing, her old colors—trouble, beauty, earnestness—rising in its place.

"I'd like to read it," she said softly. "You aren't the only

one to have visited the tragedies so recently. My dearest
mama has been nothing short of a nervous wreck and, as you
can see, her antics have driven me to drink. I've found particular solace in the sufferings of Tybalt."

"Ah, yes. Jolly fun fellow, that Tybalt, if not a bit . . . oh, I
think bloodthirsty's the right word. *Italians*." Hope shook his
head. "Never fear, Miss Blaise, the murderous rage shall pass
in a few weeks' time. You must refrain from using any sharp
objects in the interim, letter openers and the like, lest your
dearest mama end up like poor Mercutio."

Sophia laughed, the kind of laugh that made the skin at the
edges of her eyes crease with pleasure. "And *we* must take
care, lest God smite us for plotting my mother's demise."

"Bah! God hath smote us already. Smite away, I say. Smite
away."

For several heartbeats, Hope watched as Sophia's shoulders moved in time to her laughter. He knew without asking it
was the first time she'd laughed in weeks, since Violet's accident that terrible morning at Farrow Field. He saw the tension
in her neck relax, the sinews of her sloping shoulders loosen
with her delight; her surrender, if only for a moment, to him.

He remembered with startling clarity the feel of those
muscles and sinews beneath his hands as he worked his way
across every inch of her body, the sensation of her sinking
beneath him into the warm softness of his feather bed. How
sweet it had been then, her surrender; how he'd reveled in it,
worshipped it, while drowning in his own.

A breeze tickled his skin; the light from the window was
softening now, burning the silken strands of Sophia's hair a
fiery white. She caught him watching her; their eyes met for a
long moment. She was so beautiful it made his belly hurt; he
was lost in her gleaming skin and wild hair and almond-
shaped eyes.

And then they were leaning toward each other, her lips
parted just enough for Thomas to make out the white gleam
of her pearlescent teeth. Her scent invaded his every sense,
clean air with a hint of soap, his eyes fluttering shut as he
inhaled whatever parts of her he could. He couldn't, they
shouldn't, but . . .

They both jumped back at the sudden racket at the door.

Sophia managed to spill what was left of her port on her cotton dress, a very unladylike curse escaping the mouth he'd been about to kiss as she brushed at the stain with the back of her hand.

"Hello?" came Violet's voice, thin and tired. She was at the door in the arms of a rather diminutive footman, who sputtered and panted as he wove his way into the room beneath the weight of his burden. "Is that port I see on your dress, cousin? Damn you both, why didn't you wait for me?"

"Forgive me, Lady Violet, I was about to take my leave . . ."

". . . was in the library, looking for a book . . . Shakespeare, you know the one, star-cross'd . . ."

"I didn't know you'd be down . . . I was just visiting, er, the house . . ."

". . . dreadful headache after listening to Mama complain for an hour about the roads . . . terrible this time of year . . ."

Gasping with pain, Violet unwrapped her arms from about the poor footman's neck as he settled her on the nearby settee. She surveyed Hope and Sophia, her eyes narrowed with suspicion or pain, he couldn't quite tell.

"You're up to something," she said. "What is it?"

Hope cleared his throat, as if to speak, but Sophia interjected before he could begin.

"Mr. Hope was calling to ensure you received all the letters he'd sent you. He heard you had woken and was merely concerned for your well-being. Ah, the letters, there they are!"

The footman, poor chap, panted as he bent down to place a neat stack of correspondence on Violet's lap. Lady Violet blanched a whiter shade of—well, white as she looked down at the pile.

Mr. Hope took that as his cue to leave. "Miss Blaise," he bowed to Sophia, "I do so hope you enjoy the gift. Remember what I said about sharp objects. Good evening. Lady Violet."

He stalked from the room, Violet clutching the back of the settee as she turned to watch him go. "Sharp objects?" he heard her say. "What the devil does he mean by that? Sophia!"

Hope took his hat and gloves from the footman and charged through the front door, the blood marching in his ears so loudly he did not notice the Earl of Harclay bounding up the steps until it was too late.

They ran headfirst into one another, the earl drawing back as Hope muttered his apologies.

"Hope! Just the man I was . . . er . . . hoping to see! Do you have a moment, old man?"

Hope cleared his throat for what felt like the hundredth time and pulled at the wrists of his gloves. He had no patience for the earl this afternoon; he was as liable to ram his fist into Harclay's face as he was to give him a moment.

"I'm afraid not, my lord."

"Trust me." Harclay slung an arm about Hope's shoulder and pulled him close. "You're going to want to hear this news."

Hope went stiff, arching a brow. "News?"

"I've found it!" the earl whispered. "The French Blue. I've found it. Not only that—I've devised a plan, rather ingenious in my humble estimation, to have it back in your pocket by week's end."

Twenty-nine

—◆—

S ophia had every intention of keeping her distance from
Thomas. No matter her dreams of him at night, the delicious wanderings of her thoughts by day; no matter the ache
in her heart or the heavy weight of the diamond ring about her
neck. Sophia swore to focus her affections, and her thoughts,
on the Marquess of Withington, and to do so required removing Mr. Hope from her heart and her head.

With the French Blue lost, the family's fortune dwindled;
her uncle was in debt to the tune of thousands of pounds. First
they lost their credit with the grocer, the fishmonger, the shops
on Bond Street. Next, they would lose the house.

Guillaume Cassin was still at large. The threat of expo-
sure, and subsequent ruin, was very real indeed.

If ever there was an opportune time in which to agree to
an opportune offer of marriage, this would certainly be it.

Sophia had every intention of doing right by her family,
she did. But fate, in the form of an unexpected visit from that
scalawag Earl of Harclay, had other plans.

He'd found the diamond, or so he claimed. And his scheme
to get it back—well, it was nothing short of absurd, as it
involved multiple steps, multiple disguises, and crimes that
were punishable by medieval sorts of death. Like his plan, the
earl was either cracked or utterly brilliant; Sophia could not
yet say which it would be.

"I was at White's, a few evenings ago," Harclay panted. He
paced before the grate in the drawing room, Cousin Violet
laid out upon the sofa, Sophia perched at her feet.

"As I was drinking myself into a stupor I happened to

overhear King Louis—yes, *that* King Louis, the one who's been living so high on the hog in exile, here in England—and his brother the Comte d'Artois discussing payment for *le bleu de France*. Seems we're not the only ones on the hunt for the diamond."

Of course Sophia knew of the French royals; they were in the papers often enough, tales of their enormous stipends and even more enormous appetites providing endless fodder for London's gossips. Brothers to the fallen Louis XVI, they lived in exile in the hopes that the new King Louis—he styled himself Louis XVIII—might one day reclaim the throne of France.

Seeing as Napoleon had no intention of ceding said throne; seeing as Louis and Artois were so fat they would sink any ship that attempted to bear them across the Channel; well, such ambitions were laughable at best.

Harclay's news did little to further their cause.

"They said a man by the name of Daniel Eliason, a jewel merchant, is in possession of the French Blue. This week they are to meet on Eliason's ship in the Docklands, and pay him thirty thousand pounds for the jewel."

Sophia swallowed, let out a breath.

"I propose—hear me out, before you object—I propose we lure the king into our possession, and force him to take us to his brother, who at this very moment is working to procure a loan for the thirty thousand. We take the money, have the royals lead us to Eliason, and—*Huzzah!*—buy the diamond for ourselves." He caught Sophia's eye and had the grace to flush pink. "For Mr. Hope, I mean. Of course the French Blue belongs to him."

Sophia furrowed her brow. "How do we set the plot in motion, then? What bait do we have to lure the king to our cause?"

"Ah!" Here the earl and Cousin Violet exchanged a knowing glance. "It's quite simple. The king likes whores. Begging your pardon, Miss Blaise, no other way to say it. I propose we—all of us, you and Hope and that one-eyed monster of his—lure old King Louis to my house under the premise it is a palace of pleasure or some such nonsense. Once he's inside, we get him drunk, very drunk, or . . . yes, or we give him a goodly dose of laudanum, just enough to make him docile.

Then he leads us to his brother, the money, and, at last, the diamond."

Sophia looked from the Earl of Harclay to Violet and back again.

Dear God, they were serious.

This senseless, dangerous, convoluted plot—they meant to put it in play.

But the plot *did* involve Mr. Hope; and before her better sense took hold, Sophia blurted, "I'm in! Count me in. Which part shall I take?"

Several days later
The Earl of Harclay's Residence
Brook Street, Hanover Square

A courtesan, as it turned out; Sophia was one of many half-naked goddesses inhabiting Aphrodite's Temple, a labyrinthine set that transformed the Earl of Harclay's well-appointed drawing room into a house of ill repute, complete with swaths of red satin and nude statues of Greek immortals in suggestive poses.

All was going to plan—Harclay and Cousin Violet managed to lure the king into the Temple, and His Highness King Louis XVIII appeared to be enjoying himself most thoroughly in his chair beside the earl—until Harclay, having sipped from a balloon of brandy proffered moments before by Sophia, suddenly pitched forward.

His eyes welled; his face matched the swaths of satin above his head.

Sophia looked down at the empty tray she held in her hands, and looked back up at the king. He appeared healthy as an ox, if not a bit perplexed by Harclay's sudden, violent movements.

She'd poisoned the wrong man.

She'd poisoned Harclay.

Across the room, Sophia met eyes with Mr. Hope, who up until that moment had been waiting in the wings. Her belly sinking, she watched his face unfurl with understanding, and then he was dashing forward, falling to his knees beside Mr. Lake as Avery, the earl's butler, held his master's head in his hands.

Sophia placed the tray on the edge of the stage and lurched toward the small knot of men, throat thick with tears. Violet was calling for a doctor; Lake, more menacing than ever in his gravity, called for mustard seed and water.

The earl's face was now a frightening shade of blue. His body was limp, devoid of any movement. Mr. Hope was shouting now, binding King Louis' hands and feet; the room pulsed into action around her.

Dear God. She'd *poisoned* the *earl.* And not just any earl. Violet's earl, the earl that was to lead them to the diamond, to sanity and salvation. What if he never woke? What if she'd killed him, killed him with her carelessness?

Sophia checked, and checked again, that the balloon with the chipped foot—the poisoned brandy—would go to His Highness King Louis. But then she'd caught Mr. Hope watching her, his blue eyes following her every movement, lingering on her every curve.

So much for keeping her distance. Such a thing wasn't possible, not when he looked at her like that; not when she felt her heart rising beneath his gaze, her heart and blood and the longing that plagued her day and night.

Sophia remembered her hands shaking as she offered the balloons to Harclay and Louis, her thoughts a riotous tangle. It was entirely possible she offered the wrong drink to the wrong man.

Her vision blurred by tears, she stood over Mr. Lake as he held a potion to Harclay's lips. The earl drank it in short, hot sputters; but time and time again his eyes fluttered shut.

He was dying.

Panic rose in her throat. Sophia swallowed it, willing herself to remain calm. She'd written scandalous memoirs, deceived a princess, dueled with sinister Frenchmen.

Surely she could bring a man back to life.

Sophia elbowed Lake aside and sank to her knees. "Allow me."

She wound up her arm and, squeezing shut her eyes, brought down her hand, hard, on Harclay's cheek.

Violet was crying out, holding the earl's head in her lap.

Sophia watched as his lips broke into a small smile; and then he was opening his eyes and turning over and emptying the contents of his stomach onto Violet's costume.

"I'm sorry," he sputtered, wiping his lips, "for ruining your toga."

An audible sigh of relief coursed through the room.

Sophia sat back on her haunches. "I'm so very sorry. I don't know how it happened—"

With a wince, William drew himself up. "Think nothing of it, Sophia. Just promise me you'll never again raise your hand to another man—you seem to enjoy it a tad too much. Bloody hurt, too."

Thank God he wasn't dead. Thank God. Through her tears she felt herself smile.

"I promise."

There was a tickle at the back of her neck. Sophia looked up to see Mr. Hope looming above her, his fingers moving to grasp her arm. Wordlessly he lifted her to her feet, branding her with the heat of his touch, his palm to her bare skin.

They stood very close. His eyes—oh, those *eyes*— searched her face. She grew warm beneath his scrutiny; when she tried to look away he pulled her closer, his fingers pressing into the flesh of her arm.

"Are you all right?" His voice was low, barely above a whisper.

"Yes." Sophia glanced across the room. The earl stumbled; Mr. Lake caught him just before he fell face-first to the floor. "Though I cannot say the same for his lordship. Poor Harclay."

"An accident." Hope squeezed her arm. "Nothing Lake and a little mustard seed couldn't fix."

"But I almost killed him! What if he's—what if he's crippled forever?"

"Darling." Sophia tried to ignore the thrill that sparked in her chest at his endearment. "If brandy could cripple a man, I daresay I'd be gnarled and stooped as an apple tree. That thieving rogue will recover, make no mistake. In the meantime, we must see to tonight's adventure."

Sophia swallowed, squaring her shoulders. Their last adventure; one last wild night. "Yes. Yes, you're right."

"Excellent." Hope smiled. He released her arm, running

his palm over her bare shoulder. "Here, let me get your shawl. It'll be chilly by the river."

She tried not to shiver at his touch. She didn't want to feel like this, not now, not when the fate of her family, of Hope and the bank, hung in the balance.

She did not want to feel this desire for him pulse through her being with every heartbeat, every breath, more potent than ever.

She did not want to feel like this.

But then she met his eyes as she ducked into the frayed cashmere shawl he held open for her. He was looking at her the way girls dreamed of being looked at; adoringly, intently, his eyes at once soft with affection, hard with desire.

No matter what she wanted, what was good and what was proper, there was no helping the way Thomas made Sophia feel.

The gentlemen, who, in their attempts to push King Louis through the doorway, had gotten him stuck, were calling for Thomas's aid; Cousin Violet was twittering about time, they didn't have much time now.

Hope reached for Sophia's hand, took it in his own. By now the gesture was familiar, but that familiarity was thrilling in its own way. It made her feel confident, and warm, as if she might count on his presence at her side no matter tonight's events. As if he would protect her no matter what happened.

He turned and made for the king, who was howling some French obscenity or another. For a moment Sophia stood, watching the roll of Hope's shoulders through the tunic of his Achilles costume.

"Sophia! Sophia," Violet snapped. "Oh, come, enough of this wallowing in self-pity. Harclay's alive, and with any luck he'll stay that way. We've got to go, or we'll miss our rendezvous with Artois!"

Sophia blinked, breaking the spell, and followed her cousin out of the room.

T heir party piled into two hackneys. With a bit of cajoling, King Louis was at last persuaded to lead them to his brother, the Comte d'Artois, who waited like a sitting duck in his carriage on King Street, a thirty-thousand-pound note tucked into his tasseled pocket.

Sophia watched the proceedings in mute fascination. At gunpoint, the king and Artois agreed to accompany Hope's motley crew to the Docklands, where Mr. Daniel Eliason, that shadowy jeweler, awaited their arrival, the French Blue in the strongbox aboard his ship.

Thomas sat across from her as the hackney rumbled through the darkened streets toward the Docklands. Outside, the night was black, complete; this side of town had no gas lamps of which to speak, and the thoroughfares were narrow and mean, bordered on either side by shuttered tenements.

Sophia swallowed, and kept her gaze studiously focused on her lap. Not only was she terrified of what was to come— this adventure, it was dangerous, it was stupid, and it would likely get them all killed—she feared meeting Thomas's eyes. She couldn't bear to see him look at her like that again. Not when she would leave him behind after tonight. Leave him behind, and all that he had made her feel, all that she had seen and known at his side.

At last the hackney creaked to a stop. The gentlemen dismounted first. Hope held out his hand, guiding Sophia out of the vehicle. Her fingers shook in the warmth of his palm; he tucked her arm into the crook of his elbow and held her close against him.

She did not protest.

The stench of the Docklands reached out to them in the humid silence. Now that summer had at last arrived the River Thames was as fragrant as ever; Sophia pressed her nose into her elbow and tried not to breathe too deeply.

So this is where it's all going to end, she thought. This is where we shall find our salvation, mine and Violet's, England's and Mr. Hope's. This is where he shall take back what is his, and restore his good name.

His body felt warm against hers as they made their way to the hackney parked in front of their own. The king and Artois were leaning against the vehicle, panting in unison like two enormous, slobbering bulldogs. Mr. Lake, menacing as ever, was pointing a pistol at the royals.

She felt Hope hesitate; he reluctantly released her from his grasp, and with his free hand he adjusted the front of his breeches, much as he'd done that night in his study at Hope & Co.

With a wince, Lord Harclay drew to his full height before King Louis and the *comte*. "You know where this man Daniel Eliason keeps his ship?"

Artois sniffed, turning up his nose. Though he was hopelessly shorter than his lordship the earl, he would not, it appeared, be looked down upon.

When neither Artois nor his brother responded, Harclay waved the thirty-thousand-pound note before them, the paper flapping in a sour breeze.

"I've already got your money. Don't make me take your manhood, too. Do you *know* where this man *Eliason* keeps his ship?"

Artois huffed. "*Oui.*"

"And you will get us to him?"

King Louis lurched forward in a huff that rivaled his brother's, and waved his curiously tiny arm at the circle of shadows gathered around him: Lake and Caroline, Sophia and Hope, Harclay, Violet. "Yes. But we cannot take all of you. Eliason is not a fool. If he sees so many coming, he will turn up his tail and run."

"Yes, he will run," Artois added. "We will only take two."

Hope stepped forward, pressing Sophia behind him. "It's a trap, Harclay. If these two won't lead us to Eliason, to the diamond, then we'll find him ourselves."

Cousin Violet, who until that moment had been unusually quiet, stepped forward and placed a hand on Hope's shoulder.

"No. Lord Harclay and I will go with the king."

Hope made a choking noise; Sophia saw his face flush pink. "The French Blue belongs to *me*, Lady Violet. I'll be damned if I make the same mistake I did that night in the ballroom. We cannot trust Harclay; not with the diamond, and especially not with your life."

He was not the only member of their party to object: Lake said something about the earl being liable to faint, to which his lordship replied he was fine, just fine, before turning to vomit quietly at Artois' feet.

"You have my word, Hope," Violet said. "I will return the French Blue to you."

His eyes flicked to the earl. "You understand why I question your motives, Violet."

"I do." Sophia watched above the ball of Hope's shoulder as her cousin looked up at him, her blue eyes wide, serious. "But you've got to trust me. Trust us. Harclay's the one who started all this—let us, together, finish it. Lake is—well, it's obvious what he is, too, too big, too mean—and liable to scare Eliason witless. And you, Hope."

Violet met Sophia's eyes. "You have other matters to attend to."

Hope opened his mouth to protest. Impulsively Sophia reached out, gathering his sleeve in her fingers. She looked at him with all the calm and steadiness she could muster. Though he remained flush, she sensed his surrender to her touch, his anger, his worry fading.

With a long, rather dramatic sigh, Hope stepped back. "Very well. But make no mistake, Lady Violet. If you're not back here in half an hour with diamond in hand, I'll search for you myself and have the two of you thrown in gaol. Do I make myself clear?"

Harclay nodded, and spoke some nonsense about being the one who fooled them all, the one who stole the French Blue from under their noses at the ball.

Hope was silent as they watched the stooped outline of the earl's figure disappear into the night beside Lady Violet's. Ahead of them, the king and Artois panted rather colorful obscenities at one another.

And then they were gone, lost to the night.

Sophia and Hope, Lake and Lady Caroline had only to wait.

Thirty

───── ❖ ─────

E verything, *everything* Hope had ever wanted, everything he'd worked for, all that he'd done for the family he loved and missed—it all hung in the balance. What happened tonight, in the minutes and hours ahead, would determine the course of the rest of his life. His failure or success—whether he would win back the diamond or not—now rested on the outcome of his enemy's foray into the great darkness spread before them. By dawn he would either have the diamond . . . or he wouldn't.

Hope should be terrified. He should be going with them. He should be ill with anticipation, or at the very least, drowning his sorrows with the flask of whiskey he'd stuffed into his breastplate.

Instead he was staring at the lithe figure beside him, electrifying his skin with the gentle probing of her fingers.

Sophia shivered in the breeze. Without thinking, he gathered her shawl in his hands and drew it tighter about her shoulders, her hand grazing his thigh as it fell from his arm.

In his belly desire curled, heady, fully formed in the space of half a heartbeat.

Not now. He must focus, concentrate what little energy he had left on the French Blue, his plans to save Hope & Co. from the brink of failure.

And the marquess's diamond ring. Sophia wore it about her neck, and soon she'd wear it on her fourth finger, where it would leave its narrow mark on the pale, tender skin of her hand.

It was useless, this desire. That night they swore they'd

leave these inconvenient longings in his room, and in his bed. Leave behind each other.

And yet he found leaving her behind more difficult than he could have ever imagined. The desire inside him was, despite his efforts, impossible to ignore.

Sophia gasped as he pulled her closer, fisting the fine fabric of her shawl in his hands. Gasped, but did not protest.

Beside him, Lake cleared his throat, rocking back on his heels. "Well, then. Jolly good of Harclay to do the heavy lifting for us, eh? Come, let's have a nip in the hack while we wait."

Grasping Sophia's shawl in one hand, Hope reached for the flask inside his breastplate with the other, and wordlessly passed it to Mr. Lake.

Lake cleared this throat. "Well, then," he repeated. "We'll just, er, meet you . . . there. Do take your time, we have all night. Half an hour, at least."

Placing his hand on the small of Lady Caroline's back, Lake led her into the darkness. Hope heard Caroline giggle, and Lake snort with laughter, before they disappeared altogether.

Lake, in love! Hope thought he'd never see the day.

Forbidden fruit indeed.

He turned back to Sophia. He should send her after them to wait in the safety of the hack. He should not move from this spot until the Earl of Harclay returned, French Blue in hand.

He should.

But he wouldn't.

Sophia looked at him, her hazel eyes gold in the half-light of the moon. He slid his hand into the inviting curve of her jaw, his fingers brushing the baby-fine hairs of her neck. She shivered again.

He ducked his head, lips brushing her ear. "Let's go."

H ope led Sophia down the quayside, bowing in and out of shadow as they passed bawdy houses, bawdier taverns, and the dark, nameless facades of weathered warehouses. The gaping blackness of the Docklands yawned over Hope's right shoulder. He held her closer.

"D'you think they're all right?" Sophia whispered. "I trust

Harclay to keep Violet safe, but seeing as I poisoned him an hour ago . . ."

"He's recovered. They'll come back to us in no time at all. Besides. With Artois' thirty thousand in their pockets, I hardly think this Eliason fellow will refuse them."

Even as he said the words, Hope winced. Though the Docklands were mostly deserted, the devil knew what characters trolled about this time of night: pickpockets, cutthroats, lightskirts. King Louis' beringed fingers and Artois' gilt costume certainly did their party no favors.

If Sophia saw Hope wince, she said nothing.

"Ah, here we are."

He drew up before a whitewashed warehouse, its facade covered in bold, black letters: HOPE & CO.

"Here? Really?" Sophia wrinkled her nose.

"No," Hope said, pointing toward the river. "There."

Her gaze followed his outstretched arm to the bulkhead at their right; a sturdy ramp led from the quayside down to the water, where a dozen gleaming, full-rigged ships bobbed silently in their berths.

He felt her stiffen. "Those are yours?"

Thomas scoffed. "Depends on the outcome of tonight's events. They may be heading for the auction block first thing in the morning, so I figure we may as well enjoy them while we have the chance."

He looked down and met her eyes. They were open, storm-tossed, moving from his gaze to his lips and back again.

"Please," he said. "Please, Sophia, come with me."

His heart drummed an erratic rhythm in his chest as he waited for her reply.

"Thomas, we shouldn't. I cannot—" She swallowed, hard, and looked down at their clasped hands. "I promised myself I wouldn't. I've made every attempt to keep my distance, I have, but I—"

"But you can't." The words came out in a rush of relief. "Neither can I, Sophia. I cannot keep away from you."

She looked at him, pleading. "We shouldn't."

"If you tell me to stop," he said, sliding his hand up her arm to rest on her neck, "I'll stop."

"Please." Her voice was barely above a whisper. "Please don't ask that of me, Thomas."

"Tell me," he pressed a kiss to the place where ear met jaw, "to stop."

He trailed his lips along the slope of her neck, breathing in her scent: water, soap, air. Each kiss was soft, lingering, sweet. It was madness, this embrace; it went against every rational thought, everything he could and should be doing.

But once his lips touched her skin he couldn't help himself.

Sophia arched against him, head lilting back in offering. "Thomas," she breathed. "Oh, Thomas."

"Do you want me"—another kiss—"to stop?"

She met his gaze with heavy-lidded eyes. "No. No, don't stop."

"Good," he said, pulling back. "Come with me. We shall have to be quick; half an hour, remember."

One side of her mouth curled into a grin. "Let's not waste a moment, then."

He tugged her down the ramp to the water; she let out a breathless laugh. Their bodies collided at the sway of the dock beneath their feet; Hope caught Sophia and held her against him. She looked up, lips half-open; her shawl fell, revealing the ball of her bare shoulder.

Hope took a deep breath, let it out. The river sighed with him, the dock rolling beneath them: raising them up as a wave crested, sending them down as it ebbed.

Planting his feet on either side of Sophia's, Hope bent his neck and gently pressed his lips to her shoulder. She tasted clean.

Sophia sucked in a breath, her body rising to meet his caress. He wasted no time; he moved his mouth along the ridge of her collarbone, nipping the tender flesh at the base of her throat. Beneath his lips her pulse took flight, an insistent fluttering like the wings of a bird.

His desire flared, filling every fiber, every thought and every space of his being. If he wasn't careful he'd take her here, now, against the bulkhead, hard and fast and rough. Not at all what he wanted for her; not at all what he wanted for this, their last night together. Even if they only had twenty minutes to themselves, he wouldn't take her like that.

He prayed the others—Hope and Violet, most of all—didn't come back, catch him and Sophia. He prayed they took the full half an hour he'd given them.

"Thomas," Sophia repeated. "Please. *Don't stop.*"

Above them loomed one of Hope's triple-masted merchant ships. From a cursory glance, Hope gathered it was vacant; the windows in the aft cabin were dark.

Or at least he hoped it was. Somehow he very much doubted Sophia would yield to his touch while a dozen toothless sailors looked on.

There was no ramp of which to speak, only a series of slatted indentions carved into the side of the vessel.

Hope pulled away. Sophia's pretty features creased in confusion. Pressing a kiss between her brows, he murmured, "Not here. Follow me."

Together they made for the ship. Nestling Sophia in the circle of his arms, he climbed up the ladder one rung behind her; he winced as the curve of her backside brushed far too invitingly against the bulge in his breeches. Again his desire flared, burning a hole in whatever logic he had left; whatever worry he had over being caught.

That Sophia was here with him; that she would again be his, after he thought he'd never get a second chance—his chest welled with gratitude.

She heaved herself over the banister onto the ship. She turned, wiping her palms together in satisfaction, and held out a hand; Hope took it, her grip firm as she helped him onboard.

He leaned back against the banister, catching his breath. Sophia placed her elbows on the railing beside him, her arm brushing his. He listened to her quiet panting; they did not meet eyes, but he sensed her every movement, the curling of her hair about her head in the breeze.

The ship undulated slowly beneath his feet, the river plunking against its bow some feet below. As far as Hope could tell, the ship was deserted. The deck had been recently swept, and appeared to be vacant of any cargo, empty save for a coil of rope and a pile of carefully folded canvas tarpaulins.

Relief washed through him. Catching his breath, he turned around and placed his elbows on the banister beside Sophia's. The River Thames stretched out before them, the moon setting alight a wide blue ribbon of radiance on the water's surface; the city glowed dimly at its banks.

How many pairs of eyes, he wondered, had filled hearts to bursting at this very sight. A hundred, a thousand years ago, had the Romans looked upon the Thames in the dead of night and found in its quiet, insistent rush, the glow of the moon upon its surface, solace or sorrow? How many hearts were broken in this place, how many healed? Generations of love lost, love thwarted, love quiet and dangerous; so many stories begun and ended here, at the edge of the River Thames.

Hope turned to find Sophia looking at him, her eyes soft about the edges. He wondered what she was thinking, if she felt her own heart, full and swollen, beginning to crack.

"Are you all right?" His voice was quiet.

Sophia reached out and tucked an errant curl behind his ear. "No. Not in the slightest."

He rose to his feet, running his palms up the length of her arms as he turned her to him. "Good." He tucked his hand against her cheek as he leaned in. "Neither am I."

His lips found hers, full and warm and yielding. She tilted her head to better match his movements, her arms rising to circle his neck as together they fell into the kiss. He slipped his tongue between her lips; she let him in, moaning as he pulled back, taking her bottom lip between his teeth.

He cupped her face in his hands and pressed his mouth to hers, harder this time. He felt her body rising to meet him, running her tongue along the slick seam of his lips. His blood ignited as she dug her fingers into the hair at his neck, his cock pulsing between his legs, painfully enormous.

Hope ducked, deepening the kiss. Her tongue was warm and deliciously wet tangled with his; her eyelashes fluttered against his cheek, featherlight. Her hands were on his face now, pulling him closer, closer, as if she might swallow him whole.

Please, he prayed silently. *Please.*

The breeze moved around them, tickling the hair on Hope's bare arms. He wrapped them around her, trailing his hands from her face down the slope of her back to rest on the rise of her buttocks. Her pert flesh yielded to the press of his palms; she gasped into his mouth and he nipped at her lip, a low growl in her throat as she bit back. He tasted blood and grinned; she was wicked, more rascal and seducer than painfully proper debutante.

Sophia began to attack the straps of his breastplate with her fingers; his body went up in flames at her impatience. He covered her hand in his and loosened the strap, breaking their kiss to quickly shrug out of the costume. Dropping it with a *thud* at her feet, he darted forward and crushed his mouth against hers. The tips of her hardened nipples pressed against the thin fabric of his tunic as the kiss became messy, urgent.

The pressure between his legs became too great to bear. He needed her here, now, before he was obliterated by the weight of his desire.

Hope pulled away, and as he stood to catch his breath, Sophia tucked her head into the curve of his neck.

His heart swelled against his ribcage as if it might expand through sinew and bone to meet her caress. It killed him, the tenderness of her gesture. How vulnerable she felt in his arms; and he—he was defenseless, holding her to his heart, the both of them knowing all the while that in the end they would betray one another.

He lowered his lips to the top of her head and left them there as he led her across the deck. With the toe of his ridiculous gladiator-style sandal, he coaxed the tarpaulin to unfold into a nestlike circle and guided Sophia to its edge. She was breathing hard; even in the darkness he could make out the luscious curve of her swollen lips, the prick of her nipples against the gauzy fabric of her costume.

Hope swallowed, gritting his teeth at the anticipation that coursed through him. He grasped the edges of his tunic and made to pull it off; in his haste it got stuck on his head, and no matter how he tugged, he couldn't untangle himself.

Sophia laughed softly; he felt her hands on his tunic, gently removing his hands from the fabric before pulling it over his head.

"Thank God," Hope breathed. He shook out his curls, wiping them back from his forehead, and lowered his gaze to see Sophia staring openmouthed at his naked chest. He felt himself harden even further—really, how was that even *possible*?—as her eyes traveled to the front of his drawers.

He made to cover himself with his hands, lest he frighten her away, but Sophia snatched his wrist.

"No," she said. She stepped forward and slipped her first finger into the waistband of his drawers. "Let me, Thomas."

Before he could stop her, Sophia dropped to her knees, digging the fingers of both hands into the waistband. With her thumbs she caressed the jutting points of his hip bones, slowly, *oh God*, so very slowly pulling down his drawers.

She coaxed them over the bulge; his cock pounced free, the drawers dropping silently to his feet. For a moment she drew back, her eyes widening as she took in his length, the enormity of his desire for her.

"Really, Sophia, you don't have—"

"Shh." Splaying her palms over the hardened flesh just above his groin, she drew up on her knees. "I *want* to."

He thought he might scream at the feel of her hands scraping down, down, *down* the length of his groin. She encircled the root of his cock in one hand, the shaft in the other; and then she was bending forward, pressing her lips to the head, kissing him as she looked up, curiosity sparking in those wicked, *wicked* eyes of hers.

He let out a long, slow hiss, drawing his thumb across her forehead.

"You feel so lovely," he breathed. "So goddamn lovely, Sophia."

Sophia did not hesitate, sliding open her lips instead, slick with the first show of his seed. Carefully, very carefully, she took his head into her mouth, one engorged inch at a time.

Hope sucked in a breath at the feel of her tongue on the very tip of his manhood, languorously, slowly caressing him. He watched as her lips stretched to accept him, digging a hand into her hair. He saw God, he saw stars, he had to hold on, she was so lovely, so beautiful, he wanted to remember every moment, every caress . . .

Her mouth felt hot and gloriously wet against him, tightening as she began to move, taking him deeper and deeper. He covered her hand at his root with his own, tightening her grip on his shaft, and together they moved, an easy, back-and-forth motion that had him growling with pleasure.

Sophia's rhythm increased, her eyes fluttered shut; he

watched as she lost herself in him, her toga slipping from her shoulder. That *shoulder*. There was something distinctly erotic about her bare shoulder, the way her skin glistened in the gray-blue light of the moon.

He felt himself coiling with pleasure inside her mouth, the familiar tightening almost unbearable as he watched himself disappear past the silken caress of her lips. He was tugging at her hair now, the braids wound about her head falling free under the ministrations of his fingers.

Wave after wave of sensation washed through him, each more potent than the last. She was here, she was *his*, for a little while, anyway, and she was giving herself to him without reservation, without regret. Again his heart swelled. How he ached for her; how he would ache after all was said and done, when he belonged to the bank and she, to another.

He bit his lip, the stirrings of his climax becoming more insistent with each stroke of Sophia's tongue. He cupped her face in his hand, her eyes flying open as he guided himself out of her mouth.

His eyes on hers, he sank to his knees before her. His blood jumped at her heavy-lidded gaze, her swollen lips parted to reveal the tiniest sliver of white teeth. She looked beautiful. She looked . . . aroused.

He kissed her lips; he could taste the tanginess of his body in her mouth and on her tongue.

That tongue. He caressed it with his own, great, sloping circles that had her moaning into his mouth. She arched against him, wild with need; he felt the insistent press of her hips against his cock.

Hope released her lips, trailing his own down to her shoulder. His fingers brushing her skin, he coaxed the toga off her arm and down her chest, his hands on her breasts as they surged free above the bodice of her toga. For a moment he held their heaviness in his hands, pressing his fingers into the silken skin; her nipples pleaded against the center of his palms.

"Thomas," she whispered. "Please."

He slid his left hand to the back of her neck and gently led her down onto the tarpaulin, leaning on his elbow above her as he rolled her nipple between his thumb and forefinger. They landed softly on the deck, the tarpaulin sighing around them in the breeze.

Sophia arched against him, moaning softly into the darkness. She was clawing his chest with her fingertips, her nipples brushing against his skin as he brought his mouth down on hers. The kiss was savage and hard, mindless as they lost themselves to their pleasure.

He reached down, drawing up the skirts of her toga. He parted her legs and found the slit between her drawers; his fingers first encountered the curls of her sex, silken and slick.

And then.

And *then*.

Hope groaned, his desire spiking. She was very wet, her flesh swollen with need; she gasped as his fingers grazed the apex of her sex, the nub engorged and hard.

His cock throbbed against her leg; his blood was screaming.

He bolted upright, grabbing Sophia by the waist and settling her on her knees above him, her hair swirling around them in the breeze. Her legs were spread just above the tip of his hardened prick, so aroused, the anticipation so great it hurt.

"*Thomas*," she was breathing, her fingers finding purchase on his naked shoulders. He placed his hands on her thighs and squeezed her flesh.

"*It's all right*," he whispered in her ear, his lips catching on the sloped ridge of her jaw. She tasted of sweat, salt. "*I want you, Sophia. Let me have you.*"

He took his cock in his hand and held it upright. With his other hand he coaxed her legs wider, guiding her down.

She reached down and covered his hand with her own, nestling the tip of his cock into the cleftlike opening of her lips. He cursed aloud, pressing his forehead against hers as they fought for the air between them.

Slowly, with excruciating tenderness, she sank onto his length. She felt exquisitely tight, stretching to take in the enormity of his desire. She sucked a breath through her teeth, but before he could ask if she was in pain she threw back her head and thrust downward, swallowing him to the hilt.

For a moment they sat motionless; he didn't want to hurt her, didn't want to ruin these last moments together, and so he waited to take her lead. When at last she brought her head up to look at him, her eyes were dark and wet. He saw a bit of pain there, pain that quickly faded to wild desire.

"Are you all right?" he asked, breathless.

Sophia dug her hands into the hair at his neck and rested her forehead against his. "Never all right. Never, never. Please, Thomas, don't stop."

Hope slid his hands up her thighs and placed them on her hips. He gently coaxed them up and down, up and down, small motions at first that had him gritting his teeth to keep from climaxing then and there.

With his thumb he brushed the engorged space at the tip of her sex, now spread wide to accommodate his girth. As if he'd lit her body on fire, Sophia began to move on her own, rocking her hips against him.

He saw stars as he slid in and out, *in* and out of her slick warmth. His heart was beating so hard, felt so big in his chest, he thought he might explode. He dug his hand into her hair, fingering her loose curls down the length of her back.

Sophia arched against him, her head falling back as she bared her body to the night. Her breasts moved in time to her hips, and he bent his head to catch a pink nipple between his teeth. She moaned; he pulled back and swallowed.

Heavens, but she was beautiful. The way her skin shone beneath the light of the moon, the abandon in her dark eyes; her hair and her passion and the musky scent of her desire. He wanted her, he wanted her more than he'd ever wanted anything. He wanted her now and he wanted her after, he wanted her tomorrow, next week, next year.

Hope wanted her with him always.

His throat tightened. It was all too much; he couldn't breathe against the force of his emotion, the force of his body as Sophia swallowed him whole.

Hope was no fool. She was not his, never had been his. All he had was this moment, and their joined flesh. The exquisite sensations thrumming through him.

He felt her tightening around him, the first signs of her release. His pulse drummed in his ears. The tarpaulin fluttered in the breeze beneath their bodies.

He closed his eyes, willing her rising pleasure to blot out his grief.

Thirty-one

---❖---

H ead thrown back, Sophia gazed at the night sky above through the heavy-lidded haze of her desire. She felt so full, so completely lost in Thomas and the rising beat between her legs, she imagined herself bursting into a white-hot spatter of stars, the force of her climax banishing her to the far reaches of the blue-velvet sky.

His hand was at her neck, pulling him toward her. She smelled his desire, sweat mingled with sandalwood, lemons. She tugged at his hair with her fingers, her hips rolling of their own volition over and through and with him.

Thomas was so large with desire it had hurt at first to take him inside her; even now her pleasure was tinged with pain, each stroke a lesson in patience. But with this thumb working her sex where their bodies joined, the pain only increased her desire.

And now he was trailing his lips down her throat, skipping to her shoulder before taking her nipple in his mouth. He ran his tongue over its hardened tip, scraping it with his teeth, *oh God, oh my God, I can't, I can't wait much—*

Pleasure, blinding, complete, ripped through her, her legs bucking against the hardened plane of Hope's thighs. Sophia cried out, and cried out again, her blood rushing through her in a frenzied explosion of poignant sensation. Her limbs pulsed, painfully rigid against the force of her climax.

Vaguely she sensed herself pulsing around the length of Thomas inside her. He bit back a cry, as if she'd hurt him; and then he was lifting her off of him, his movements quick but gentle as he withdrew. She watched as he covered his manhood with both hands. He winced, face screwed tight with pain as he was overcome by his completion.

His seed pulsed through his fingers; she felt its warmth on the exposed flesh of her thigh.

"I'm sorry," Thomas whispered, wiping it away with the edge of the tarpaulin. He was breathing hard, his massive chest rising and falling rapidly, the dark, curly hair sprinkled across its expanse tickling the tips of her breasts.

Sophia let out a breath, her heart suddenly heavy in her chest. She reached out, brushing a curl from his temple before taking his chin between her fingers.

"Look at me, Thomas."

He looked at her from under his dark lashes. She saw her own pain reflected in the translucent depths of his blue eyes. Already she felt her desire rising again, her body's thirst for him only heightened by their coming together. She'd never known pleasure and happiness like she had with Thomas inside and around and with her. The completeness of it, the sheer expanse of it was terrifying. With his arms wrapped around her and his mouth on hers, she succumbed to who she was, whom she wanted. The worries of the world, the marquess and her family's falling fortunes, dissipated into the evening breeze. In those moments there was nothing and no one but she and Thomas and the love they shared between them.

Love.

Sophia blinked at the jagged pain that sliced through her chest; her eyes pricked with tears.

"Thomas, I—"

"Don't." He held a finger to her lips. "Please, don't."

And then he was taking her in his arms again, pulling the tarpaulin over them as he lay atop her. The canvas rippled above their heads in the breeze, blocking out the night sky.

Sophia stretched out her legs, stiff from exertion, as Thomas pulled her body against his. He pressed a kiss into her cheek, her chin, her forehead; he pried her lips open with his own, a depthless kiss, a desperate kiss, as if he knew it would be their last.

She melted beneath the weight of his body, the fleshy warmth of it. She closed her eyes and ran her palms over his shoulders down to his chest, memorizing every inch of his skin, every muscle and curlicue of hair. A tear escaped from the corner of her closed eye, trailing into her hair.

Sophia broke the kiss, pressing her cheek against Hope's as he wound his arms about her.

"I love you, Thomas," she whispered.

Thomas started, drawing back to look in her eyes. His were wide and full, gleaming as if they might be wet. His eyes, they were so beautiful; so beautiful it made her ache.

He parted his lips, swollen from kissing her.

"Fire!"

The cry rent the silent night air, a strangled thing that echoed through the endless expanse of the Docklands. Hope's eyes widened; he threw back the canvas and sniffed the air. Sophia inhaled, the crisp odor of burning wood invading her nostrils; above Hope's head she saw the dim outline of smoke curling into the night sky.

Thomas snapped upright and was already shrugging into that ridiculous tunic of his.

"Bring water, quick! Fire!"

Sophia's heart turned over in her chest. If the night's previous mishaps were any indication, then this fire had everything, *everything* to do with their plot; she could only pray that Cousin Violet and the earl were far from it, though her every sense told her otherwise.

With trembling fingers, she tried to set her costume to rights, dropping the sleeve of her toga once, twice, damning it to hell on the third try.

Thomas reached over and tugged the sleeve back into place; Sophia barely managed to tuck her breasts into her bodice before Hope was lifting her to her feet. Together they scanned the horizon, the smoke growing thicker now.

"There." Sophia pointed to an ember of color at the far edge of the void. Plumes of smoke rose to meet the sky; the back of her throat burned just looking at it. She could discern the dim outline of a ship, the tall shadows of its masts strangely angled, as if they were tilting into the water.

Thomas met her eyes.

They didn't have much time.

Scrambling down the makeshift ladder, Sophia leapt into Hope's outstretched arms. He caught her effortlessly, his thick arms holding her close for one breathless moment before he set her on her feet.

They took off at a sprint, Sophia working double to keep up with Thomas's enormous stride. She followed the outline of his shoulders through the maze of the Docklands, both of them slowing as their lungs filled with smoke.

For what felt like the hundredth time that night, Sophia panicked. She could hardly see on account of the darkness, and as the smoke thickened she worried she would be lost, and would never get to Violet, and Violet would be caught on a burning ship with no one but that bounder the earl to save her.

"Are we," she coughed, "getting close?"

"Yes!" Thomas called over his shoulder. Seeing her distress, he slowed his pace and wrapped an arm about her shoulders. "Stay close, Sophia. I don't want to lose you."

Shouts rang out around them; the crackle and snap of burning wood filled the summer air, the once-cool breeze now humid with sweat and smoke. Sophia struggled to breathe, her eyes watering as the haze surrounded them. It was too painful to keep them open, and she stumbled blindly at Hope's side, leaning further and further against him the more her lungs burned.

"Sophia." Hope drew to a stop. Choking, he took her hands in his face. "Open your eyes. Are you all right?"

"I can't," she panted. The smoke was suffocating; she felt faint. "Leave. I won't leave Violet."

"No." Despite the thickness of the air, his reply was savage, sure. "I'm taking. You back."

"You can't. Leave the diamond. And what. Of Violet!"

Sophia stumbled back as something—someone—ran headfirst into her chest, knocking what little wind was left from her lungs. She let out a strangled cry; an eerily similar cry rang out at her feet.

Violet. "Violet!"

A stroke of implausible luck at last.

Sophia bent and helped her cousin to her feet, doing her best to wave the smoke from Violet's face as she coughed and sputtered.

Thomas was at her side in a moment, wrapping an arm about Violet's waist as she swayed dangerously close to the edge of the dock. "Are you. All right?"

Violet met Sophia's eyes through the increasingly opaque haze. "We've got. To go." She waved a limp arm in the direction of—well, Sophia frankly couldn't tell up from down, left from right, so Lord knew where Violet was pointing—but she knew it was *away* from the French Blue.

Sophia looked at Hope. "But the. Diamond," she panted.

Violet was shaking her head. "No, no. The ship. Is in flames. And sinking. With William—"

She collapsed against Hope, head lolling on the broad expanse of his shoulder. Violet, who only abhorred swooning ladies more than swooning itself, had *actually swooned.*

Sophia's panic returned full force. This was serious. More so because Cousin Violet had referred to the Earl of Harclay by his given name, a name even his sister Lady Caroline did not use in public.

Really, what the *devil* had happened in the hour since they parted company on the quayside?

Sophia moved to help Mr. Hope carry Cousin Violet, but he waved her away, scooping her into his arms instead.

"But the. Diamond," Sophia said again.

Thomas shook his head. "Later. Let's. Go."

They retraced their steps along the dock, Sophia keeping her eyes trained on Hope's bare heels lest she lose him in the thickening smoke. She could tell by his sagging shoulders that he was exhausted, but he trudged forward, their pace slowing to a mere crawl by the time they miraculously reached the quay. Sophia's eyes blurred even further with tears of gratitude. Only a few more feet, a few more steps, and then they could collapse into the hack, and after that it was only a few miles to home, to bed . . .

"The hacks." Hope's head snapped left, snapped right. "They're gone."

The breath left Sophia's body as she took in the empty lane before them. She dashed about in the darkness, peering past the warehouses into alleys and hidden alcoves. Nothing. She glanced over her shoulder; the burning ship was now fully visible, the flames licking the top of its mainmast as smoke billowed into the sky, obscuring the moon and stars. Somewhere in the darkness she heard the wailing of a siren; the fire brigade was on its way.

Behind Sophia, Hope cursed none too gently in a language Sophia was grateful she didn't quite understand. Something about pigs, and Mr. Lake's—was that *bones* or *stones*?

"Wait here," she whispered, trolling further into the darkness.

"Don't you dare move, Sophia, it's not safe. Anyone could be about, what with those ruffians the king and Artois at large . . ."

Sophia ducked through an oiled canvas door that hung between two weathered clapboard buildings, finding herself in a dim, damp alley. Wading into the darkness, Sophia held her hands out before her.

Was that a muffled giggle? A beat later she heard a noise that sounded suspiciously like a man's playful growl of pleasure.

"Hello?" she called out weakly, coughing. "I don't want to, er, interrupt . . . whichever activity in which you are engaged . . . but I'm looking for my friends, you see . . ."

Sophia's outstretched hands encountered a hard, smooth surface, and a moment later the looming shadow of a hack came into view.

"Oh. Oh, thank God." Sophia went to open the door. "Mr. Lake, I—*Mr. Lake!*"

He tugged his buckskins over his bare behind, clamoring to the edge of the bench inside the hack. His hair, usually clubbed back in an immaculate queue, was disheveled, sticking straight up around his head like a halo; though he shrugged into his coat, Sophia could see the smooth skin of a well-muscled chest peeking through the lapels.

"I'm sorry to, er, disturb you, but we need to go. Violet is ill—"

Lady Caroline glanced over the slope of Lake's enormous shoulder. Her hair looked even worse for the wear than her paramour's. "Is she all right?"

"Yes, I'll explain everything, but we *need* to *go,* now."

"Right-ho." Lake held out his hand, sniffing the air. "I say, what's that dreadful smell?"

By the time they reached Thomas and Cousin Violet, Lady Caroline was hopelessly tangled in her toga after Sophia's attempts to get her dressed; across from the cacophony of the makeshift dressing room, Lake fumed silently, his forehead gleaming with perspiration in the light of a passing lantern.

"Where the devil did you go?" Hope spat, handing Violet's limp body inside the hack. "What if we'd been tailed, and attacked on the quay? Don't tell me—" Hope's eyes slid from Caroline to Lake and back again, narrowing with suspicion. "Never mind. I don't want to know."

Hope squeezed onto the bench beside Lake, called for the driver to keep moving. "No word of the diamond?"

Thomas shook his head. "The ship will sink, if it hasn't already. Violet told us virtually nothing; for all we know, Artois could've run off with the diamond before the fire started, or that Eliason chap could've jumped ship with it in his pocket. The French Blue could be anywhere by now."

Lake pounded the wall with his ham-sized fist, and called for the driver to make haste. "Bloody perfect. We came so close. So *bloody close*."

An enormous crack, round and deep as thunder, reverberated through the vehicle, the horses screaming as the cobblestones shook beneath their hooves.

Hope flung out his arm, pinning Sophia to her seat; in her lap, Violet's head lolled openmouthed, limp. The hack drew to a sudden, violent stop, and in a flurry of movement Lake was leaping from the hack, his voice hoarse as he called to the driver.

What the devil? What happened? What the devil was that?

Sophia shook in her seat at the driver's reply as the acrid odors of smoke and splintered wood filled the hack.

"Can' rightly say, sir, but all ov a sudden I seen a big explosion like, out there in th' river."

She looked down at Violet, smoothing the hair from her face, and blinked at the unexpected prick of tears. The ship on which Cousin Violet and the earl had hoped to reclaim the French Blue was sunk, or, at the very least, had erupted into a ball of fiery flames.

Sophia reached across the bench and took Lady Caroline's hand. Her brother was on that ship, as was Sophia's family's fortune, their future, too. The dowager duchess sat still as a statue, her long, swanlike neck bent toward the window. Lake and Hope stood outside, hands on their hips, their heads turned toward the black pit of the Docklands.

Sophia wanted to offer Caroline words of comfort, declare

her brother was, surely, far too wily to be caught flat-footed on an exploding ship. But in her mouth her tongue felt thick and dry as ash. There would be no comfort for Caroline, not until she knew her brother the earl was in one piece, and in her arms.

And so Sophia merely squeezed her hand. How many times Violet had done the same for Sophia before stepping into Almack's, or a wedding breakfast attended by far too many eligible dukes, she could not count; but the small gesture had always calmed Sophia's nerves. An unspoken promise of support, a pledge to gossip shamelessly about said dukes' foibles and follies when the breakfast was done; it was hope and faith when Sophia needed it most.

Lady Caroline squeezed back. *Thank you.*

Sophia watched out the window as Hope pressed a handful of guineas into the driver's palm; a moment later he was at the door of the hack, his blue eyes hard.

"I've given the driver instructions to take you home," Hope held up a hand as Sophia leaned forward to protest, "under pain of death. Lake and I will see to things here. Go home, Sophia, and take care of your cousin. If—*when. When* Harclay returns, he will come to the house for Violet. You'll do that for me, won't you, Sophia? Keep watch?"

Sophia bit her lip. He was right, of course. Thomas was *always* right.

But as she was *always* wont to do, Sophia longed to stay. And though she usually longed to stay for the promise of adventure and port, tonight she wished to say for an altogether different reason.

She wanted to stay with *him*. Her heart ached with it, with the knowledge that this would be their last night together, before they won or they lost and went their separate ways. It would end here, tonight. And she didn't want to let him go.

"Sophia." Thomas's voice was soft now, his eyes, too. "You must do this."

Falling back against the seat, Sophia swallowed the lump in her throat. "Yes. I'll do it."

"Thank you."

A beat of silence passed as their eyes met. Behind Hope, Sophia was vaguely aware of Lake's rather vile curses, something about bloody time and not having bloody enough of it.

But Thomas, all but oblivious, leaned into the hackney, opening his mouth as if he might speak.

Sophia, too, was leaning forward in rising anticipation. Would he confess undying love? Pledge his heart and soul to her honor? Say he could not bear to be away from her for more than a moment, reach for her and fling her over his shoulder and begin their grandest, most daring adventure yet?

Instead Thomas fell away, looking over his shoulder to shout, "All right, you cranky old goat, I'm *coming*!", before meeting Sophia's gaze one last time.

Sophia's belly turned over, and turned over again, at the smoldering desire burning his eyes a darker shade of blue.

With a stiff bow he closed the door, banging his fist against the side of the hack to signal the driver.

The horses jerked into motion. In Sophia's lap, Violet moaned; Lady Caroline bumped and jolted in silence beside her.

And then Thomas was gone.

Thirty-two

---·◆·---

Two weeks later
The Residence of the Marquess of Withington
St. James's Square

Sophia toyed with the thin strand of matching yellow diamonds that snaked about her wrist. The bracelet was lovely, understated yet glamorous, and of the latest fashion; yellow diamonds were, it seemed, all the rage this season. Considering feathered turbans and a ghastly shade of puce were also a la mode, Sophia had good reason to be wary of such a gift; but it *was* a gift, and from a marquess at that.

Even so, Sophia could not summon the gasps of gratitude and virgin blush with which any debutante worth her salt would accept such a gift. She was no virgin—a fact that, conversely, *did* made her blush—but more importantly, the diamonds, *of course*, made her think of Hope.

Mr. Hope, and the extravagant diamond they together filched from the Princess of Wales. Sophia remembered the silence that settled over Caroline's puce-painted drawing room (really, that dreadful color was *everywhere*!) as Her Royal Highness opened the lacquered box. She remembered the way the French Blue glittered in its puddle of white silk velvet, its watery transparency taking captive Sophia's imagination.

She remembered being afraid to touch it; foolishly she believed it cursed, the apple in the Garden of Eden. Surely something so beautiful, so transcendently indulgent, was not meant to be plied by mere mortals. She wondered at its story, the first stirrings of a tale coming to life as she'd looked upon it, Hope at her side.

And his history! How they'd laughed that night in his study. An adventure to end all adventures, surely, if not a bit overzealous in its style and sense of doom.

"Sophia, my dear." Withington flushed pink, twitching nervously on the settee beside her. "May I call you 'my dear'?"

Sophia swallowed. "Of course you may."

He jerked his head to the side, brow furrowed as he looked at her. "Do you not like it? We might bring it back to Rundell and Bridge, if you'd like, and exchange it for something better suited to your tastes?"

Sophia looked up from the bracelet, and tried again to swallow the tightness in her throat. Here was a marquess, offering a diamond bracelet to match the diamond *ring* he'd given her. Very earnest, very expensive tokens of his affection.

Here, sitting anxiously with his hands on his knees, was exactly the sort of man, offering exactly the sort of match, for which mere months ago she would've sold her soul.

Sophia stiffened her spine, and tried to ignore the throb of pain in her chest. *Remember who you are. Remember what you want, all that you've fought for.*

"It's lovely," she said, extending her arm. "Would you put it on?"

Withington brushed the sliver of exposed skin at her wrist as he took the tiny gold clasp in his fingers. After several failed attempts, he slid the clasp into place and pulled away with a sudden jerk, as if she'd burned him. His blush went from pink to purple, rising from his clean-shaven neck up to his cheeks and, impossibly, to his forehead.

"I'm . . . er, terribly sorry, Sophia."

She wiggled her arm so that the bracelet caught a beam of late afternoon sunlight, blinding them both as the diamonds flashed and winked, throwing a spray of translucent shadows about the walls. "You've nothing to be sorry for. They're beautiful, Withington. A beautiful gift."

From the far corner of the drawing room, Lady Blaise exclaimed her pleasure, the dowager marchioness cooing a reply. Withington glanced over his shoulder as if to admonish his mother, and Sophia watched with a smile as the ladies returned to their tea with suspect scrupulousness, Lady Blaise going so far as to compliment the biscuits around a mouthful of said confection.

Withington let out a long sigh, turning back and smiling at Sophia with a roll of his dark eyes. "Shameless, aren't they?"

"Terribly. I've had your cook's biscuits, and I mean no offense when I say they are anything *but* deliriously delicious. My mother, you see—she has a flair for the dramatic."

"*Your* mother? Your mother's a warm, fuzzy puppy compared to my own."

Sophia's grin deepened. "I sympathize, I do."

A beat of silence stretched between them as the marquess's gaze wandered to the base of her throat, where his diamond ring rested in the small cleft between her collarbones.

"I thought I might take a page from my mother's book and be a bit shameless myself." He looked down at his hands, clenched over the balls of his knees. "I was hoping the bracelet might convince you to wear my ring on your finger at last. They will look better together, after all."

Sophia's heart turned over. By now Withington's face was the color of an eggplant.

His willingness to bare his heart to her, to be honest and kind and good, was lovely, and more than a little endearing. So much so the lump in Sophia's throat grew until it was large as the moon, her heart in her chest so swollen with affection for this new companion she could hardly breathe; with affection, and a special kind of self-loathing that she would drag *his* heart, as honest and kind and good as it was, through the mud of her own indecision.

Withington deserved better than a woman who loved another. She wanted more for him; she wanted him to know the wild, senseless love she knew for Thomas. Withington deserved to be the *one*. He deserved to love fully, and *be* loved fully in return.

He deserved better than what Sophia had to offer him.

Even now, with her family on the brink of bankruptcy— the diamond was still missing, as was the Earl of Harclay and his butler, Mr. Avery—even as Violet quietly dismissed their household servants and sold off their possessions; even as she debated putting the house up for auction; even then, Sophia could not deceive her admirer the marquess.

Not like this. Not with his pride, his future, his heart in the balance.

She brought her fingers to her neck, tangling them in the fine gold chain. With a gentle tug she pulled it from her throat, folding the ring in the palm of her hand.

The marquess, brow furrowed, watched Sophia reach for his wrist, pulling out his hand. She unfurled her fingers and dropped the ring into his palm, curling his fingers around it. As the chain wrinkled into his grasp, Sophia felt her heart gasp for air as the great weight of her indecision was lifted from it.

She was nameless and even poorer than when the season began some months ago.

She'd never felt more free, more sure, or more frightened than she did at this moment.

"But." Withington's eyes flicked from his hand to Sophia and back again. "I don't understand."

Sophia held his fist in the cradle of her hand. She leaned forward, ignoring her mother's pointed look of warning over the slope of Withington's shoulder. "You honor me with your proposal, Withington, and your friendship. I hold you dear in my heart. I adore that you love port. I adore your easy laugh and the kindness you show your family. I adore our conversation and your good nature. I adore you, but—"

"But," he repeated.

"But," she said thickly, "not like you deserve to be adored. Whomever's heart you capture—it won't be long for you— she will love you as you should be loved, and you will understand me then."

Withington scoffed, meeting her eyes. "But I want you."

Sophia's face pulsed with heat. She blinked at the sting of tears. "One day, very soon, you'll be glad it *wasn't* me. It was a close scrape, our courtship. A scrape with disaster, unhappiness. You must believe I am saving you from these things."

For a moment Withington was very still. At last he began to nod slowly, his shoulders sagging. Behind him, the matrons gave up all pretense of tea and conversation *about* tea, and were watching Withington and Sophia with naked interest.

"Sophia. Sophia!" Lady Blaise's voice rose with panic. "Is

everything all right? I hate to see his lordship distressed thus—"

Withington turned abruptly and offered a tight smile over his shoulder. "Quite all right, Lady Blaise, *thank* you."

Sophia's mother flushed and turned back to the dowager marchioness, applying herself with great care to her teacup.

"Hardly fair, that my mother listens to you," Sophia whispered. "Tell me, how do you manage it? Witchcraft? Deals with the devil?"

The marquess's smile loosened. "I would gladly trade my soul if it meant mother dearest kept her pretty nose out of my affairs. Alas, I do not think my soul would prove sufficient payment. It *is* a lot to ask."

Together they scoffed; and then that terrible silence again. Withington's fingers flexed and unfolded around the ring in his hand.

"My only wish is that you find happiness, Sophia." Withington kept his voice low. "If I am not the man with whom you find it, so be it. As long as you are content—that is all that matters to me."

For a moment, Sophia was speechless. He was a good man, Withington, and a better friend.

Friend. Sophia wanted to laugh at the absurdity of it. No self-respecting debutante made *friends* with the season's most eligible bachelor; it was akin to the spider befriending the fly before ensnaring him in her web and eating him for supper. Women and men were not *friends*.

Not in England, anyway.

But here they were, Sophia and the marquess, laughing mean-spiritedly at their mamas, confessing wishes for each other's happiness, reminiscing over their shared love of port.

It was enough to make a girl cry.

And that's exactly what Sophia did.

"Thank you." She grasped his hand and squeezed. "I wish the same for you, Withington. And I have no doubt you will find great happiness. I can think of at least a dozen debutantes who would gladly consider—"

Withington held up a hand and laughed. "Please, for the love of God, spare me! There's a reason I chose you, Sophia. A reason I chose you above all the others."

He made to rise, jerking to his feet, but Sophia pulled him by his sleeve back onto the settee. "If I may be so bold—why *did* you pick me?"

Withington sighed, running a hand through his close-cropped hair as his blush crept back up his neck. "It's rather simple, actually. You are . . . different from all the rest. I knew the moment I met you that you were not cut from the same cloth as the fortune hunters, the heiresses. You wanted so badly to be ambitious, Sophia, to make the same match that all the others wanted. But you are too honest. Too passionate. I like that about you, very much."

He scoffed, shaking his head in that abrupt, nervous way of his. "I suppose those are the same reasons why you *won't* wear my ring. But that doesn't . . . doesn't mean I admire you any less, Sophia. To do the honorable thing, the hard thing, is no small feat. You could very well be the best friend I've got, considering the scalawags and seducers that populate the clubs these days."

By now, tears fell so profusely from Sophia's eyes she could hardly see. Somewhere in the blurry dimness of the room, she heard Lady Blaise's cries for smelling salts and a snifter of brandy; none of it registered as she flung herself into Withington's chest.

"Thank you," she breathed. "Thank you for all that you've done, and all that you are."

Withington was stiff at first; but then he reached around and patted her gently on the shoulder. He stood, pulling her up with him. He stepped away, holding her by the arms, and smiled into her eyes.

"Save your tears for Lady Blaise." His gaze flicked to the tittering ladies across the room. "I think you're going to need them."

Sophia took a deep breath, returning his smile; and was about to gather what was left of her mother when the glint at her wrist stopped her short. "Oh. Oh, here, don't forget this."

She unclasped the bracelet and held it out to him.

"Keep it," he said, waving her away. "It is my gift to you."

Sophia rolled her eyes. "You know me better than that, Withington. I can't keep it."

"I insist."

"And I insist you take it back." She glanced over her shoulder. "Perhaps give it to the dowager marchioness; who knows, it might buy you a little luck. I think you're going to need it."

Withington smiled, taking the bracelet with a sigh of defeat. "Until next time, then."

Sophia reached out and squeezed his hand. "I look forward to meeting all those scalawag friends of yours."

"Scalawag. Such a diverting word."

"More so over a bottle of port. Let's skip the theater next time, shall we?"

Withington groaned with pleasure. "I thought you'd never ask."

Sophia released his hand. His brown eyes were kind but full; and not everything she saw there was joyful or relieved. Even so, he bowed low, tucking the jewelry into his waistcoat pocket; and when he rose, he leaned in and pressed a soft kiss into her cheek.

Behind them, Lady Blaise hit the floor with a dull *thud*. Withington pulled back, a secret smile on his lips.

"Told you to save those tears."

L ady Blaise made a miraculous recovery the moment the musty family coach pulled away from Withington's well-appointed pile.

Sophia sat very still against the squabs, waiting for the assault to begin. Mama opened and closed her mouth several times, her small, heart-shaped face white with anger; Sophia drew several deep breaths, though they did nothing to relieve the knot in her belly.

Lady Blaise focused her gaze on the street outside the grimy carriage window. When Sophia, unable to bear the silence any longer, moved to speak, Mama pinned her to the seat with an icy glare.

"I never pressed this dream upon you, Sophia," she said. "Whatever you desired, I desired, too. You are my only daughter, my only child, and I wished to give you the world. If that meant remaining a spinster like Violet, so be it; a match with a poor vicar, I would have supported you. But you came to desire this match all on your own; you became the creature you are on your own. I wanted what you wanted. And I still want this match, this title, whether you do or not."

Withington was right; the tears came. Sophia had no reply. She was not fool enough to believe her decision would come without consequence; still, the shame that washed through her, the guilt of disappointing her mother; these things were not easy to bear.

Still. She would have to bear them. And hope that in time her mother might forgive her.

B efore the carriage drew to a full stop in the mews behind the house, Cousin Violet appeared breathless at the coach door. In her right fist she held a crumpled piece of paper; her cheeks were wet with tears.

"It's him!" she cried the moment Sophia swung to the ground. "It's *him*, Sophia, he's alive!"

Sophia's eyes widened as a fresh wave of weeping threatened to break. "Lord Harclay? The earl is alive?"

"Yes!" Violet thrust the page into Sophia's hand, choking on the words as she said them. "Look. Look what he—what he sent."

Sophia held Violet against her as she attempted to smooth the wrinkled surface of the paper. "What? What is it?"

But Violet had collapsed into noisy sobs, and could hardly breathe, much less speak.

Sophia glanced down at the page. It was smaller than standard letter paper, about the size of a flimsy; it brought to mind the banknote Mr. Hope had set down on Princess Caroline's marble-topped table the night they bought the French Blue.

But this couldn't be a banknote, certainly not one worth much money, anyway; it was wrinkled almost beyond recognition, and one corner appeared to be missing entirely. The paper itself felt coarse, and crumpled, as if it had come into unwanted contact with water.

Sophia scanned the first few lines.

Banco Giugliano di Firenze . . . 23 June 1812 . . . pay to the bearer . . .

"Thirty thousand pounds." Sophia's head snapped up. "*Thirty thousand pounds*! Good God, Violet, this is the Comte d'Artois' note, isn't it? The money he was going to use to buy the diamond?"

Violet merely nodded, and appeared ready to swoon for the second time in as many weeks.

Sophia felt a swoon coming on herself. "This means—does it mean—heavens, Violet, it's a gift! Harclay's giving you the money as a gift!"

T he earl's invitation arrived the next morning:

> To His Grace the Duke of Sommer
> and all the Ladies of his house,
> His Lordship the Earl of Harclay
> requests your presence
> At a Masquerade Ball
> This evening, at half past eight o'clock.
> A prize shall be awarded
> To the jewel who shines brightest.

Thirty-three

---◆---

Later that night
Brook Street, Hanover Square

Mr. Thomas Hope gave his hat a vicious tug, but to no avail; his curls were as wild as ever, and no matter his best efforts, the beaver hat atop his head would not stay put.

Not that he was surprised. The French Blue was still missing; by Hope's estimation it was lost forever, disappeared into the tumult of history as it did some twenty years ago, in Paris.

And because Hope had yet to miraculously recover the diamond, proving to his clients, investors, and those nasty editors at the papers that yes, he was a capable man of business, and yes, he would safeguard the wealth of those who depended upon him with his very life, he was seen as exactly opposite that: a careless, vulgar idiot.

As Hope's situation deteriorated and Hope & Co. slid further into debt, he'd spent the week at his desk mired in panic, tugging his hands through his hair as if he might pull it out by its very roots. By Friday his dark curls stood on end, lending him the appearance of a wide-eyed street urchin who'd been struck in the arse by lightning.

"Really, old chap, you should try to get some sleep," Mr. Lake had counseled. "We'll find the diamond. When that rascal the earl resurfaces, I'll take him by his—"

Hope had cut short that thought with the wickedest glare he could muster. *Sleep.* Ha! As if he could afford such luxury. Besides, whenever his exhausted eyes fluttered shut—even for a moment, a second, a heartbeat—he saw Sophia's face tensed with passion, screwed tight in pain. Her eyes full as he closed the door on whatever it was they had shared these past weeks.

Even now it stole his breath, the memory of that unspoken good-bye; regret pressed heavy on his chest. He'd never had the chance to tell her that he longed, more than anything, to hold her in the circle of his arms and make her his.

To tell her that he loved her.

The coach pitched to a sudden stop, nearly launching Hope headfirst into the opposite row of velvet squabs. He was going to miss this carriage, yes, but the driver? Not quite.

Hope let out a sigh. The time for regrets had passed. Tonight was his last chance to gain back all that he'd lost. If Harclay, as his invitation suggested, had indeed returned from the dead, then perhaps he'd managed to bring the French Blue back with him. And perhaps—though this was highly, *highly* unlikely— he might feel, after his trip to the underworld, the compulsion to atone for his sins and return the diamond to its rightful owner.

Perhaps.

He glanced out the window; the Earl of Harclay's house was ablaze, the twinkle of crystal and shine of satin-clad ladies peeking through the massive front doors, which were flung open to greet an impossibly long line of guests that snaked along the perimeter of the drive.

For a brief moment his heart rose with hope. Hope, not for the earl to give back what he'd taken, but for Sophia to be there, at the door, her gold eyes alight with mischief. Would she be wearing that pale pink gown of hers, the one with the rosettes embroidered about the neckline? Or, more daringly, the gauzy confection she wore to his own soiree? The invitation *had* said something about a masquerade . . .

Heart pounding, Hope tugged the strings of his white leather domino into some semblance of a knot at the back of his head, his fingers for a moment getting lost in the tangled nest of his curls.

Regret be damned. If he was going to see Sophia tonight, or win back the diamond—he wasn't stupid enough to hope for both—he could not afford to waste a single moment.

Mr. Hope waited rather less patiently than was polite in the receiving line. While he understood that this was the first ball the earl had hosted since he'd come into the title some years ago, it did not excuse the snail-like progression of introductions.

After waiting a lifetime—five minutes, actually, but who was counting?—Mr. Hope ducked into the shrubbery and strode through the front doors beside his grace the Duke of Devonshire, who, as the infamous bachelor duke, arrived alone, and started in that baffled, Labrador-like way curious to the English.

"Hope, old boy, out to avenge your honor?" The duke wagged his heavy brows. "I've been reading up on your diamond, ho ho!"

"My honor's been shot to hell, your grace."

The duke pulled back so violently he nearly fell down the stair, his face wide with horror. "Good God, but what will you do?"

Hope shrugged. "Die, I suppose."

The duke gaped at him as if his brain had just exploded inside his skull. Only after Hope slapped him, hard, on the back, did his good humor return. "Ho, ho, it can't be as bad as all that. You, without honor. Ho ho! What will you live for, old boy? What *will* you live for?"

Hope turned to glance up the stair. There, standing at the top of the landing as if God himself had sent her down from heaven to answer the duke's idiotic query, stood Miss Sophia Blaise.

She was wearing the gown of gauze; the nymph gown. Her dark curls were gathered loosely at the back of her head, a stray lock or two brushing her temples as she smiled at something Cousin Violet was saying.

Hope's gaze darted to the fingers of her left hand. Damnation; she was wearing gloves. But there was no hint of the ring through the fine satin, and he'd seen no mention of the engagement in the papers or gossip sheets.

Not that he'd been looking, of course . . .

Stop.

It took a special kind of idiot to believe a debutante as wicked, and as wickedly pretty, as Sophia would ever refuse the season's most eligible bachelor.

Bah. Even thinking the words *most eligible bachelor* made Hope recoil in distaste. Really, he had to stop reading the gossip sheets.

The Marquess of Withington was heir to a family that traced its lineage back to some hideously handsome medieval knight, who, after saving England from those devil-worshipping Yorkists at Bosworth Field, built the family's current rambling seat with his own two hands and the help of six strapping sons. His title was ancient and his fortune enormous; almost as enormous as his fashionably furry sideburns.

His was the name that every debutante whispered into her pillow at night. Sophia, with her dreams of a brilliant match, was no different. She'd be a fool to pass up the chance to marry the *Marquess* of *Withington*. What with the prince regent being more akin to a hippopotamus than King Arthur, a match with the marquess was even better than a match with royalty.

Hope climbed the stairs slowly, Devonshire breathing heavily beside him.

Sophia turned to him, her smile fading as if in his gaze she could read his dark thoughts. In the molten light of the chandeliers above her eyes burned a deep shade of amber, depthless pools of passion. Whatever she was feeling, she felt it acutely, wholly; she teetered on the edge of something nameless, and it bothered him that he could not assuage it.

His grace the duke bowed low, murmuring some nonsense about the weather and its effect on his delicate knees before excusing himself as one of his mistresses, this one decked out in head-to-toe peacock feathers, tickled him on the ear as she passed.

This left Hope flat-footed and openmouthed before Lady Violet, Sophia, and Lady Blaise. He felt Sophia's presence beside him as one might feel heat from standing too close to a fire. The urge to touch her, to look her shamelessly in the eye, overwhelmed him.

Stop.

Hope pulled off his ridiculous mask, attempting to quell the rapid beating of his heart with thoughts of the diamond, the earl, the bank. He was here to get back what Harclay had taken from him. He was here to protect all those who depended on him.

He was here to fight back in the name of his family.

He turned to Lady Violet.

"Our plot is still in play, yes?" he asked, a bit more breathlessly than he intended.

With no little impatience Violet replied that yes, the plot was still in play, and yes, if Harclay did not hand over the French Blue, she would have him arrested. From the way her eyes wandered toward the crush of the ballroom, looking for the earl, waiting for him to make his move, Hope didn't believe her, not for a second.

Especially not with the slip of paper held in the hand she clutched to her breast. It peeked out between her first and second fingers, a small sliver of fine, smooth-edged stationery. He peered closer, trying to make out the embossed seal half-hidden by her glove.

His weary eyes betrayed him; years spent poring over ledgers in the dark had ruined his sight. But he knew, he *knew*, it was a note from the earl.

Harclay was here.

Hope scanned the ballroom that thrummed beyond the arched threshold, parsing through the masked and feathered and bejeweled faces. Damn him, Harclay had done it on purpose; with everyone in disguise, that devil could move freely about without anyone the wiser.

Well. Two could play this game, Hope thought with a harrumph, and went about refastening the ties of his mask.

Only they kept getting tangled in the wild mass of his hair.

"Here," came a voice, soft, from beside him. "Let me help you, Mr. Hope."

He froze, casting a sidelong glance at Sophia as she raised her arms.

"Thank you." He let his arms fall to his sides as her fingers went to work.

"It is my pleasure."

Hope sucked in a small breath as her fingertips grazed his scalp; a wave of goose bumps broke out on his neck and arms.

The silence between them was broken by Lady Blaise's twittering about moving on, why, look, the dancing's begun, and is that the Dowager Baroness Hat-Wittlesby . . .

"There you are." Sophia patted him lightly on the shoulder. "Does the white suit me?"

"Not at all."

Sophia smiled. Hope's heart lurched.

"I thought I might stand out from all those would-be rogues in their dashing black leather." He sighed. "I suppose one can't win them all, Miss Blaise."

She blushed, her eyes never leaving his. "I suppose not."

For a moment they stood, eyes locked, at the top of the stairs, guests prodding and elbowing their way past them. The music had started; somewhere in the back of his mind, Hope registered the *one-two-three* of a waltz.

He felt desire welling up inside him, grief, too, a kind singular to the sort from which he'd suffered all these years for his family. His heart was full enough of mourning; he did not want to have to mourn Sophia, too.

Stop.

The French Blue.

The bank.

And that bloody bastard the earl.

When he opened his mouth to speak, Sophia rose with hope, eyes wide and willing. Pain ripped through him, pain and rage and the desire to throw her over his shoulder and leave this place forever, the rest be damned.

Stop.

He tore his eyes from her as he fell into an awkwardly stiff bow; and because he could not bear to see her disappointment, he turned and without another word stalked into the ballroom.

For a moment the edges of his vision blurred. Stop, stop, *stop* you bloody fool, stop; the words came in time to the savage pounding of his heart. The agony of leaving Sophia alone, of leaving her so rudely and abruptly to chase after that bloody jewel, left a bitter taste in his mouth.

Hope stole a coupe of champagne from a passing footman and downed it in a single gulp. There, that helped; the ballroom materialized around him, the lilting music, the scents of sweat and spilled wine, the honeyed light of twinkling chandeliers above. He returned the coupe to the gaping footman's tray and stepped into the crush.

The ballroom appeared to be evenly divided: half using the waltz as an excuse to grope one another, half yelling above the din that said dance would lead them all straight to hell. Yes, yes indeed, the waltz was the harbinger of the apocalypse, and did you see the way the Earl of Harclay swept into the ballroom, that dashing black leather mask of his . . .

"Pardon me, Lady Featherstone." Hope watched with no little satisfaction as *both* her chins flushed at his smile. "Did you say the earl has at last made his appearance?"

"Oh, Mr. Hope, yes, yes indeed!" Lady Featherstone leaned in, the wisps of her wig flying in the furious batting of her fan, and lowered her voice. "He's *dancing* with *Lady Violet Rutledge*! Out of all the girls in England, he picks a degenerate gambler, and did you know she openly professes her love for liquor! . . ."

"Thank you," Hope said, peering in the direction of her outstretched arm. Ah, yes, there they were; there was no missing them, pressed against one another as if these were their last moments on earth. The heat between them was palpable, even from here.

Indeed, a small circle of observers had gathered around them, staring incredulously. From the crowd there rose an audible gasp, loud enough to cause the musicians to falter. Hope's heart went to his throat; he pushed toward Violet, desperate to see what was happening, what would happen next.

The crush here was thick and stubborn. No one, it seemed, wished to relinquish their position at the forefront of what was sure to prove this season's greatest scandal.

Hope ducked; he leapt into the air; still he could see nothing.

At last, squeezing between two potbellies, Hope found himself inside the circle.

His eyes fell on Lady Violet.

There, strung from a collar of glittering white diamonds, was the French Blue, nestled just above the overeager rise of Lady Violet's bosom.

The French Blue.

Disbelief pulsed through him, along with a wave of panic so strong it made him nauseous. Without thinking he leapt into motion, pushing bodies out of the way as he made for Violet, the diamond, his salvation.

The Earl of Harclay was nowhere to be found; it seemed he'd vanished as quickly, as inexplicably, as he'd appeared some moments before.

The crush was terrible, and even with the advantage of his height and breadth he could make little headway. His heart raced. He was close, so close, he couldn't let the diamond out of his sight . . .

If only for Sophia. If only to save her family's meager fortune, her cousin, her mother, and her uncle. If only for Sophia, he would reclaim the diamond, make it his once more.

When at last he trampled his way to the middle of the room, Lord Harclay had, predictably, disappeared; Violet was nowhere to be found. He frantically searched the sea of faces that surrounded him on all sides, thousands and thousands of masked people he did not recognize. Was that the back of her head there? Or her skirts, was she wearing blue, or had it been white? No, no, he thought, ticking off faces as he looked, not her, not her, *definitely* not her . . .

But then he caught sight of a small ripple on the sea's surface, a parting of bodies as if someone were snaking between them. He followed the movement as it made its way across the ballroom and into the gallery beyond; as the figure rounded the corner, he caught the glimmer of a gauzy gown, followed by the flash of diamonds.

It was Violet. She was going after the earl, wherever he'd disappeared to.

Hope pushed and prodded his way after her, ignoring the cries and gasps of outrage as he went. He wasn't about to lose the French Blue, not after he'd come so far; not after all he'd lost, and still had to lose.

He stumbled into the gallery just as Lady Violet ducked through the narrow servants' door at the far end of the hallway. Hope paused, catching his breath, his mind racing with options, his chances, what his next move should be; and as he stood there, his eyes of their own volition settled on a shapely figure in an alcove to his right.

Sophia stood dutifully next to her mother as Lady Blaise

chatted with a circle of flush-faced matrons. Watching Sophia, face studiously blank as if she were about to weep, eyes darting over her mother's shoulder in search of him—he *knew* she was looking for him—something inside Hope broke and began to bleed. He felt the poison seeping into his lungs, weighing down his limbs and his will to move on.

But he had to move on. *Move*, but his feet remained planted on the parquet floor of Harclay's high-ceilinged hall.

Hope gritted his teeth. There would be time enough for grief. Right now he *had to move*.

Only with tremendous effort did he coax his body into motion. Down the gallery, through the door, he nearly fell down the darkened corridor of the servants' stair. His unexpected tumble lent him momentum, and the cacophony of the kitchens passed by in a whirl of scents and shouts and the clatter of pots.

He heard Violet's voice, soft and breathless, followed by the burly cook's booming reply: "He's thataway, my lady. Just missed 'im, you did. You'd best hurry!"

He followed Violet into the servants' quarters at the back of the house. Violet was calling for Harclay, *William, William, wait*, as her footsteps quickened on the cold stone floor.

Hope followed her through the back kitchen door and out into the night, skidding on the loose gravel of the drive. Lady Violet was several paces in front of him; she was cursing, something about damning said William to hell; in answer to her curses, an enormous coach silently materialized out of the darkness.

Hope plastered himself against the house's far outer wall, peering through a thorny tangle of a rosebush. The vehicle slowed but did not stop; the door flung open, and with a little yelp, Violet was swept from her feet and into the carriage, the door clicking quietly shut behind her.

His blood rushed as he bolted out into the drive. Had Lady Violet, with that fifty-carat diamond about her neck, been *kidnapped*? Hope was as tired of that plot as anyone, but it *did* make sense; it wouldn't be the first time the French Blue was thieved out from under his nose.

Or had the Earl of Harclay—*William*, Lord Townshend—

defied everyone's wildest expectations and actually done the honorable thing? Had he swept Lady Violet off her feet so that he might take her to the *altar*, the diamond aside?

And could Harclay even speak words like *honor* and *altar* without bursting into flames?

Only time would tell.

And Hope didn't have very much time at all.

He leapt out into the drive and burst into a sprint, his heart hammering as he gunned after the coach. The gravel slipped and skidded beneath the fine soles of his pumps; his chest and throat burned.

He was so close. So very, very close to getting back what was stolen from him those weeks and weeks ago. The diamond was within his grasp; he could feel its cold weight in the palm of his hand, the thrill of his triumph.

But it was slipping further and further away, the coach disappearing into the darkness as the pair of matching blacks was urged into a gallop.

The drive curved into the lane up ahead. Hope watched as the coach pulled into the evening traffic, disappearing into the seamless tangle of horseflesh and lacquer that heaved just beyond the gates of Harclay's property.

And then, as if it had never existed at all, the coach was gone.

His heart burst with pain and Hope doubled over, hands on his knees as he fought to breathe. He tried to curse the vilest curses he knew, in every language he spoke, but all he managed were a few pitiful wheezes.

The diamond was gone. That bloody jewel was gone *again*.

He felt sick at the finality of it, the irony of it. Hope knew better than anyone that the French Blue brought misfortune to those who owned it—first Shah Jehan, then that wily traveler Tavernier, the kings of France. And now it brought misfortune to Thomas Hope; a hideously classic example of mankind being doomed to repeat its terrible history.

Doom. Even the poet in Hope winced at the word. It was 1812, damn it, and no such thing as doom existed anymore. Everyone knew it died out with the Tudors, or, at the very least, with wart-faced Oliver Cromwell.

Even so. Watching the innocuous push and pull of traffic in the lane, the slow turning of the moon in the night sky above, Hope could not shake the sense of dread knotting in the pit of his belly.

He was about to collapse in defeat and, with any luck, roll into a ditch somewhere when a familiar hiss—*psst! Psst!*— sounded from over his shoulder.

Hope rose, chest releasing with relief at the sight of La Reinette leaning out a carriage door, her face obscured by a red satin domino.

"Venir, monsieur, vite!"

She waved him over to the coach in that singularly elegant way of hers, her eyes on his face as he trotted toward her.

"We've got," he wheezed, pointing in the direction of the lane. "To go."

La Reinette held out her hand. *"Oui, oui*, I know, come!"

Thank God.

Thank God she was here to save him. He still had a chance.

Hope fell heavily onto the fine velvet squabs. It was dark inside the coach, the lanterns having been extinguished; the better, he figured, to slip through London's streets unnoticed.

"Oh, Marie." He gasped. "I cannot tell you. What a relief. It is. To see you."

He saw the flash of her teeth as she smiled. In the dark they appeared small and sharp, like the talons of a falcon.

He paused. "Wait a. Moment. What are you. Doing back in London?"

"It was time," she replied. He waited for her to say more but she remained silent.

"Well then," he said uneasily. "Shall we be off?"

The voice that answered did not belong to La Reinette.

Or any woman, for that matter.

"Oui, we shall." The voice was like gravel; the accent heavy but clear, clipped.

Hope recognized it at once.

Beside him, Guillaume Cassin pounded the roof with his silver-topped cane. The carriage heaved into motion.

Hope jerked to life, leaping for the door; but the man who had indeed come back from the dead, whose neck La Reinette had sliced open in that sour-smelling room in Paris, stopped him short, using his cane to thwack Hope soundly in the head.

Hope fell face-first to the floor with a ringing *thump*.

In his head his blood rushed.

And then, nothing.

Thirty-four

Thankfully Lady Blaise had wept herself into a stupor over Cousin Violet's sudden disappearance at the ball, leaving Sophia to face the black evening ahead in blessed solitude.

After helping Fitzhugh, one of the few servants left at the house, carry Mama upstairs to her bed, Sophia pleaded exhaustion. With promises that she would wait up for any word of Violet's whereabouts, she ducked into her room and closed the door behind her.

She stripped off her pale satin gloves and loosened a particularly painful pin that had assaulted her right ear all night, allowing them to fall through her fingers to the floor.

And then she fell back against the door and let out the breath she'd been holding all night, tears welling as she sank slowly to the ground.

She wrapped her arms around her knees and allowed herself at last to cry, her hurt and her anger and her grief pouring from her eyes, the tears hot as they slid down the length of her neck.

It was the sort of cry reserved for prima donnas on stage and hapless heroines in novels.

But Sophia would not be thwarted; she had wronged, and been wronged in return, and hang it all if she wasn't going to get a good, solid, one-for-the-ages cry out of it.

Mr. Hope had looked handsomer than ever tonight; and while he would've looked better in black leather rather than white, her heart had skipped a beat at the blue of his eyes, the boyish curve of his lips. He'd excused himself so abruptly on the landing of the top of the stairs; as she watched him walk away, intent on seeking out the French Blue, her heart, so exultant moments before, sank into the depth of her disappointment and seemed to dissolve altogether.

It would be the last time. The last time he would bow over her hand and her blood would pulse with the knowledge that he was hers and hers alone. The last time she would look into his eyes and see her own desire, the love she bore him, reflected in the wide, startling blue irises.

On ne peut avoir le beurre et l'argent du beurre.

Sophia remembered the faraway look in La Reinette's eyes as she said the words.

One cannot have one's cake and eat it, too.

The madam had been talking about some lover or another, one who broke her heart; one she loved above all the others. Now Sophia understood La Reinette's pain, her regret. By setting her cap at London's most eligible—and often most lackluster—gentlemen, Sophia had neglected men like Thomas.

Passionate men, handsome men, men who made her feel alive, adored.

Men who loved her, and whom she loved in return.

What a fool she'd been! To even *think* of choosing the Marquess of Withington, sweet natured as he was, over Thomas Hope.

Thomas hadn't broken her heart; no, Sophia had done smart work of that herself.

And now she was alone in a crumbling house, no money or future of which to speak; it would only be a matter of time before that Cassin fellow, wherever he'd disappeared to, revealed her identity as the author of some of the most scandalous memoirs England had seen in decades. What little she had left—family, reputation—would be ruined.

Again the tears threatened; but even as Sophia was tempted to give in, and give up, and resign herself to a thankless and gray spinsterhood in some thankless, gray place like Scotland—for surely Mama's exhibitions of grief would force all of them into exile—she found herself wondering what La Reinette would do.

La Reinette. Yes, thinking of Madame always made Sophia feel better; and in the early, heady days of her courtship—if one could call it that—with Mr. Hope, the Little Queen's adventures occupied her thoughts often.

Sophia glanced toward her bed, the single taper on the table beside it. Its flame wavered sluggishly in the still air of the room.

Barely enough light by which to read.

But it was enough.

Sophia wiped her eyes with the heel of her hand and scampered to the side of the bed. Drawing up on her knees, she pushed aside the bedclothes and ducked to peer into the dark space below.

Admittedly not the cleverest of hiding spaces, but then again Lady Blaise was not the cleverest of mamas. Besides, if anyone needed watching, it was Cousin Violet; no one suspected Sophia of much beyond the usual sins of youth: vanity, a proclivity for gossip and flirtation.

Harmless things, really, when compared to her usual nighttime activities. If her mother only knew! Lady Blaise would be dead of apoplexy in five seconds flat.

The tattered hatbox scraped across the floor as Sophia drew it out into the small circle of light. She traced the familiar lettering, now faded, with her fingers: LOCK & CO HATTERS. 6 ST. JAMES'S ST. LONDON.

Carefully she placed the box on the bed and climbed up after it, her slippers falling to the floor with tiny, hollow *plunks*. Drawing near the taper, she opened the box, inhaling the animal scents of leather and fur that still clung to it so many years later.

Inside, a scattered pile of fine paper lay strewn about the box's silk-lined interior. Each page was covered in Sophia's careful copperplate handwriting, La Reinette's extraordinary life boiled down to a series of looping *p*'s and *g*'s, the grand arch of an *A*.

Sophia read the first line of script at the top page—*It had been a cold winter, a terrible winter, and I knew the duke's warm embrace could not last forever*—and only when the taper's light sputtered, the wick having burned down to a blackened nub, was La Reinette's spell broken.

Sophia looked up, blinking. She sat up, running a hand

along the stiffness in her neck, and set the pages down on her lap.

Goodness, but the memoir was good; Madame's stories were intoxicating; the romance and the bare-chested barons and long, naked nights spent before roaring fires made for some exquisite reading.

Sophia glanced out the window; outside the night was black, no sign yet of dawn or sleep.

Settling a few pillows against the headboard, Sophia leaned against them and bent her knees, propping the pages on her thighs. She still had a few minutes yet of light, and the story was just getting good . . .

> *The spy had no name but the bluest eyes I had ever seen in my short life. With his gaze alone he could fell any woman, rich or poor, royal or common . . .*
>
> *Tonight he played the part of pirate, leaping from his ship on the Seine, his billowing shirt open, his eyes alive with danger. It took all my strength not to swoon at his feet. His dark hair was wild in the wind, the curls held back by a red handkerchief . . . I waited for him to touch me, for the stars in the blank sky above to answer my urgent prayers that he love me as I loved him . . .*

Sophia pulled back, her thoughts sparking with a vague sense of recognition, of familiarity. Blue eyes, fallen woman, dark, curly hair.

Dread snaked up her spine; her body went stiff. It couldn't be; couldn't *possibly* be him. He and La Reinette were no more than strangers back then, two people brought together by a series of exciting, if unfortunate, events. She couldn't be in love with him, not after what they'd done together . . .

But Sophia knew better. She recalled her conversation with La Reinette the night Mr. Hope had interrupted their meeting at The Glossy:

I enjoyed this week's tales. Thoroughly. That spy you knew, back in France—the one with the curls, who could fell a girl with his gaze alone? He is my favorite gentleman yet.

La Reinette had smiled; a smile Sophia now understood to

be the secret sort, the malicious sort. *Yes. He is my favorite, too.*

Blue eyes, fallen woman, dark, curly hair.

It could only be one man.

It could only be Mr. Thomas Hope.

Sophia leapt to her bare feet, her mind racing as she tore into her armoire in search of her boots.

Of three things she was certain.

First, La Reinette was in love with Mr. Hope, had been since they'd first met nearly a decade ago.

Second, Hope was not in love with La Reinette, never had been.

And third, La Reinette was French. She said herself the French were possessed of vengeful hearts. As a woman spurned, Sophia had no doubt Madame would do everything in her power to destroy the object of her unrequited affections.

Everything, like colluding with Hope's enemy, Guillaume Cassin, to mastermind a plot to bring Hope to his knees.

A plot to bring the woman Hope *did* love to her knees, too.

It made perfect sense; Sophia was angry at herself for not seeing it sooner. La Reinette was the only one other than Thomas who knew Sophia was writing scandalous memoirs. The madam was the missing link; *she* was the one who sold Sophia out to the gossip sheets.

And now that La Reinette and Cassin had Sophia by the short hairs, they would turn their attention to Mr. Hope.

It was, ironically enough, just the sort of plot, of adventure, that populated the Little Queen's memoirs. Only now, the madam would use her cunning and wily nimbleness against Sophia; it was no longer an adventure but a duel, a race to ruin.

Sophia quickened her steps, and was about to scuttle down the stairs, when she caught sight of the narrow door that led to Uncle Rutledge's dressing room. She paused, but only for a moment; she darted into the room, emerging moments later wearing only her chemise, a ball of clothes tucked into the crook of her arm.

She skipped down the stair as she tugged one leg, then the other, into her uncle's rather voluminous breeches; she tugged a shirt over her head, tossing aside a musty waistcoat after tangling her arms in its armholes. Too much work, that, and no one would notice, anyway.

At least she *hoped* no one would notice.

Skidding out the kitchen door, Sophia shrugged into a jacket. She topped off her costume with a hat that was two sizes too big and twenty years out of fashion.

She tucked the last of her pilfered finds into her jacket and, tipping up her nose so that she might run without the hat falling into her eyes, Sophia took off at a sprint.

There wasn't much time. She had to stop La Reinette and that rat-faced Frenchman Cassin from getting to Thomas.

If they hadn't already.

Thirty-five

———◆———

The Glossy was a far less pleasant place, Hope found, when one was bound and gagged and dragged none too gently down the stairs to a dark, smelly room behind the kitchens.

His senses returned slowly. He was vaguely aware of the murmured conversation between La Reinette and Cassin as they followed him into the basement; every word, spoken in crisp, clipped French, made the pain in his head pulse sharply.

When at last he opened his eyes, the darkened room swam languidly about him; he was suddenly aware of the chafe of rope against the skin of his wrists, his arms bound behind him to the rickety chair in which he sat. A handful of stray curls had fallen into his eyes, and the impulse to push them away made his fingers itch.

He managed a glance about the room. It was a pantry, its shelves lined with flour and turnips and cellars of salt; a trio of cured pig haunches hung listlessly from the ceiling, lilting back and forth, back and forth, as if they, too, were impatient to know what the *devil* this was about.

Aside from the pig haunches and turnips, the room was bare, illuminated by a single lamp La Reinette had placed on a nearby shelf.

Umberto, seemingly unscathed from his run-in with Hope's pursuers some weeks ago, was tying Hope's legs to those of the chair. Marie urged him *faster, faster*, then shooed him from the room when the task was done; quietly she closed the door behind him, turning to Hope.

Her eyes were alive, joyfully triumphant as if she'd wagered her last guinea on a no-count featherweight and won. Hope swallowed. He didn't like that look, not on La Reinette; it made her look wild, like she might do or say anything and Hope would be none the wiser.

From behind her, where Cassin moved in the darkness, there came ominous scraping sounds, metal against metal; he was sharpening something, a blade. Hope swallowed, his belly turning over. He did not care to know what Cassin was up to back there.

Not yet, anyway.

La Reinette sauntered toward him, crossing her arms over her chest. She wore a robe of watery Japanese silk that was so fine as to be transparent, showing every curve, every sinew, highlighting especially the hardened points of her nipples.

Hope looked away, annoyed. Had she come to slay or seduce him? How like her to confuse the two.

"Thomas, look at me."

His gaze snapped to meet hers. "Don't call me that. I am not Thomas to you."

The triumph in her eyes faded somewhat; she chewed the inside of her lip as she considered him. He gently tugged at his bindings, only to find they wouldn't budge. Umberto, it seemed, knew his way around tying innocent men to rather uncomfortable chairs.

Hope swallowed the panic that rose in his throat. He'd faced worse odds than these and had somehow managed to survive. Tonight will be no different, he told himself. Think. *Think.*

"So you and Cassin." Hope nodded at the figure that moved in the shadows behind La Reinette. "What an unlikely alliance, considering you killed him eight years ago. Tell me, Marie, how'd you manage such a feat? The mind boggles. Really, it does."

The madam twisted her lips into a sour smile. "I am perhaps a witch. That answer, does it satisfy you?"

Hope scoffed. "Don't insult me, Marie."

She tilted her head; after a moment she uncrossed her arms and pulled up her sleeve, fingering a ribbonlike scar that ran up the pale flesh of her inner arm.

"It was my blood on his throat. I went to Cassin before,

and told him you meant to kill him. And to myself I thought, let Hope think his enemy is dead; what a surprise it will be, yes, when he knows he is alive! And my friend Cassin. A very good actor he is."

Hope felt the damp break out beneath his arms and along the edge of his scalp; if he didn't feel ill before, he definitely did now. Though he knew the answer, he asked the question anyway.

"Why?"

Marie smiled. She let down her sleeve, resting her hands on the arms of his chair.

"And you." She bent over him and brushed her lips to his ear. "Do not play stupid. These things I do not want to say. Don't make me say them, *Thomas*."

He winced. It was all wrong, that name on her tongue. Thomas belonged to Miss Sophia Blaise.

Thomas was dead.

He looked La Reinette in the eye. "Answer the question, *Marie*."

The movement behind the madam stilled; she turned and murmured something soothing in French. After a beat, Cassin resumed his sinister doings, and Marie turned back to Hope.

He sensed her hesitate when she met his eyes; for a moment her own went blank, as if she were lost, under a spell.

"My God," he breathed. "You can't still—no. Not after all these years. Surely there have been others."

Marie blinked; her eyes went hard again. She rocked back on her heels, gaze trained on Hope's feet. "You. You I loved from that first time we met. There has only been you."

Understanding rolled hard and heavy through him. "Marie. I made clear to you my feelings—"

"Your feelings." She scoffed, meeting his eyes. "That is it, you see. You never had them for me. Not the feelings I had for you."

Hope swallowed. The bindings at his wrists and ankles felt unbearably tight. "I'm sorry, Marie. I am. We had a jolly bit of fun, you and I, I thought we were partners, friends, even. I gave you everything I could—"

Her eyes flashed with anger now; for the first time ever he

saw color rise to her cheeks. "What about that time, in the, how do you say? *Vignoble*."

"Oh, God, Marie, that was *one* time. We were drunk. I was drunk. I should have never—"

"Yes. You should have never. I will make you regret it, Thomas. Tonight. You will regret what you did to me."

Hope let his head fall back, closing his eyes. "It was a mistake. I apologized for it. I regret what I did, I do. Christ, Marie. Out of all the men who have loved you all these years. Kings and princes and tsars—you could've had any man you wanted, and still you wanted *me*?"

Again that wry twist of her mouth. "Ah, yes. I am always wanting what I cannot own. And you know the tsar, he was, how do you say it?" She made a pinching gesture with her first finger and thumb.

"Tiny."

"Ah, yes, tiny."

Hope swallowed for what felt like the hundredth time. He straightened, opening his eyes. "We could've never been together, you and I. We were partners. An entanglement . . . it would've gotten in the way. I had a job to do, Marie. You knew I was running for my life. Mr. Lake saved me, but only on the condition that I help him—"

"Mr. Lake. Do not use him as the excuse, Thomas. No. You used me, my brain, my body, as if I was nothing to you, the dirt under your boots. My heart, you broke it. And so I decide to make the score even, make you bleed the way I bleed."

Hope glanced over her shoulder. "So you went to Cassin. Allied with my enemy, plotted my demise in the most epic and medieval fashion you could think of, cursed my black soul. All the usual tomfoolery, yes? Except you didn't kill me. You could have, right then and there in that room in Paris, and been done with the whole business. Why wait until now?"

La Reinette's smile deepened. Turning to the shelf, she asked, "Wine?"

"Thank you, Madame." Hope rolled his eyes. "But my hands are, at the moment, otherwise occupied."

Madame shrugged, pouring red wine into a fine Murano glass tumbler. She brought it to her lips, her dark eyes dancing with glee. Damn her, she was enjoying this a tad too much.

"I wait all this time," she said, "because I believe in taking, what is the expression? Two eyeballs?"

Because it appeared he would not have them to roll much longer, Hope rolled his eyes again. "Eye for an eye."

"Ah, yes, eye for an eye! I have been waiting all this time for you to fall in love, to love someone as deep as I loved you these years. I bide my time so that I might take from you what you take from me."

Hope started, his vision blurring as rage engulfed his carefully practiced nonchalance. He gave his bindings a vicious tug, hardly feeling the rope as it scalded his ankles and wrists.

"Leave Sophia out of this," he growled. "She did nothing to deserve your wrath. She is innocent. Punish me if you must, but leave Sophia alone."

The viciousness of his defense of her, the wild pulse of his blood, the violent urge to do violent things to keep her safe—it shocked him. He loved Sophia, had loved her since he pressed her body against his in that dreadful closet; but now he suddenly, devastatingly knew just how much he *loved* her.

"She did nothing!" La Reinette threw back her head and laughed. "Nothing but steal the heart that was meant for me! No, Thomas. If I cannot have you, no one will. Especially not that silly girl Sophia."

At the sound of her name on La Reinette's poisoned tongue, Hope lurched forward, straining against his bindings with all his might. So wild was his assault that Hope would have toppled the chair if Marie had not reached out a hand to steady him.

"It all was so perfect, yes," she said. "Cassin at last was in London, here to seek his own revenge against you. And then you fall in love! It is too perfect. The missing diamond, I did not plan that, but it was, as you English say, the ice on the biscuit."

Hope didn't bother correcting her. "Cassin is a traitor and a murderer, Marie. When he has his way with me, what the devil do you think he'll do to you?"

As if on cue, Guillaume Cassin's unshaven face appeared over La Reinette's shoulder. His wolfish grin revealed slimy green teeth—really, did the French practice any sort of dental hygiene at all?—and when he spoke, his cigar-ravaged voice raised goose bumps on Hope's arms and the back of his neck.

It was *him*. Understanding unfurled as Hope thought back to that first night in Mayfair, the night he and Lake had gone out looking for the French Blue.

It had been Cassin who'd given Hope and Lake chase; Cassin, who'd followed Hope up to La Reinette's rooms in The Glossy. Hope recalled La Reinette distracting Cassin as he and Sophia escaped. Now Hope understood that Marie had merely told her partner in crime to hold back, be patient, wait for the right time to strike.

Cassin, who'd penned that nasty note to La Reinette to throw them off her scent. He imagined them, heads bent over the page, cackling gleefully at their *savoir-faire* as Cassin scrawled his filth.

"He-*llo, Mees*ter Hope." Cassin stepped forward around La Reinette. He was bigger than Hope remembered; his teeth blacker, skin sallow. "What I am going to do to you, I have been saving, for only you. It has been many long years, after all. Many years to plan your pain, *Mees*ter Hope. You kill me, you kill my man. And I now—haha! You know the rest."

He held something that glinted silver up to the low light, reverently fingering its surface as he would a woman's body. For a moment Hope was blinded by a metallic flash; blinking, he made out the long, pointy shape of a French-style rapier, complete with overly bejeweled handle that swooped out in a series of gilded loops and swirls.

Hope swallowed. Again. And somehow managed to muster a scoff. "Ah, *monsieur*, I admire your sense of humor! Does it have a name?"

Cassin swung the sword through the air in a high, dramatic arc; the weapon made an equally dramatic *whoosh whoosh!* noise as he did so. "Of course. In France, our weapons are like our women. Beautiful, lithe, very deadly. This one I have given the name Bernadette."

"Bernadette?" Hope wrinkled his nose. "You're really going to kill me with a sword named *Bernadette*? Surely you can do better than that."

Cassin pursed his lips, offended. "You insult her," he said, polishing the blade of the rapier with his cape, "and you insult me. *En garde!*"

The Frenchman squatted into a lunge, and before Hope knew what he was about, Cassin charged forward, bringing the blade down on his face so quickly he hardly felt it slice through his cheek.

Hope did, however, feel the sting of the cut a moment later, followed by the warm drip of blood down the slope of his face. He smelled its sickly sweet scent above the must of the pantry; it filled his nostrils, thick, nauseating.

Two cuts, in nearly the same place: first La Reinette's hedgerow, poking his cheek that night weeks and weeks ago; and now Bernadette, making mincemeat of his face.

Maybe Cassin would poke his eyeballs out next. Soon Hope and Lake would be twins.

He would've laughed at the thought if panic didn't slam through him. It struck him, suddenly, that he faced death; *he would die here, tonight.* Before it had been petty games and witty banter, trading barbs with La Reinette as she told her tale of woe.

But now.

Now the diversion was done, leaving only the vengeful hearts that beat in the bodies standing before him.

Hope was going to die, and by a *rapier* named *Bernadette*, no less. No honorable death for him; no battle-scarred sword to the neck. Cassin would kill him and throw his body in the Thames, and that would be that.

It was a rather sobering thought.

He closed his eyes against the rage, the regret, and the hurt that welled up inside him. All he could think of was Sophia; all he could see in the vast blackness behind his eyelids was her face, the tender indent in her bottom lip as she bit down on it. More than anything he wanted to see her one last time, to tell her that he loved her above all things, above the bank and his grief and the family he left behind.

To tell her that *she* was his family now. That they should start one of their own.

To tell her he should've never let her go. That he couldn't bear the thought of another man, no matter her dreams of a brilliant match, touching her, having her, marrying her.

God, what he would give to kiss her one last time. He remembered that first kiss in Princess Caroline's puce-colored drawing room, the way Sophia had yielded to him, invited his touch. Her sense of adventure, her wit, and her honesty.

While his heart was glad to have known her at all, to have loved her and held her when he did, he cursed himself for never telling her. For letting her go.

And then his brothers—why did he never apologize, try, and try again until things between them were right and good? They were the only family he had left, and Thomas had kept them at arm's length, virtual strangers.

He would go to his grave regretting these things.

Hope opened his eyes. Cassin was raising his rapier, his dark eyes gleaming with malice. He swung Bernadette in the air, winding up for the deathblow.

Sophia, he pleaded silently. *Sophia, I am sorry.*

Cassin brought down the blade. Hope flinched, his heart lurching in his chest.

Was it to be heaven or hell for his soul? Probably hell, all things considered; surely the devil enjoyed his liquor more than all the angels and saints . . .

"Stop!"

There was a great racket by the door; Hope's eyes flew to the threshold to see a disheveled lump of a man dart into the pantry, tossing his ridiculous feathered hat to the side as he launched himself at Cassin.

The Frenchman's eyes went wide; and then all Hope could see was a tussle of a black cape and long, shining curls, Cassin grunting and La Reinette screaming and Umberto falling face-first to the ground just inside the door.

Bernadette fell, too, with a scraping clatter that did not bode well for its bejeweled handle.

Cassin had somehow managed to take the man by his curls, tugging him viciously against his chest so that the intruder now faced Hope, his head caught in the crook of Cassin's rather massive arm.

"Sophia?" Hope breathed. "What the devil do you think you're doing?"

"Yes." Cassin panted. "Yes, what is she doing here?"

La Reinette swooped down and retrieved Bernadette, placing

her in Cassin's outstretched hand. "Guillaume, it is perfect. We will kill them both, and poof! All our problems, they are gone."

Hope's blood surged as he watch Cassin pull Sophia against him, holding the blade of the rapier at her throat.

"You foolish girl," Cassin murmured into her ear. "You think you might save him, all by yourself? Haha! You make us laugh."

Sophia's eyes were wide; she grasped Cassin's forearm as if that might keep him from slitting her throat. For a moment she met Hope's gaze; he could not tell what she was thinking. There was nothing she could do, nowhere she could go. They were done for, as good as dead.

Without warning, Sophia winked—at least he *thought* he saw her wink. And then she let out a hot, distraught sigh, her hand moving from Cassin's arm to her face before she crumpled against him, eyes rolling up into her head before they closed altogether.

Dear God. She'd *swooned*.

And she'd looked just like her mother as she'd done it. Learned from the best indeed!

Cassin froze; La Reinette drew back, brow furrowed.

It was just enough of a pause for Sophia to leap into action. Her eyes flew open as she slammed her elbows into Cassin's gut, and he doubled over with a shout of pain. His rapier once again clattered to the floor; at once Sophia and La Reinette dove after it.

With his heart in his throat, Hope watched the women wrestle each other to the ground, Sophia yelping as La Reinette tugged at her hair. His own limbs pricked to join the fight, to shield Sophia from the madam's wrath.

La Reinette got the better of Sophia, rolling on top of her as she drew back her fist and slammed it into Sophia's cheek. Hope burned with white-hot rage, tugging at his bindings with a viciousness that made his wrists bleed in sympathy with her bloody lip.

Cassin was still rolling on the floor, whining meekly in unintelligible French. Sophia continued to struggle, but La Reinette had the clear advantage. Pinning her to the ground between her knees, Marie reached over Sophia's head and snatched the rapier from the ground.

She climbed to her feet, breathless, and held the point of Bernadette to Sophia's throat.

"Don't," Hope snarled. "Leave her be, Marie."

Marie ignored him, using the rapier's tip to tilt Sophia's chin. "So pretty," she murmured. "So very, very pretty. I see why he loves you, *mademoiselle*. Your charms are many."

Sophia glanced toward Hope. She held her hands by her ears in surrender; but as he watched, she lowered her right hand slowly, very slowly, toward the waist of her suspiciously enormous black-satin breeches.

"Marie." Hope turned to face La Reinette. "Point your blade at me. I am the one deserving of your anger. Besides. Disposing of one body is one thing; but two bodies is a different matter altogether. Isn't that so, Cassin?"

Cassin moaned his consent.

La Reinette met Hope's gaze. "Before, yes, I to—"

Sophia pulled the gleamingly ornate pistol from her breeches and held it in her right hand, releasing the safety as she pointed it at La Reinette.

Hope's heart went to his throat. Out of all the things Sophia could have been hiding in those breeches, he never guessed she'd hide an antique dueling pistol that looked to be a relic of Queen Elizabeth's court; but the trick worked.

La Reinette stumbled back in horror, Sophia rising to stare down the barrel of the gun at Marie's pale face.

Sophia nodded at the rapier. "Drop it."

Marie did as she was told. Holding up her hands, she said, "*Mademoiselle*, listen to me. Listen, yes? I let you go. We let you go, forget the gossip sheets and the memoirs, we forget everything we did to you. Keep your honor, your reputation. Marry whatever lord you pick. I give you this if you give me *him*."

Hope's pulse stilled at her words. He glanced at Sophia; he could not tell what she was thinking. But La Reinette was offering her everything she ever wanted: the peace to pursue her marquess, and marry him without event, her reputation and her pride intact.

His throat tightened. At least he got to see her one last time.

It was too enticing an offer. Sophia should take it and run. She was on the verge of making her dreams come true; this one last push, and it would all fall into her lap.

Sophia should leave Thomas and never look back.

But she didn't.

Instead, she said, "Untie him."

"But, *mademoiselle*, I—"

"Un*tie* him," Sophia thrust the pistol against La Reinette's temple, "or so help me God I'll put a bullet through your head. I am not a soulless lightskirt like you; I won't leave Thomas. I can't leave him."

After a beat, Marie stooped before Hope, head down as she went to work at the ropes that bound his ankles.

Relief washed through Thomas as she untied one leg, then the other. Perhaps he would make it out of here alive; perhaps he and Sophia had a fighting chance.

He glanced up to meet Sophia's eyes. They were hard, still full of alligator tears, but hopeful.

Venturing a smile, Hope opened his mouth to speak when a flash of movement behind Sophia caught his eye.

Too late did he see Cassin rising to his feet, reaching through the gloom with his broad-fingered hand for Sophia's throat.

Thirty-six

———— ✦ ————

I t all happened so quickly Sophia hardly had time to think. She was pulled, hard, from behind, a hand wrapping around her neck and squeezing shut her windpipe. Cassin's warm, foul breath filled her nostrils as he tugged her around to face him.

With trembling hands she jabbed the pistol into his ribs, but he merely smiled down at her, tightening his grip on her throat.

"Do it," he hissed. "I remember your shot, it is not very good. I was there, remember, when you could not shoot me?"

Sophia swallowed. Of course she remembered. If only she had remembered to have Thomas teach her how to properly fire a pistol in the meantime. Damn him, she'd been too distracted by his body, his hands, specifically, to waste what precious time they had on so mundane a thing as *shooting*.

Still. Such knowledge would've come in handy at a moment like this.

Sophia fingered the trigger. Dear God, was the gun even loaded? She'd snatched it as an afterthought from a drawer in Uncle Rutledge's dressing room. For all she knew it could be a prop from Drury Lane, an ancient heirloom that hadn't been fired in two hundred years.

Well.

Whatever it was, Sophia was about to find out.

Screwing shut her eyes, she gritted her teeth in anticipation of the discharge and pulled the stiff trigger.

There was a great rushing sound in her ears as her heart

leapt to her throat. She opened her eyes, and Cassin was staring at her, his dark eyes inscrutable.

And then his face creased and the gruesome seam of his mouth opened and he laughed, a loud, triumphant sound. He let loose her throat and wrenched the pistol from her hands, tossing it to the floor where it landed with a decidedly hollow *clunk*.

Sophia glanced at Hope, eyes widening with panic.

This was bad.

He sat very still in his chair. Behind him La Reinette dropped his bound hands—*blast, his hands were still tied*—and slowly rose, her doe eyes brimming with triumph.

"I gave you the chance," she said, grinning. "I gave you the chance to go but you do not take it. So now, we will have the two bodies."

Sophia glanced at Hope, feeling the heat drain from her face. His blue eyes sparked; her heart skipped a beat.

Before she knew what he was about, he reached out and with his foot kicked the rapier up into the air. With bated breath Sophia watched it arc through the room; reflexively she reached up and managed to catch it, thoughtlessly, by the blade.

Ignoring the searing burn that burst across her palm, she took the sword by its rather ridiculous handle. This time she did not hesitate; she whirled about and, praying she was better with a rapier than she was with a pistol, slashed the weapon in the general direction of Cassin.

She sensed the blade finding purchase in the hardened flesh of his arm. He cried out, more a girlish scream than a shout, and fell back. She slashed again and again, so many times until she was breathless and sure Cassin would stay put crumpled there in the corner.

From behind her she heard a scuffle and a decidedly female groan. Sophia turned just in time to see Hope take La Reinette's legs between his own and haul her to the floor.

La Reinette screamed, *No, no!*; her head came down on the floor with a liquid *thud*; she was silent, suddenly.

A strange, heady sort of quiet descended upon the room as Sophia met Thomas's eyes. He was breathing hard, the muscled expanse of his chest straining against his shirt, stained with blood and sweat.

Sophia dropped the rapier.

It was just the two of them. The only ones left standing. Or sitting, in Thomas's case.

She began to shake, her eyes warming with tears.

"Thomas," she breathed, throat so tight with relief she could hardly breathe.

His blue eyes were soft as he spoke. "Don't cry, Sophia. You know how I feel about you crying. Untie me, and I shall see to the rest."

T hey remained in the shadows, stalking through the dark-ened streets of Mayfair much like they had done that first night those weeks and weeks ago.

Only this time, Thomas held Sophia's hand firmly in the warmth of his own, their arms brushing as they walked the familiar route side by side.

She felt as if she were walking on a cloud, or perhaps among the stars. Everything felt different; everything looked and smelled and *was* different with Thomas moving quietly beside her. He swallowed her whole in the great bulk of his shadow. Sophia felt safe here, warm, as if nothing and no one could touch her. Nothing and no one mattered, not when she was with Thomas.

It would hurt to let him go; she was no fool, and knew that despite their victory over La Reinette and Guillaume Cassin, the matter of the missing French Blue still remained. Thomas belonged to Hope & Co. He would need to see the matter through to its bitter end, and she knew there was not time enough in his days for her.

Still.

Still her heart hoped.

She squeezed his hand.

I love you.

Sophia waited for him to squeeze back, but he did not.

Her throat tightened with disappointment as they turned into the familiar alley that led to the lane on which her family resided. A chill ran up her spine at the memory of the kiss she shared with Thomas; yes, it was this very spot where he turned . . .

Sophia nearly tripped over his boots as Thomas drew to a sudden stop. With his body he pressed her, hard, against the wall, the scrape of the brick against her bare neck a welcome foil to her pounding heart.

She sucked in a breath as he pulled her against him, his touch rough and riotous and urgent. In the space of a single heartbeat her body went up in flames, the blood rushing hot and wild beneath her skin as he cupped her face in his hands.

And then he was kissing her, his lips gentle as they pulled and teased and stroked her own. His hands were in her hair and his nose was brushing hers and she surrendered to the inescapable tug between their hearts. He surrounded her, her legs nestled between the hardened mass of his thighs, his arms brushing her shoulders as with his hands he moved her face in time to his lips.

Sophia let out a moan; whether it was pleasure or distress, she could not say; but Thomas pulled away, his breath hot on her cheek as he touched his forehead to her own. His eyes were closed.

"Sophia," he breathed. "Sophia, I love you."

Despite herself, she felt the corners of her mouth edging up into a grin.

"What?" he whispered. "What's so amusing?"

"I thought I'd never hear you say it."

He pulled back, looking into her eyes. "And do you have anything to say in reply?"

"Perhaps," she teased. "Perhaps not."

"The anticipation is killing me."

Sophia glanced down to where their hips were pressed snugly against each other. "I know."

"Well?"

She looked up and met his eyes, face creasing with happiness. "You fool. Of *course* I love y—"

He captured the words with his mouth, his kiss in his excitement, his relief, adorably clumsy. Her heart turned over in her chest.

Lovers, let them love.

Thomas pulled back, his eyes serious. "Don't marry the marquess, Sophia. I beg you, don't do it."

"You don't have to beg." Her grin faded. "I couldn't."

"Couldn't? Couldn't do what?"

She looked down at her hands. "Withington is a fine fellow. Better than that. He is kind and generous, and deserving of greatness. I desire for him the love that I know for you. I refused his proposal. I gave back his ring."

"You did." Hope let out another breath. "But he's the season's greatest catch! Everyone wants to marry the marquess, including your mother."

Sophia scoffed. "Everyone, it seems, but me."

Hope couldn't help himself; he smiled. "Marry me, then. I don't have a title, nor do I have a castle; and my fortune—well, I don't have much of that left, either. But I love you. By God, Sophia, I love you more than is proper, more than I should. I love you, and I want you with me all the days of my life."

Sophia swallowed the ominous tightening in her throat even as her heart leapt. "But the bank—the diamond . . ."

Hope shook his head, brushing back a handful of rogue curls. "I was blinded by my grief. My greed. But I don't want to be blind anymore, Sophia. You've opened my eyes to a kind of happiness I never thought I deserved. That I never thought I'd know. And now that I know it, I cannot live without it. I want to do right by my brothers, and by you. Marry me, Sophia. Please do me the great honor of becoming my wife."

The tears were warm as they streamed from the corners of her eyes. "Yes," she said, wiping her cheeks with the lapels of his jacket. "Yes!"

Thomas kissed her long and hard after that, the sort of kiss that left her breathless, lips throbbing, her body alive with the desire for more, *more*. She tangled her hands in the wilds of his hair, pulling him closer; he could never be close enough.

"We're going to have to tell my mother, you know," Sophia said, when at last Thomas had released her, draping an arm about her shoulders as they strolled bonelessly toward the house.

"I know." Thomas pressed a kiss into her forehead. "I'm decently handsome, or so I've been told. Perhaps I might use my masculine charms to woo from her a blessing?"

"You're not *that* handsome," Sophia teased.

They turned out onto the lane, and Sophia looked up from

the scuffed tips of Hope's boots—her *betrothed's* boots!—to
see her family's ramshackle house ablaze with light.

"What the devil?" Sophia quickened her pace, Thomas
trotting in time beside her. "I hope everything's all right."

"Perhaps Lady Violet has returned?"

"Perhaps."

Together Thomas and Sophia flew through the front door.
The hall was empty; the quiet was punctured by a distant
chiming, or was that laughter she heard, a vaguely familiar
trill?

Sophia tugged Thomas through a pair of French doors at
the back of the house that opened onto a derelict rose garden.
There, on the crumbling stoop, sat Lady Blaise and Uncle
Rutledge, each of them puffing on the most enormous cigars
Sophia had ever seen.

"Mama!" she gasped, blinking in disbelief. "What's happened?"

Lady Blaise waved away Sophia's words, chewing thought-
fully on her cigar.

"Your cousin," she said, releasing a plume of smoke from
between her lips. "She's run off with the Earl of Harclay.
Gretna Green, she told us. Can you imagine?"

Sophia glanced at Hope. "Oh, dear, Mama, I am so very
sorry."

"Sorry?" Uncle Rutledge's hairy white brows shot up.
"What's there to be sorry for, dear girl? We're celebrating!"

"Celebrating?"

"Yes," Lady Blaise said. "The circumstances of the marriage are not ideal, of course, but neither of us thought Violet
would ever be wed, much less to the *Earl* of *Harclay*! Ha! To
think she would be the one to tame that wicked rogue."

Lady Blaise turned to Thomas and started, as if seeing
him for the first time. "Oh! Before I forget. Violet left something for you, Mr. Hope. The box is on the table inside, in the
drawing room."

Thomas and Sophia exchanged a glance. A beat of breathless silence passed between them.

Then, without further ado, they skidded into the house and
through the hall, their footfalls giddy as they echoed through
the empty rooms.

There, on the round pedestal table in the center of the drawing room, rested a plain wooden box. It was small and square, its hinges oiled bronze.

"Dear God," Sophia breathed, eyes glued to Hope's fingers as they feathered across the lid, at last lifting it open. "Is it—"

"Yes." Thomas held the French Blue between his thumb and forefinger. It glinted in the light of the chandelier above, sparkling wildly as he turned it over in his hand. "Yes, Sophia, it is."

"Well." She took a step forward. "Perhaps you might woo mother dearest, after all."

Thomas lobbed the stone into the air and caught it in his palm. He met her gaze, his eyes alight with mischief as he took her hand, turning it over in his. Carefully he set the diamond in the middle of her palm, curling her fingers around it.

"It's for you. A necklace, perhaps. We'll call it the Hope Diamond." He traced his fingers lightly over the edges of her collarbones, his thumb grazing the edge of her bodice.

Sophia gaped. "But Thomas, I couldn't possibly . . . it's far too large, and precious . . ."

"What was it I said in Princess Caroline's drawing room? Oh yes: 'Only such a stone would be worthy of your beauty.' I meant what I said then, and I mean what I say now. It's yours."

Sophia blinked at the sudden prick of tears. Really, the weeping was getting a bit excessive; but she couldn't help it. This kind of happiness, it was unspeakably wonderful.

"What is it?" he said, brow furrowed with concern as he looked at her. "I know my poetry's terrible, but it's the thought that signifies, isn't it?"

"Yes," she said, burying her head in his chest. "Yes, Thomas, it is. Thank you."

Beneath her ear his heart beat a steady rhythm, strong and assured. "But we *are* going to have to work on your poetry."

"I thought you'd never ask." He grinned. "Might I inquire after your services? I've a memoir—well, a history, really— that needs. Er. Your professional touch. I have nary a penny to my name, you see, but I *am* able to pay you in diamonds."

Sophia smiled. "In that case, let us begin straightaway. I've a desk in my room, right beside the bed . . ."

Thomas swung Sophia into his arms, pressing his lips playfully to her throat as he carried her up the stairs.

Historical Note

The French Blue vanished from historical record following its theft in Paris from the Royal Warehouse in autumn 1792. It reappeared some two decades later in 1812 London, in association with French émigré and jeweler John Françillon; in his papers, Françillon described an enormous, and enormously unique, blue diamond that was at the time in the possession of another jeweler (you may recognize his name from the dockyard scene!)—Daniel Eliason.

There are a variety of scenarios that point to the French Blue's whereabouts between 1792 and 1812; according to Richard Kurin's excellent *Hope Diamond: The Legendary History of a Cursed Gem*, it's possible Caroline, Princess of Wales, inherited the stone from her father, the Duke of Brunswick. If this had indeed been the case, Kurin posits the duke—under duress while at war with Napoleon—had the stone recut sometime around 1805, before sending it to his daughter in London for safekeeping.

While it's impossible to know, exactly, how the French Blue crossed the Channel, I'd like to think this the most likely scenario. It was also a fabulous opportunity to incorporate Caroline into the story—she's an incredibly divisive, fascinating figure (if you haven't noticed yet, I adore having real-life historical giants make cameos in my books!).

That Thomas Hope and his paramour, Lady Sophia Blaise, purchased the French Blue from Princess Caroline under false pretenses—well, that was a delicious twist provided by my imagination.

The diamond disappeared again, mysteriously, for another two decades. It resurfaced in 1839, when it was recorded as being part of Henry Philip Hope's impressive collection of gems. The Hope who is the hero of this book is *Thomas* Hope, Henry's elder brother.

So why not Henry? For starters, I found Thomas a more compelling historical figure; as you learned reading this book, he was an intriguing, well-traveled member of London society, and an author in his own right.

I'd like to imagine that, as heirs to the immense Hope & Company banking empire and expatriates marooned together in London, Thomas and his brother Henry worked together to build their collections—art, books, *jewels*. Perhaps they even comingled their possessions; in *Hope: Adventures of a Diamond*, Marian Fowler suggests that Thomas's wife wore the French Blue to a ball in 1824.

Thomas was well-connected in royal circles and would likely be among the first to know when such a unique stone came up for sale. While no written records exist, it's possible Thomas was involved in the purchase, and perhaps at some point even the ownership, of the stone—after all, Thomas's sons would go on to inherit it.

The theft of the French Blue by a daring—and daringly handsome—earl, however, is entirely the product of my imagination (well, my agent's, too, but that's neither here nor there).

It is true King Louis XVIII and his brother, the Comte d'Artois, lived in exile in London following the Revolution. They would return to France in 1814 during the Bourbon Restoration. That they frequented White's—and had a penchant for nubile women—is, as far as my research tells me, purely fiction.

For more on the Hope Diamond, check out Richard Kurin's *Hope Diamond: The Legendary History of a Cursed Gem* and Ms. Fowler's *Hope: Adventures of a Diamond*, both of which proved indispensible to my research for this trilogy.

—— — ——

Turn the page for a preview of the next book in
Jessica Peterson's Hope Diamond Trilogy

The Undercover Scoundrel

Coming in June 2015 from Berkley Sensation!

—— — ——

Oxfordshire
Summer 1800

T heir vows echoed off the chapel's mottled ceiling, rising and swooping like birds to surround the couple in soft whispers of faith and hope and love.

"Rings?" the Vicar said, arching a brow.

For a moment the groom's eyes went wide; and then he plucked the pale green ribbon from his queue, releasing a curtain of red hair about his shoulders. He used his teeth to cut the ribbon in two. Tying one length into a small circlet, he slid it onto the bride's fourth finger.

A sea of flickering candles held the darkness at bay as Lady Caroline Townshend was kissed for the first time by her husband. Joy welled up inside her and she smiled against the warm press of Henry Beaton Lake's lips.

He kissed her far less chastely than was proper at a wedding, even a secret one. He kissed her as if every stroke, every pull, every move of their lips roused, rather than satiated, a growing need inside him.

Henry held her face in his hands, guiding her toward him as he pressed a kiss to one corner of her mouth, then the other. Breathless, Caroline stood on the tips of her toes to meet his caresses, streaks of light and bursts of color illuminating the backs of her closed eyelids.

The Vicar, a rather less romantic fellow than Romeo and Juliet's priest, shut his ancient Bible with a censorial *thwunk*.

Blushing, Caroline fell back from Henry, their hands entwining between them.

Lips pursed, eyes wide, the Vicar glared at them. "God. Sees. *Everything*."

In a whirl of black he turned and stalked down the aisle, shaking his head at young people these days and their carnal proclivities. Caroline's lady's maid, Nicks—the one and only witness—hurried after him.

Beside Caroline, Henry shook with repressed laughter.

"How much did you pay him?" she whispered.

"Clearly not enough."

"Will he tell our parents?"

Henry ran his thumb across the back of her hand. "In the morning, yes."

"Then we haven't much time."

"Do you mean to ravish me, Mrs. Lake?"

"I do indeed."

"Let's get on with it, then," he said, and swung her into his arms.

C aroline grasped the windowsill and, as Henry gave her a boost from below, somersaulted into his bed chamber. Inside the room it was warm and quite dark, save for a single lit taper on the bedside table.

"Really," she panted, wiping her hands on her skirts. "Why. Not use. The door? Your parents are. Still at my house for the. Ball."

Henry landed noiselessly on his feet, closing the window behind him. "Where's the challenge in that? Besides, I like all this sneaking about. Suits the secret marriage bit, don't you think?"

He took her outstretched hands and pulled her a smidge too enthusiastically to her feet. Her nose bumped against the hardened center of his chest.

"Oh," he said, thumbing her chin. "Oh, Caroline, I'm terribly sorry. Are you all right? I only meant to, um . . . I forget sometimes that you're so little, you see, I'm used to my brothers, as you know they're rather large . . ."

Caroline looked up at Henry. Large was an understatement;

like his older brothers, Henry was a broad-shouldered, ginger-haired giant with the wickedest cheekbones she had ever seen. His green eyes were even wicked*er* (if that was a word), so brightly suggestive, so darkly penetrating, Caroline feared she might burst into flames every time he looked at her.

"I'll have a devil of a time explaining that to my mother."

Henry angled his neck and brushed his lips to her injured nose. "Bloody business, marriage."

"Mm-hm," she said, burrowing further into the circle of his arms. Her ring of ribbon slipped from her finger—it was a tad too large—and she coaxed it back into place.

His hand slid from her cheek to cup the back of her neck. With his thumb he tilted her head and caught her mouth with his. He kissed her deeply, passionately, as if he were out to steal not only her heart but her soul, her body, her being.

Henry took her bottom lip between his teeth. She saw stars.

His hands were on her face now; Caroline clung to his wrists, fearful the rush in her knees might cause them to give out. She felt the scatter-shot beat of his pulse beneath her fingers, the jutting architecture of his bones. Strength rippled beneath the surface of his skin; strength she felt him struggling to restrain.

And yet he touched her with great care, gently, as awed by her shape as she was of his. His fingers tangled in the hair at her temples as his mouth moved to her neck, working the tender skin there with his lips.

Caroline let out a breath, desperate, suddenly, to be free of her stays and ridiculously ruffled muslin gown. She couldn't breathe, couldn't think; she was lost in the longing she'd felt for Henry from the moment they met eyes across the garden, three weeks before.

She was hardly seventeen, set to make her debut at St. James's the following spring. Even so, Caroline knew the intensity of her feelings for Henry was a rare thing; rare and fragile, as the world seemed fanatically intent to nip such reckless affection in the bud before it ever had a chance to bloom.

But Caroline was intent to bloom. Beneath Henry's careful, confident touch, his insistent caresses, she felt herself unravel and open, giving as Henry took, and took, and kept taking.

She slipped her hands beneath the lapels of his jacket. Henry rolled back his shoulders and shrugged free of the garment, tossing it aside. He began to move forward, pressing his body into hers as he guided her farther into the room. His fingers found purchase in a row of buttons between the blades of her shoulders, working them free one at a time.

"Hold up your arms, darling," he murmured against her mouth, and gently coaxed the gown over her head.

It fell with a rustling sigh to the floor. The night air felt coolly potent against the bare skin of her arms. She shivered.

Henry gathered her in his arms, surrounding her body with the heat of his own. She could smell his skin, the clean, citrusy spice of his soap. Her desire soared.

In a hushed frenzy of movement they unclothed one another: his waistcoat, her stays, his neckcloth; his head caught in his shirt, and after several futile attempts to remove it, Henry ripped it open. Buttons ricocheted about the room, landing with small *pings* as they rolled across the floor.

Caroline stared at his bare chest. She swallowed.

Henry took her hands and placed them on the center of his breastbone. She inhaled at the shock of warmth that met with her palms, the spring of wiry hair. She could feel his heart beating proudly within the cage of his ribs. Proudly, wildly, an echo of her own.

In the darkness she bent her neck, and pressed her lips to his chest. He inhaled sharply, his chest rising and falling beneath the working of her lips across his collarbone, up the corded slope of his neck.

Heavens, but she hoped his parents would not return for some hours yet; Caroline couldn't have kept quiet if she'd wanted.

His fingers tugged at the neckline of her chemise, taking her bare shoulder in his mouth. The heat between her legs burned hotter. Henry coaxed the garment down the length of her body, releasing one breast, then the other. Quickly his mouth moved to take her nipple between his teeth, rolling it in the velvet touch of his tongue. The sensation was so poignant it hurt.

"Henry," she breathed, tangling her fingers in his hair. "Please. Show me."

He raised his head, eyes luminescent, translucent; they were warm and soft and they were on her, gleaming with desire.

"I was hoping you'd show me," he replied.

"You've never? Never . . . you're almost twenty, I thought . . ."

"This is to be the first time for both of us, I'm afraid."

"Then I really *am* to ravage you."

He grinned. "If you don't mind terribly."

His mouth came down on hers, and he was digging at the pins in her hair with impatient fingers. She heard them fall, one by one, until at last her hair tumbled in soft waves about her shoulder blades. Henry drew his hands through its tangled mass to rest on the naked small of her back. He pulled her to him, skin to skin; the hardened knots of her nipples brushed against his chest, and she nearly cried out in agony, in desire.

The backs of Caroline's thighs met with the bed. Henry grasped her hips, and her breath caught in her throat as he tossed her lightly onto the mattress. The coverlet felt cool and deliciously soft against her bare skin.

Henry looked down upon her with narrowed eyes, his face suddenly tight.

"Caroline," he said roughly, slowly. "You are so . . . so very lovely. Beautiful."

He ran a hand up the side of her ribcage, cupping her breast; he thumbed her nipple and she arched into his touch.

And then both his hands moved to her legs, sliding off her stockings; his fingers were in the waistband of her pantalettes, tugging them over the smooth expanse of her belly, her knees.

Caroline was naked. She winced at the sudden rush of cool air against the beating throb of her sex. *Please*, she prayed. *Please let it be soon.*

Henry unbuttoned his breeches and swept them down to his ankles. He rose; Caroline stared at his cock, heavy with need, as unrepentantly enormous and thickly veined as the rest of his body. It jutted out from the sharp angle of his hips, unembarrassed, and she was at once hesitant and terribly curious.

"Caroline," he said.

She swallowed. "I'm all right."

"Caroline," he said again. "We don't have to do this. I couldn't bear it if I hurt you, if you weren't ready."

For a beat he did not move, as if waiting for her to change her mind; waiting for her to roll over and demand he escort her home, take back all they'd said and done this night.

"I want to," she said. "We're married now, remember? We get to do this at last."

Caroline sat up and reached for him. He drew a breath as her hand followed the narrowing trail of hair down his hardened belly; his whole body tensed when she wrapped her hand around his cock. He felt hard and soft all at once, the skin impatiently hot and silken. She put her mouth on his belly. One of his hands went to her hair while the other moved down to cover her own around his manhood.

"How?" she whispered.

"Like this," he said, and together their hands moved up and down the length of his cock, once, twice, until he groaned and pulled away, suddenly, as if she'd hurt him.

"Caroline," he said, his face in her hair. "I love you."

"I love you," she whispered.

"I can't wait much longer. I want—I need you. Badly. Here." He reached behind him, producing his rumpled shirt. "Lie down on this, love. I'm afraid you might bleed."

Bleed?

She swallowed for what felt like the hundredth time that night. He wasn't kidding about marriage being a bloody business.

Wedging the shirt beneath Caroline's bottom, Henry coaxed her back onto the bed. He took her knees in her hands and moved them apart, stepping forward so that he was wedged between her legs. She was wide open to him; she was afraid; she was overwhelmingly aroused.

Henry reached down and they both drew a breath when his first two fingers slipped between her slick curls, revealing a warmth, a wetness, that neither of them expected. Her desire soared; she ached for him to be inside her.

"You're," he swallowed, "ready?"

"Yes," she panted. "Please, Henry."

"Once we . . . I can't stop then."

"I don't want you to stop."

He stepped forward. The bed was set high, so high that, even while standing, Henry's hips were level with hers. He put his hands on the inside of her thighs, pushing her legs even wider.

"Bend your knees about me," he said.

Caroline did as she was told. He wrapped her bent legs about his hips, hooking her feet at his buttocks. She felt his fingers on her sex, holding her open as, with his other hand, he guided his cock into her folds. He nudged against her, wincing.

"Is it . . . are we going to work?" she asked.

"Yes," he breathed. "It's very small in there."

"Is it. Um. As it should be?"

He closed his eyes, lips curling into a pained half grin. "You're perfect."

She tried not to recoil as pressure mounted between her legs. She felt herself stretching. Her pleasure was edged with pain.

"Caroline," he said. He was looking at her now, eyes wide with concern. "Tell me how you're feeling, all right?"

"I'm all right."

He guided himself farther against her, using his fingers to keep her open to him. He moved his hips, pressing into her. He pressed harder, sucking in a breath as the first bit of him entered her.

The pleasant throb between her legs heightened to burning discomfort. Her eyes smarted. Henry was saying her name but she told him to keep going, and he did. Slowly he slid into her wet warmth; they both paused when he met the barrier inside her. He looked at her. She nodded, overwhelmed by the sting; by the sense of fullness he brought her.

I'm all right, Henry. Keep going.

He inhaled through his nose, and then he bucked his hips. In a single heartbeat he sunk to the hilt. A sound escaped Caroline's lips, something between a cry and a whimper.

He was bent over her then, taking her cry into his mouth as he set his forearms on either side of her head, surrounding her. His body was wound tightly; she could tell he wanted to move between her legs, but he waited.

He grit his teeth.

The sting began to subside, her pleasure—her heart— rising in its place. Oh, this felt lovely. A little full. But lovely.

Her hips began to circle against him, asking for more. Henry let out the breath he'd been holding and gently rocked his hips, withdrawing, entering again. Their skin, damp with sweat, slid and stuck.

She surrendered.

She surrendered to the pounding beat of her passion. To the heavy weight of her love for him.

She surrendered to Henry.

They moved against each other ardently, lost in a whirl of pain and limbs and pleasure. Her hands moved over his shoulders, marveling at the roping and bunching of his back muscles as he worked between her legs. His lips trailed over her jaw and throat.

He slowed, suddenly, and then his eyes fluttered shut; he stilled and she could feel his cock pulse inside her.

"Christ," he said when the pulsing subsided. His lips fluttered over her eyelashes. "I'm sorry, Caroline, I didn't mean . . . I meant to be more careful, but you felt so good, I couldn't stop. I wanted to stop."

"I didn't want you to stop," she whispered. "I don't want you to ever stop."

Slowly he withdrew from inside her; she felt his seed seeping warmly from between her legs.

He cursed again when he looked down at the shirt beneath her.

"What is it?" she said.

"Blood," he replied, mouth drawn into a line as he used the shirt to clean her. "A lot of it. Are you sure you're all right?"

Caroline flexed her stiff legs. She felt very sore between them. "All right. Sore. A little sore."

He crumpled the shirt between his hands and tossed it to the ground. He tugged the coverlet aside, holding it open for her. "Here, lie down. I'll get a towel."

She crawled between the bedclothes, smiling as she drew them up to her nose. They smelled like him. Like her husband.

He returned from the washstand with a damp towel, climbing into bed beside her. Thankfully he was still naked as the day he was born; he pressed his body against hers as he coaxed her legs apart, pressing the towel between them. It felt blessedly cool.

"I love you, Caroline," he murmured in her ear, nicking the lobe with his teeth. She felt him smiling against her skin. "*Wife.*"

She smiled, too, a wide, irrepressible thing she felt in every corner of her being. Despite everything—despite how it appeared, her ten-thousand pound dowry and his lack of position—despite their youth, their parents' disapproval—despite all that, she knew this was where she was meant to be.

Caroline loved him. She felt loved by him. And wasn't that the end of everything?

Henry spun her around and tugged her against the hardened mass of his body, her back to his front. He pulled the sheets over their heads and she, giggling, yielded to his hands as he took her body again and again and again, until the sun burned away the darkness.

I t happened the next afternoon. As she was wont to do when in need of solitude and space, Caroline disappeared into the garden. Henry—her *husband!*—had a habit of sneaking from his father's house to meet her there besides; she had half a mind to toss him beneath a bush and ravage him soundly, as she promised she would last night.

She was on her knees, digging at a half-dead holly, when she heard the telltale rustle in a nearby boxwood. Her chest lit up with excitement; she was smiling, hard, when she brushed back her hair and turned toward the noise.

Only it wasn't Henry. George Osbourne, Viscount Umberton, heir to the wildly wealthy Earl of Berry and Henry's very best friend, emerged from the hedgerow. Caroline's joy hardened in her throat at the sight of Osbourne's well formed, if slight, figure. His face was hard, his dark eyes soft.

A tendril of panic unfurled inside her belly. She didn't like that look; something was amiss.

"My Lord," she said hopefully, as if she might will good news with the tone of her voice. "What an unexpected surprise. Have you . . . er . . . come for tea?"

Osbourne bowed. "My Lady, I am sorry to meet you like this, but I came straightaway."

"What?" So much for the soothing tone of voice. "What is it?"

He wiped the sweat from his thick eyebrow with a trembling thumb. When he spoke his voice was low, hoarse.

"He's gone. Henry—Lake—he's gone. I—" Here Osbourne looked away. "I thought you should know. I understand the two of you have . . . become quite close this summer, and I—"

The brass-handled garden trowel fell from her gloved hand to the earth with a muted *thud* of protest. "Gone? Where? But how . . . I don't understand!"

Osbourne's face was tensed with pain as he looked down at her. He swallowed. "Emptied his drawers into a valise—there's nothing left, and he took the five pounds his older brother was hiding in his pillow. He left a note, something about duty, and not coming to look for him. He said he wouldn't come back. Lady Caroline, Henry is gone."

Caroline's vision blurred; tears burned her eyes, and she fell back on her haunches. "Perhaps it's a mistake," she said. "A misunderstanding with his father, or maybe it's a joke, or—or—"

"I know Henry," Osbourne said. "He's gone, Caroline. I don't know where, and I don't know why. But he's gone."

She was sobbing then, and George Osbourne fell to his knees beside her and held her to his chest. They sat like that, damp with the heat of one another's tears, until the garden was tawny with twilight.

That was the last Caroline heard of Henry Beaton Lake, her husband, before he disappeared from Oxfordshire, from England, from her life.

Before he disappeared forever.

*In an era when ladies were demure and men courtly,
one priceless treasure set England ablaze with scandal
and passion—the Hope Diamond.*

FROM
JESSICA PETERSON

*The Gentleman
Jewel Thief*

The Hope Diamond Trilogy

Heir to an impressive title and fortune, Lord William
Townshend, Earl of Harclay, is among the most dis-
reputable rakes in England. Desperately bored by dull
heiresses and tedious soirees, he seeks new excitement—
starting with a dangerous scheme to steal the world's
most legendary gemstone from its owner, Thomas Hope.
To his surprise, it's not the robbery that sets his blood
burning but the alluring lady he pilfers the gem from...

jessicapeterson.com
facebook.com/JessicaPetersonAuthor
facebook.com/LoveAlwaysBooks
penguin.com

M1534T0714

FROM AWARD-WINNING AUTHOR

ANNE GRACIE

THE

Autumn Bride

A Chance Sisters Romance

Governess Abigail Chantry will do anything to save her sister and two dearest friends from destitution, even if it means breaking into an empty mansion. Which is how she encounters the neglected Lady Beatrice Davenham, who agrees that the four young ladies should become her "nieces," eliminating the threat of disaster for all. It's the perfect situation, until Lady Beatrice's dashing and arrogant nephew, Lord Davenham, returns from the Orient—and discovers an impostor running his household...

"I never miss an Anne Gracie book."

—Julia Quinn, *New York Times* bestselling author

"Treat yourself to some super reads
from a most talented writer."

—*Romance Reviews Today*

annegracie.com
facebook.com/AnneGracieAuthor
facebook.com/LoveAlwaysBooks
penguin.com

M1389T1013

LOVE
ROMANCE
NOVELS?

For news on all your favorite romance authors, sneak peeks into the newest releases, book giveaways, and much more—

"Like" Love Always on Facebook!

f LoveAlwaysBooks

M1063G0212

*Enter the rich world of
historical romance
with Berkley Books . . .*

Madeline Hunter

Jennifer Ashley

Joanna Bourne

Lynn Kurland

Jodi Thomas

Anne Gracie

Love is timeless.

berkleyjoveauthors.com